Eleanore of Avignon

Eleanore of Avignon

A NOVEL

Elizabeth DeLozier

DUTTON

DUTTON
An imprint of Penguin Random House LLC
penguinrandomhouse.com

LIBRARY OF CONGRESS CATALOGING-IN-PUBLICATION DATA

Names: DeLozier, Elizabeth, author.
Title: Eleanore of Avignon : a novel / Elizabeth DeLozier.
Description: [New York] : Dutton, 2024.
Identifiers: LCCN 2023047005 | ISBN 9780593475034 (hardcover) | ISBN 9780593475041 (ebook)
Subjects: LCSH: Black Death—Fiction. | Midwives—Fiction. | LCGFT: Historical fiction. | Novels.
Classification: LCC PS3604.E44737 E44 2024 | DDC 813/.6—dc23/eng/20240110
LC record available at https://lccn.loc.gov/2023047005

Printed in the United States of America
$PrintCode

BOOK DESIGN BY LAURA K. CORLESS

For my mother and aunt,
who have been so generous with
their love of history and literature

But the stars that marked our starting fall away.
We must go deeper into greater pain,
For it is not permitted that we stay.

—Dante Alighieri, Inferno Canto VII

Eleanore of Avignon

Chapter One

November 1347

The sun is low by the time I reach the woods. I pause at the crest of the hill and look back the way I came, pulling my cloak tighter against the wind.

The river below winds a ribbon of molten gold around the city walls. The bone-white steeple of Notre-Dame des Doms reaches over the rooftops like a scolding finger, the scaffolding of the Palais Neuf rising daily beside it. Even from this distance, frantic hammer blows and the shouts of stone masons echo across the water. When Pope Clement VI arrived in Avignon five years ago he was not sufficiently impressed with the newly built palace of his predecessor, Benedict XII—no, Clement's palace must be the largest in the world, the most elaborate.

It is a blessing to be out of the city, to breathe the sweet smell of earth instead of urine and woodsmoke. I step off the cart-rutted road into the dappled shadows with my empty basket swinging.

I could sleepwalk this invisible path my mother trod through ancient oak trees, past crumbling Roman walls and forgotten olive groves.

Dusk comes early to the woods this time of year; I must work quickly to be back before the city gates are locked at nightfall.

Under the cool shade of the oaks, comfrey grows. I spot the tiny purple flowers and kneel, pull my knife from the waistband of my skirt, and slide it through their slender stalks. I review my mental list: comfrey for Anes's swollen knees, fennel for the baker's fussy baby, pennyroyal to keep the fleas at bay. They are relentless since the rain started, and Margot keeps me up all night with her scratching.

The thought catches like a canker sore. *Margot.*

Our argument from the morning plays in my head, the words worn smooth as river stones with repetition.

"Why must it be him?" I'd demanded, pacing our room like a cat. "You could have anyone, Margot. Any merchant or solicitor or physician. Why must it be Erec Dupont?"

My twin sister sat on our bed, spine straight and hands folded. "Because I love him," she said simply.

"And it doesn't hurt that he is rich," I retorted.

"That is unfair," she said, the color rising in her cheeks. "You know I do not marry him for his money."

In a few short months she will leave me and our comfortable home in the rue des Lices for the echoing Dupont mansion, where her future mother-in-law presides like a pale, spiteful spider. From our family pew I shall watch the back of my sister's dark head bent meekly beside the other merchants' wives with their wealth evident in the lace at their cuffs and the jewels in their ears. And I will patch my skirts, dry herbs and brew tonics, make ointments for kitchen burns and set broken bones. It will be my fate to care for my father as he ages, watch as my own reflection becomes tired and lined.

"All those years when you and Mother were together in the woods, or making house calls, or bent over your medicines, where was I?" There was no anger in the turn of her mouth, only a surprised kind of hurt.

The memory of a hundred mornings came rushing back like something dreamed: Mother's knuckles against the Duponts' elaborately carved front door, Erec's pale hair glinting in the gloom of the hall. Before we could afford to hire Anes, Margot spent many days in that cold house.

"You had Mother," my sister continued. "And I had Erec."

"You could have come with us," I said, holding the guilt away. "We asked you, I remember. And you did come, once or twice." But even as I said the words, they sounded hollow. I saw Margot as a little girl squeezing her eyes shut, clutching Mother's skirts with bunched fists, sent to wait outside with the other children while Mother and I pulled their new brother or sister into the world.

"You know I was never much for blood, Elea," Margot said. "But I did like holding the babies."

And most of all I dread the day when I am called to Margot's bedside as her midwife. I pray she will not die as Mother did, with the blood soaking the fine down of her marriage bed and I helpless, again, to save her.

A howl cuts through the cold air.

I freeze. I scan the woods around me, alert as a rabbit, but nothing moves between the dark trees. Images of wolves from some book of chivalry spring into my head, but no wolf has been seen in Avignon in decades.

The animal howls again, low and desperate, ending in a whimper.

It came from the meadow.

I reach into my basket, pull out the battered tin spoon I use for digging up fennel bulbs and hold it before me like a weapon. I walk forward, aware of my raucous breathing, the suck of my boots in the wet ground. Ten steps. Twenty. Thirty. I reach the thin trees and pooling golden light at the edge of the forest.

Long ago, some industrious peasant hewed this clearing out of the woods. In the middle of the meadow sits the skeleton of a cottage, crumbling walls with no roof and vines creeping through the stones like ladies' hair. It was my mother's favorite place. And at the side of the cottage, where the wild fennel grows, stands a wolf.

I step reflexively behind an oak with my pulse tripping. Did it see me? Should I run? I am about twenty paces away, but if I step lightly . . .

The animal whimpers, a pathetic canine sound that tugs at my chest. Ignoring my wiser instincts, I peer around the edge of the tree.

The creature has not noticed me. Its great head is bent, worrying at something in the grass. I examine the ridges of its loose body, the powerful haunches, the shape of its head. A dog, not a wolf—but unlike any dog I have seen. This is an animal caught between its wild ancestors and the friendly creatures that lie beneath tables and beg for scraps. Its black hair stands like quills between ridged shoulder blades, its face is long and angular.

The dog cries out again. With a sinking feeling in my belly, I realize its leg is caught in a trap.

I have seen the victims of poachers on Queen Joanna's land—rabbits, foxes, the occasional genet—but never, before, alive. They lie with glassy eyes, their muzzles stained with blood from trying to gnaw off the trapped limb, their precious pelts picked by vultures.

I say a prayer, return the spoon to my basket, and abandon my hiding place for the brassy light of the meadow.

The dog swings its head toward my sudden movement. It jumps back, yelps as the iron bites deeper. I steady the blood thrumming in my ears and put a hand on the oak trunk. I reach out to the dog the way my mother taught me, imagining the words and actions in my mind.

Hello, brave creature. I am sorry you are in pain. I will not hurt you. I can help, if you let me.

The dog stares back at me, ears flattened against the long skull. I note the powerful muscles, the thick pointed claws. But he—yes, it is a he—is still. He is listening.

I can open the trap and release you. But you must trust me.

His wild eyes hold mine for the space of ten heartbeats. Then, slowly, he inclines his head. When he lifts his gaze again, the wolf is gone. Only the dog remains.

I hold my breath and step through the dead grass.

Just out of his reach I kneel down, bring my face level with his. I am not my mother. Once free, he could rip out my throat, leave me to bleed out on the leaves beside him.

Inch by inch I raise a hand, stretch it toward him. His breath is hot on my face, my nose fills with the wet wool of his coat. He flinches as my hand meets his breastbone. Through the thick fur and muscles his heart throbs in its cage of bones.

He takes a deep breath. His shoulders relax, ears soften. Beneath my fingers his heart slows, and he is still.

"Good," I whisper. "Good dog."

Satisfied he will not hurt me, I turn my attention back to the trap. Under the dog's paw, at the center of the device, there is a pin. If I can free it from its coupling, I should be able to wrest it open. Gently, carefully, so slowly, I place my left hand on the base to steady it. With my right hand I grab the end of the pin; it is slippery with blood, caught in the metal. I wrap the hem of my skirt around it, twist and pull. The pin starts to move. I slide it all the way out, take another breath, and wrench the jaws of the trap apart.

The dog cries out again as the iron teeth separate from his leg, pulling dried blood and fur with them. He lifts his paw out gingerly. It hangs limp at the end of his leg, white bone visible through the gore. He tries to put weight on it and yelps. Without thinking I reach my hands out toward him. He turns and runs, limping, into the trees.

I stand up, shaking, and call to him in my gentlest voice. I unwrap the loaf of bread Anes insisted I pack, hold it high so the breeze might bring the scent to him. I walk a wide circle around the cottage, hoping he will reappear. But he is gone.

He would have come back to my mother. He would have placed his head in her lap, allowed her to stroke his ears. He would have followed her home.

Animals do not love me, not the way they loved her. When I am out in the woods, I never look down to find a snake wound around my ankle, as though enjoying the way my skin feels under its scaly belly. Deer do not disentangle themselves from the shadows to rest their velvet noses in my open palms, as if I am the priest at Saint-Agricol, my hands holy water.

But sometimes, I feel someone following me and glance over my shoulder to catch a cat curling around the corner with his tail high. Or watch a bird land too close, then hop closer, bright black eyes surveying me with interest. It always ends the same, though: the cat runs off with a hiss, the bird flies away, chirping a warning to her friends. I am not who they thought I was.

I try to shake the ache in my chest that accompanies memories of my mother. It comes unheralded: I'm washing dishes with Anes or walking between the market stalls with Margot and suddenly I remember. *My mother is dead.* It sweeps through me like the winter mistral and blows out all the candles I have lit against it.

Two hollow years have passed since she was here, swinging her skirt, humming a ballad, touching my arm to point out some growing thing and explaining its use if it had one or why it should be avoided. *Everything is strung together,* she said. *Once you know that, you are never alone. Look around you. The earth is calling.*

And if it weren't for Mathilde Dupont, Erec's mother, she might be beside me now.

The wind picks up, hurrying dark clouds across the sky. On the ground along the south wall of the ruined cottage, shielded from the wind and coming rain, I lay the loaf of bread and two apples from my basket. Thinking of the dog in the wet night with his wounded leg, I pull the cloak from my shoulders and fold it into a neat square against the wall with a prayer to Saint Francis that he will find this offering.

I turn back toward Avignon, to Father and Anes. And, for a bit longer, Margot.

I am almost to the road before I realize I forgot the pennyroyal and curse under my breath. Another week of flea bites for Margot and sleepless nights for me.

The wind reaches cold fingers up the cuffs of my sleeves and down the neck of my dress as I join the press of people entering the city from the Pont Saint-Bénézet. The flags mounted over the gate snap in the wind: the red-and-white triple tiara of the pope, Queen Joanna's blue-and-white fleur-de-lis. The scarlet-uniformed guards stare straight ahead, sword handles and scabbards glittering in the last of the light.

Inside the walls, the sounds of the city eclipse all thought: voices call in greeting or advertisement, dogs bark and mules bray, cartwheels clatter over cobblestones. Townspeople scurry through the narrow streets with hats clutched to heads against the wind. I turn onto the rue des Lices as the first blaze of lightning splinters the sky.

Voices carry from the open windows of the house on the corner along with the smell of cooking meat. A booming laugh—Father. A light contralto—Margot. And a third voice, mellow and masculine. Erec.

I want to run back to the woods.

"There she is!" Father says as I enter our home, getting to his feet with some difficulty; his bad leg bothers him with the change in weather. He is a slight man, an athlete in his youth, the fastest runner, the surest swimmer, all wasted when his horse sunk a foot in a rabbit burrow and trapped Father's leg beneath him. My parents met when

Mother's father—a physician, she his young assistant—came to treat my father. He is balding now, but his face is still handsome, still suntanned and youthful despite the hours hunched over the pope's ledgers by candlelight.

Margot and Erec stand across from him, their coloring a pretty juxtaposition of dark and light. I always forget how tall Erec is: although he is eighteen, a year older than me and Margot, in my head he is still eight, or ten, or twelve, throwing apples at passersby from the roof, knees scraped by tree trunks or smeared with river mud. This broad-shouldered man in fine black wool is a stranger. Only his hair is unchanged since childhood, the same pale gold as his mother's.

"You're late," says my sister, a frown clouding her forehead. "We feared you would be caught in the rain."

Although identical at birth, after the age of three or four no one mistook us. Our eyes are Father's, wide-set and hazel, our noses narrow and straight above small mouths. But under Mother's dark widow's peak, Margot's skin is pale and creamy as milk, mine as brown as Father's and freckled across nose and cheekbones. When my rough hands bump against my sister in sleep, I am always surprised at her softness, the fine grain of skin and flesh beneath her chemise.

I hold out my arms to show I am dry. "As you see, I have returned unscathed."

"Where is your cloak?" Margot asks.

I think quickly. They would not understand the feral dog, how I knew he would not hurt me. Only Mother would.

"It was warm in the meadow," I lie. "I hung it on a branch while picking herbs and forgot it."

"That was foolish." Margot looks through the open window at the low sky, her hair gleaming in its complicated braid. "It will be ruined by tomorrow. You can use Mother's until I have time to sew you a new one."

I can tell by the set of her jaw that she is still angry with me from this morning, but she makes her voice pleasant for Erec's sake.

"We are celebrating!" says Father exuberantly, gesturing to the wine jug and cups on the table.

I raise my eyebrows in a question, although in the twisting of my guts I know the answer.

"Margot and I have set a date," Erec says.

My sister turns to him, happiness spreading over her face like a sunrise.

"We will marry in spring, when my father returns from Paris."

I had feared they would marry sooner. But it is set. Funny, to dread spring.

They are all staring at me, and I realize I have not responded. I bare my teeth in a smile.

"That's wonderful news," I say. "Congratulations."

Father sits ungracefully on the bench. "Take a seat, Elea," he says, pouring more wine.

I shift the basket on my arm as though it is heavy, although it contains only a few sprigs of comfrey. "In a moment," I say. "I'll unpack my basket and see if Anes needs help with supper."

Without waiting for a response, I cross the hall and turn down the narrow passage that leads to the kitchen.

Anes bends over a pot on the fire with her back to the door, sampling the contents with a wooden spoon. I step over the threshold and drop my basket on the scrubbed oak table with a thud.

Anes starts, bumping her head on the low mantel.

"Oh! Sorry, Anes." I hurry over to where she stands, rubbing her forehead.

"Saint's blood, child," she snaps. "You nearly sent me into the fire!" I wipe away the smear of soot on her temple and inspect the pink skin beneath.

"I expect you shall make a miraculous recovery," I say solemnly, kissing the spot.

She pushes me away. "Those carrots need peeling."

Grateful for the distraction, for something to do with my hands, I get to work.

Anes cooks like she does everything, with the Provençal love of simplicity partnered with a passion for perfection. She hovers around the kitchen like a plump fairy, tasting and salting and spicing with abandon. The results are always delicious.

At ten, Anes lost her entire family to the pox. She was left no money—her parents had been tenant farmers—so she was shipped off to the nearest, poorest convent to be raised by nuns. But she always had a gift in the kitchen. At sixteen she left the convent with a young baroness whose family plucked her from religious life to marry a wealthy wine merchant. The girl could rescind her lifelong vows of chastity, but she could not live without Anes's tarts.

Anes moved from house to house across the city as fortunes waxed and waned. When Margot and I were eleven, she came to live with us and quickly became a member of the family. Despite the countless hours spent in the kitchen with her, I have none of her culinary magic. When she was sick last winter, I made chicken soup—something I have helped her cook countless times—but when I brought her a bowl, she took one spoonful and spat it out. My concoction tasted like soap.

I look up now to see Anes surveying me, hands on wide hips.

"What's the matter with you?" she demands, looking me up and down. "Why so glum?"

"Nothing," I mutter. "I'm just tired. I walked up Mount Andaon."

"Not just today. The past few weeks. Since the engagement."

"It's all the rain," I lie, placing the last naked carrot in the bowl. "Tomorrow I'll brew a tea against melancholy. What else needs to be done?"

Twenty minutes later we emerge, sweating, from the kitchen, each bearing a heavy tray. Anes made pork and apple pie, the flaky golden crust decorated with pastry leaves and egg wash, boiled carrots tossed in butter and thyme, and courgette and onion soup.

"It smells delicious, Anes," Erec says, lifting the tray lightly from her hands. She beams at him.

We take our places at the table: me beside Father; Erec across from me, beside Margot. Anes cuts and serves us each a generous slice of pie, then excuses herself. As always when we have guests, she will eat her supper in the kitchen.

Father fills the cups without watering down the wine for me and Margot. It is his finest, deep red and complex, reserved for the specialest of occasions. Father is exuberant. The only son of the city's wealthiest wool merchant: a better match than he could have prayed for. Beautiful and accomplished though she may be with her Latin, her household accounting learned at Father's side, her perfect needlework, Margot is still the daughter of a papal notary and a dead midwife. Every burgher's wife and even some of the minor nobility clambered to match their girls with Erec Dupont. But for him, there has only ever been Margot. He will dress her in velvet and silk, keep her larder full of sugar and spices, buy meat for the table every day of the week. Never mind the madwoman upstairs, filling her head with poison.

Father bows his head to say grace. "Bless us, oh Lord, and these thy gifts, which we receive from thy bounty, through Christ our Lord." He pauses. "And thank you, Lord, for the forthcoming union of Margot and Erec. May their lives be long and happy, and may they be blessed with many children. Amen."

"*Amen,*" we chorus, crossing ourselves.

I sip my wine, taste the grapes ripening in the hot summer sun, the dark rich soil in which they grew, and swallow the image of Margot, lying pale and sweat-soaked as blood blossoms between her legs.

"What news of Allistair?" asks Father after a few appreciative bites of pie.

Allistair Dupont, the eldest son of a middling cloth dyer, was blessed with a head for numbers and an eye for a good bargain. At the age of sixteen he took over the family business and quickly expanded a small storefront in the rue des Teinturiers to a successful trading company with holdings in Paris, Bruges, and Lille. His marriage into Mathilde's family—one of the oldest in Provence—gave him connections in Navarre and Aragon when King Philip's war made it impossible to buy cheap wool from England. He is haughty, loud, and self-important. My mother quietly despised him.

"Father is well," Erec says, setting down his fork. "He is in Navarre, finalizing a contract. Then he travels to Paris. These rumors of illness and unrest have been good for business—people are buying wool as though the world is ending."

"And Mathilde?" asks Father.

I feel Margot's eyes on me and busy myself with my plate.

Erec takes a long sip of wine. "Mother is weak and feverish," he says, "which is not uncommon for this time of year. Dr. Laurent has been by to bleed her daily. He says she will improve when the weather turns. But the fever will not break."

"You did not tell me," says my sister, concerned. "I would have visited her."

"I did not want to worry you unnecessarily, my love. She is so often ill. But this affliction seems different." Erec turns, unexpectedly, to me. "I was hoping that Elea might come by to examine her."

The food turns to chalk in my mouth.

"The fever will not break," he repeats. "She passes in and out of reality. Today, she called for Bietriz."

My mother's name sends a shiver through me.

I glance at my sister, see my own disquiet mirrored in her face. Two years have passed since the last time I saw Mathilde Dupont, twisted in scarlet sheets. *I know what you are.* And my mother, in her deep, understanding love, forgave her.

"I am not my mother," I say, meeting Erec's blue gaze. "If her condition is as serious as you say, you should send for another physician."

He shakes his head. In the worried angles of his face, I catch a glimpse of the boy I knew. "We have had three physicians examine her. Father even brought one from Paris. The only medicines that made a lasting difference were Bietriz's."

"Elea," says Father, his mild voice laced with a warning. "I'm sure your other patients will understand. Madame Dupont's illness sounds serious."

"I realize what I ask," Erec interrupts gently. "And would not ask it if the circumstances were not grave."

In their yearlong courtship I have done my best to avoid Erec, turned from the door when I heard his voice as often as I could without drawing attention. He has never mentioned what transpired between our mothers. Their sisterly bond broken in a night, the poisonous rumors that followed. Father, like Mother, forgave Mathilde, called her slipping mind a tragedy, and when Erec first asked to walk Margot home from mass on Sundays, Father welcomed him with open arms. But Erec must guess what I think of his mother.

I glance around the table, meet my sister's pleading eyes and Father's disappointed ones.

"She asked for Bietriz," Erec repeats. "Please."

And suddenly my mother's voice rings through my head as clear as a bell, speaking the words she spoke that night.

Take pity on her, Elea. She knows not what she does. She is a prisoner of her own mind.

I think of the dog in the trap, who would have gnawed through the bones of his own leg to be free.

I have all the herbs for feverfew tonic. For Margot, who will soon live under Mathilde's roof; for my mother, who would want me to ease her friend's suffering, I will try.

"I do not know that I can help," I say, already regretting the words, "but I will make the medicine and come by tomorrow."

"Thank you," Erec says, relief bright in his face. "Thank you, Elea."

Lightning flashes through the open windows, followed by a boom of thunder. The clouds finally release their burden of rain.

Margot and I jump up and hurry to the casements to draw the mullioned panes together. As I drive the iron fastening home, Margot reaches out and covers my hand with hers. I pull my fingers free, not ready to make peace.

We settle back to our meal. For a few moments there are no sounds but the rain on the stone shingles and the scrape of cutlery.

"There is news of Queen Joanna," says Father lightly.

Margot and I lock eyes, the tension between us momentarily forgotten. Joanna, queen of Naples, Sicily, and Jerusalem. Countess of our own region, Provence, through her Capetian blood, and the great-great-great-great-great granddaughter of my namesake, Eleanor of Aquitaine. Fierce, famously beautiful, a woman in a man's world, she was Mother's favorite, the heroine of our bedtime stories.

"She has married her cousin Luigi of Taranto—"

Margot gasps.

"Without the pope's dispensation."

I choke on my pie.

"Pope Clement is so furious that he has been confined to his bed all week with indigestion, and Surgeon de Chauliac is at his wit's end for how to cure him," Father finishes, refilling his cup happily.

Three Septembers ago, Queen Joanna's first husband, Andreas of Hungary, was murdered. Strangled and hung from a balcony with his genitals mutilated, to be precise. Everyone believes Joanna arranged his death. The only reason she married him in the first place was to stave off a Hungarian invasion of Naples; Joanna was always supposed to hold the true power in the region. But petulant, childlike Andreas decided he wasn't content as royal consort and must be crowned king.

I understand why she might have done it: there are few ways out of an unpleasant marriage. But I would have counseled more subtlety in the execution.

"What will Pope Clement do?" asks Margot. "Will he excommunicate them?"

Father laughs, swirling the wine in his glass so it catches the light. "Oh, no. He will do nothing but seethe in his chambers. The papacy only makes its home in Avignon at her pleasure. Clement can excommunicate them and limp back to the crumbling ruins of Rome to be murdered like Boniface VIII, or he can stay put in his ridiculous new palace and bide his time. It is said that there will be a trial."

"A trial?" Margot and I repeat together.

Father nods. "Queen Joanna and her new lover will come to Avignon to stand trial for the murder of her husband."

"But Andreas died years ago," I say. "Why is the queen being prosecuted now?"

Father shrugs. "The pope did not want to choose a side. But Louis of Hungary, Andreas's brother, has forced his hand; Naples will descend into civil war if he does not announce a verdict."

Margot's face is pink with excitement. Our fearless queen, in our city, *her* city, for the first time. There will be a parade. We will see her.

"Joanna needs the vocal support of the papacy," Erec cuts in. "Louis has sworn vengeance upon her. He and his army have already taken Alba." The words sound rehearsed, likely his father's. "And it is said he will take Naples by winter. Unless the pope declares her innocent, the Hungarians will ransack the city and execute both the queen and her lover."

"Luigi of Taranto may be fair game," agrees Father, happy to be discussing matters of the world with a man. "But Queen Joanna cannot be murdered. Louis of Hungary knows this. He is the upstart king of a kingdom of peasants. He has neither the heft nor the pedigree to change the course of Europe's future."

The talk shifts from Queen Joanna to France's endless war with England, to the rumblings of earthquakes and illness in the East. I allow my attention to drift in and out, lulled into a stupor from the wine and food, and try to ignore the dread gathering in my mind like the storm clouds above. Tomorrow I will see Mathilde. Father throws back his head to laugh at something Erec said: a low belly laugh I haven't heard in ages. Margot watches Erec, her skin glowing like the moon.

Anes shuffles in to clear the plates, and Father pushes back from the table. I realize how late it is, how deeply tired I am.

"Please accept my thanks for tonight," says Erec.

"A match such as this deserves celebrating," Father replies, getting to his feet unsteadily. His wine cellar is emptier than it was this morning. "When Allistair returns, we must all dine together. It has been too long." He clasps Erec's hand, then he turns and walks carefully up the stairs to his room.

Erec takes his cloak from its hook beside the fire and says good night to my sister. I busy myself clearing the plates, trying to ignore their aching eyes, the way their hands meet like a drowning man reaching for the shore.

I take my time helping Anes in the kitchen in the hope that Margot will be asleep and I might crawl into bed beside her without talking. The dishes are washed and dried, the flagstone floor swept, and tomorrow's bread left to rise by the fire when I finally climb the stairs.

A ribbon of candlelight flickers under our door. I turn the handle and enter.

Margot sits up in bed with Mother's dog-eared copy of *La Commedia* open in her lap, her unbound hair tumbling over her shoulders like raw silk. I sit heavily in the chair in the corner and unlace my muddy boots.

"Thank you," says my sister quietly.

I tug a stockinged foot free and avoid her eyes. "If three licensed physicians couldn't cure Mathilde Dupont, I don't know what an herbalist will do. Despite what your soon-to-be mother-in-law may believe, I have no unnatural powers save Mother's tinctures and common sense."

Margot closes her book. "What is the matter with you?"

I don't reply. I pull off my second boot and shove it under the chair.

"Ever since Erec and I announced our engagement you have been horrible to me. You're behaving like a child."

"And you're behaving like a hound, waiting for her master at the door."

A mean hit. I regret the words even as they leave my mouth.

"Is it Erec you despise?" Margot asks, her voice climbing higher. "Or is it Mathilde? Because I've told you over and over again that Madame Dupont is to be pitied, not feared. You are holding on to this hatred because it feels good to have someone to blame. It's not her fault that Mother died, Elea. And you know it."

"It *is* her fault that Mother died without the care of a physician or midwife," I retort. "With no one but a frightened girl to help her."

Margot sighs, turns her eyes to the ceiling in the expression of the long-suffering. In the uneven light she looks so much like Mother that my chest aches. "We've been through this a hundred times. No one could have saved her. The baby was too big."

"And Father Loup?" I snap. "Did he not repeat Mathilde's lies when he stood over her deathbed and cursed her?"

I see the priest's long, curled spine, his reek of unwashed old age eclipsing the smell of rain and lavender and blood.

If she were not already dying, I would burn her myself. And you, girl. Your time will come. The devil has his claws in you, I see it.

I look up to find my sister watching me. The expression on her face suddenly makes me feel very young.

"He's gone." Margot's voice has lost its heat. "Shipped off to Arles, remember? Maybe dead. You know what Mother would say. Cut out this hatred before it poisons you. It is time to let the past go."

A voice deep inside me whispers that she is right. But Mother is not here. Her body lies beneath the stones of Saint-Agricol; her unshriven soul, if the priests are to be believed, wanders the flat plains of purgatory.

Margot snuffs the candle and curls under the blankets. I sit stupidly in the dark for a moment, then stand and shuck my clothing, my skin prickling under the thin chemise. I lift the bedclothes and lie with my back to Margot, taking up as little of the mattress as possible.

Across the cold inches between our spines, my sister slips into sleep. I listen to the step of the heart that, for three seasons, grew beside mine in the red sea of our mother. *Home*, it whispers. *Home. Home.*

I will miss her like the dead miss breathing.

Chapter Two

Morning dawns misty and cold.

Anes leaves early for the market. Father, as always, has been sitting in the notary offices at the papal palace since daybreak. Without a word to me, Margot sweeps out the door for her charity rounds at La Pignotte, Saint-Agricol's poorhouse. My sister spends her days in the mundane tasks of all bourgeois young women. First, she carries yesterday's stale bread and softening vegetables to the less fortunate. At the city's almshouses she often meets friends—girls who would stab her in the eye with an embroidery needle for a chance to marry Erec Dupont—and they gossip about who is pregnant and who is in love and whose husband was caught in one of Avignon's eleven houses of ill repute. Back at home, Margot balances the market receipts against the monthly household budget, helps Anes with chores, and spends the rest of the afternoon sewing the contents of her marriage chest. It seems to me that she already has enough sheets and nightgowns for several lifetimes, but still she bends her head over the yards of cream-colored flax that were Erec's betrothal gift, making her tiny, enviable stitches.

Alone in the kitchen, I eat a breakfast of bread and cheese and consult my mother's book for her feverfew recipe. The book is my most prized possession. Dog-eared and water-stained, it contains all her remedies: medicines to start contractions when a baby will not come, for toothaches and gripe, to soothe winter coughs and ease swelling in painful joints.

I find the page and trace her letters with a finger.

Tonic for Fevers

Grind one handful feverfew with pestle
Add one spoonful valerian root powder
Add one spoonful willow bark powder
Add five drops each elderflower syrup and honey
Mix with aqua vitae

I lose myself in the contentment that always envelops me when I make my mother's recipes, following her spidery script and remembering the sure movements of her hands.

When the church bells chime for terce, I pack my basket. I stare at the empty hook where my cloak usually hangs before remembering that I left it in the meadow for the dog. Margot was right; that was foolish.

Upstairs in Father's room, I lift Mother's cloak from its peg at the back of the wardrobe and stand for a long moment with my nose buried in the gray wool. The house seems to listen, silent and heavy around me.

I walk north through the city under heavy rain clouds, dread tugging at my feet like a lodestone.

The houses grow taller and finer as I approach the rue Dorée. Some of them are the city seats of lesser nobles, but the grandest are the homes of the new merchant class. Through trade, these families have grown far wealthier than the solicitors and notaries who, like my family, live along the rue des Lices, and they style themselves after the old noblesse in opulence if not elegance. Intermixed with the old coats of arms are the new emblems of legacy, available for purchase if one only has enough gold.

The Dupont home is beautiful and spacious and drafty. It looms over the rue Dorée like a disapproving scarecrow, its white stone facade discolored with soot. I regard it from the opposite side of the street as I wait for a break between rattling handcarts and burdened donkeys. The mullioned windows stare back, giving nothing away.

Before I was old enough to accompany Mother on her house calls without getting underfoot, she left both me and Margot with Erec while she attended her patients. The three of us hid in every corner of this house, climbed the roof to throw rotten apples at passersby, hunted for ghosts in the cellar until Erec's tutor caught us and forced him back to his lessons. Then one day Mother and I turned together toward the open streets and forests and left Margot here, in Mathilde Dupont's cold mansion.

Memories overlay one another like a flock of pigeons taking wing. Me, Erec, and Margot digging for worms in the garden dirt; Erec laughing from the tallest tree branch; Erec chasing Margot through the door, tripping on the threshold and cutting his chin open. He was so brave when my mother stitched it up, jaw clenched, squeezing my hand so tight I did not think I could stand it.

Erec's face the day my mother died, reflecting my own pain like a mirror.

"Move back, girl!"

A cart laden with turnips rumbles past, and I step out of its path. At the next break in the traffic, I zigzag across the street to the door, raise the heavy bronze knocker, and let it fall.

After a moment, a narrow-eyed woman opens it. She takes in my wet cloak, the mud on my shoes. Her apron and bonnet are stiff with starch and very white. Like Mathilde, like everything about this house, she has an air of unpleasant superiority.

"Good day," I say, mustering a smile. "I am an old friend of Erec's. He asked me to visit his mother."

"Indeed," she says with a disapproving sniff. "The young master told me to expect you." And then, rather regretfully: "Come in."

She steps back without opening the door wider, and I squeeze past her into the entrance hall. As my eyes adjust to the dim interior, the young shades of me and Erec scatter like rats.

"May I take your cloak?" the woman asks. The words are polite but the tone chilly.

"Thank you." I unclasp the fastening and hand it to her reluctantly. I feel naked without it, as though it offered some form of protection.

"I shall inform Master Dupont that you have arrived," she says, holding the fabric at a distance as she leaves the room.

The hall is unchanged since I was last here. Expensive tapestries cover the walls. A long table with carved legs—which I would bet my boots has never seen a feast—takes up the center of the room. Before me the ostentatious banister ascends to the first floor, embellished with curling ironwork ensconcing the Duponts' recently purchased coat of arms.

My heels send up sweet clouds of straw and lavender. It smells the same. My mother taught Mathilde that trick, to toss herbs in with the rushes.

Saints gaze out at me from their tapestries, faces flat and blank. The stink of candles burning in the chandelier mingles with the lavender. Tallow, not the much more expensive but sweet-smelling beeswax. No matter how rich, Allistair Dupont will always be the son of a wool merchant.

When we were children, a cat from the stable had her kittens under this table. Erec, Margot, and I lay on our bellies for hours and watched her lick them clean. When Mathilde found them, she had the stable boy tie them in a sack and throw them in the river.

"Elea?"

I turn. Erec stands in the arched hallway leading to his father's study in a dark green doublet that makes his bright hair shine.

"Thank you for coming," he says, crossing the hall in a few long strides. "May I take your basket?"

I hand it to him. "How is Mathilde today?"

"Her fever worsened in the night," he says. "She does not know where she is, does not recognize me. I am glad you are here."

I see, now, the marks of a night passed without sleep: the blue crescents under his eyes, the wrinkles in his white undershirt.

"How long has she been ill?" I ignore the apprehension settling like a rock in my stomach and adopt the matter-of-fact tone my mother used to hide her concern. "And how has the illness progressed?"

"She has not been herself since the rain started in September," Erec replies. "She is distant, unquiet. Prone to sharp turns in mood. Last Tuesday Dr. Laurent performed his twice-weekly bloodletting. She was weak the following day, which is not unusual. On Thursday she awoke with a fever, and I called the doctor back. He recommended a bland diet of bread and milk and said something about how her symptoms were due to . . . Jupiter in Sagittarius, perhaps? I can never keep that astronomical nonsense straight."

The narrow-eyed woman reappears in the hallway leading to the servants' quarters.

"You've met Madame Cromier," says Erec, gesturing toward her. "Mother's lady's maid."

She curtsies stiffly; I can nearly hear her bones creaking.

"She will fetch anything you require. Shall we go up?"

I nod, my mouth suddenly dry.

As we ascend the staircase, Madame Cromier following a few

discreet steps behind, the memory of my last visit to this house pounds through my thoughts like a fist on a door.

"Mother called for Bietriz again this morning," Erec says quietly.

It is for her, for Margot, that I am here. Fever can masquerade as madness, I remind myself. Perhaps it is just a fever.

We reach the landing, walk down the long hall, dark as twilight, to the door of Mathilde's rooms. Erec knocks with an ear to the wood. I see his boy's face again, earnest and frightened. He turns the handle and gestures for me to follow.

Heat hits my face like a blow.

The fire is built midwinter high and illuminates the room with a red glow. The thick velvet curtains are pulled tight against the daylight. Sticky incense fills my nostrils, followed by sweat and human waste and something fouler.

A woman kneels, feeding the fire. I recognize her as the Duponts' cook, red-cheeked and sweaty, quick with a wooden spoon to the bottom. Two other female servants, kitchen maids judging by the soot on their hungry faces, stand by the high four-posted bed. They curtsy as we enter and step away to reveal a form in the white sheets, slight as a girl.

Erec places my basket on a table and bends over his mother. He extricates a limp hand, lifts it to his lips, murmurs something soothing. Motions for me to come closer.

But I am in another room, where bright morning light shines on blood-soaked sheets and my mother lies so still, her eyes open.

Erec speaks again. The scene before me slides into focus.

"Mother," he says tenderly. "Eleanore is here to care for you."

I feel the wheels of fate turning like one of Monsieur Dupont's water mills. I force my feet to take the steps to the bed.

The change in Mathilde Dupont stops my breath. Only two years have passed since I last saw her, but it might be twenty. Her fragile beauty is wasted: the white skin of which she was so vain sags around colorless, crusted lips. Her once gold hair is brittle and dull as dead grass, gummed to her brow and pillow with sweat. I can smell the sickness through her skin, the way one knows milk has just turned. Something rots within her.

Just a fever?

I unpack my basket. Erec stands behind me, watches as I lay out my medicines. I hope he cannot see my hands shaking.

"When was she last bled?" I ask the question mostly to quiet the panic in my head.

"Three days ago." Sweat beads his upper lip; the room is stifling.

I feel at Mathilde's clammy neck and wrist for her pulse. It is rapid and shallow. Her right arm, the one Erec pulled from the sheets, is wrapped in white gauze. The vein inside the elbow is a common bleeding site.

I unwind the bandage to reveal six horizontal slashes in the white flesh, the skin patterned like a snake's with dozens of old scars. I cringe, imagining the cold lancet slicing through the delicate skin of my forearm. My mother hated bloodletting; she thought it barbaric, that it weakened the patient. These wounds are in different stages of healing: a thin scab marks the topmost cut, bright red blood congeals at the clean and open edges of the lowest.

"Did Dr. Laurent bleed her only from this arm?" I ask.

Erec shrugs.

I walk to the opposite side of the bed and lift the sheet to reveal Mathilde's left arm, wrapped in older, grimier bandages. I find an edge and start to peel the gauze away. The arm feels bloated and heavy in my hands. As the layers come away, the smell of rot grows stronger, the gauze is glued to itself. Erec pulls a scented kerchief from his pocket and holds it over his nose.

I peel the last of the bandage free. A cut, the length of a needle, festers just below the crease of the elbow. The incision is blue gray, the surrounding flesh is swollen, mottled purple and yellow.

I gently grip Mathilde's arm, one hand above and the other below the cut, and squeeze. Pus floods the cleft edges of skin. Behind me, Erec retches. Mathilde groans, her eyes flickering behind bruised lids.

I am not my mother, but I know that this wound is putrid and needs to be cleaned immediately. Even so, even if my mother were here herself, I am not sure that Mathilde will survive this corruption, nor the amputation that any barber-surgeon would likely advise.

I turn away from the specter of my nightmares, reduced to this: a sick old woman.

Erec's face is pale in the red glow of the fire.

"It's corrupted. This is too advanced for my skills," I whisper. "You should call her physician."

"Dr. Laurent would have killed her." The words come through clenched teeth. "He did not think to examine his last cut, or worse: he saw the putrefaction and thought he could drive it out with more bleeding. That man shall never enter this house again."

"Then you must call a different physician. I make teas for head colds, Erec. I am not my mother."

Erec steps closer, drops his voice. I look up into the face of my old friend. The face my sister loves.

"That idiot doctor has been here every day and failed to realize what you did in an instant," he says. "She asked for your mother. Her knowledge and skills live in you. *Please*."

At least I can do no worse than this doctor, too blinded by pride to question his initial diagnosis. Yes, I knew what was wrong. Yes, I watched my mother stitch up a hundred wounds.

"I will do my best to clean and suture the wound," I say reluctantly, "but the *moment* I tell you to fetch a physician, you must run like the devil himself is chasing you. Do you understand?"

Relief washes over his face. "I understand."

Despite my hesitation, the steps jump into my head as though they were waiting to present themselves. I send Erec to the cellar for a bottle of his father's aqua vitae and Madame Cromier and the kitchen girls to fetch hot water and clean linen. I ask the cook to stoke the fire high enough to keep the water hot. I open all the windows.

In the bottom of my basket is a small purse with my mother's instruments: an awl, a set of sewing scissors that I stole from Margot, and a skein of thread made of sheep's intestines for suturing. As I lift Mother's scalpel, the light flashes off the metal like fish scales. I blink away a vision of the last time I used it, when it bit through my mother's flesh like butter and I could not stop the hemorrhage that killed her.

When Erec and the women return, I have cauterized the scalpel and awl in the fire with a pair of tongs.

"Lay out the supplies," I instruct Madame Cromier. "Be ready with hot water and cloths."

I place Mathilde's arm on pillows in the light of the open window. First the putrefaction must be cleared.

I pull the cork free from the bottle of aqua vitae, tempted to take a swig for courage. "Will you hold her, Erec?" I ask. "This next part will hurt. She may jump."

Erec places his hands on his mother's frail shoulders as I dribble the alcohol into the cut. Mathilde writhes for a moment, tossing her head on the pillow as though caught in a nightmare. Then she is still.

The edges of the wound are my next task. With Margot's sewing scissors I painstakingly remove the dead skin. Mathilde does not move again, although bright red blood dribbles down her arm. Madame Cromier stands at my elbow and dabs the wound clean between snips. She is an intuitive assistant, and despite her earlier coldness, I am glad she is here.

I thread the awl with sheep's gut thread, thinking self-consciously of my hasty needlework and Margot's perfect stitches. I remember my mother's steady hands and will mine to not tremble.

With some difficulty, I pierce the skin and join the two sides with a tight suture. The first two attempts are a bit sloppy, but I find my rhythm, and by the time I close the wound, the stitches are neat and uniform, almost as pretty as my mother's. It seems to take an eternity. My fingers cramp with the effort, and my back and neck ache from craning over the bed.

When I step back to admire my handiwork, I am filled with pride. I was never meant for embroidery.

"Well done!" says Erec, throwing an arm around me and pulling my shoulder against his. "I told you, you are as good as Bietriz."

"She is not free from danger," I say, turning out of his half embrace to clean my instruments. "Far from it. I will do all I can, but she must fight the corruption herself."

I dab an alcohol-soaked cloth over the wound once more, then apply an ointment made of rose oil and egg whites. I wrap the arm loosely with gauze and, with Madame Cromier's help, spoon two measures of feverfew tonic between Mathilde's parched lips.

"What now?" asks Erec.

"Now," I reply grimly, "we wait."

Erec and I pull up chairs to the bedside while the servants tidy the room, whisking away the soiled bandages and bloody linen.

We spend the afternoon watching the rise and fall of Mathilde's narrow rib cage. I stand at intervals to drip water between her lips, feel the pulse below her jaw. Bit by bit her breathing becomes deeper, her pulse stronger. Erec falls asleep in his chair, head lolling on his shoulder. I watch him, examine the face that will kiss my sister, will take her from me. But my jealousy has cooled.

I doze as well, lulled to sleep by the quiet room and warm fire. When I start awake, I am uncertain, for a moment, where I am. I gaze around the room blearily, take in the slanting golden light through the windows, the fire reduced to embers.

Erec's chair is empty. I am alone.

I stand, sore-backed after so long in one position, and approach the bed. Faint color blooms in Mathilde's sallow cheeks; she inhales and exhales with the steady cadence of sleep. I check her pulse and temperature and sigh with relief: the fever has broken.

I pack my supplies and head for the door, planning to find Erec, give him the good news. Behind me, the bedclothes stir.

A creeping feeling spreads up my spine, like cold water seeping into fabric.

"Bietriz?"

Mathilde's eyes are open, the same summer-sky blue as Erec's. She blinks, trying to bring my face into focus. "Bietriz?" she croaks again. "You have forgiven me?"

It takes a moment for the words to sink in. Beside them I hear my mother's voice, as I did last night. *Forgive her, Elea. She is a prisoner of her own mind.*

"Not Bietriz, Madame Dupont," I say soothingly, setting down my basket and moving to the bedside. "I'm Eleanore. Her daughter."

She stares at me, lips moving silently. Open and closed, open and closed.

"I'm going to find your son." I reach down and cover her cold fingers with mine. "I'm going to get Erec."

Mathilde glances down at my hand on hers. When she raises her eyes again, it is not the gaze of my mother's friend that meets mine. It is that of an untethered mind.

"You sneaking witch," Mathilde spits, wrenching her fingers free. "You dare enter my home, Bietriz? After what you did?"

I stagger backward, nearly tripping over my basket.

"You killed my child!" she shrieks. "Get out of my house!"

I grab my supplies and run to the door, her words pelting me like arrows. "Get out, *witch*! Get out! GET OUT!"

I nearly collide with Erec on the landing.

"Elea!" He glances over my shoulder at the door.

Through the wood, his mother's screams have melted into moans.

"What happened?"

I want to push past him. I want to run down the stairs and through the streets and not stop until I am in my bed with the covers over my head.

"Her fever broke," I say. "She awoke and mistook me for my mother."

Erec examines my face, sees the fear and rage written there. He runs a hand over his jaw. Shakes his head. "I'm so sorry, Elea. She's not . . . she's not herself. She has not been herself for many years."

Beneath its frantic pounding, my heart aches for him. His mother may still be living, but he has lost her, too.

"Come on," Erec says, turning his back on the closed door. "Let me walk you home."

The late-afternoon sun casts the cobblestones in an amber patina. The streets are busy with peasants leaving the city markets, basket weavers and leather workers and wool dyers on their way home to their families or the tempting anonymity of a tavern.

Erec and I do not speak. I am unsettled, tangled in the memory of Mathilde's shift, the sudden wildness in her eyes. By the set of his mouth, I guess Erec, too, is thinking of his mother. But he is a perfect gentleman and offers his arm over broken cobbles, places his body between mine and the street. As we approach the rue des Oranges, he stops suddenly and turns to face me, his profile edged like a saint's in the coppery light.

"Do you hear that?"

My ears fill with the daily cacophony: the rattle of carts, the calls of peasants selling their wares, the lowing of lucky beasts who survived another market day.

But then I hear it. A harsh voice stretched to its limit to carry through the narrow streets. A voice that makes the hair on my forearms stand on end.

Erec grabs my hand and pulls me toward it, down the twisting rue des Oranges.

The passage is dense with other people emerging from homes and businesses, searching, as we are, for the source of the commotion. Erec tries to press forward, but the crowd is thick; he cranes his neck, taller than nearly everyone by a head, but the abrupt turn in the street only allows him a view of ten paces. Shutters creak open overhead, faces appear at windows.

"The end times are here!" screams the ragged voice, growing closer now. It is a voice that should speak only in whispers, its unnatural projection scraping painfully through windpipe and across tongue. "It is written that the day of the Lord will come like a thief, that the heavens will pass away with a roar, and the heavenly bodies will burn and dissolve!"

In the hush that descends, I hear the shuffling of many feet.

The crowd at the turn of the street ahead splits, presses against the walls to make space. Erec inhales sharply as the first figure rounds the corner.

A boy, no more than thirteen, shirtless and filthy. His ribs and breastbone press beneath bruised skin, his bare feet on the cobblestones are cracked and bleeding. In his hands, he holds a leather whip.

"He shall send famine against you, and wild beasts to rob you of your children!" the bodiless speaker shrieks. "Pestilence and blood will pass through the land, and the Lord shall bring the sword upon all sinners!"

The boy is a few steps away from us. I cannot tear my eyes from the hollows of his face, the sores around his mouth. His eyes are lightless; he lifts the whip overhead and brings it down behind him with a terrible slap on the bare skin of his own back.

Erec reaches his arm across my chest protectively, presses me against the wall. I am grateful, for I do not trust my feet to hold me.

"Flame and sulfur will rain from heaven, and flood will clear the sinners from the earth!" The voice is almost upon us now, cracking in desperation.

A long line of penitents follows the boy, none as young as he but all with the same dead expression, all carrying tools of self-mortification. All their backs slashed and bleeding.

"And as for the cowardly," the voice rasps, "the faithless, the sorcerers, the followers of the false prophet, their portion will be in the lake that burns with fire." A tall, stooped figure rounds the corner, draped in a black cassock.

I gasp.

There is the long, hungry face, the eyes dark as dungeons, as devoid of kindness as the holes in a hangman's hood.

"They shall burn with the devil who deceived them and be tormented day and night forever more!"

It is Father Loup.

Chapter Three

Flagellants," Erec says to Father as Anes takes his cloak. "About two dozen by my count."

"Those lunatics," Father says roughly, "traveling from city to city, chanting and beating themselves to a bloody pulp. Believing they can stop the end of the world through their suffering." He scoffs. "Madness. The pope will spit when he hears. They will be ejected from the city by morning, mark my words. You are too young to remember, but they have passed through Avignon before. A rash of crimes always follows them: the lynching of single women, Jews, gypsies."

"Are you all right?" Erec asks, guiding me to Father's high-backed chair beside the fire. "You're white as a sheet."

Father Loup passed inches from me. Close enough to mark the liver spots on skin as pale as a body pulled from the river, the broken fingernails.

Margot comes downstairs with a question in her face, and Erec pulls her aside. I hear him tell her in a low voice what we witnessed, feel her concerned gaze on me but cannot meet it. Father hands me a cup of hot wine. I take it with shaking hands.

Perhaps it was not him. But of course it was. His gaze roved over my face and past without recognition. How could he not remember?

"Why so pale, Elea?" Margot places her palm on my forehead the way Mother used to, although my sister would not know a fever if it burned a hole in her hand. "It is not like you to weaken at the sight of flesh and blood."

If she were not already dying, I would burn her myself.

"It was Father Loup," I say.

Margot and Father lock eyes over my head.

"Father Loup?" Erec repeats, unaware of the sudden tension in my sister's shoulders, the muscle working in Father's jaw.

I nod.

"Was he not your old priest at Saint-Agricol, before Father Germaine? The one shipped off to Arles after delivering a sermon calling for the expulsion of the Jews from Provence?"

I nod, not trusting myself to speak.

"That must have been, what? Three years ago?" Erec asks.

"Two." There is a rare edge in Margot's voice.

"Father thought his idea had some merit," Erec continues obliviously. "By banishing the Jews and confiscating their property, King Philip paid his debts and helped fund his war with England. The pope could launch another crusade."

"He is a cruel man," I say. "A cruel, violent man."

"The Jews provide an essential service to Avignon," says Father, steering the conversation out of dark waters. "Only they can provide the loans that Pope Clement and King Philip already desperately need. Throwing them out and confiscating their money would be shortsighted, not to mention unchristian."

"If it was Father Loup," says Margot quietly, kneeling beside me, "he will be gone tomorrow, as Father said."

"What happened?" asks Erec.

Behind his turned back my father shakes his head imperceptibly, signaling that the subject is closed.

Anger wells up inside me. "He was the priest called to Mother's deathbed," I say. "He refused to read her last rites. He called her—"

"Elea," interrupts my father, a warning in his voice.

"But, Father—"

"That is *enough*."

That night, Margot slides into bed beside me, stealing the heat of my body like a housecat. I scoot away from her, but she follows, moving into the warm vacancy and tucking icy fingers under my waist.

"Stop it!" I hiss. "You're freezing!"

"And you're hot as a chimney brick. You'll miss my cold fingers when I'm gone."

"I will not."

Silence. My lie settles over us like snow.

"Are you all right?" she asks.

I shut my eyes, but Father Loup's voice reverberates inside my skull.

If she were not already dying, I would burn her myself. And you, girl. Your time will come.

"I will be."

My sister presses her forehead against my back. "You'll never see him again."

"That's what we thought when he was sent to Arles. But he is free, Margot. He is out in the world preaching hatred."

"Did he see you?"

I shake my head, remembering the cold crawl of his gaze. "He looked right at me. But he didn't recognize me."

"Thank God Erec was with you," Margot says.

"Thank God," I echo.

Margot tucks her knees tighter behind mine. "Did you hear Father say that the last group of flagellants lynched single women? Pulled them from their homes in the night and killed them. No trial. No hearing. And the papal guard didn't even hear of it until it was over."

I laugh at her transparency. "Here we are again. You want me to wed some pox-nosed clerk who will forbid me from going to the woods."

"A husband would protect you, Elea."

"Marriage is a cage."

"It is freedom." Her voice is sharp. "Not the same freedom as running through the forest with your skirts tucked into your belt, perhaps. But a more secure freedom."

Freedom to share a home with Mathilde and her madness. Freedom to plan each meal to the measure of wheat and number of eggs. Freedom to die with a child trapped between her hips.

"I want you to be safe," my sister says. I hear the tight squeeze of fear in her voice.

If only I could tell her of Mathilde's sudden turn, how the madness slithered from her like a snake in the spring. I imagine the impatient sound my sister would make, the disappointment in her voice. *How many times must we go over this, Elea? She is to be pitied, not feared.*

I ignore the dread thrumming through my veins like a chord with a sour note and cover Margot's hand with mine. "That is my prayer for you, too."

Her chest expands against my back as she inhales. "Perhaps," she says, "we must try to trust each other to make our own way."

I close my eyes and breathe my sister's smell, the female scent of her body and hair, the old fragrance of lavender. I distill bottles of it every summer but can never bring myself to wear it. It is Mother's smell. But somehow it smells right on Margot and does not make me sad.

"*Tu es moi-même*," I whisper. Our childhood endearment, consolation, apology.

"You are myself," she repeats.

The night tiptoes past, each hour marked by the gloomy clang of the bell at Saint-Agricol.

Margot's soft snores fill the room, but there is no sleep for me. Father Loup's voice slips over my skin and into my ears, punctuated by the thud of leather on flesh. Behind shut eyelids Mathilde waits for me, spitting like a viper. Here, too, is my mother, pale-faced and still.

Just before dawn, my father's feet hit the floor in the room beside me and limp down the creaking stairs. The front door opens and shuts as the bells chime for prime.

I climb out of bed, careful not to wake Margot.

"You look ghastly!" exclaims Anes as I enter the kitchen. She lifts my chin and examines my bloodshot eyes.

"Thanks, Anes," I mutter.

She places a hand on my forehead. "No fever, thank the Virgin," she says. "The air is bad. Far too wet for November." She pours me a cup of hot ale, which I take gratefully, feeling warmer and more fortified with each sip.

Anes bustles about and brings me a helping of bread and sausages, which I move around the plate without appetite. I watch her stoke the fire, chop celery and carrots and onions for stew. When she turns her back, I slide a beef bone from her pile and tuck it in my apron pocket. Perhaps I can steal away to the meadow.

"Will you visit Madame Dupont today?" Anes asks.

I avoid her eyes. "She has my medicine. I can do nothing more for her, I fear. And I have my own patients to see."

I pack my basket and leave the house before Margot is awake.

Of my thin list of clients only the baker's wife, Madame Vielle, is up and dressed at this hour. In the cramped, hot tenement over the bakery in the rue de l'Épicerie I massage the baby's swollen belly and give Madame Vielle a balm of chamomile and lanolin for her sore nipples.

"Que Dieu vous bénisse, mademoiselle," she says, as always, handing me a warm loaf of bread.

"May God bless you, too," I say, tucking the fragrant gift into my basket.

Outside, the rising sun peeks valiantly through ragged clouds. The city is coming to life, the streets full of carts, people and animals headed to market. I lose myself in the crowd heading north toward the palace up storm-clean stones. Last week I set the broken arm of a woodworker's son in the rue de la Grande Fusterie. There is no harm in stopping by; I have nothing else to do, and the boy's mother always knows the juiciest town gossip, which I repeat with relish for Anes.

In the shadow of the palace walls, Avignon's principal market rises from the cobblestones. Donkeys and horses stand patiently beneath their bundles of merchandise, stall poles lie forlornly beside bright squares of tent fabric. The air is redolent with the smells of animal dung and cooked meat.

"Apples!" a woman calls half-heartedly as I pass, pushing a wheelbarrow full of firm pink fruit. "Last of the season!"

Their perfume makes my mouth water. "How much?"

"A *denier* the dozen," she replies.

A ridiculous price. But then I imagine the tart Anes might make of them. "I'll take a dozen."

As I fish in my purse for the silver coin, the woman leans closer and lowers her voice conspiratorially. "Did you see the commotion?"

I frown. "What commotion?"

"Those religious fanatics, them that whip themselves. The papal guard ran them out of the city." She points toward the south gate. "Passed this way not five minutes ago, herded like so many sheep. Led by a priest shrieking about the end of the world."

I follow her finger, but the street is empty of Clement's scarlet livery.

"And good riddance," the apple seller continues, spitting on the cobblestones. "Mortifying their own flesh. Just children, some of them were. What would Christ say about that?"

I make some reply and pay for my apples.

He is gone, I tell myself. He has left Avignon.

But as I turn to face the wide Magna Carreira, I can't shake the disquiet from my head. Father was right. Margot was right. I will likely never see Father Loup again. Still, the thought of returning home, to Anes humming happily in the kitchen and Margot embroidering beside the window, makes my skin feel too tight around my bones.

A drop of rain falls on my cheek.

I put a hand in my apron pocket for my handkerchief, and my fingers encounter something hard and rough. The beef bone.

I turn my feet west and walk toward the river.

Chapter Four

The mud around the cottage is riddled with paw prints and the bread is gone. My cloak is where I left it, drenched in the rain of two nights ago, covered in long black hairs and rusty bloodstains. The dog slept here, ate my bread. He must be close.

I sit on the ruined fabric and lean my back against the warm stone wall of the cottage. I close my eyes and shut my mind against the memories of Father Loup, of Mathilde, and focus instead on the sounds around me.

Wind whispers through naked branches. Birds call to one another as they journey south for winter. A twig snaps.

I open my eyes.

Another crack of wood beneath weight, the crunch of leaves under heavy feet.

My head swivels. The meadow is empty, the tree line dark and still. Whatever it is, it is behind me, on the far side of the ruined cottage.

More footfalls; the sucking sound of a boot sunken in mud. A muttered curse.

Not long ago these woods were filled with vagabonds: groups of roaming peasants from the north who abandoned their barren homesteads during the Great Famine. Hungry and desperate, with no skills save working the land, they became criminals. They lived meanly off what they could forage, robbed merchants on their way to the markets of Avignon, raped travelers' wives and daughters until Pope John XXII sent armed guards to patrol the land surrounding the city. My mother remembered bloated bodies hanging from trees lining the path to town, a warning to other would-be bandits. Since then, the woods are generally safe and empty, save the odd peasant foraging for mushrooms or trapping rabbits.

The footsteps grow fainter. When a few silent minutes have passed, I get to my feet and peek my head around the wall of the cottage.

There is no movement from the forest.

I wait for another moment, then lift my basket and cross the open meadow.

In the shadows of the trees, I pause again, listening. Silence greets my ears. Whoever he was, whatever he was doing here, he is gone now and so clumsy in the woods that I will hear him if he comes again. I spot a footprint in the mud below a pine and kneel, examining it. The outline of the heeled boot is massive, sunk deep into the earth. A big man in fine shoes: no peasant's hide slippers.

The bushes behind me rustle. I jump backward and lose my balance, fall on my wrist. I try to push myself to my feet, to run—then something big and four-legged emerges from the undergrowth.

It is the dog.

He limps toward me cautiously, his long nose lifted and quivering, hunger calling louder than fear. He does not put any weight on the lame paw but holds it high and dangling.

I reach into my pocket, pull out the beef bone, set it on the ground before me. He sniffs suspiciously, takes another limping step forward with his eyes on mine.

I have bandages and ointment if he will let me bind his leg. How will I win the trust of this wild animal?

Speak to him, my mother would say. *Tell him the truth.*

I close my eyes, clear my mind of chattering thoughts, and focus on the wounded creature before me.

I will not harm you. I visualize cleaning the wound, binding it. *I can help. But you must come closer, you must trust me.*

I open my eyes and nearly fall backward again. The dog sits before me with his lame paw lifted, just as he would have done for my mother. Between rows of white teeth, saliva glistens in ropes, but his long ears are raised to me curiously. Something tame glimmers in his brown eyes.

Barely breathing, I reach out my hand until my fingers close over the fur of his foreleg, then pull my eyes from his to examine the wound.

The fur is matted with blood, and it is difficult to see the depth of the cut, but the bones do not appear to be broken. With my free hand I reach into my basket and feel for the bottle of aqua vitae and cloth. To calm the dog and myself, I speak out loud.

"This will sting," I say quietly. "But it is important to first cleanse the wound." I soak the rag, take a deep breath, and place it over the cut. The dog yelps as the alcohol burns and tries to pull his leg from my grasp, but I am ready for it and hold him tightly. After a moment he stops struggling, but his eyes are wide, his breath quick and shallow.

"Good boy," I whisper. "Good dog. That is the worst bit over."

The alcohol dissolves the coagulated blood. I move the paw slowly through its range of motion; the dog whines but does not cry out again. The sharp teeth of the trap bit through skin and muscle, but the deep ligaments and bones appear undamaged. Thank God.

"You're being very brave," I say. "Now for some ointment, which will help with healing."

I pull out a jar of oregano and garlic ointment and remove the clay lid. It is smelly stuff: the dog's nose wrinkles distastefully.

"I know," I say. "The other forest creatures will mistake you for an Italian. But it will keep the wound from souring." I smear the ointment over the wound in a thick layer.

I locate my roll of bandages: an old bedsheet torn into strips. I wind the fabric around his ankle like a figure eight to support the joint and tuck the end in tightly, then set his foot on the ground. He sniffs my handiwork curiously, places tentative weight on the bandaged foreleg, takes a few steps. It works better than I hoped.

The dog looks up at me and moves his tail awkwardly, as though he is trying to wag it but does not know how. I hold out my hand, turn the palm down. He lifts his great head until the soft fur between his ears meets my skin. Slowly I slide my hand down the back of his neck, across his powerful shoulders, down his spine to the base of his tail. He tries to wag it again.

"You need a name," I say. "A strong, noble name." I repack my basket as he settles on the ground beside me and helps himself to the beef bone. "I think 'Baldoin' suits you. It means 'brave friend.'"

Baldoin and I share an apple and the baker's bread, and I tell him about my medicines; how I made them and what they do. "And this, Baldoin," I say, uncorking a glass bottle of wolfsbane tincture and holding it out to him, "eases pain and swelling from bruises and falls." He takes a sniff and sneezes.

It is midday when I stand and brush the crumbs from my skirt. "I will come back in a few days with food, and to change your bandage."

Baldoin gets to his feet, too, a little unsteady on his front leg.

"Be careful," I say, scratching him between the ears. "There is a man somewhere in these woods. He may think you a wolf, until he sees the bread crumbs on your face."

I walk back toward the path, glancing over my shoulder every few steps at Baldoin, who watches me with ears and tail high but does not follow. Soon the trees eclipse him, and I am once again alone.

I have nearly reached the road when a patch of hawthorn catches my eye, the red berries bright against dark leaves. It is late for them, and after the short, wet summer, this is the only fruiting bush I have seen. The berries are sour and sweet, perfect for cordials or pies, but they also have a myriad of medicinal qualities. The fruit is cleansing and acidic; it decreases swelling and produces copious urine in someone with too much water in their body. My mother made a tonic of hawthorn berries to ease the swelling in my father's leg. Remembering his painful step on the stairs this morning, I pick the bush clean and place the berries on a cloth over the apples so they will not be squished.

I step onto the muddy path and begin my descent to the shining Rhône. The road is empty—no pilgrims climbing to the shrine of Saint Casarie, nor peasants peddling their wares at the abbey.

As I walk, another sound becomes apparent over my own quiet step. It grows louder and louder until the click of heeled boots on packed earth echoes off the mountainside. A shape has appeared at the curve of the hill behind me, huge and black against the steep road. The man from the woods.

"Girl!" he calls.

I pick up my pace.

"Girl!" he repeats. I glance back; he is twenty yards away now, every footfall like a drumbeat in my ears. "Slow down!"

The bridge is a ten-minute walk, at least. I slide a hand in my basket under the cloth, feel for the handle of my scalpel.

"I wish to see what's in your basket!"

He's breathing like a winded ox. If I turn into the woods and run, I can outpace him. As I scan the bank of bushes for a break in the foliage, the undergrowth beside me shudders. A shape moves parallel to me through the thick leaves and branches.

It is Baldoin.

"Are you deaf, girl?" the giant calls, nearly upon me now. "I shall give you a *sou* if those are hawthorn berries!"

I stop. Behind the cover of bushes behind me I feel Baldoin freeze, lift his long nose to catch the man's scent.

Slowly, I turn. The giant stands ten paces away, catching his breath. He takes off his hat to mop the sweat from his forehead with a lacy handkerchief. His clothing is wildly expensive: a coat of purple velvet cut long in the Italian fashion, pointed leather boots coated in mud. A gold pendant swings on his neck. His visage, however, is anything but noble. He looks like a Provençal farmer with his big bones, swarthy skin, curling black hair, and thick beard. His nose is very large and covered with big pores, a few black hairs springing from the tip. A boar in fancy clothing.

When he has collected himself, he shoves his purple hat on his sweaty curls and gives me a courtier's bow. "Forgive me," he says in a deep voice that matches his size. "I did not intend to frighten you. I have scoured the markets, these damned woods, and the abbey garden for hawthorn berries but have not had your enviable luck. I shall give you a *sou* for your basket. I require them for a patient."

Of course. I am irritated with myself that I did not realize it immediately: doctors wear purple. This man is a wealthy physician, likely attached to a cardinal's or nobleman's household.

"I will give you some," I say carefully, not wanting to anger him. "But I, too, have need of them."

He snorts. "You would turn down a *sou*? What will you use them for, a pie?"

I stand up taller, bristling. "My father's leg swells and pains him with changing weather. A tincture of hawthorn helps clear the water."

The man eyes me sharply, his piggy eyes suddenly bright and intelligent. "That is true," he says, "and what else would you use them for?"

Suddenly I am full of fierce pride for my mother, what she knew and taught me. This man attended medical school, but my mother once told me that physicians do not study even the most basic techniques of midwifery. They think the miracles of pregnancy and birth beneath them, that such messy matters should be handled only by women.

"Hawthorn berries have many purposes," I recite. "A tea can ease disorders of the heart or blood. A tincture can decrease swelling in the body by increasing urine."

He blinks. "How do you know this?"

"My mother's father was a staff physician for Pope Benedict. He taught her everything he knew. She was the best herbalist and midwife in Avignon."

He considers this, considers me, steps back a pace, and looks me up and down.

"I would like to see how you make that tincture," he says. "Would you accompany me to my laboratory and allow me to watch you work? I have all the supplies you need, I'm sure, or could easily have them fetched."

I regard him with suspicion. Why would a clearly successful physician deign to learn from me?

"Of course I will pay you handsomely for your time," he says, sensing my hesitation.

"I am not an herbalist, nor an *apothicaire*," I say, my hasty pride deflating. "I have no formal training. There are many skilled healers in Avignon, certainly one of them—"

"Folk medicine is old," the giant says, cutting me off with a smile, "and the roots run deep. Modern medicine has many applications, but the discipline is young—we have much to learn yet. Sometimes the simplest remedies are the most effective. And they did not teach me how to make a hawthorn berry tincture at the medical school at Montpellier. I would like to learn."

When I say nothing, he takes another step toward me, holding his palms open.

"Please." There is a note of desperation in his voice now. "My patient is very important and very ill. I have done everything I know to do, as have other learned physicians. But thus far our knowledge has failed us. I read in an ancient text that hawthorn may ease his affliction but do not know how to prepare it. I shall leave no stone unturned if there is a chance of helping him. I came here today praying for wisdom and guidance. Praying to find hawthorn berries. And I met you. Perhaps you have been sent by God to help me."

There is no guile in the big, open face. "Please," he repeats.

I feel, somehow, that I can trust him. "Very well," I say. "I will go with you."

He beams. "I am Guigo," he says, bowing.

"Eleanore," I reply. In the woods behind me I feel Baldoin slip away, confident I am not in danger.

Guigo and I walk side by side down the pitch of the mountain. He speaks incessantly, offering his opinions of the position of this and that planet and their effect on everything from the war with England to the mysterious disease in the East.

"My colleagues at the Paris medical school and I agree, for once, on this," says my new friend. "This eastern pestilence is a result of poisonous air released during an earthquake, which was then ignited by the hot and dry vapors of Mars and Jupiter. We in Europe have nothing to fear, having very few earthquakes ourselves."

In the brief silences between his thoughts, he whistles tunelessly through the gap between his front teeth. My mother rolled her eyes at this astrological nonsense, said diseases were more likely caused by poor hygiene and hunger than the distant movement of stars. But I say nothing, just nod or agree politely when he pauses for breath and wonder if I have made a mistake by agreeing to help him.

As we walk down the path toward the Pont Saint-Bénézet, Guigo gives me a brief background of his patient: a nobleman in his late fifties, vigorous, intelligent, and hardworking. He has been recently afflicted with pain on the right side of his back, a weak pulse, and a fever. Guigo bleeds him daily, prescribes a diet of nothing but bread soaked in milk, and administers a tonic of coriander and willow bark to reduce the fever. Nothing helps. This morning there was blood in his urine. Guigo speaks confidently about his treatment of his patient, says the man should improve when Jupiter's position changes at the end of the month, but I can tell beneath the veneer he is very, very worried. Worried enough to ask a strange girl in the woods for help.

As we approach the bridge, the path thickens with peasants leaving the markets and Avignonese braving the wind to escape the bad city air. Everyone we pass, it seems, wants to stop and speak with Guigo. They thank him for his care of a relation, offer him gifts from their carts, ask his opinion on everything from a weeping ankle sore to Queen Joanna's guilt.

"Queen Joanna is a paragon of womanly virtue," my companion answers to this last question, asked by a nobleman in a parti-colored doublet. "And we all, I am sure, pray for her safe arrival in our fair city. I believe the stars should fall from the sky before she is convicted of murder."

As Guigo turns away, he winks at me.

No one pays me any heed; I may as well be invisible. I observe my new friend's interactions with curiosity. He treats peasants and nobles with equal courtesy, listens to their stories and answers their questions thoughtfully, leaving them with a funny anecdote or a slap on the back. It takes us an age to cross the bridge; by the time we reach the northern gate Guigo carries a bunch of radishes, a vial of rosewater, and a new straw hat. I think of my mother, so skilled in the healing arts. She never received this kind of praise or respect.

"What do you require to make your tincture?" he asks as we approach the street that branches to the market.

I spot the arched doorway of a merchant's house, protected from the bustle in the street, and make for it. "I need to look at the recipe," I say over my shoulder.

I lean against the thick oak doors, crosshatched with iron and emblazoned with the merchant's coat of arms—a rather sickly phoenix rising over a castle turret—and search my basket. Guigo watches with interest as I pull my mother's book free. I turn my back to him, shield her pages from his prying gaze, and flip to the recipe for hawthorn tonic.

"I'll need a mortar and pestle, cheesecloth," I say, tracing my fingers over her letters. "Parsley, dandelion, lemon, aqua vitae."

"Eyes of a toad?" Guigo offers. "Arsenic? Gold? Elephant dung? Powdered pearl?"

I wrap the book in its linen cover and tuck it back in the bottom of my basket. "I'm no witch," I say, meeting his eyes.

He laughs. "No more am I," he says. "Those were remedies recommended by the most preeminent physicians in Europe. But for your recipe we need only send to the kitchens." He shakes his head. "God above, it's the cheapest medicine I've ever heard of."

Guigo leads me through the crowd and up the steep Magna Carreira, toward the pope's palace and the homes of important clergymen.

At the foot of the palace, we stop to catch our breath. As Guigo swabs the sweat from his face with a lace kerchief, I gaze up at the gray facade of the Palais Neuf. The wind carries the smells of mortar and varnish.

Clement began this new construction when the paint of Pope Benedict's palace was still wet and Pope Benedict himself barely cold in his tomb. All of Christendom clicked their tongues over the unnecessary cost, and my father lost most of his hair trying to balance the accounts. We call it a palace, but it is a fortress. The windows are small and high, the only entrance the size of our front door, reinforced with iron and surrounded by guards. The pope has many enemies. He is wary of King Philip to the north, the Aragonese to the south, the bickering Italian city states to the east. I have never been inside, of course, but my father works here—all the men of Avignon work in the palace or for the pope in one way or another: slaughtering his animals, carving his furniture, counting his money, and paying his bills, as Father does.

"Follow me." Guigo stuffs his handkerchief into his pocket and makes straight for the palace, his purple coat flapping behind him.

I hurry after, my mind racing. *Who is his patient?* A bishop? A cardinal? A visiting nobleman?

"Good day, Jean," says Guigo to one of the guards. "This is Eleanore. She is an *herboriste*, here to assist me in my care of His Holiness." Jean scans me from cap to skirt hem then, sensing no threat, raises a chain mail–encased hand. The guards beside the door uncross their lances, the door opens, and I follow Guigo into the papal palace.

It is not until the iron latch clicks behind us that Guigo's words register with a sickening rush.

His Holiness. Guigo's patient is the pope. Which means—Holy Mother of God—this great beast of a man is Guy de Chauliac: a doctor of great renown, born a peasant, who by his own skill and intelligence became the pope's personal physician.

Which means—sweet Virgin—I am about to make my mother's hawthorn berry tonic for Clement VI, under the eyes of the most famous physician in Christendom, with mud on my dress and dog blood under my fingernails.

My knees start to shake.

The interior of the palais passes in a blur. I follow Guigo through an arched passageway, then left down a covered walkway. It's so much larger than I expected, a walled city within a walled city. To my right, across an enormous courtyard, looms the central tower of the complex. The Tour des Anges. I know from Father's descriptions that this is where the pope has his private apartments. Through one of those windows lies God's vassal on earth, feverish and weak. And I am here to help him.

Black-clad notaries hurry past, carrying stacks of documents. The air thrums with men's voices and the distant sound of music. *My father is here,* I realize suddenly. *Perhaps I can find him, make some excuse*—but even as I search for him in each face that passes, my desperate hope deflates. There are thousands of men here. Hundreds of rooms, staircases, corridors. I could search for weeks and never find him.

Guigo pauses before an unassuming door about halfway down the wall of the courtyard. He fiddles in his pocket, draws out a brass key, unlocks it. I follow with my insides in knots.

I expected fine personal chambers—an anteroom, a bed, perhaps. But this is some sort of . . .

"Welcome to my laboratory," Guigo booms.

The room is long, with a large window overlooking the courtyard. Papers and pools of candlewax cover a long table in the center of the room, where a rimmed wine cup sits atop a medical illustration of trepanning. Glass jars hold gray organs suspended in liquid and colorful powders better suited for a painter's workshop. Along the far wall a fire crackles merrily in the grate between a washbasin and a rumpled cot. And the back wall—

I inhale. The back wall of the room is covered by floor-to-ceiling shelves crammed with manuscripts and scrolls, leather-bound volumes and piles of parchment. Never have I seen so many books. I did not know there *were* so many books.

Guigo clears a space for me at the table. I set down my basket but cannot take my eyes from the shelves.

"Ah, yes," says Guigo happily, following my gaze. "My library. It is impressive, no?"

"Where," I stammer, "how did you—"

"I have been collecting for a long time, since I was your age," he says. "Mostly medical texts. But all physicians study mathematics, astrology, history. I have buyers all over Europe. And people send them to me as gifts."

"You have read them all?" I ask incredulously. The firelight flickers over spines embossed with alphabets I do not recognize.

"All of them. I read Latin, Greek, Italian, of course. There are some in Arabic, which I do not read but have had translated. Can you read and write?"

"Just Latin and French."

He nods, pulls out a chair. "Have a seat. I'll apply to the kitchens for your ingredients."

The door closes behind him, and I am left alone with nothing but the popping fire and my screaming thoughts.

It was a mistake to come here. I have no business making medicines for Guy de Chauliac, no business bringing my mother's knowledge and intuition into this place of dead philosophers and power. And Guigo deliberately kept his patient's identity from me until I was already inside the palace, knowing I never would have agreed to help him against stakes this high. If I leave now, disappear through the gates and into the city, he will never find me. I should go.

But when Guigo returns with my supplies, a plate of sausages, a flagon of ale, and two cups, I am still sitting at the table. He takes the seat across from me.

"One cannot work hungry." He pours a cup of ale and hands it to me. "So," he says, spearing a sausage, "what else is in that book of yours?"

I take a gulp. "It was my mother's," I say by way of an answer. "She was a great healer, as I have said—"

"May I see it?"

Reluctantly, I pull the book from my basket and unwrap it. The leather binding is stained and scratched, but I hold it like a relic.

Something in my face must convey the value of the item to Guigo. His eager expression changes to a grave one. He wipes his hands with a kerchief and takes it as gently as though it were Venetian glass.

He lights a candle and opens the book. I watch his eyes pass swiftly over the words, the lists of ingredients written in her delicate hand, the notes and drawings in the margins. His plate lies forgotten beside him.

By the time Guigo closes the cover, the fire wants another log. He holds the book out to me with two hands.

"You spoke truthfully, mademoiselle," he says quietly. "Your mother was a great healer. These pages are full of old folk wisdom and new medicines, combinations and ratios I have never seen before. You are right to cherish them."

My throat feels tight. I wish I could tell Mother that Guy de Chauliac thought her a great healer.

"Thank you for letting me read it," he says. "I am honored that you trusted me with such a treasure."

As I wrap the book in its linen shroud and tuck it away in my basket, the church bells chime for none.

"God's teeth," says Guigo, pushing back from the table and getting to his feet. "Is that the time? His Holiness will send for me after vespers. Come, mademoiselle, and let me observe you make this tonic."

I roll up my sleeves and unpack the ingredients on the empty space he has cleared for me at the table. I start by grinding half the hawthorn berries.

"Why grind them?" Guigo asks. "Why not juice them, or make an infusion with alcohol?"

I shoot him a black look from under my eyebrows.

"I'm sure there's a reason," he says quickly, holding up giant palms. "You're the expert. You and your mother. I shall promptly shut up."

And, to his credit, he does.

Guigo watches the process from over my shoulder. I feel him shift his bulk from one foot to the other as questions burn on his tongue, but he does not interrupt. When I empty the ground berries into the vial, he runs his finger along the lip of the mortar and sniffs the grainy residue. When I finish chopping the parsley and dandelion, he takes an unused sprig of each and chews them thoughtfully. I pour the last of the lemon juice into the glass vial, fill it to the top with aqua vitae, stopper it, and shake it. It is so sour that the smell alone floods my mouth with saliva.

"Let it steep overnight," I say, handing the tonic to Guigo. "Tomorrow, strain out the sediment through the cheesecloth. Give His Holiness three spoonfuls on an empty stomach morning and night."

"How many days will it last?" he asks, holding the murky substance up to the light.

I consider the little bottle. "About a week," I guess.

"And if it works? If I need more?"

"You know how to make it. I'll leave you the rest of the hawthorn berries."

Guigo grins. "Ah, mademoiselle, I fear I do not have your skills. At least direct me to where I might find you, should I require your knowledge again."

An hour ago, I couldn't wait to leave this place. And now I don't want to.

"Where the rue des Lices crosses the Magna Carreira," I say, "the big sandstone house on the corner."

Guigo jots the address on a piece of parchment, then unties the purse strings at his belt. I hear the clink of metal on metal and feel the warmth drain from me like water from a tub. He is going to pay me like a servant and send me home. The miraculous door that was opened this afternoon will once again close to me forever. Margot will begin her new life. I will care for Father, deliver babies, make ointments, and set broken bones until I die.

Guigo hands me a *sou*. "And if I require your services in the future, there will be more coins for you. Think of the cloth you could buy"—he looks at my filthy frock with pity—"and make yourself a new dress!"

I stare down at the cold gold in my hand.

"Come now," Guigo says, opening the laboratory door. "I'll walk you to the gate."

My mind moves frantically. This gift—any wisdom in my hands, any knowledge of herbs—is nothing without the formal training my grandfather passed to my mother. She taught me everything she could, but there is so much I do not know. I am called to healing as my mother was, as Guigo is, but I am a woman. Without the protection of a respected physician, I am nothing. At best, a midwife. At worst, a witch.

I run across the courtyard after Guigo. He has nearly reached the arched passageway when I touch his hand.

"Guigo."

He turns in surprise.

"Can I come back? Will you teach me?"

I think, for a nauseating moment, that he will laugh. But he doesn't. He bends down so his face is level with mine.

"You are a woman," he says gently. "You can never be a physician."

"I know that," I reply, frustration bubbling up inside me. "I don't need a license to help people. But I need experience under a trained *médecin*, like my mother had with her father."

Guigo eyes me sharply. "Being a doctor is hard work," he says. "People refuse to follow your advice and then curse you when they do not get better. Your clothes reek of shit and piss and vomit. Your dreams are haunted by the patients you could not save. A physician's task is not to heal the sick but to stand between the living and death, armed with nothing but books and a little knowledge. You would choose this life? You, a pretty girl with your whole life ahead of you?"

I nod.

"Why?" he demands.

This might be my only chance to pursue knowledge and skill without fear. Guigo's respect and association, won through hard work, would offer far better protection than a husband. I feel Father Loup's cold eyes on my face.

"When I was a girl," I begin quietly, "my mother was a healer and midwife of great skill. She apprenticed with her father, but she was a better doctor than he. She took care of everyone, often without payment. And people—the same people she helped—spread cruel rumors about her. When she needed them, they did not come. She died alone without physician or midwife, with only me to care for her, because she was an educated woman who sought more from life than motherhood. They feared her; they hated her. They thought she deserved what she got."

He says nothing.

"And I wish I could have saved her," I say bitterly. "More than anything. I wish I could have saved her."

Guigo considers me for a long moment, kindness and understanding in his face. His voice, when he speaks again, is soft.

"I do not take apprentices."

His words puncture the swelling hope in my chest. I drop his gaze before he sees my tears spill. I walk alone to the gate, turn back to my life like a dog that has been sent from the door.

Chapter Five

It is nearly dark when I open the front door.

My father gets to his feet, looking angry but relieved. "Where have you been? We almost called the Dupont guards to search for you."

Across the table from him, Margot and Erec stand. My sister's face is creased with worry.

"I am sorry to have frightened you," I say, pulling off my cloak. "Truly I am. But when you hear my story, you will forgive me."

An hour later I sit answering my family's endless questions with my belly full of Anes's eel pie.

"Do you think the medicine will work?" my sister asks. The same question that has been pacing back and forth across my mind since I left the palace.

"I don't know," I say. "I pray that it does. When Mother attended patients, she put her hands on them, felt the parts that pained them. The hawthorn tonic will clear excess fluid from the pope's body, but I wonder if Dr. de Chauliac and the other physicians, in all their learning, missed something simple that Mother would have known in a minute."

"That reminds me," says Erec, leaning across the table to pass Father his empty cup. "I must thank you, Elea. I don't know what magic you performed, but when I returned home this afternoon, Mother was nearly her old self, cursing the maids and complaining her dinner was oversalted."

My stomach somersaults. Yesterday feels like another life.

Bietriz, you have forgiven me?

I shake the memory and take a sip of wine.

The days that follow pass like a year.

I walk the city like a street cat. I haunt the markets, run my fingers down stacks of muslin, dip my hands into bags of oats and beans.

"May I help you, mademoiselle?"

"Just looking," I reply, but really, I am listening. Praying for any mention of the pope's health, any hint that his condition has improved with my medicine. I eavesdrop on peasants selling vegetables, merchants gossiping on the street outside their guilds, women washing clothes along the banks of the Sorgue.

"They say in Constantinople, the dead outnumber the living. Tumors all over them, like mushrooms on a log."

"God willing the Calais truce holds. We cannot continue to pay this much for silk; it will bankrupt us!"

"I have it from my cousin, who knows someone in the royal household in Naples. Our queen bathes in milk mixed with the blood of virgins to preserve her beauty. Of course she killed him, coldhearted witch that she is."

I cannot bear to be home. Margot and Anes sit together in the hall under the light of the windows, stitching sheets for my sister's marriage chest. Erec visits often, always with a gift—candied fruits, ribbons, hairpins—and he and Margot sit before the fire with their heads together, cooing like roosting doves. My sister's happiness lingers in the room like perfume and amplifies my own nail-biting anxiety for the future.

I climb Mount Andaon every day.

Baldoin takes to lingering in the trees along the road and slips like a shadow from the undergrowth when he's certain it's me. He leads the way to the cottage, limping ahead and stopping at each turn to be certain I follow. Under my ointments, his leg heals well, and on the fifth day I remove the bandage. We sit together on my ruined cloak, and I tell him about Margot, about my mother and Mathilde and Father Loup. But mostly, like fingers to a flea bite, my thoughts return to that heady afternoon in Guigo's laboratory.

I make certain I'm home when Father returns from the palace each night.

As the bells chime for vespers, I sit at the table with a book or something to mend. But my eyes will not focus; my fingers are clumsy.

I stand when I hear his uneven gate on the cobbles. He opens the door, hangs his hat and cloak on their hooks. Then he turns to me and shakes his head. Night after night, the same words.

"No news."

One week after my meeting with Guigo, I accompany Margot and Anes to the rue des Teinturiers to choose the fabric for my sister's wedding gown.

"A blue velvet," Anes says for what must be the tenth time. The day is clear; the sun shines cold and bright through bare sycamore branches along the canal. "Blue for purity."

"We'll see," Margot says noncommittally. "Mother wore green."

"I *know*, my lamb, but blue's traditional, and the Duponts are a formal family. I'm sure Madame Dupont would prefer you in blue. . . ."

I shut my ears to their tedious conversation and listen instead to the sounds around me. The river rushes; the mills creak. Shouts of men ride the air with the animal smell of indigo.

In the Duponts' small, cheerful storefront—*Of course we're purchasing from them, Elea! Can you imagine the talk if we went to another cloth merchant?*—a short man with plump pink hands pulls out a stool for Margot and rushes from the shelves to the basement storage room and back again with stacks of fabric in every color, nearly tripping over his shoes in his eagerness to serve his master's soon-to-be daughter-in-law.

"And this red brocade, mademoiselle, with the roundels? Since Madame de Sade had a cotehardie made of it last summer, I cannot keep it in stock! But I hid my last bolt away for you, just in case. . . ."

Mother should be here, not me, with my wandering mind and indifference to this sort of beauty. I can nearly see her beside Margot, holding the colors up to the winter sunlight and asking all the right questions about weight and stitching.

I force my face into expressions of consideration as Margot runs her fingers over velvet and silk, echo Anes's *ooohs* when she holds the jewel tones up to her face, but my attention wanes. I stare up at the shelves of folded fabric. My sister speaks of yards and girdles and veils with metallic thread, but it is Guy de Chauliac's voice I hear as he pressed the gold into my palm. *Think of the cloth you could buy and make yourself a new dress!*

But when Margot raises a piece of gray-green velvet from the pile, I can't keep the grin from my face. It has the silvery sheen of olive leaves. Above it, Margot's eyes are the brown green of the river shot through with summer sun, and her hair gleams like burnished walnut wood.

"That's the one," I say. "That's it, Margot."

The little man's eyes dart between me and my sister. "An unusual choice," he says quietly, almost to himself. "A most unusual choice. If I may, mademoiselle—"

He lifts the folded fabric from Margot's hands and, with a flourish, opens the bolt so it fills the small room like a shining wave.

"Silk pile velvet," he says. "From Lucca. Just off the ship last week. And—if you will forgive my liberty for saying, mademoiselle—such is your beauty that were you to wear a dress made of this, every lady between here and Aix would come battering my door down for the same fabric."

Margot eyes the cloth and sinks her teeth into her bottom lip. "How much, monsieur?"

The man smiles, the happy messenger of good news, and I am suddenly filled with warm affection for him. "There is no charge. My express instructions from young Master Dupont were to give Mademoiselle Blanchet whatever she likes."

Margot and I walk side by side through the midday winter sunlight, our arms laden with bolts of fabric: linen for new chemises, cream-colored muslin for Margot's wedding veil and a thick wool, the same pine-needle green as Mother's wedding gown, for a traveling cloak. Anes huffs a few steps behind, carrying the sage velvet.

"It will be you next," Margot says.

I had been eyeing a contingent of papal guards on the corner of the rue Saint-Michel and wasn't paying attention. "What?"

"When you are betrothed, I'll be the lady of the house with a purse full of coins. We'll go to the Dupont storehouse together and you can choose whatever you'd like."

I swallow the old reply about wanting more than the life of a caged songbird; this is her day. "As long," I say, "as it's not blue velvet."

But Margot doesn't laugh. She is staring at the house on the corner—our house—where Pope Clement's scarlet livery stands bright as blood against the gold walls.

We walk the last block in silence. I feel my sister's anxious eyes on me, but mine are fixed on the blot of red that, as we approach, materializes into the form of a papal page. He is about our age, pale-faced and freckled. He sweeps his hat from carrot-orange hair as he bows.

"Bonjour, mademoiselles. I am looking for Mademoiselle Eleanore Blanchet."

I step forward. "I am she," I say, relieved that my voice does not waver.

The page casts a wistful look at Margot before turning his reluctant attention on me. "Dr. de Chauliac sent me to fetch you, mademoiselle." He places the velvet cap back on his head and smooths the feather self-consciously. "He requests your presence."

Anes steps between me and Margot, eyeing the page suspiciously over her stack of fabric.

"Is it His Holiness?" I ask eagerly. "Is he better?"

The page's mouth turns down at the corners. "It is not my place to ask questions, mademoiselle. Only to follow orders."

"Wait here," I say, stepping past him.

Margot and Anes follow. At the door I remember my manners.

"Please."

In the kitchen I pack my basket haphazardly, throwing in everything I can think of. Cobwebs to staunch blood. Bundles of yarrow root and willow bark, jars of rose hips, sage, henbane, wormwood, goatweed. My mother's book, tucked safely in the bottom with her surgical tools. I hoist the wicker handle onto my shoulder and pray that the page will demand, for chivalry's sake, to carry it for me.

He does not.

At the door, I kiss Margot and embrace Anes. "Don't worry," I whisper. "He would not send for me if my medicine did not help."

But I cannot help imagining terrible possibilities as I follow my impatient escort through the city: the pope dead or dying, and I, his poisoner, marching to my end like a sheep to the Grande Boucherie.

At the gates of the palace the guards search my basket and decide to let me keep my scalpel. I follow the page through the arched hallway and down the length of the courtyard, where he raises a fist to the laboratory door and knocks.

The door swings open. Guigo stands on the threshold. His eyes are hung with dark circles, and his clothing is creased as though he slept in it, but he manages a weak smile. "Mademoiselle." He bows. "I have been waiting." Then, to my escort: "Thank you, Phillipe."

The redheaded page bows and turns abruptly on his heel, glad his errand is complete.

Guigo ushers me in and closes the door. "Thank you for coming," he says. "May I take your basket?"

"How is the Holy Father?" I ask, handing it over. "Did the medicine—"

"Your tonic gave His Holiness more relief than any of my treatments," he says.

I could melt onto the flagstones like butter in a pot.

"The vial lasted until the day before yesterday. His fever reduced, his urine was clear and copious. As God is my witness, I thought him out of danger." Guigo sets my basket on the table and stands facing me, his expression grave. "But yesterday the fever returned, and the pain. Will you make your tonic again? I know I have your recipe, but I am an amateur in herbalism and prefer to leave it to a professional."

I consider what Guigo has told me: relief, then the return of the same symptoms in a day. "We have only enough hawthorn for another week's worth of medicine," I say, "and there will be no more berries this year. What if the tonic is merely covering up the underlying cause of the malady?"

Guigo's gaze sharpens. "What else do you suggest?"

"Let me examine him myself. I cannot work blind."

Guigo rubs a hand across his cheek. After a moment, he lifts his eyes to mine. "Very well."

But I am not finished.

"And if I determine what's wrong and heal him," I say, "you take me as your apprentice."

For a second—do I imagine it?—a smile flickers across Guigo's lips. Then he holds out his hand, his face once more somber.

"You have a deal, mademoiselle."

I follow Guigo across the courtyard to the Tour des Anges, my insides writhing. With a few words from my companion we pass between the guards, across a chamber, past a second set of guards. At the third checkpoint my basket is searched, my scalpel now confiscated. We climb a staircase, lit only by flickering torches.

Guigo reaches the landing and opens a door. I am so nervous that I do not, at first, register the sound filling my ears. Birdsong.

The room is long and high-ceilinged, illuminated by twin fires on opposite walls. It smells musty, familiar. Golden cages cover the floor and the many long tables, swooping voices echo between tiled floor and frescoed walls and high ceilings. Nightingales.

Guigo takes a lit candelabra from a table and crosses the room to a small door that must be a servants' entrance. He opens it—a lightless, gaping hole in the wall—and disappears into the dark. I have the sudden, mad hope that this is a dream and soon I will wake beside Margot.

I follow Guigo into a tunnel as close and black as a tomb. Under the doorjamb, ten paces away, firelight twinkles. Guigo knocks.

"*Entrez,*" comes the croaking reply.

Guigo opens the door. With my heart in my mouth, I follow.

The room is not large, but it is airy. Painted walls support a vaulted ceiling, ribbed like a cathedral. After the claustrophobic passageway the rimmed light of the closed curtains feels like breath in my lungs. Fingers of incense thread the air, thick and sweet.

Guigo bends over a small bed at the far side of the room and speaks to the man lying there. The same hoarse voice answers. I cannot make out the whispered words, but I recognize pain in them. I stand a respectful distance away, waiting to be summoned, and turn my eyes upon the frescoes.

My mouth falls open.

White hounds, their bodies outstretched in mid-leap, chase a stag against a backdrop of fruit-laden trees while their courtly owners look on. A lord holds a gloved fist aloft to an alighting hawk. Children play ball; peasants fish in an aquamarine river. Maidens dance; the thin stuff of their dresses floats in the breeze. The forest floor is covered in flowers. A Provençal paradise.

The art in my family's church of Saint-Agricol is all sour-faced saints, expressionless Jesuses and Marys. This is art for beauty's sake alone, reflecting the joy of earthly life. I have never seen anything like it.

"Mademoiselle Blanchet," Guigo calls.

I turn, the blood fluttering under my skin like a thousand trapped moths. I force my feet to take the steps to the bed, where the most powerful man on earth lies, suffering.

In the dim firelight I make out a hooked nose and an imperious, down-turned mouth with full lips. The skin of his face is yellow and unshaven, but his eyes are bright and intelligent. I bunch my hands into fists to stop them from shaking.

I have seen this face before, of course. Our aristocratic pope, who adores clothing and jewels and spectacles. I have seen him in parades surrounded by an army of cardinals, throwing gold coins to the crowd. I have seen him preach from his balcony—*this* balcony, I realize—to a packed square of onlookers, extolling the virtues of piety and poverty while wearing an ermine cloak and diamond-encrusted tiara.

"This is the girl, Your Holiness," says Guigo.

I curtsy on trembling knees.

"Come closer, child," says Pope Clement VI. I obey, stepping into the yellow circle of candlelight. "What is your name?"

"Eleanore Blanchet, Your Holiness."

"Blanchet," the pope repeats. "From where do I know that name?"

Guigo shrugs. I answer impulsively, "Please, Your Holiness, my father is one of your notaries."

Clement inclines his head. His eyes seem to flick through files in his mind.

"Ah, yes. Blanchet . . . *Bernard* Blanchet is your father?"

Shocked, I nod. In my mind I see Father taking off his boots by the fire, exclaiming over Clement's one thousand ermine skins, his staff of four hundred, the lion and bear procured at great expense for the papal menagerie. I gulp.

"He is an excellent notary," says Clement. "One of my best. He has been in the employ of the papal household since the time of my predecessor, has he not?"

I nod again.

"Surgeon de Chauliac tells me that you made the tincture that relieved my symptoms."

"Yes, Your Holiness."

"And how did you acquire this knowledge of herbalism, child?" he asks. His tone softens, sensing my nervousness.

"My mother was a healer, Your Holiness," I say. "She learned from her father, who was a staff physician for Pope Benedict."

Clement appraises me for a long moment. Then he turns to Guigo. "Very well, Surgeon. I will permit Mademoiselle Blanchet to examine me, if you feel it may be useful. But I am not a medical specimen to be ogled and studied. There will be no more visitors in my private chambers, do you understand me?"

Guigo bows his head, looking abashed. "I understand, Your Holiness."

I, too, look at the floor. Gone is all the bravura I wielded in Guigo's laboratory. I am just a girl in an old dress, standing before the pope. I do not belong here.

Clement settles back onto the pillows with a pained grimace. My mind is blank. I have no idea what to do. Guigo nods at me encouragingly, anxiety bright in his eyes.

I fight the urge to run from the room.

"Where does it hurt, Your Holiness?" I ask, forcing myself to step closer.

Clement groans, lifts a shaking hand to hover above his right flank. "Everywhere," he says. "But the worst is here."

My mother told me that real physicians perform analyses of urine; examine the color, the smell, even the taste. Just by looking at a patient, they can surmise which humors are out of alignment and prescribe bleeding or purging to balance them. I have none of these skills, none of this knowledge. But then I think of what I said to Margot, the night after I met Guigo, that he might have missed something that Mother would have known as soon as she laid hands on skin.

I lift my hands over the richly embroidered nightshirt. Clement jumps a little as my palms touch his abdomen through the fine cotton. My mind races. *I am touching the pope.*

I close my eyes and tune out the sounds of the crackling fire and distant whistling of birds, the smell of incense and the sour body odor from this sick old man, God's vassal on earth. The flesh is swollen and thick and presses back into my hands. This illness, whatever it is, has made him boggy. There is too much water in the tissue, like dough without enough flour.

And then I feel it—a pull, like a tug on a string, a fish on a line. It is strong and insistent, drawing me back, through the skin and muscle of his abdomen, past slippery organs, to just below his ribs on the right side. I don't know what it is, but I know I must follow it. It is the source of the pain.

"Your Holiness, could you please turn onto your stomach?" I ask.

Clement slowly makes his way onto one side, then rolls onto his belly with a groan. Guigo watches over my shoulder, shifting his weight from one foot to the other.

Clement flinches again as I place my hands under his right ribs. I sink in, feel the same organ, whatever it is, under my fingers. It is about the size of a fist and feels swollen and tender. I trace the outlines of it; two curves, one large and one small, the shape of a bean.

I stand up straight and turn to Guigo, my hands still on the pope. "What organ is here?"

He looks at my hand placement. "The right kidney," Guigo says, a note of surprise in his voice.

I think of kidney pie, the texture of the organ under my teeth, the chewiness of it. "What does it do?"

"It has many functions," Guigo answers. "It draws humors from the liver. It filters the blood and urine and provides heat and seed to the testicles. It is a lusty organ."

I consider this information, the implication of what I am about to tell the pope's physician. "Well," I say, removing my hands from Clement, "there's something wrong with this one." The confidence in my voice surprises me, but I know I am right.

Guigo snorts. "Is that so, Mademoiselle *Médecin*?"

Clement's eyes are on me, sharp and clear in the swollen face. The sensation of the engorged organ lingers in my fingers. I did not attend medical school in Paris, do not understand what I felt, but I trust my hands.

"Yes," I say. "There is too much fluid in this kidney. Something is stopping it from . . . doing what it does. From draining properly."

Clement makes his way painfully back onto his side. "The child is right, Guigo," he says. "It feels like tiny stones, or shards of glass."

Guigo nods. "What do you advise we do about it?"

I think about tiny stones blocking the way, slicing through delicate tissue. What would break them down?

"Ox bile," I mutter out loud. I can see the page from my mother's book. *For Pathologies of the Kidney.* "His Holiness should take the juice of a lemon in the morning and evening on an empty stomach," I say to Guigo. "And a tonic of ox bile, goatweed, celery, and thyme."

Guigo smiles at me like a proud father. "I agree with Mademoiselle Blanchet's prescription, Holy Father," he says with a respectful nod. "Sometimes in afflictions such as these, the old folk remedies are more effective than the teachings of Galen. Are you willing to try another of her medicines?"

Clement winces again and clutches his side. "I will try nearly anything," he says. "The pain is intolerable."

"I shall send to the kitchens for the juice of a lemon immediately, to take before your supper," says Guigo. "And will return this evening with Mademoiselle Blanchet's tonic and a dose of opium and willow bark for the pain."

Clement closes his eyes. Guigo glances at me from beneath his bushy brows, and I know it is time for us to leave. I recover my basket with a curtsy for the pope, but he does not see it.

My mind reels as we retrace our steps through the dark passageway and into the large chamber beyond, past the whistling nightingales, down the stairs to the guardroom where Guigo recovers my mother's scalpel, and out into the courtyard. *I just met the pope. Touched the pope.* Blessed Virgin, let my medicine work.

Back in the laboratory, Guigo sends to the kitchens for all my ingredients, except the goatweed, which I brought from home, and watches me make my mother's kidney tonic.

The bells chime for none when I stopper the glass vial of yellow-green tincture and hand it to Guigo. "Three spoonfuls. Morning, noon, and night."

Guigo wraps his meaty fingers around the little bottle, eclipsing its contents. "If this concoction turns His Holiness into a lizard, the church will need someone to burn," he says with a wink. "So, to save my own sorry skin, I want you here tomorrow at prime."

It takes a moment for the words to register. "I—I can come back?" I stammer. "Tomorrow?"

"We had a deal," Guigo says. "If your medicine works, I will take you on as my apprentice. But be warned that if you disobey me, if you displease me in any way, you will be dismissed immediately. Do you understand?"

I nod, hardly able to believe my luck.

"Be here at dawn. I'll tell the guards to let you in."

After another dinner where I am peppered with questions, I stay up until midnight grinding herbs and cutting roots while Anes cleans the kitchen. She says nothing but scrubs the dishes so savagely I fear she will crack them.

When I can fit no more jars in my basket, I cross the room to where Anes sweeps the floor as though it has personally offended her. She is suspicious of Guigo, of the danger I might be in if something goes awry. I wrap my arms around her waist. She stiffens under the embrace.

"I know you're worried," I whisper. "It will not be like Mother. I promise."

"I only worry for you, you know that," she says gruffly. "And if either this physician or the pope himself gets you into trouble, they shall have to answer to me."

I laugh, imagining Pope Clement and Guy de Chauliac seated at the kitchen table like schoolboys while Anes shakes a finger over them.

I barely doze for excitement. With every chime of the church bells I lie awake with my heart thudding, certain I have overslept and wasted the incredible opportunity. The window is still dark as pine pitch when I pad downstairs in my stockings, carrying my shoes.

As I climb the rain-slick stairs of the Palais Neuf, the bells of

Notre-Dame des Doms chime. The guards search my basket and let me pass.

"There she is!" Guigo says, opening the laboratory door on the dawn-dark courtyard. "Have you had breakfast?"

He installs me at the table with a cup of warm ale and a slice of chicken pie. I am too excited to eat, but I move my pie across the silver until Guigo pushes his empty plate away from him with a satisfied sigh.

"Come now, mademoiselle." Guigo stands and reaches for his cloak. "It is time to discover whether your medicine worked."

Clement sits up in bed in the frescoed room, reading a letter by the early light of the open window. He is still pale, and there are dark pouches beneath his eyes, but he greets us with a wan smile.

"Surgeon," he says. "Mademoiselle Blanchet."

"Good morning, Your Holiness," Guigo says with a deep bow. "How did you pass the night?"

"I hardly slept a moment for passing urine," says the pope. "Careful with the chamber pot. It is nearly overflowing."

Guigo kneels and pulls an engraved urn from beneath the bed. He lifts it carefully and carries it to the window, where he removes the lid and examines the contents.

"I see no blood," says Guigo with relief. "And a healthy bowel movement." He tips the contents through the open casement, where they splatter on the cobblestones below. "How is the pain, *Éminence*?"

Clement shifts on the embroidered pillows. "It is a bit better today."

I breathe a silent sigh of relief.

"It seemed to ease a little each time I relieved myself."

Guigo measures out three spoonfuls of my tonic into a bone cup beside the bed and holds it out to the pope. "Another dose, Your Holiness."

Clement swallows the sour concoction in a great gulp. "Let us pray that the foul stuff continues to work," he says, grimacing. "Now, if you will excuse me, I shall try to rest, as so little sleep was afforded me during the night."

Guigo sets the chamber pot beside the bed, and we take our leave.

Back in the laboratory, Guigo is boisterous over the pope's improvement. He asks to examine my mother's book again as we wait to be summoned by our next patient.

"Magnifique!" he declares, reading her recipe for a tonic for gout. "Autumn crocus, really?"

While Guigo is engaged, I survey the titles of books on the shelves: encyclopedias, medical atlases, canons. Dictionaries, astrology and history texts. Greek philosophers, of course: Galen, Hippocrates, Socrates, Plato. Dante's *La Commedia*. A surprising number of romances.

An hour passes before someone knocks on the door. I open it as Guigo still has his nose buried in my mother's pages and does not seem to have heard.

The page on the threshold is clearly surprised to meet a woman, but hides it gracefully by sweeping off his cap and bowing. "Good morning, mademoiselle. Is Surgeon de Chauliac in?"

Two minutes later Guigo and I follow him through a maze of corridors and staircases. Cardinal Romana has a terrible toothache and we have been called to examine him. Guigo slid a nasty-looking pair of pliers into his bag. I packed all the necessary herbs to make a poultice as well as a wad of cobwebs to staunch the blood in case Guigo has an opportunity to use the pliers.

We stop at a guarded door on the third floor. "Surgeon de Chauliac and his assistant for Cardinal Romana," announces the page.

Surgeon de Chauliac's assistant. Pride lightens my feet as we pass through an antechamber into a room the same size as Clement's bedchamber. Here there are no wondrous frescoes, only a life-size crucifix hanging above the bed where a very fat man lies moaning, a hand pressed to his cheek.

"Good morning, Cardinal," booms Guigo with a bow. "Another toothache, eh?"

He pulls open the heavy drapes and floods the room with light. The cardinal winces.

"The blasted thing has bothered me for weeks now," he grumbles, moving his mouth as little as possible. "I haven't eaten solid food in three days."

Guigo approaches the bed. I follow.

"This is Mademoiselle Blanchet," Guigo says with a nod in my direction. "She is a skilled herbalist." The man looks at me for the first time, suspicion gleaming in his rheumy eyes.

"Open your mouth please, Cardinal," says Guigo, holding a handkerchief over his nose.

The cardinal obeys. I stand behind Guigo, careful not to get in the way of the light, lift my own kerchief to my face, and peer into the cardinal's mouth.

The teeth are all stained and cracked; I see at least five empty sockets where others have been extracted. Even through my kerchief, drenched in Margot's sweet lavender oil, the old man's breath is noxious. On the right side of his bottom jaw, I spot a molar, black and rotten.

Guigo backs away and lowers his handkerchief. "It is corrupted, Your Eminence. It must be removed."

"I feared as much," says the cardinal with a sigh. "Do what you must, Surgeon."

Guigo pulls the pliers from his bag and turns to me, opening and closing the iron pincers like a self-satisfied crab. "A poultice?" he asks, "for the swelling and pain?"

I hurry to a table beside the window and unpack my basket.

There will be blood, of course. I pull out the cobwebs and place them on a clean piece of linen. Now, for a simple poultice. Peppermint to soothe the gums, cloves and oregano for swelling. Garlic to guard against corruption. I grind the ingredients together and walk back to the bed with the cobwebs in one hand and my mortar in the other.

Guigo hands the cardinal a bottle of aqua vitae and an empty cup. "Swirl the alcohol around the tooth and spit, please."

The cardinal takes a swig, grimaces, and spits. Guigo hands the cup to me. The liquid is pink with blood; I set it down hurriedly.

"Are you ready, Cardinal?" asks Guigo, holding up the pliers.

Cardinal Romana nods reluctantly, closes his eyes, and opens his mouth wide. Guigo leans over him. The pliers disappear, he moves his arm in a skillful twist and pull, and the cardinal screams a horrible gurgling scream. Guigo raises the pliers: a long-rooted tooth, the top sunken and black, drips blood on the fine carpet.

"Your patient, mademoiselle," Guigo says with a wink. Cardinal Romana moans.

I push up my sleeves.

"I have prepared a poultice, Your Eminence, which will help with the pain and swelling." I hold out the bottle of alcohol and the cup. "But first you must clear the wound of blood." The cardinal complies, wincing again as the alcohol fills the wound, and spits into the cup.

"Now lie back, please," I command, "and open your mouth." I hold the handkerchief over my nose and examine the angry socket. As gently as possible, I pack the cobwebs over the pit and apply the poultice with my fingertips, then wad up a piece of gauze and wedge it between the teeth on either side.

"Finished," I say, straightening up and lowering my kerchief. "The ointment will need to be reapplied tomorrow. And here is a pain-relief tonic." I hold out the medicine: comfrey, willow bark, yellow root. "One spoonful—morning, noon, and night."

Guigo takes the bottle from me, uncorks it, and sniffs. "Get some rest, Cardinal," he says, placing the tonic on the table. "Only broth and water for the next few days."

The old man moans again as we leave—whether from pain or sadness over his supper, I do not know.

We are next called to attend a kitchen maid with a broken toe (Guigo splints it deftly; I give the girl comfrey tonic), a stable boy with ringworm (Guigo recommends bathing the boy's head with his own urine), and a French ambassador with gout in the joints of his hands and feet (I take the lead and recommend he avoid rich foods and wine).

At midday our growling bellies lead us beneath the south wall archway in search of food. Guigo knows everyone in the bustling kitchen by name, and the head cook himself packs my basket full of cakes to take home for Margot. We bring our flagons of ale and bowls of stew back to the laboratory and eat in companionable silence.

Once Guigo has mopped the bottom of his bowl with the last piece of bread, he leans back in his chair and interlaces his hands behind his head. "You did very well today, mademoiselle," he says. "Only God knows if your medicines will cure the pope, but I think I may enjoy having an apprentice."

I bite the insides of my cheeks to stop from grinning.

After a final examination of the pope, who slept through the day and has more color in his cheeks, we return to the laboratory together in the cool press of twilight.

Guigo stretches his arms overhead and yawns as I gather my things. "I believe I shall dream before my head meets the pillow," he says. "I hope my valet has lit a fire."

"Is this not where you sleep?" I regret the words as soon as they leave my lips.

Guigo laughs. "Oh, no, mademoiselle. I am the personal physician to the pope. Do you think because I was born a peasant, I would not have fine rooms and servants?"

I blush. Guigo follows my gaze to the disheveled cot in the corner by the fire.

"Ah," he says, his tone kinder. "As I have said, a physician's days are long. Sometimes I rest my eyes between patients. But my own chambers are much finer and far from this room. Only the pope's messengers and a few kitchen staff who bring me my breakfast know where I sleep, otherwise I would get no rest at all."

Guigo walks me to the gate. "*Bonsoir,* Mademoiselle Médecin. Same time tomorrow?"

Chapter Six

I am happier than I remember being in my life.

My eyes open each morning before the bells of Saint-Agricol peal for lauds. I close the front door just as my father's feet hit the floorboards overhead and turn to face the wide Magna Carreira alone. Woodsmoke joins the mist of the Rhône and tangles around my ankles while I climb the cobblestones toward the papal palace. Around me, the city stirs. The talk of servants carries from kitchens and stables, the cries of roosters herald the gray-pink stain spreading up the eastern sky. With every step my anticipation crescendos, accompanied by the pounding of my heart.

Each time I announce myself to the palace guards as Eleanore Blanchet, assistant to Surgeon de Chauliac, I believe it a bit more. Guigo arranges for me a salary of one *sou* per week, to be collected on Saturdays, but any payment seems ridiculous. The opportunity to learn from him is an inestimable gift.

After a hearty breakfast (sometimes meat and cheese, sometimes spiced honey cakes with cream), Guigo and I present ourselves at the pope's chambers. I watch as he takes Clement's pulse, listens with an ear to his chest to hear the work of his lungs, and inspects the contents of his chamber pot. To my immense relief the pope improves a bit each day, and on the fifth day he shoos Guigo away after his examination is complete.

"Go, Surgeon," he says, waving a pale, patrician hand. "Attend your flock. It is time I attended mine."

Back in the laboratory, Guigo lifts a worn leather bag from its hook behind the door.

"His Holiness is out of danger, God willing," he says, grinning at me. "So today, mademoiselle, we take to the streets to care for the good people of Avignon."

We start at the Hôpital Saint-Antoine, a stone's throw away from Saint-Agricol. I came here a handful of times with my mother to administer care and medicines to women in need.

The peaked door resounds under the impact of Guigo's fist. After a moment a monk, not much older than I, opens it.

"Good morning, Brother Louis," Guigo says, smiling.

"Surgeon de Chauliac!" the monk exclaims, flushing from the black collar of his robes to his tonsured hair. "We have not seen you in some time. Is the Holy Father . . . ?"

"His Holiness is much improved," Guigo says proudly. "Thanks to the work of this young woman."

Brother Louis's eyes move over me with interest, then return to Guigo reproachfully. "And the mercy of God."

"Yes, yes," Guigo says hurriedly. "And the mercy of God."

After a quick introduction, I curtsy and follow Guigo through the door.

Brother Louis leads us into a room as large as the chapel next door but not nearly as pleasant. As my eyes adjust to the dim light trickling in from the few high, grimy windows, my head fills with the sounds and smells of sick humanity.

Beds stand in rows so tight that there is barely space to pass between them, and each holds two or three patients. The flagstones under my boots are slick. It is the scene I remember from childhood, but then I had my mother, upright and steady, beside me.

Guigo scans the room. "Ah," he says, pointing to the far wall, where an elderly monk stands with a ladle and a water bucket. "Let's join Brother Christophe."

We cross the room, Brother Louis trailing us eagerly. The old monk raises a face like one of the gargoyles on Clement's new palace as we approach, but his eyes are bright and gentle. His wrinkled face cracks into a smile as he recognizes Guigo through the gloom.

"Surgeon de Chauliac," he says in a gravelly voice. "We are blessed to have you back among us."

"Are you well, Brother Christophe?" Guigo asks, clasping the monk's age-gnarled hand in his.

"I am, praise be to God," the monk replies. His gaze shifts from Guigo to me. "And who have you brought?"

"This is my assistant," Guigo says, "Eleanore Blanchet. An herbalist and midwife."

Brother Christophe's eyes search my face. They remind me of the monkeys in the papal zoo, brown and intelligent, questioning.

"Not the daughter of Bietriz?"

My hackles rise like Baldoin's. How foolish of me to think the past would not find me in my new position. What rumors might have reached their corruptive fingers here? But there is only kindness in the old man's face.

"Ah, mademoiselle," Brother Christophe murmurs after a moment. "Of course it is you. How you have grown."

The monks of the city's hospitals blur together in my memory, black-cassocked and featureless. My mind fumbles for something to say.

"You would not remember me," Brother Christophe says, saving me from the embarrassment of admitting I do not recognize him. "You were so young. But I remember you. And, of course, I remember your mother." He does not step closer, does not reach for my hand, but his warmth is like a brazier. "Bietriz was a great healer and a friend to me. I was away on pilgrimage when she died and was so sorry to hear of it when I returned. But you do honor to her memory, following in her footsteps."

My throat burns with unshed tears. I cast about for something to say, but again, the old monk rescues me.

"Now," he says, turning his eyes back to Guigo and pressing his arthritic hands together. "Mademoiselle Blanchet. Surgeon de Chauliac. I require your assistance . . ."

A moment later we approach a cot that has been pushed some distance away from the others and contains a single patient: a red-faced, sweaty man who cries out as soon as he sees us making our way to him.

"It's the pestilence!" the man howls. He is about my father's age but ill-kempt; a few strands of rank hair escape his filthy cap, and his nose is red and bulbous with years of drink. "The eastern pestilence!"

"Keep your voice down," growls Guigo, with a quick glance over his shoulder to where a few of the more lucid patients are sitting up in their beds, craning their necks toward the source of the commotion. "And tell us what happened."

"My brother-in-law's a boatswain," the man whispers. "Just come in from Naples. And he says the pestilence is rotting the nethers of every Italian, and, oh, God, it burns like the fires of hell—" He breaks off with a swallowed sob and shuts his eyes.

Guigo shoots me a sidelong look, and my heart beats an unpleasant tattoo. All the rumors rush back to me, heard in the market, repeated by Erec and my father. *They say in Constantinople, the dead outnumber the living.*

"Your nethers, eh?" Guigo says gruffly, rolling up his sleeves. "I assume, sir, that you refer to your generative organs. Let's have a look."

Brother Louis steps forward. "Allow us, Surgeon," he says. "The mademoiselle should not assist with undressing a man."

Guigo raises his eyebrows at me, and I repress a mad urge to laugh. Have I not seen the pope himself with his pants around his ankles? The male anatomy, once uncloaked of its mystery, is not as awe-inspiring as I was led to believe.

"The mademoiselle is my assistant," he replies. "There is no part of the body she has not seen."

The young monk shifts uncomfortably but does not speak again. Guigo motions me to his side. I copy him, holding my handkerchief over my nose as he raises the man's long nightdress.

The man's testicles and member are covered with small red boils. They look like pox; I stop myself from stepping backward. But the marks are localized on the genitalia and do not extend onto the pale skin of his thighs.

Guigo lowers his kerchief. If I didn't know better, I'd swear he was fighting off a smile.

"Do you enjoy the enviable state of matrimony, monsieur?" he asks, dropping the hem of the nightdress.

"Eh?"

Guigo's mouth twitches. "What I mean to ask is: Are you *married?*"

He grunts an assertion. "Nigh on fifteen years now."

"And have you and your wife been blessed with children?" Guigo folds his kerchief and returns it to his pocket.

"Eight," the man replies proudly. "Five still living. And another on the way."

"Am I correct to assume, during this delicate period, that you have abstained from your marital duties?"

The man blinks.

Guigo sighs. "What I mean to ask, monsieur, is when was the last time you visited a bawdy house?"

The man flushes from his chest to his cap. He looks from Guigo to me, then back to Guigo. "Two weeks ago."

"And when did the boils arise?"

"Yesterday morning."

Guigo turns to me with an air of self-congratulation. "Many physicians recommend cutting away the corrupted flesh," he says, loudly enough for the man to catch every word, "followed by the application of quicklime. Others advise the injection of mercury directly into the member itself."

I hazard a glance at our patient. He has gone very still and pale. "But I have seen great success with a less-invasive cure." He smiles broadly at the man in the bed. "Wash your nethers daily with equal parts water and vinegar and stay off your wife until the sores have healed."

Outside the hospital, afternoon shadows lie long and cold on the cobblestones.

Guigo begins a monologue about different treatment techniques for venereal afflictions as we wind our way back to the palace. "Of course, it is an affliction of overindulgence. Hyperexcretion of the phlegmatic humor. And as such must be treated by increasing the volume of the choleric humor . . ."

I try to pay attention to his lecture, but my mind keeps turning back to Brother Christophe, to his bright eyes in their nests of wrinkles, the warmth of his worn voice, and the certainty that here, at least, was someone who admired my mother.

Chapter Seven

For once, Erec is not at the table when I open the front door.

"He said he would come for supper," Margot says, helping me out of Mother's cloak. "Some business must have kept him. But never mind Erec; tell us of your day!"

"Come, sit," Father says, patting the bench beside him and filling my wine cup.

As Anes trundles to the kitchen to dish up supper, there is a knock at the door. My sister rushes to open it.

"Here you are at last, my love."

The wind bends the candle flames as Erec brushes past her. Something is wrong.

"Erec?" Margot asks. "Erec, what has happened?"

Erec's hair stands on end as though he has run his hands through it a thousand times. His cloak is only half-clasped, the untied laces of his boots drag on the floor.

"What is it, son?" Father asks, standing in alarm.

Erec does not respond. His eyes are fixed on the rushes, but his expression is that of a man lost at sea.

"Fetch some cognac, Elea," says Father.

I sprint to the cellar door. Mathilde. It must be Mathilde.

When I return with the bottle, Erec and Margot are sitting together on the bench. His hat and cloak are still on, his unfocused eyes locked on the knotted wood of the table. My sister loops an arm around him, but the hard line of his shoulders does not soften under her touch.

Father pours a cup of cognac and places it before Erec. "Drink, son," he commands.

Erec lifts the cup to his lips like a sleepwalker. He takes a long sip.

Is she dead? I think back to the last time I saw her. The wound was free of putrefaction. What did I miss, in my frantic desire to leave that room?

When the cup is empty, Father takes it gently from Erec's hands.

"You have clearly suffered a shock," he says. "We are your friends, Erec. Soon to be your family. Tell us what happened."

Erec covers his face with shaking fingers.

I want to scream. I want to run. I do not deserve to be Guy de Chauliac's apprentice. I am a midwife, not a doctor. I told him to call a licensed physician—

"My father is dead," he says.

Margot gasps. A terrible relief floods my veins. *Not Mathilde. Not my fault.*

"How—" Father begins.

"A drunken brawl," Erec interrupts, closing his fingers into fists and lowering them to the table. "At an inn. He was stabbed and his purse was stolen."

"My love," says Margot, taking both his hands with hers, "I'm so sorry."

"That is not all." Erec's voice is ragged with rage. Still, he does not look at my sister. "As I was consoling my grieving mother, not an hour after I received this news, a group of moneylenders knocked on my door. These men—these *Jews*," he spits out the word like a profanity, "came to collect. They informed me that my father did not leave me the booming business he boasted of. No." He laughs; a cold, high laugh that raises the hair on my neck. "He left us nothing. Worse than nothing. He left us debts we cannot pay. Toledo silver and Antwerp velvet bought on credit. Foolish ventures in Paris. Gambling debts. I must sell the house, the horses, the tapestries. Everything."

A suffocating silence falls. I know what he must say next. I stare at my sister, wanting to somehow shield her from this blow, but her eyes are fixed like lifelines upon the man she loves.

Erec raises his miserable face and, for the first time, meets Margot's gaze. "I cannot marry you," he whispers.

Margot recoils as though he'd slapped her. "What?"

Father takes a deep breath. "He is right, Margot."

"I do not care if you are poor," she says, her knuckles hardening over Erec's. "We do not need money, my love. So long as we have each other."

Erec stares at his lap, shoulders hunched against my sister's words.

"You can sell your family's possessions," Margot says, her voice climbing higher in desperation. "Father can find you work at the palace, can't you, Father?" Her eyes are huge, pleading.

I feel her panic as though it were my own. Her love, the happy life she planned. Stamped out like a spark.

"I can find work as a lady's maid," Margot continues frantically, "and there is my dowry . . ."

"*Enough.*" Father's voice is laced with the authority he so seldom uses. "Erec is right. He cannot marry you. Penniless. Disgraced. That is no way to start a family."

"But, Father—"

He holds up a hand. "I know you love him," he says, a little more gently, "but even if you do not believe it now, you will grow to resent him when you are living in a tenement with three other families. You will resent him when you are old and tired and no longer beautiful and you see how your life has been wasted. As your father, it is my duty to ensure you marry well. And because of Allistair's foolishness, Erec will never be able to provide you the life you deserve."

Erec looks like he will be sick.

My father gets to his feet. "You were brave to come here tonight, Erec," he says. "Brave for realizing that you can no longer marry my daughter."

My sister's despairing eyes shift from Father to Erec, who still does not apologize, comfort her, make any acknowledgment that she fought for him. I want to scream at him. I want to take him by the shoulders and shake him. With a sob, Margot pushes away from the table and runs up the stairs.

I follow her, leave my father to assure Erec that he acted with honor while my sister shatters into a million pieces.

Margot lies face down on the bed. Sobs shudder through her like gusts of wind. I close the door softly and climb into bed beside her.

She cries for a long time.

Below us, the front door opens and closes. A while later I hear Father's uneven step on the stairs. His footfalls pause at our bedroom door before continuing to his room at the end of the hall.

When the house is silent, Margot lifts her swollen face from the pillow. She looks so young that my throat catches.

"What am I going to do, Elea?" she whispers. "What will my life be now? He was everything to me. Everything. And now I have nothing."

I want to tell her that she is young and beautiful, that she will find happiness with another man. That she can still have the qualified freedom and safety that she yearns for. But now is not the time.

"You are myself," I whisper.

Margot's face crumples. She collapses into me.

I hold her tightly and stroke her gleaming hair as Mother would have. I lie awake a long while after she has cried herself to sleep, listening to her breath and feeling her heartbeat against mine, like the reflection on the other side of a mirror.

When the first cock crows the next morning, I slide out of bed. Margot does not stir as I pull on my dress and stockings. My stomach aches at the thought of her awakening alone, facing the hopeless day with only Anes for company. But I am Guy de Chauliac's apprentice and cannot be late.

There is no answer when I knock at the laboratory at dawn, but the door is unlocked. I let myself in, feeling like a burglar, and look around for Guigo. Candles burn at the casement, and a fire crackles in the grate, but there is no other sign of him.

I pace back and forth, debating what to do. I am not late; should I walk to the Tour des Anges and ask the guards if Guigo is already with the pope? Should I stay here and wait for him to return?

As if in answer to my question, the door opens, kicked by a booted foot. Guigo turns sideways to walk through the door with something heavy slung over his shoulders. He crosses the room to the table, hauls his burden overhead with a grunt, and drops it onto the table where it crushes quills and sends loose parchment soaring.

It's a pig. A very large pig.

"Is this breakfast?" I ask. Guigo laughs and mops his brow with a lacy sleeve. He looks like his mother dressed him, forced him into an embroidered undershirt and fussy brocade doublet, and the second she turned her back he ran out into the yard and got them filthy.

"No, Mademoiselle Médecin," he says with a wink, "or shall I call you Mademoiselle *Surgeon* today?"

I look at the beast, realization dawning. Its eyes are closed, long blond eyelashes still on pink cheeks, humanlike mouth turned up a little at the corners. There is a gash across its throat from ear to ear where the butcher drained it of blood and ligature marks on its legs from where it was hung upside down. I can almost hear the flies buzzing in the Place de la Grande Boucherie.

Guigo starts pulling books from the shelves.

"A pig is very similar to a man, mademoiselle," he says, handing me a stack of manuscripts. "A surgeon who does not know his—or her—anatomy is like a blind man trying to carve a piece of wood." He chuckles, sensing my fluttering apprehension. "So, a pig it is. Unless you prefer to raid the graveyard for corpses by the light of the moon? Human autopsies are outlawed by the church."

"Is this how you learned?" I ask.

Guigo nods. "When I studied anatomy with Nicola Bertuccio in Bologna, I ate so much bacon I began to think like a pig," he says. "I dreamed I was hunting for truffles."

We ready the supplies, place a linen tarp underneath him—it—to catch the blood and gore and fill bowls with water from the cistern to rinse our hands.

Guigo brings me his set of freshly sharpened surgical knives. "Until vespers," he says, handing me the instruments, "this is our work."

We dissect all day. The only evidence of time passing is the movement of the square of sunlight across the floor and the growing pile of offal beside the table. Guigo dons an apron, and I cannot help but think it suits him; he looks more at ease in bloodstained linen than velvet.

We lay the pig on its back, stiffening limbs splayed. I butcher it under Guigo's direction, first making a vertical incision through the abdomen from pelvis to rib cage. Clear liquid spills from over the sides of the table and splashes on my shoes.

"Peritoneal fluid," explains Guigo. "Now you and the viscera have both bathed in phlegmatic humor. It is the cold and moist element of the body, associated with maturity, patience, and winter. It originates in the brain."

The organs are visible now, the intestines expand out of the cavity and onto the table. They are so long, so voluminous, that I wonder how they ever fit inside the animal to begin with.

Guigo stops me frequently to take over, showing me the proper way to disengage an organ from its nest of connective tissue or crack the ribs with iron pincers to get to the heart and lungs, pulling out his old notes and drawings to help me make sense of the anatomy. He does not stop talking the entire day—he clearly loves to teach and is good at it.

"This, mademoiselle," Guigo says, placing a hand on a dark, wet organ, "is the most important part of the body. Galen writes that the liver is the first organ formed in a fetus; it is the source of all veins. The liver creates blood, the moist and warm humor, associated with air and spring. A sanguineous person is enthusiastic, charismatic, restless, impatient. His Holiness's humors are almost perfectly balanced—"

"Eucrasia," I interrupt eagerly. "Equal amounts of the four humors. The ideal state."

Guigo nods. "But occasionally he has an excess of the sanguineous humor and requires bleeding from this vein."

He indicates a thin blue line along the inside of the pig's elbow, where Mathilde's cut festered. I shudder.

The purposeful layout of the body fills me with wonder. I dissect the kidneys, marvel at the tiny hollow tubes that filter blood and urine and black bile. I feel the bouncy tissue in my hand, so much lighter than it looks, and remember Pope Clement's swollen organ under my fingers.

I ask occasional questions, but mostly I try to soak up Guigo's knowledge like a sponge, feeling each body part with my eyes closed to discern its essence. The strong muscles that still yearn to contract around gelatinous joints, the nerves like lute strings under my fingers, the heart with its many chambers, aching to throb again. This pig was still alive this morning, sniffing the air and anticipating his breakfast. The tissues are dead, but the imprint of life remains, like the brightness of the sun after I close my eyes.

The gore is in my hair, under my fingernails, everywhere, by the time the chapel bell rings for vespers. Guigo and I both look up from the carcass, surprised at the time. He takes in my wild hair and blood-stained apron and laughs.

"Go home," he says. "I will give His Holiness your tonic and make your excuses; you are in no state to see him. Be back tomorrow at dawn."

I am too weary to argue with him. I pass a damp towel over my face and hands, hang up my apron, gather my things while Guigo cleans his knives in the basin. Tomorrow the pig will be cold on the table, the secret language of his body silent, dead as ashes. I pause over the mangled animal and place my hand on a hoof.

Thank you. Thank you for giving your life so I could learn. I wish you peace.

I say good night to Guigo and open the door onto the busy courtyard.

I step backward in surprise.

A page in the red-and-white livery of Clement's personal staff stands before me with a hand raised, ready to knock.

"His Holiness requires the immediate presence of Dr. de Chauliac."

A fist tightens around my heart.

Five minutes later Guigo and I stand before the nightingale room, waiting to be admitted. *This is the end,* I think miserably. *My medicines did not cure the pope after all.* I glance at Guigo, hoping he will say something comforting, that no matter what happens, I may stay, but he stares ahead with his jaw clenched.

The door opens. I follow Guigo over the threshold, praying with all my might that it is not the last time.

Clement sits in a high-backed chair by the fire with a letter in his hands.

I scan his face anxiously: the signs of his illness are still there but fading. He glances up at us, eyes widening as he takes in my blood-speckled hair and Guigo's scarlet shirt cuffs.

"Your Holiness," says Guigo with a bow. "Forgive our appearance. Your summons found us in a porcine dissection. Are you unwell?"

"I am well." He hands his letter to Guigo. "But there is news. From Marseille."

Relief warms me like a hot drink. I will return tomorrow. I am still Guy de Chauliac's apprentice. But as I watch the color drain from Guigo's face as he reads, my elation is replaced by cold ripples of dread.

Guigo drops into the chair across from Clement without invitation, the letter gripped between white-knuckled fingers. "Is this true?" he asks.

"I fear it is." Clement turns, surprisingly, to me. "Can you read, mademoiselle?"

I nod.

"Give her the letter, Surgeon. Everyone will know soon enough."

Guigo hands me the parchment, and I raise the elegant, slanting script to the candlelight.

To His Holiness Pope Clement VI from his most humble servant Cardinal DuLac, on this the fourteenth of November, the year of our Lord 1347.

No doubt you have heard reports of the illness decimating India, China, and the Far East. It is my sorry task to inform you that it is no fictitious rumor. It has arrived in Europe.

Three Genoese galleys, bearing spices and other riches, put in at Genoa after being storm-driven from the East on a stinking breath of wind. Once it was realized that many of the sailors and any man who conversed with them had died suddenly and without remedy, the survivors of the fleet were driven from the port with flaming arrows. One of the galleys arrived at Marseille on All Saint's Day. The port authority of the city, ignorant to the danger, lowered the harbor chain and allowed them to dock.

Soon it was discovered here, too, that the Genoese and their cursed merchandise were the cause of the illness afflicting so many. We, like Genoa before us, drove them from our harbor. But it was too late.

The disease attacks in two strains: The first, a fever, terrible cough, and the spitting and coughing of blood. The second, a continuous fever with swellings in the armpits, groin, and neck, which sigh and squeak like demons and then burst, erupting with bloody pus. Both forms of the pestilence are equally deadly.

Marseille is dying in droves. A man may wake healthy in the morning and be dead by nightfall. By the next day, his servants, wife, children, and livestock will be dead or dying. It is a plague surely sent by God to wipe the race of Adam from Earth for our sins.

Yours, in faith,
Francis DuLac

My insides turn to ice water.

"I will search the texts in my library," Guigo is saying, "for any mention of pestilence. This illness may be new to us, but Avicenna wrote that every disease except old age has a cause and a cure. There must be something we can do."

I must get home. I must tell my family.

Tell them what? That a terrible illness has already landed in Provence, that it may already be within the city walls?

"In the meantime, you must stay inside, Your Holiness," Guigo says. "If it is a corruption of the air, as seems likely, you must keep the windows closed and burn the fire day and night. Mademoiselle Blanchet will supply herbs to clear the miasma."

I think quickly: rosemary and sage are sweet and cleansing. I rifle through my basket until I have located the bundles and place them beside the fire.

"Go," says Clement, waving a bony hand. "Read and research. Arm yourselves with whatever knowledge you can find. Speak to other physicians. And I shall pray, may God hear me, that this pestilence spares our city."

Chapter Eight

Guigo and I reenter the laboratory in silence. The metallic smell of blood hangs in the air; the floor is littered with scarlet rags and discarded organs. We have both forgotten the pig.

"Go to the scullery," says Guigo, crossing to the bookshelf and running a finger down the titles. "Call for servants. This room must be cleaned before we begin our study. And send a messenger to your family. Tell them you will spend the night at the palace."

I obey, hurrying through the cold darkness to the kitchens, which are so alive with cooking smells and chatter that I want to cry.

I chase down one of the pope's pages to send home. As I write the direction and the message, I feel my sister's sorrow like a distant, aching muscle. Margot passed one of the worst days of her life today. I should be with her. But if this disease is as deadly as it seems, there is no time to waste in finding its cure or cause. For my family's sake, for Avignon's sake, I must stay here and work. *I'll go home tomorrow,* I tell myself. *No harm will befall them in just one night.*

When I return a few moments later with four sooty kitchen boys, Guigo sits reading at the far edge of the table, heedless of the mess. The pig's hooves rest on a compendium of Galen's treatises. A stack of books awaits me before the opposite chair. As the boys clear the gore—the buckets of bloody water, the piles of organs, and finally, together, hoist the pig from the table and carry it through the door—Guigo and I read.

The night creeps along in uneasy silence.

I start with Avicenna's *Canon of Medicine*, Guigo with the passages on the plague of the Philistines from the book of Samuel. It is tiring work; the fine lines and artistic curls make for difficult reading. Is that an *S* or a *G*? A *T* or an *I*? I strain to make out the words in the candlelight, and Guigo stops every few minutes to yawn or scratch his beard. I open the window onto the courtyard in hopes that the cold night air will keep us alert.

Finally, my itching eyes pass over the word.

"Pestilence!" I exclaim.

Guigo looks up at me in surprise, as though he had forgotten I was there.

"Listen," I say. "From the plague of Mesopotamia. Avicenna writes, 'The pestilence was borne by poisonous air, released by upheavals in the crust of the earth, which entered the body by way of the breath to first rot the complexion of the spirit and then rot the heart itself.'"

Guigo nods. "I recall that passage; not one of the medical faculty could give me a straight answer when I asked what 'the complexion of the spirit' was. We have heard of earthquakes in the distant east. Any mention of treatment or cure?"

I read the passage once, twice, three times. I shake my head.

"Ah, well," says Guigo with a half-hearted smile. "They couldn't make it easy for us, could they?"

A short while after the bells chime for midnight, I realize I have read the same paragraph three times without comprehending a single word. The candle beside me drowns in its pool of wax. I push the chair back from the table and get to my feet.

"I'm going to the kitchens for more candles," I announce.

Guigo doesn't seem to notice I've spoken; the crease in his forehead is so deep that his eyebrows are almost touching. I take my mother's cloak off its peg and open the door.

"Bring some sausages and bread, will you?" calls Guigo without looking up. "And some cheese?"

"Yes."

"And some wine?"

I close the door, laughing a little. Only Guigo could think about food at a time like this.

The walk to the kitchens in the freezing air revives me as much as the food revives Guigo. We take a few moments to eat and drink and discuss our meager findings.

"It seems," says Guigo through a mouthful of sausage, "there are many vague accounts of pestilence and plague, but the three that seem most similar to this new disease are the plague of the Philistines, the plague of Mesopotamia as described by Avicenna, and the plague of Justinian. All we know from the book of Samuel is the Philistines were beset by 'tumors in the groin,' but we know no treatment nor cure—only that they were believed to be a punishment from God. Avicenna, as you have said, describes terrible earthquakes that released poisonous gases in the air, which caused the plague of Mesopotamia."

"And the plague of Justinian?" I ask, helping myself to a piece of bread.

Guigo riffles through his manuscripts until he finds what he's looking for. Handwritten on vellum, the lines of cramped writing are visible through the material as he holds it up to the candle: a copy of Procopius's *History of the Wars*.

"It was a disease like this that began with a fever and a cough," says Guigo, taking a swig of wine, "which then progressed to swellings in the armpits and groin, bloody vomit, and diarrhea. Most afflicted died within a day or so. It struck suddenly and killed many, regardless of age or nobility, and infected dogs, pigs, and cattle, too, just like this new illness."

He traces his finger along the page. "'The graveyards and tombs of Constantinople overflowed, and the bodies were thrown into pits or into the sea.'" He looks up at me over the edge of the manuscript, the candlelight trembling in his tired eyes.

"According to Procopius, who lived through the plague of Justinian, one out of every three people died."

The bread is chalky in my mouth, my saliva gone. One out of every three. I count on my fingers. Me, Guigo, Anes, Father, Margot.

The cathedral bells awaken me with a terrible jolt. Across the table Guigo starts. He rubs fists into his eyes and gauges the gray light at the casement.

"Prime," he croaks.

My back aches, and one side of my face is numb from sleeping on it. I wipe a spot of drool from the pages of Galen's *On the Natural Faculties* and glance at my meager paper of notes on which is written, *Earthquakes: poisonous air. Swellings in the groin and armpits. Will of God.*

"We will do no good by sleeping through our study," says Guigo, pushing his chair back with a squeal of wood on stone. "Go home for the morning. Rest a few hours. Come back at midday and we shall resume."

I think of opening the front door, facing my family with the terrible news and no answers. "What should I tell them, Guigo?"

Guigo considers me with bloodshot eyes. "Tell them to stockpile what they can. To do it discreetly, from several different merchants, so as to not cause suspicion. Flour, dried meat, salted fish. Anything that will keep. Avoid any goods that may have come from Marseille or Genoa. And stay far away from anyone coughing."

As I walk home through the cold breath of the river, the city awakens around me. Smoke spirals from chimneys, cocks crow, windows open and shut. Life carries on, ignorant of the terrible knowledge reverberating in my head like a clapper in a bell.

I pause in front of the house on the corner and take a deep breath, steeling myself. Father will already be at the palace—I should have searched for him in the labyrinth of notary chambers, told him first—but Anes will be in the kitchen, and Margot will be sleeping.

I open the door. The smells of baking bread and the faint medicinal aroma of herbs greet my nostrils. I walk like a ghost through the hall to the kitchen.

Anes jumps when I enter, raising her wooden spoon like a sword. Her face relaxes when she sees me, then tightens again as she takes in the blood on my clothes.

"What has happened?"

"I'm fine. It's pig's blood," I say as Anes pulls the stiff hair from my forehead, searching for a wound. "A dissection. But I have unhappy news. The eastern pestilence has arrived in Marseille. The Genoese brought it from their trading posts in the Orient. It may already be here in Avignon."

"God help us," she whispers. "What should we do?"

"Go to the market," I answer, remembering Guigo's advice. "Buy all the firewood and dry goods you can carry. And do it today, while there is still food to be bought."

An hour later I climb into bed beside my sleeping sister, scrubbed within an inch of my life in the big copper tub in the kitchen. Margot stirs as the mattress sinks beside her.

"Elea?" she murmurs.

In answer, I loop an arm around her waist and press my nose against her neck. She smells of lavender and clean linen dried in the sun.

"Are you all right?" she whispers, still half asleep.

I want nothing more than to tell her everything I know, unburden myself of the words burning a hole through my tongue. But the pillow under my cheek is damp, and the memory of two nights ago returns to me in a dull rush. Margot has just suffered a terrible shock. She deserves a few hours of peace before another.

"Yes," I whisper back. "I'm all right."

An uneasy sleep engulfs me, filled with terrible dreams.

I dream a chasm opens in the bedroom floor, splintering the floorboards like a shipwreck and cracking the ceiling open to the sky. Margot and I are trapped on opposite sides—the breach is too wide, I cannot reach her. I watch in silent horror as poisonous gases escape the fissure like snakes and slither into my sister's open mouth.

When I open my eyes, the room is flooded with light, and the bed beside me is empty. I walk downstairs in my chemise, my head still thick with nightmares, to find Margot sitting at the table. Her face is pale, the skin around her eyes and mouth swollen and mottled.

"Anes told me," she says. "She is at the market now."

It is such a relief to see her safe and whole after the terror of my dream that I sit on the bench and wrap my arms around her. "I'm sorry," I say into the perfumed cascade of her hair. "I'm so sorry, Margot. About Erec. About all of it."

"That does not matter now," she says evenly, but I hear the tightness in her throat. "If this pestilence has arrived in Provence, we will have more to grieve than a broken engagement."

I take a deep breath and release her. "I fear so, too."

My sister helps me dress and pack my basket. She stands at the mullioned window and watches me walk up the rue des Lices. When I turn back to wave at the crest of the hill, I see a flicker of movement, like the white belly of a fish through water, as she raises her hand.

Word of the illness in Marseille spreads like fire.

The unease is evident in the empty streets, the way the few pedestrians avoid one another's gaze and hold kerchiefs to their faces as they pass. The guards at the city gates do not admit anyone from Marseille nor the infected cities of Italy. A curfew is set between sunset and sunrise, enforced by the papal army; anyone caught in the streets at night is heavily fined or tossed in the stocks.

Apothecaries hawk from their storefronts. "Desiccated toads! Ground unicorn horn! The only proven cures against the pestilence!" On every street corner, mountebanks sell counterfeit relics and amulets that promise to safeguard the wearer from illness. Some peasants spend hours with their heads down latrines, inhaling deeply, hoping the bad air will counteract the miasma that carries plague.

Townspeople buy wheat and salt at exorbitant prices; the markets are stripped bare of dry goods. Fishmongers come door-to-door with desperate faces, their carts heaped high with fresh fish that no one will buy for fear of corruption from bad air. The spice sellers, normally the busiest stalls in the market, stand behind their fragrant wares calling out desperately, "Cinnamon! Clove! Spikenard!" No one will buy them, afraid that they were carried on Genoese galleys. The panic is augmented by stories—some factual, others fantastic—of travelers from Marseille and other ports.

Every morning I peer through my bedroom shutters at the predawn sky, as though I could see the plague coming, a black fog on the southeastern horizon.

Guigo and I still begin each day attending the pope, who is recovered from his illness but daily grows more impatient over his quarantine. Then we return to the laboratory to study. We have read every book on the shelves that might contain a passage on plague. The only constant—the only reliable thread running through contemporary and historic accounts—is the poisonous effect of bad air. Where does the bad air come from? Procopius attributes it to the wrath of God, Avicenna to geologic forces, Hippocrates and Galen to the alignment of the planets. Gentile da Foligno, the most famous living physician after Guigo and his frequent correspondent, believes that bad air can come from the sea, the south, or sealed places such as crypts or cellars.

For treatment, Hippocrates recommends swallowing Armenian clay to draw out the poison. Maimonides warns against the consumption of fresh fruits and vegetables. Galen himself was cured of the plague through bloodletting. Gentile da Foligno recommends a powdered emerald taken in wine.

Guigo and I shake our heads at this lack of consensus. Surely when it arrives, we say to ourselves, we will know what to do with it. How many cases of winter fever, pleurisy, and sweating sickness have we treated between us? Surely medicine has come so far in the last five hundred years, all it will take is one breakthrough—one brilliant rereading of an ancient text in which a cure or cause is illuminated—and we shall stop this disease in its tracks. We hang in limbo, knowing the news is coming, dreading it and hoping for it, wanting to meet it head-on, rush it in the streets, have something to do with our hands and our minds and our time other than wait and read and worry.

I take any opportunity to escape the city walls and visit Baldoin. Together we walk through the winter-bare trees, the frost crunching under my heels and my breath billowing behind me. Baldoin bounds from one rabbit burrow to the next, then back to my side. I dig roots in the frozen ground, peel bark from willows and elms, fill my basket with herbs and my lungs with clean air.

At the end of each visit, he accompanies me farther and farther down the mountain. A few days before Christmas, he follows me all the way to the bridge.

"You cannot come," I say, scratching his ears. "My father would turn you out on the street. I couldn't bear to see you begging for scraps."

He shakes himself from nose to tail, then turns and trots back into the protection of the woods.

Guigo insists I spend the holiday with my family.

I have barely seen them, sneaking in after dark and sliding out of bed before dawn each day. Under my embrace on Christmas Eve morning Margot is thinner than I remember, her smile forced.

"You are well?" I ask, peering anxiously into my sister's pale face. Her eyes are overlarge in their delicate orbits, the skin beneath them stained with fatigue.

"It has been a long month," she replies. "But I am well."

"The city has lost its mind," Father says, installed in his favorite fireside chair with a cup of hot hippocras. "There is no sense left. A man was killed in the market yesterday over an amulet. The thief who stabbed him truly believed it was unicorn horn and not a horse hoof trimming! And the wealthy have bought up all the flour and sugar, they with their larders already full. People will die, from disease or starvation or a panic stampede if not from this illness."

"Many will die from this illness, Father," I say. "It is said in Marseille that five hundred people perish each day."

Father nods. "I have no doubt that it is deadly. But we have weathered disease before. It is no excuse to lose Christian courtesy."

We try our best to be cheerful, toasting cheese and playing cards, but the threat of plague hangs over us like a rain cloud. It is a gloomy holiday.

I watch my sister from the corners of my eyes. Her smile does not warm her face; her laugh comes too late.

I corner Anes while she spices the wine. "How is Margot?"

Anes peers over my shoulder at the empty doorway and clicks her tongue.

"Poor chick," she whispers, sprinkling a handful of anise into the pot. "The broken betrothal, then this plague. Shut up in the house all day with none but me."

"Is there any news," I ask, "of the Duponts?"

Anes casts another furtive glance toward the hall and nods. "Your father found Erec a position in the palace stables. They sold the house on the rue Dorée and are living with Allistair's cousins in the rue Banasterie."

Rue Banasterie, the basket weavers' street. Mathilde never spoke of this side of her husband's family, ashamed of his humble origins. And now she relies on their charity.

"Come," Anes says, handing me a stack of cups. "We have but a few more hours together. Let's be merry."

After supper we gather around the fire to exchange gifts. Father, as always, gives everyone three silver *deniers*. Mother used to roll her eyes at this. *It is meant to be a gift, Bernard, not a tax.*

"I don't know what ladies like," he says to me, Margot, and Anes, like he does every Christmas. "Buy yourself something nice." As we murmur our thanks, I catch Margot's eye and grin.

Anes's gifts are sugared fruits wrapped in wax paper, mine bottles of scent that I made last summer: rose for Anes, lavender for Margot, bay and clove for Father. Margot gives embroidered handkerchiefs to Anes and Father, then disappears upstairs for my gift.

A moment later she is back, hiding something behind her back. "Close your eyes," she says.

I comply and hear a woosh of unfurled fabric.

"All right. Open them."

I gasp.

It is a cloak, spangled from hood to hem with flowers, leaves, and berries in Margot's exquisite needlework. The wool is thick but light, the color of pine needles, finer than anything Father could afford. With a pang of sadness, I recognize it from the bolts of fabric chosen for Margot's wedding chest.

I take it from my sister and hold it up to the hearth light: here is a bunch of feverfew, the cheerful yellow faces surrounded by white petals; there a spike of rosemary topped by tiny blue flowers. Red hawthorn berries, gray-green lamb's ear, purple campaniles of comfrey, lacy milkweed, sprigs of lavender. All my herbs. All my medicines.

"Margot," I breathe, "it's wonderful."

"Do you like it?" she asks. "It's what I've been doing most days. I copied Mother's illustrations and the herbs in the kitchen."

"I love it." I wrap it around my shoulders and admire the fall of fabric, the delicate needlework more precious, more beautiful than lace and gems. And the cost to my sister to hold the fine fabric in her hands for hours each day, reminding her what she lost. "It is the most beautiful cloak in the world."

In the icy darkness Margot, Father, Anes, and I, wrapped in my new cloak, join the mass of worshippers on their way to Notre-Dame des Doms to hear the pope's midnight mass.

I do not think it wise to be trapped indoors with every soul in Avignon, breathing the same air for four hours when one of the few things we know of this disease is that it travels from one person to another with just a breath. But Guigo laughed when I voiced my concerns.

"Do you believe God would permit the plague to enter his house and infect his followers on the night when we celebrate the birth of his son?" he asked. "Besides: Do you wish to be the one person who is notably absent?"

This shut my mouth, and I agreed, reluctantly, to go.

Margot's shoulders are straight, her hair coiled and perfumed, but the last weeks are stamped in the set of her mouth, the sharpness in her cheekbones. I watch her gaze drift through the crowd, smiling and nodding to acquaintances. But I know she is hoping and dreading to see a glimmer of gold hair among the throng.

I imagine Erec in cramped apartments above the street-level shop, surrounded by cousins he does not know. Does he pine for Margot, as she pines for him? Does he mourn the life that was stolen from him, or is he too preoccupied with his father's debts to spare her a passing thought?

I sit between my sister and father, listening to Clement's deep voice roll through the Latin, and take little sips of air, holding my scented kerchief discreetly between my palms and jumping every time someone coughs. The service is soothing in its familiarity, the smell of incense and the chorus of voices replying *Amen*.

Father nods off, his chin lolling on his chest. Margot tenses beside me. Turning, I follow her gaze to the back of the nave. And there, just inside the doors, is Erec. He sits beside a small, bundled woman who must be Mathilde, betrayed by his height and the brightness of his hair. His eyes are on my sister, wearing the same starving expression as she.

Margot takes a deep breath and turns back to the pulpit. She does not look over her shoulder again but keeps my hand clutched between hers for the remainder of mass.

As the altar boys enter with trays of communion bread and the congregation prepares to spring from the pews and jostle for an early spot in line, Clement's voice rings through the cathedral once more.

"My children," he says in French.

Father starts awake.

"It is no secret that a pestilence has invaded the fair shores of Provence and, even as I speak, torments our faithful brothers and sisters in Marseille. Thus far, our fair city has been spared. I pray that we will emerge from this threat untouched by their suffering. We have taken actions to protect ourselves and our city, but the greatest assurance of all is prayer. It is God alone who has sent this plague, and God alone who has the power to redeem our souls."

The mood of the crowd trickling from the cathedral doors two hours later, with stale bread and cheap wine on their tongues, is hopeful. "If it hasn't come yet," whispers a merchant's wife to her husband, "perhaps it won't come at all."

But, of course, it comes.

Chapter Nine

January 1348

"The plague isn't here," Pope Clement snaps during our morning visit to him on a frosty January morning. "God has spared us. Apart from Christmas mass, I have been locked in these rooms for over a month. I am ready to see a face and hear a voice that does not belong to my surgeon."

"Pestilence still rages in Italy and Marseille," says Guigo soothingly.

"It has not stopped the Hungarians," Clement says. "The plague ravages Naples. But Louis of Hungary and his army are camped in Benevento, ready to lay siege to the city."

"And Queen Joanna?" I ask before I can stop myself. "Is she safe? Is she still coming for the trial?"

Clement shrugs. "Her soul is in God's hands. But it appears to me that he has made his divine judgment on the queen's guilt."

My heart plummets, thinking of Margot. Her heroine might be dead already, felled by her brother-in-law's sword.

"Once the plague has passed," Guigo says, returning to his earlier argument, "Your Holiness may return to feasting and processions. But until then, we cannot risk it. The world needs you: without your wisdom and guidance we are lost."

Clement reluctantly allows Guigo to bleed him, and we leave him pale-faced and gloomy. As we walk together back to the laboratory, a voice rings over the cobblestones.

"Dr. de Chauliac! Dr. de Chauliac!"

A boy I have seen about the kitchens, no more than eight or nine, runs toward us.

"Dr. de Chauliac," he pants. "There is a monk at the gate to see you. He said to tell you there is a sick man at the Hôpital Saint-Antoine. From Marseille."

My stomach dives.

Five minutes later, armed with his surgical instruments and my medicines, Guigo and I pass beneath the crossed lances of the palace guards to find Brother Louis pacing the foot of the stairs, the icy mistral lifting his black cassock like a skirt.

"Surgeon de Chauliac, Mademoiselle Blanchet," he says, raising a pinched face as we descend. "I wish I met you with better tidings."

"Lead the way, Brother Louis," says Guigo. I feel a nervous excitement in his voice, echoed by the bounding of my heart. "And tell us of our patient."

"Last night," says the young monk, guiding us across the plaza, "a man collapsed in the street not far from the hospital. One of the brothers saw him fall. We brought him in, gave him the usual medicines for such ailments, but nothing improved his condition. By midnight he was delirious. This morning he began to cough. While he could still speak, he told us his name was Arye Ravelle and admitted he was from Marseille. We believe it is the plague."

"And now?" asks Guigo. "How is he now?"

Brother Louis stops at the mouth of the rue Saint-Antoine and faces us, his features aged beyond his years by the expression they wear. "I have seen nothing like it, Surgeon. Last night he was feverish.

But walking, talking. Now, it will be a miracle if he lives to see another day."

As the monk turns toward the gold stone walls of the chapel and Hôpital Saint-Antoine, I glance at Guigo. His face is set like that of a man going to war.

At the hospital doors Guigo pulls a perfume-drenched kerchief from his pocket and ties it behind his head. I copy him, tugging free a square of muslin embroidered with Margot's tiny violets, doused in her lavender oil.

"Have you a scented handkerchief, Brother Louis?" he asks. "Mademoiselle Blanchet and I have researched the pestilence throughout history. Strong scents block the bad air."

The young monk shakes his head. "God will protect me," he says. "There is no greater security than prayer."

Together, we pass through the arched doorway into the hospital. It is unchanged, the air thick with the sounds and smells of sickness. I think of the last time I was here, when the man in the corner cot cried out that he had the plague. The relief when we realized his sores were a bawdy house affliction.

At the end of the hall, Brother Louis pauses before a large door and fumbles a key into the lock. We follow him into a narrow hallway lined with doors: the monks' quarters. I realize distantly that I, a woman, should not be here. At the last door on the left, the young monk stops and raises a fist to knock.

"Enter," comes the response through thick oak.

The cell is low-ceilinged and sparsely furnished. A sliver of blue sky gleams through the narrow window. In the bed beneath a carved crucifix, a man lies gasping.

Arye's closed eyes are sunken, the skin around them a ghastly gray. As Guigo and I enter the room, a coughing fit overtakes him. It is small at first: the cough of a winter cold. But it grows, moves deep into his chest with a horrible rattling, then explodes through his mouth with a spray of bloody mucus. Guigo and I recoil, clutching our tied kerchiefs tighter. An old monk leans over Arye and wipes his face tenderly. It is Brother Christophe, my mother's friend.

"Surgeon," he says, turning his wrinkled brown face toward us. "Mademoiselle Blanchet. Thank you for coming."

Despite the horror in the bed, my shoulders relax. When I was small and prone to nightmares, my mother lit a candle in the hall and let it burn all night. Finding Brother Christophe in this room is like opening my eyes to the flicker of light beneath the door.

"Thank you for your work, Brothers," says Guigo. "I have the unhappy task of telling you that your assumption is correct. This illness has all the symptoms of the first form of the pestilence we have heard described: fever, coughing, and spitting of blood. The only countermeasure that has been proven is clean air. I recommend we all wear scented kerchiefs, as Mademoiselle Blanchet and I have done. Open the window, burn herbs in the grate. I will conduct a thorough examination, then we will try everything we can think of to save this man."

Brother Louis rushes to the window. I pull dried sage and rosemary from my basket to crumble over the brazier.

"Before you begin, Surgeon," Brother Christophe says in his warm, grating voice, "there is something you must know."

He raises the linen to expose Arye's inert left arm on the mattress. Against the brown homespun, as stark as a wound, shines a circle of yellow felt.

"We didn't know until we had already brought him in, and he was too sick to move," Brother Christophe says softly. "We will do all we can to help any of God's children, of course. If he dies—God forbid it come to that—but if he dies, he should have his own people with him."

Guigo stares at the piece of yellow fabric for a long moment, then turns to Brother Louis. "Go to the Place Jérusalem," he says. "Knock on any door and ask for Dr. Farissol. When you find him, bring him here. Tell him I sent you."

Brother Louis nearly runs from the room.

I watch as Guigo listens to Arye's chest and lungs, places a hand to his forehead, measures pulses at throat and wrist. He straightens up, shaking his head.

"I've never felt a hotter fever," he says. "We shall check for the swellings that Cardinal DuLac described as symptoms of the second form of pestilence, just to be certain, then he must be bled before he is cooked alive. You may perform your own examination, Elea."

As Guigo readies his bloodletting supplies, I approach the bed. Arye's labored breathing fills the room with the smell of rotting meat. I hold my kerchief against my nose and take a deep breath of my sister's scent.

I place my other hand above Arye's heart and fight the reflex to withdraw it: Guigo is right, he is as hot as a stove. Under my fingers, through skin and muscle and ribs, his heart pounds, his chest expands and contracts desperately. The image of a sailor bailing water from a sinking ship springs into my mind.

I pull my hand away. This is not an ill body. It is a body battling tooth and nail for a slipping fingerhold on life. And I know in my bones that Arye will lose this battle. The invisible enemy that has breached the walls of his body is more potent, more deadly, than any disease we have ever encountered.

I see my same useless fear reflected back at me in Guigo's eyes. But in the determined lines in his brow, I understand that our work is unchanged. Guigo's words come rushing back to me, from my first day at the palace: *a physician's task is not to heal the sick but to stand between the living and death, armed with nothing but books and a little knowledge*. Perhaps there is nothing we can do to save this man, but we must try.

Guigo and I pull back the bed linens and begin to undress Arye.

There are no swellings in his groin or armpits, but his skin is drenched in stinking sweat. Guigo ties the tourniquet around one arm while I fetch the bloodletting bowl.

Guigo bleeds Arye from both arms—so heavily that the bowl is nearly full—and I dab the incisions with healing ointment before binding them with gauze, as I did Mathilde's. Guigo rubs vinegar and rosewater on Arye's head, which does nothing for the fever but makes the smell more tolerable.

A knock sounds on the door.

"*Entrez,*" calls Brother Christophe from his seat beside the bed.

Two men enter. The first is around Guigo's age, with dark hair and a beard beneath his kerchief, tied like Guigo's. They might be brothers but for his pointed hat and the yellow felt circle on his sleeve, identical to Arye's. The second is younger, slender and tall, and lingers behind on the shadowy threshold.

"My friend," says the first man, striding toward Guigo. "It has been too long."

"Far too long," Guigo repeats, clasping the man's proffered hand warmly. "How are you, Jacob?"

"I am well, as is Sarah, praise be."

I shift my weight beside Guigo, and he remembers I am here. "This is my apprentice, Eleanore Blanchet. Elea, this is my friend Dr. Farissol."

"*Enchantée,* mademoiselle." Dr. Farissol returns my curtsy with a courteous bow. The skin around his brown eyes is crinkled with laugh lines. If he is surprised that Guigo has a female apprentice, he does not show it.

"This is my apprentice," Dr. Farissol says as the second man steps beside him. "And my nephew. David."

David is young—only a few years older than me, I would guess—and nearly as tall as Guigo. His limbs, in their simple black garments, are long, and my gaze falls on the pale hands escaping their sleeves. They are gracefully formed, the fingers arching and tapered. An artist's hands. His eyes are dark above his tied muslin mask, but they do not meet mine. They stare in terrible recognition at the man in the bed.

"He, too, is from Marseille," Dr. Farissol says sadly, following David's gaze. "He watched his whole family die of this cursed plague."

"How long?" asks David suddenly, turning to Guigo. "How long since he fell ill?"

Brother Christophe, getting slowly to his feet beside the bed, answers the question. "He collapsed in the street last night. About twelve hours, I would guess."

"And you've examined him?" Dr. Farissol asks.

Guigo nods. "Examined him, bled him. But I'm interested to hear your opinions." He nods at David. "Both of you."

Guigo and I watch from the far wall as Dr. Farissol and David approach the bed. They perform the same examination we did, listening to Arye's lungs, feeling his pulse, lifting the bedding to search for swellings in his groin and armpits. After a moment they straighten and exchange a few words. I can't catch Dr. Farissol's low voice, but David's whisper, as he lifts his face to his uncle's, sends a shiver down my spine.

"*We will be blamed for this.*"

Guigo starts speaking eagerly as they join us in the sweet, herbal cloud by the brazier. "We have heard of two kinds of pestilence. The first, the fastest moving, passed from one man to the next as easily as breath. And the second—"

"The second moves more slowly," David interrupts. His voice is deep but melodic. "Fever, vomiting, black stool. And the swellings at groin and armpits. This man has the first kind."

"Are you certain?" Guigo's gaze is sharp on his face. "Think hard, young man, of what you're about to say."

"I am certain." David turns his dark eyes back to Arye. A brightness burns in their depths I did not see before. "This is how my family died."

A silent moment passes. David's words sink in like rain.

Dr. Farissol raises a hand to his nephew's shoulder. "They are in the place of eternal light," he says. "Their suffering is over."

But I know how empty these words fall on the ears of the living.

"I'm sorry," I blurt out.

David's head swivels from Arye to me. They are all looking at me, Guigo and Dr. Farissol and Brother Christophe, but I keep my eyes on David. My face flushes under the intensity of his gaze, but I meet it, hold it.

"I'm so sorry," I repeat, this time nearly a whisper.

The room around us seems to blur. It is just him and me, two mourners, standing in our grief together. David's face softens. He drops his chin in acknowledgment but doesn't let go of my eyes.

"Did anything help?" Guigo interrupts, bringing me back to myself with a jolt. "Did you hear of any treatment, any cure?"

David breaks my gaze to turn to him, shakes his head. I force myself to focus on his words and ignore my heart, which is suddenly beating very fast.

"None," he says. "I protected myself as best I could, with handkerchiefs drenched in scent and herbs to burn on the fire, as you have done here. But many followed these precautions and did not survive. I do not know why God spared me."

He utters the last sentence almost dreamily, and I know he has wondered this every day, perhaps every moment since he watched his family perish. *Why them and not me?*

"But we had no doctors," he says. "They would not come, when they knew what it was. But you, Surgeon de Chauliac, you are the greatest physician alive. Perhaps you will discover a cure."

Guigo is saved from responding by Arye, who suddenly convulses with a deep, gurgling cough.

"Shall we compare the findings of our examination, Jacob?" Guigo asks. "David can take notes while Elea prepares her medicine."

While the three men gather around the cot, I lay out the contents of my basket on the table. Brother Christophe vacates his chair creakily and crosses the room to stand beside me. He has tied no cloth about his mouth and nose; perhaps he, like Brother Louis, believes prayer is all the protection required.

"May I watch you work, Mademoiselle Blanchet?" he asks, eyeing my vials curiously. "I was always fascinated by your mother's medicines. How she harnessed the healing powers of God's herbs."

"Of course." I feel myself relax a little despite the creaking of Arye's breath like a ship in the wind, the lingering fever heat in my fingertips.

I measure the tinctures one by one into my bone cup. "Two draughts of willow bark tonic and one of comfrey tonic," I say, pouring in the pale purple liquid, "for pain. One draught each of mint and fenugreek to ease his coughing. Three of feverfew, to break the fever." Although I know that this fever will not be broken. "And honey, to coat his throat."

I add a heaping spoonful of summer honey and stir the mixture until it dissolves, thinking of bees and sun on my face. Thinking of anything but Arye's fight for life.

The sweet florals cut through the poisonous air. Brother Christophe closes his eyes and takes a deep breath. "It smells like a summer afternoon, mademoiselle. Is nature not wonderful?"

I do not answer him. My throat tightens with sudden hopelessness. Arye will die, just as David's family died, and there is nothing any of us can do to stop it.

After a moment, the old monk shifts in his chair. "I would very much like to learn the recipe for this medicine," he says gently. "Would you write it down for me?"

I swallow hard, pushing down the despair, and force myself to meet his eyes. "It is simple, really," I say. "My mother always said our task is to prepare the herbs in the most potent way possible and then step back and let them work."

Brother Christophe nods thoughtfully. "God has given us so many gifts. I believe that no matter how far medical science comes, how much doctors turn to the heavens for explanation and guidance, the cures to all men's maladies, the answers to all those questions, lie right here under our feet. The natural world is miraculous."

I lift the cup like a communion chalice. "Let us pray," I say, "that these simple herbs perform a miracle now."

Guigo and Dr. Farissol help Arye to a sitting position so he can swallow my medicine. His eyes, bright and bloodshot, flutter open for the first time and search the room in dazed confusion.

"Haquin," he croaks through cracked lips. "Where is Haquin?" He starts to say more, but another cough erupts up his throat and chokes the words.

It's like no cough I've ever heard, like a chain dragged across cobblestones, and with each convulsion blood spatters the counterpane and dribbles from his chin to his chest. At first the blood is bright, mixed with spittle, but with each new paroxysm it is darker and thicker until he spits black tissue into his lap.

When it is over, there is a thick silence.

I look down at the cup in my hands filled with mild medicine. It will do nothing, I know, to stop the disease. But I must try to ease this man's terrible suffering in the only way I have. And I know that it cannot hurt.

I approach the bed.

Arye now lies motionless on the pillows, eyes closed, filling the room once more with the sound of his stertorous breathing. I look at Guigo for guidance, but his eyes do not meet mine.

"Arye," David says, staring not at our patient but at me, the light of an idea illuminating his face. "It's Haquin. You've been ill, my friend." He takes the man's ashen fingers in his hand. "We are here to help you."

Arye's head swings toward David like a drunk's, the fading eyes flickering open again.

"Arye," David says again, "can you hear me? You must take some medicine. It will make you feel better." He looks up at me, nods. "Open your mouth, my friend."

Arye obeys like a child, and I am ready; I tip the medicine down his throat and say a prayer as he swallows.

Blessed Virgin, grant this soul peace.

"Good work, Haquin," Guigo says humorlessly.

"What did you give him?" David asks me.

But I do not have the chance to respond. A burbling sound fills the air, followed by an eye-watering smell. Arye has soiled himself.

David helps Brother Christophe roll Arye on his side to clean him. When his nightshirt and linens are changed, and the soiled cloth taken by Brother Louis to be burned, we lay Arye back in the fresh bed.

No sooner is he supine than his belly convulses and he vomits up all my medicine, still smelling like honey and flowers and tinged pink with blood.

We clean him again, change the bed linens once more. He coughs so hard the blood vessels burst in his eyes.

The day—clear and blue through the window—lasts forever.

I watch Brother Louis and Brother Christophe begin to comprehend what I realized when I touched Arye. This man will die a terrible death, with no friends or family, and there is nothing any of us can do about it.

We stop changing his linens and leave him in the filthy bed, do our best to sponge the gore off his face and chest in between coughing fits. The fever rages, with so much stinking sweat I could wring it from the sheets, and then delirium. Arye raves, calls over and over for Haquin, but David doesn't answer him. He seems to have retreated deep inside himself, perhaps to a memory of another night like this one, when he marked the passing hours alone, and the face in the bed belonged to someone he loved.

When shadows stretch like bruises across the courtyard, Dr. Farissol stands beside the cot and lays a wide hand on Arye's stuttering chest. Through his protective handkerchief the prayer comes, low and gentle, in a voice chosen to lull a baby or calm a horse. The words are foreign—Hebrew, I realize distantly—but the sentiment is clear as air.

Peace. Peace. Peace.

Dr. Farissol's voice fades. He steps away from the bed, candlelight catching on the tears on his face, and does not approach it again.

Around midnight we fall into a sort of stupor, transfixed by the terrible sounds from the cot. Death is seated on Arye's face now, his cheekbones craggy edges under gray skin, his eyes pits.

Finally, gratefully, a choking sound deep in his chest. A gurgle. And his chest rises no more.

I lean on the pillar outside the hospital doors and rest my forehead on the cold stone. The stench of the last few hours clings to my hair, my clothing, and the realization hits me: the disease may already be rotting my lungs as it rotted Arye's, turning my insides to black blood. I take a steadying breath, focus on the ground under my feet, but it's no good—I am sick, vomiting up food I don't remember eating, then yellow bile, then nothing, and still I heave, my stomach twisting, my body trying to purge the memory of the night and the foulness I may already carry inside me.

When it is over, I crouch beside the column and shiver. River mist curls through the silent graveyard, the mounds of earth and wooden crosses peaceful and still in the light of the moon.

This moment, right now, is just the beginning.

Chapter Ten

Guigo and I walk together through empty streets. Behind closed windows and locked doors, the people of Avignon lie safe and warm in their beds while we pass like wraiths.

"What will they do with him?" I ask dully.

Guigo and I watched in empty silence as Dr. Farissol and David, with the help of the monks, bundled Arye's body in bed linen and carried it between them to a handcart. We didn't say goodbye to them. There was nothing to say.

"Bury him according to their customs," Guigo says. "Try to find his people, I suppose."

We reach the wide rue des Lices. I think of my loved ones, sleeping, ignorant of the enemy already inside the city walls. My feet freeze.

"Guigo," I say, "I have to tell my family."

Guigo's mind is far away, and it takes a moment for him to answer. "Very well," he says. "I shall walk with you."

"My home is just there," I say, pointing at the next block of houses.

He follows my finger, eyes still distant. "Try to sleep a few hours."

I nod. "You do the same."

Guigo places a palm on my shoulder. I think he will say something, offer some word of encouragement, but he just takes a deep breath, shakes his head. Then he lifts the comforting weight of his hand and turns back toward the palace.

As Guigo's footsteps fade and silence falls, the same terrible thought comes back, drowning out all reason. What if I am already corrupted? What if I carry this plague home to my family? Were the burning herbs, the scented kerchiefs, protection enough? David said they were, but he also said—oh, God—he also said that many that followed these protections died as Arye did, as his family did. An image of Margot coughing blood flashes through my mind. I place a hand to my forehead. No fever. I bring up phlegm and spit in my hands, hold them up to the distant moonlight. No blood. Not yet.

I glance over my shoulder as though death follows me from the hospital: a beggar in black rags, watching me from empty sockets.

My heart stops.

No beggar, but at the last of the street, dim in the light of the lamp, a shape moves toward me on four feet.

I step backward, a scream rising in my throat—but then I recognize him.

"Baldoin?"

At the sound of my voice he picks up his pace, ears and tail high. It is him: loose-limbed and wild, covering the cobblestones of the rue des Lices in silent strides like one of the panthers in Clement's zoo.

He trots up beside me, tail wagging. Without stopping to wonder how he slipped past the guarded gates into the city walls, how he found me, I kneel, wrap my arms around his neck and bury my face in his thick coat.

The stifled emotions claw their way out. Baldoin does not move, does not pull away as tears roll down my cheeks and bead his fur: tears for Arye. Tears for my family, who do not know how frightened they should be. And tears for me and Guigo, who must fight this war with no weapons.

Baldoin turns to lick my face, and I am returned to myself like someone waking from a nightmare. I know what I must do.

I get to my feet and place a palm on Baldoin's head.

"Thank you," I say. "I don't know how you found me. But thank you."

Baldoin looks up at me with his mouth open, the lines of long white teeth giving the appearance of a smile.

"It's not safe here," I say. "And I cannot bring you home with me. Go back to the woods. I'll visit when I can."

Baldoin gives me one last tail wag and turns back the way he came, trotting into the thick darkness.

I watch the street for a long time after he has disappeared. Then I set my shoulders resolutely toward my home.

I pass the front door and walk around the house through the side yard, disturbing a few chickens, to the backyard. Along the wall of the chicken coop sits a rusted metal trough for watering horses. I drag it to the well.

I lower the bucket, hear the shattering of ice as it breaks the surface, and bring up enough frigid water to fill the trough. My breath billows around me, and my fingers are numb by the time I finish. Beside the back door I find a piece of black wood-ash soap Anes uses for pots and pans. Then I strip off my filthy clothing and step into the freezing water.

The shock takes my breath away. I feel my courage evaporating, and I know I must act quickly. I take a deep breath and sit down. Water sloshes over the sides of the tub. Shaking with cold, I dunk my head, wet my hair, and reach for the soap.

I am standing in the middle of the yard in the horse trough, covered in gray soap bubbles, when Anes opens the back door.

If it weren't for the circumstances, the expression on her face would have made me laugh. She looks wildly around the yard and then runs toward me, pulling the shawl off her shoulders.

"Are you mad?" she hisses, holding the mantle in front of my naked body.

I take another gulp of air and flop back down in the tub like a fish. I splash the icy water over my skin, dunk my head a few more times for good measure, then stand up and step into the warm circle of wool.

"What are you doing?" she whispers.

My teeth are chattering too hard to answer her. She pushes me toward the open door and stoops to pick up my discarded clothes.

"Leave them," I order. She looks up, alarmed. I have only two other dresses. Something in my face convinces her, though, and she drops them back in the mud.

"And wash your hands," I say. "Those clothes are poisonous."

When the first gray light creeps through the casement, I gather my family around the table. Margot is bleary-eyed and pale, Father grim and alert. Anes flits from kitchen to hall with cups and a jug of hot ale like an anxious swallow. When we are all seated, I begin.

"The plague is in Avignon. It has claimed its first soul."

Margot covers her mouth with her hands. Father nods, grave but unsurprised.

"It was only a matter of time," he says.

"Is it as bad as they say?" asks my sister.

"It is worse." There is no sense in lying to them; they must know the enemy we face. "A healthy man in his prime died a terrible death—a death I would wish on no one—within a day." I feel the pounding of Arye's dying heart under my fingers and squeeze my hands together beneath the table.

"Is there anything to be done?" Anes asks. "All these amulets and powders, does anything help?"

I look around the table at the frightened faces of my family, turned to me for guidance. An unwanted honor, a weighty burden. But I chose to walk this path. I think of Baldoin standing so still and find a deeper courage.

"The course of this disease and what might cure it are unknown to us," I say evenly. "But if anyone can discover this disease's cause and cure it is Guigo, and I will do everything I can to help him. Until we know more, you must stay inside. Burn rosemary and sage on the brazier. Admit no one. Father, stay far from the other clerks and close to the fires. Anes, Margot, don't leave the house, not even for the market. I'll arrange for the kitchens to bring you food and firewood."

"And what of protecting yourself?" asks Margot. "How will you stay safe, attending the sick?"

"My herbs and kerchief," I say, hoping my voice exudes a confidence I do not feel. "I will sleep at the palace and visit when I can, with news. But I must leave soon. Guigo is expecting me."

Margot gets to her feet, pale but steady. "I'll help you pack your things."

"And I shall walk with you," says Father, "when you are ready."

Margot and I stand on stools in the kitchen and cut down bundles of dried herbs until the ceiling is barer than I ever remember seeing it. I crowd my basket with clinking vials of tonics and tinctures. Then I turn to my sister.

My twin wraps her arms around me. "Please be careful," she whispers. "I cannot afford to lose you, too."

In the press of her heart against mine I feel the echoed throb of my own fear.

In the pink light of dawn, Father and I walk through the streets together. We do not speak. My father's face is somber, his mouth a hard line.

Once inside the palace walls, my father squeezes my hand and turns toward the notary chambers. I resist the childish impulse to call him back—as though my invincible father could keep reality at bay, the way he once dissolved the monsters of my nightmares.

When I open the laboratory door, Guigo sits at the table surrounded by the usual stacks of books and manuscripts. His eyes are bloodshot, his hair wild. I close the door quietly behind me so as not to startle him.

"Did you sleep at all?" I ask.

"What?" he says, looking up distractedly from his worn compendium of *The Hippocratic Corpus*. "It's you. Oh. No."

"Have you seen the pope?" I ask.

"Not yet," he says, absorbed once more in the yellowed pages. "I requested an audience at prime."

"Guigo, the sun is risen," I say in alarm.

"What?" He blinks in dismay at the bright window.

"Yes," I say gently. "Wash your face. Eat something. You look dreadful."

"I'm not prepared," he says blankly. "I have no answers."

Someone raps at the door.

"Enter," Guigo calls. The door creaks open.

It is the sooty-faced boy from the kitchens. "*Bonjour,* Dr. de Chauliac, mademoiselle," he says brightly. "The monk left a message for you at the gate. He said to tell you Brother Christophe is ill. He asks if you will please come to the hospital quickly."

"*Bon Dieu!*" Guigo bellows, smashing a fist on the table so hard the windows rattle.

The boy jumps.

"Thank you," I say, pulling a coin from my purse with shaking fingers.

When the boy has run off with another frightened glance at Guigo, I stomp to where the most famous living physician stands, his hands on the table, his massive shoulders hunched under an invisible burden.

"Listen to me," I say, thinking of Margot, of Anes. "You have a duty. You, more than anyone else in this city—including the pope—can make a difference. The people are going to turn to you and your medical knowledge to lead them. You can be a voice of reason. You can help staunch the panic. We have no idea what to do, what medicines or precautions will stop this disease. But people need guidance. They need to feel they have weapons against it. Even if they are not real. Even if they don't help."

I point at the book under his fist.

"*Primum non nocere,* says Hippocrates. First, do no harm. What can you advise the pope to do today that won't cause any damage and may help? Something the people can see and take comfort in?"

The gears of Guigo's brilliant mind start to turn. He paces the length of the table, running a hand through his beard. "Yes," he mutters after a moment. "Yes. What do we know? We know that illnesses are born of bad air." He points to the open book. "We know that to cleanse the air during the plague of Athens, Hippocrates recommended fires be lit in every house. But the people of Avignon cannot all burn fires in their homes; it is much too expensive, and many do not have fireplaces. . . ."

He smacks a palm down on the table. "Bonfires! Bonfires at all the major thoroughfares. They will see the smoke and the flames and take heart that something is being done to protect them."

He takes both my hands and squeezes them, his face once more grave.

"I must speak with Clement. Go to the hospital. Offer the monks what help you can."

As Guigo pulls on his cloak, I glance down at the book he was reading, open to a passage on the plague of Athens. The words *Cito, Longe, Tarde* are underlined in scrawling ink.

I swallow. Fly quickly, go far, return slowly.

Light gilds the highest windows of the tenements and town houses as I walk alone to the Hôpital Saint-Antoine, but down in the streets it is dark and cold.

The little gate of the graveyard moans as I open it. I pass between the wooden crosses, trying not to think of Arye. Is he already covered in earth, with the blood congealing in his lungs? But my thoughts are interrupted when the peaked door of the hospital opens and four monks in black sackcloth step through it, carrying something between them. I recognize Brother Louis among them.

I start toward them, raising a hand to wave, but then I see what they bear: a shrouded corpse. *It couldn't be,* I think numbly. *He was well only hours ago.*

The monks do not see me; their eyes are fixed on the ground. They carry their burden to where a new pile of black dirt waits against the golden walls of the hospital, the winter sun falling clear and bright upon it. As they set the body—small and light in death—into the grave, I take an involuntary step forward.

The abrupt movement catches Brother Louis's eye. He says something to the other monks, then walks to where I stand frozen. His expression tells me what I already know.

"Mademoiselle Eleanore," he says. His young face is a picture of weariness. "Thank you for coming."

I nod, not trusting myself to speak.

"There was nothing you or anyone could have done," he says. "No sooner did we assist Messieurs Farissol to the Place Jérusalem than Brother Christophe began to cough. He was old, as you know, but strong . . . but it did not matter. The disease worked so quickly."

He falls silent, turns his eyes upward to the blue sky. I lean on the gatepost, not certain that my trembling knees will hold me.

A long silence passes before he speaks again. "I do not know why

God has brought this pestilence upon us," he says quietly, "but I know with all my soul that the Lord called Brother Christophe home." He smiles at me through his tears. "Do not mourn him, mademoiselle. He is with God."

Brother Louis bows to me and turns back to the grave where his companions stand with heads bowed. The wind carries me snatches of their prayers.

As I open the gate, one of the monks begins to cough.

Chapter Eleven

February 1348

Are you ready?" Guigo asks, standing before the barred palace entrance.

I take a deep breath of smoke-tinged air and wrap the cloak Margot embroidered more tightly around my shoulders.

"Ready," I answer, tying my kerchief over my nose. Guigo motions to the guards.

The door opens onto a city unrecognizable from the Avignon of three months ago.

The smell hits me like a wall. I drench my kerchief each morning in lavender oil, but it does little good. Human and animal waste fills the street, mingling with the reek of rotting food. And, over everything, the sick-sweet smell of death.

Ash from the bonfires hangs thick in the air, casting the buildings in queer yellow light and catching in our hair like snow. Avignon's bells no longer ring. The only sounds in the city are the rattle of the corpse carts and the calls of the crass country peasants who push them to the overflowing cemeteries: *"Bring out your dead! Bring out your dead!"*

Twenty thousand Avignonese have perished.

Entire blocks stand vacant, their doors marked with black crosses of soot. I shiver as we pass the mouth of the rue de l'Épicerie; Monsieur Vielle the baker, his wife, their children, all gone. Remembering their baby's cries and the warm loaf of bread in my basket, I whisper a prayer that their souls are at peace.

Gone, too, are the Roches, the Sartres, the LeCleres, the Gauthiers, families from the rue des Lices who Margot and I grew up with, dined with, exchanged pleasantries with after Sunday mass. My mind cannot conceive the scale of the loss. The faces missing from the streets, the markets, the pews of Saint-Agricol. So many souls snuffed out like candles.

I play the same twisted game each day, imagining that Guigo's wide back before me is Virgil, leading me safely through the hellscape of my city as he led Dante through the circles of hell in the dog-eared pages of Margot's favorite book. *Perhaps this is not real,* I tell myself, *and soon I shall wake in bed beside her, the last months a terrible but distant dream.*

> *Thou follow me, and I will be thy guide,*
> *And lead thee hence through the eternal place,*
> *Where thou shalt hear the desperate lamentations,*
> *Shalt see the ancient spirits disconsolate,*
> *Who cry out each one for the second death . . .*

Each day is the same.

I wake at dawn in the cot in the laboratory. I have not returned home in the month since Arye died—there is too much to do.

Over breakfast, Guigo and I review our notes from the day before. We discuss any new theories, treatments, or medicines that other physicians describe in their letters, compiling them together for a treatise Guigo might someday publish. Then we go wherever we can be of service: hospitals, almshouses, mansions, and tenements. Nearly all the doctors and priests have fled the city, and Guigo and I have more work than a hundred physicians could do. The plague strikes impersonally without regard for age, goodness, or status.

Clement releases a proclamation that anyone, even a woman, may perform last rites—which makes me swallow fresh tears for my mother's unshriven soul. Still, many die alone and unconfessed, abandoned by their families or collapsed in the street where dogs and pigs, their masters dead, feed upon them.

Despite the raging plague, church services continue. Corrupted air, the clergy reason, cannot penetrate the sanctified walls of a cathedral. So on Sundays I sit beside Guigo in the cold, echoing nave of Notre-Dame des Doms, imagining Father, Margot, and Anes in our family pew in Saint-Agricol, and listen to a rotating staff of bishops give mass. It's hard not to feel sorry for these young men, barely out of cathedral school, who were clearly assigned this task because of their youth and unimportance. They materialize in a thick cloud of incense, barely draw breath as they rush through the Latin, then disappear as quickly as they arrived in a swirl of white silk vestments. I hold my kerchief over my mouth, stand and sit, repeat *amen* with the rest of the congregation. But my mind, God forgive me, is out in the city, on the death-filled afternoon to come.

We try everything we can think of. Guigo bleeds patients from this or that vein or doesn't bleed them at all. He recommends that all the windows be opened, or all closed, or only north-facing windows be open. He prescribes theriac, powdered gold, arsenic, Armenian clay. I prepare every recipe in my mother's book and many more concoctions of my own creation. Nothing helps. Nothing makes any difference at all.

It starts with a cough and fever, followed by the expectoration of blood, phlegm, and black lung tissue. The fever brings on delirium—waking nightmares and hallucinations. Many believe they are in hell, being tortured by the devil. Others call out for family, beg for an end to the suffering. Within a day, or sometimes two, they receive it. We have only seen the pneumonic form of the disease. The bubonic form, characterized by tumors in the groin, armpits, and neck, has not yet arrived in Avignon, although Guigo says it is only a matter of time.

One windy February morning, Guigo arrives in the laboratory looking worse than usual. Dark hollows encircle his eyes. He gazes off into space as I read our notes from the day before.

"Are you all right?" I finally ask. "Do you feel unwell?"

He turns his head sharply, as though just remembering I was there.

"We have saved no one," he says. "Not a single soul."

His eyes rest on my face for a long moment, unseeing, but I can nearly hear his mind turning like a millstone behind the empty gaze. He seems to make up his mind about something and pushes back from the table.

"Come," he says. "Let us appeal to the wisdom of the pope."

Guigo says nothing more as we walk across the freezing courtyard and through the guarded doors of the Tour des Anges. He waits, toes tapping the flagstones before the nightingale room, while the guard announces our presence. The minutes creep past. I am infected by his nervousness.

Finally, the door opens.

"His Holiness will see you now," says the liveried guard.

Guigo and I step over the threshold.

The golden birdcages are empty, their inhabitants long dead from the stifling heat. Pope Clement sits in a high-backed chair between the twin fireplaces, wrapped in folds of ermine.

Guigo sweeps his hat from his head and bows. "You may rise," Clement says impatiently. "What is the matter, Surgeon?"

"Your Holiness," Guigo begins, "the cemeteries of every hospital and churchyard overflow with corpses. We haven't the earth to bury them properly, and each night the pigs unearth the dead and drag them into the streets. The rotting corpses further contaminate the air. We need several new cemeteries."

Clement nods, examining his fingernails. "I received news today. Queen Joanna and her consort, Luigi of Taranto, have fled Naples under the siege of Louis of Hungary. They make their way to Avignon as we speak, where the queen will stand trial for her husband's murder as planned."

"Now?" I blurt out. "Forgive me, Your Holiness, but a sea voyage—"

"I agree," Clement interrupts, "that it is poor timing, of course, with the pestilence raging. But Louis has already begun executing the queen's closest advisers. She had no choice but to flee."

I think of Margot, imagine her face when she learns this news. Finally, something to think of other than plague. Something to dream of other than death.

"And it will not do for the first impression of our queen's city to be stacks of rotting corpses," Clement continues. "There is a field beside Notre-Dame des Miracles that would serve as a cemetery. I shall purchase and consecrate the land for the plague dead." He shifts beneath the ermine-lined cloak. "Is there anything else?"

Guigo swallows. "Your Holiness," he begins, "Mademoiselle Blanchet and I—all the doctors with whom I communicate—are no better at fighting this disease than we were a month ago. I believe the only way to stop it, or even slow its progression, is to understand it better."

The sweet anticipation of Queen Joanna's visit vaporizes. I know, now, why we are here. Why Guigo was so nervous.

Why, I fume silently, *did he have to bring me along? Make me complicit?*

The pope narrows his eyes. A trickle of sweat runs down the side of Guigo's face and disappears into his beard.

"I ask you to lift the ban on human dissection," Guigo says in a rush. "Not just for me, but for every university-trained physician in

Christendom, so we may exchange findings with the rest of the medical community. It is the only way we will learn about this disease: its progression, its cause, and perhaps its cure."

The fire cracks. The silence stretches. Clement considers, pressing his fingers together in the shape of a church spire. I imagine him rolling Guigo's heretical request over in his mind, examining every implication like a jeweler scrutinizing the facets of a diamond.

Finally, he raises his face to Guigo. "Very well," he says. "At this time of most severe crisis, I shall lift the ban on human dissection. I shall submit a papal bull making this temporary measure official. In the meantime, write to your peers. Let it be known."

Guigo exhales.

Clement turns his gaze back to the fire. "Begin with La Pignotte. Saint-Agricol's new priest has complained that the poorhouse is essentially functioning as the parish's morgue. There will be plenty of bodies to spare, may their immortal souls rest in peace."

Guigo nods. We visited La Pignotte last month. Most of the beds held corpses, their faces already stiffening, or patients too far gone for us to do more than speak their last rites.

"Father Loup writes that our city's poorest inhabitants have no one to tend them as they die, as so many monks have perished or fled, and he requests funds to hire help. I shall increase his stipend, and in exchange he will provide you with corpses to dissect."

Guigo bows. "Thank you, Your Holiness."

An awkward silence falls, and I realize they are both waiting for me to curtsy so that Guigo and I may take our leave. But my exhausted mind has just caught the pope's words.

"Father Loup?" I repeat.

"Yes." Clement frowns at me. "Did I not just say? The priest of Saint-Agricol has succumbed, and—"

"Father Germaine is dead?" I interrupt. Doddering old Father Germaine, kind to children, always sneezing from the incense.

"Yes," Clement repeats, and this time there is a sharpness in the word. "He has perished. As I have said. I have instated Father Loup in his place."

The blood chills to ice in my veins.

"He held the parish of Saint-Agricol some years ago," Clement continues, "before he became a leader of the flagellant movement. I dislike the sect—they are fanatics who misinterpret the word of Christ—but they grow in power and followers in this time of strife. Fear is a potent unifier. I would rather have them under my nose and their leader answering to me." He stands, crosses to the parchment-covered desk in the center of the room. "I shall write an official document that he cannot disregard."

Guigo and I watch in silence as Clement dips his quill in the inkwell and scratches a message onto a blank scroll, then holds a candle flame to a stick of sealing wax.

"You shall have your corpses," he says, pressing his signet ring into the scarlet puddle.

Back in the laboratory, Guigo is exuberant. He writes identical letters to all his contacts—dozens of them—and hums as he copies the brief message.

His Holiness Clement VI, in his infinite wisdom, has lifted the ban on human autopsies during this period of most severe crisis so that we may better understand and treat the pestilence. Recount this news to every licensed physician.

When the page has been called, the letters dispatched to every corner of Europe, Guigo tucks the pope's document in his breast pocket and reaches for his cloak.

"Come, Mademoiselle Médecin," he says with a grim smile. "Let us pray that from the bodies of its victims we will finally unlock the secrets of this cursed plague."

I swallow the lump of fear in my throat and follow him.

Chapter Twelve

As Guigo and I walk through the watery winter sunlight to La Pignotte, dread drags at the hem of my flower-spangled cloak like ship ballast. I considered making some excuse, finding a reason to stay behind, but my mind is paralyzed.

Father Loup will not recognize me, I tell myself. It has been years. I am changed. I am with Guigo. I am safe.

Twice we cross the street to avoid bodies, dragged out of houses or lying where they fell, waiting for the corpse cart to pass. The boarded-up windows, the marked front doors make the city feel like a huge, blighted tree; the sight of a smoking chimney or candle in a window like a shot of green leaves on a dead branch. There are few people out: we pass a contingent of papal guards, looking gaunt and undermanned; a handful of peasants who hurry past, clutching kerchiefs to their faces.

Guigo drones on about dissection techniques as we walk up the rue Banasterie to the Jewish quarter. The Place Jérusalem is empty but for a few napping cats. Dr. Farissol and David must live in one of these pleasant homes, I realize distantly, with a Hebrew number over the doorframe and upstairs windows overlooking the square. If they still live.

La Pignotte is a few streets away. The houses become poorer with every step; well-to-do Avignonese prefer to live far from Jewish neighbors, although Father told me once that nearly all Jews are lettered and Guigo says they bathe more frequently than their wealthy Christian counterparts, the solicitors and notaries who occupy the homes in the rue des Lices beside mine.

"Keeping the lungs intact is key, I think," Guigo is saying. "If we go carefully—very carefully—with the bone cutters, so as not to nick them . . ."

I am with Guigo, I repeat to myself. *I am safe.* But terrible questions repeat in my mind. What if the priest recognizes me, what if he convinces Guigo I am what he thinks I am? What he thought my mother was?

We turn a corner, and La Pignotte squats suddenly before us, nestled between tottering tenement buildings, its roof sagging a little in the middle. Guigo raises a fist to knock, Clement's letter clutched tightly in his other hand.

My heart beats at my ribs like something trapped.

After a moment the door swings open. I exhale. The man on the threshold is not, thank the Virgin, Father Loup. My first impression is of a rat. The monk is small and slight, dressed in a black habit that is too large for him. His long nose twitches, and he squints through small, suspicious eyes as he looks first at Guigo, then me, up and down.

"I am Surgeon de Chauliac," Guigo booms. "Head physician to His Holiness, Pope Clement the Sixth. And this is my apprentice, Mademoiselle Eleanore Blanchet."

Rat Face blinks.

"I have here," Guigo says, holding out the pope's document with a flourish, "a decree of compliance from His Holiness himself."

The monk peers at the document. His eyes widen as they

encounter the words *corpses* and *dissection,* then linger over the pope's signature.

"Wait," he says, retreating into the dim interior of the poorhouse. "Wait here. *S'il vous plaît.*"

The door clicks shut.

Guigo stands with his hands in his pockets, rocking impatiently from heels to toes.

I count the seconds to quell the panic rising with my pulse. *I am with Guigo. I am safe.* A minute creeps past. Two. After three minutes, Guigo makes an impatient sound, opens the door, and disappears into the darkness inside. I have no choice but to follow.

Even after the months of death, even through my scented kerchief, the smell nearly empties my stomach.

We stand together at the threshold for a moment, eyes adjusting to the gloom. I breathe slowly, fighting nausea. The room is long and, like the Hôpital Saint-Antoine, filled with beds. A single monk, his profile plump beneath a shapeless black habit, walks the aisles with a bucket of water.

The dead and dying lie together. I hear the rattling cough of the first six hours of sickness, the deep, choking gurgle of the final two. Somewhere a baby cries.

Like me, Guigo wears a cloth over his nose and mouth, but his dark eyes flit over the sheet-shrouded bodies, searching for our first corpse.

"What is the meaning of this?" The call is as sudden and hoarse as dry wind through dead wheat.

Guigo and I turn, as one, to where a tall, thin shape has materialized through a back door of the almshouse. My knees turn to gelatin.

It is Father Loup.

"What is the meaning of this?" the priest repeats.

He strides toward us between the cots, heedless of the cries and whimpers around him just as Dante passed the damned. The rat-faced monk follows at his heels like a cowed cur.

"What profanity did you speak to my servant?"

Guigo brandishes the pope's letter like a weapon. "I am Surgeon Guy de Chauliac. Chief physician to His Holiness Pope Clement the Sixth, who, in his infinite wisdom, has lifted the ban on human autopsies so that I and other licensed physicians may better understand and combat this plague. My apprentice and I have come to arrange the transport and delivery of corpses for dissection."

Father Loup's eyes crawl over Guigo's purple robes before landing, for a heart-stopping moment, on me. But again, no spark of recognition kindles. He turns his attention to Clement's elegant script.

I focus on breathing, on steadying my shivering joints.

When Father Loup has finished reading, he straightens up and stares at Guigo as if seeing him for the first time. His face twists into an expression of raw disgust.

"I am a shepherd," he spits, "charged with the protection of each soul in my flock. And yet I have no power to protect their earthly remains? Am I to sit idly by while their bodies are mutilated so that their maker himself does not recognize them? What justice is this?"

Guigo folds the document back into his pocket and shrugs. "I am a physician. As such, I am charged with keeping the souls of my flock attached to their earthly remains for as long as possible. You must appeal to God for your answer. In the meantime, I expect a new body at the palace each morning by terce. The guards will direct your men to my laboratory."

Father Loup stares at Guigo with an intensity that would wither a violet. But Guigo keeps his expression mild.

"Brothers," he says, bowing to the rat-faced monk and the plump monk a few aisles behind him, ladling water into his patients' mouths and pretending not to listen. "Father."

Guigo makes for the door. I curtsy hastily and follow him.

"*Wait.*"

I freeze like a doe before the hunter's bow.

The priest crosses the space between us in a single stride. Guigo turns back, bristling, and I slink behind him, eyes on my boots.

"I have never heard of a woman apprenticed to a physician," Father Loup says. "Let alone one of your renown, Surgeon."

Say nothing, I plead silently to Guigo. *Please, Guigo. Say nothing.*

But it is too late. Guigo pulls himself up to his full height. "Mademoiselle Blanchet has been recognized for her skills by the Holy Father himself. I am blessed to have her as my apprentice."

A strangled silence follows, punctuated by a cough from one of the beds.

I raise my eyes to the priest's.

My heartbeat stumbles. He is staring right at me, his lips curled into a cold smile of recognition.

I force myself to hold his gaze despite every nerve screaming at me to run. *He knows who you are,* I tell my stomping pulse. *Show him you are not afraid.*

"Has this girl told you what she is, Surgeon?" asks the priest. "What her mother was?"

Guigo uncrosses his arms. "Watch yourself, old man," he growls. "You may be a servant of God, but Mademoiselle Blanchet and I are servants of the pope, and you hold this parish at his pleasure."

"Ah, yes," Father Loup replies, still smiling his vulpine smile, "what times we live in! God's vassal himself encouraging the desecration of a Christian body under his roof. In less . . ."—he casts about for the word—"*modern* times, you would have been burned at the stake as a necromancer, and your assistant as a witch. How lucky you are to be under the protection of such an unorthodox ruler."

"Indeed," says Guigo. "We are blessed. Now if you will excuse us, we have work to do." He takes my arm and turns me toward the door. But Father Loup has not finished.

"'There will be great earthquakes,'" he says softly. The hair on the back of my neck stiffens. "'And famines and pestilences. And there will be terrors and great signs from heaven.' Do you doubt, Dr. de Chauliac, that this plague has been sent by God to cleanse the world of its sins? You, an imperfect sinner like the rest of us, believe you can alter the course of God's will? These are unparalleled times. God is testing his children. Do not forget, Surgeon: the devil prowls the earth like a roaring lion, placing temptations before us all. A man of learning such as yourself has more to lose from sin than most."

"A new corpse each day at terce," Guigo says without looking back. "Or you shall find yourself in contempt of the pope, with no flock at all."

Guigo does not speak to me the entire walk back to the palace. His pressure on my arm is gentle but firm, his face inscrutable. I pray, as I take three steps for each of his, that he is not chewing on Father Loup's tainted words and beginning to believe them.

In the laboratory, Guigo pulls a chair away from the table. "Sit."

I obey, falling into the seat as though my legs couldn't support me another moment. Guigo produces a bottle and cup from the cabinet beside the washbasin. He pours a hearty dose of cognac and presses the cup into my hands.

"Drink," he commands.

I take a sip. The alcohol scalds my throat; I set the cup down hurriedly.

"All of it," Guigo says sternly.

When the cup is empty and a pleasant fire burns in my belly, Guigo pours himself a measure and takes the seat across from me.

"Now," he says, in a voice very much like my father's, "are you going to tell me what that was about?"

I meet his gaze over the scrubbed wood. Guy de Chauliac, the man who took a risk on a girl in the woods. Who has treated me with nothing but respect and kindness. But I know how quickly a poisonous lie can shut doors and change hearts.

"That man," I say. "That priest. He was called to my mother's deathbed. He refused to read her last rites."

Guigo eyes me shrewdly. "Why?"

He deserves the truth. All of it. Even if he does not believe it. Even if he sends me from the palace and forbids me from ever returning.

"I've told you my mother was a gifted healer, a skilled herbalist and midwife," I begin. "That is true. But it is also true that she knew things before they happened, like when a storm was coming, or whether a pregnant woman would give birth to a boy or girl just by looking at her. She taught me all she could, but there were many things that could not be taught. Her power was rare, perhaps, but not evil. Not unnatural. I believe she was blessed by God."

Guigo says nothing, but his gaze on my face is sharp, listening.

"When I was twelve, Mother became pregnant again. She and my father had always prayed for more children." I remember Margot singing to our brother through the taut skin of Mother's belly, describing what his life would be. But that is not the story I am telling.

"My mother had a friend, the wife of a wealthy and powerful merchant, who had only one child and desperately wanted more. She conceived perhaps a dozen times but could not keep a baby in her belly. And she was jealous of my mother's pregnancy."

The miscarriages were terrible in their frequency, and it seemed with each lost child a little more of Mathilde's mind slipped away. Some days Mathilde played with us like a child herself, running after us through the long hallways of her mansion. Other times she locked herself in her room without food or water and would not emerge for days.

"My mother attended her friend through each loss. She made rose hip tonic and held her hand as she wept. But one day, when her friend called her to her bedside, thinking herself once again with child,

Mother's exam revealed something different: there was a tumor in the woman's womb."

I see my mother's hands on Mathilde's abdomen, watch her expression change.

"The bleeding started. Constant, thick bleeding. Terrible pain. Physicians were called, medications taken, blood let. But only my mother knew what to do. She made a strong tonic of wild mushrooms, angelica and buttercups—the same herbs used to end a pregnancy."

There is no surprise in Guigo's eyes. I press ahead, struggling to keep my voice even, remembering that October night when the wind shook the leaves free in showers. When my mother and I followed the Dupont servant who had woken us through the frosty streets to the rue Dorée, where the only candles burned in Mathilde's bedroom window.

"The cramping grew worse, like labor pains, as the tumor passed. My mother anticipated this and had warned her friend. But in her agony, the woman thought she was giving birth. That the growth was a baby."

I shut my eyes, but the image only becomes clearer. Mathilde in the high bed, the sheets bloody, a shapeless lump of tissue clutched to her breast. We ran through the freezing night with her shrieks echoing in our ears, the same word over and over. *Witch.*

"Then the rumors started. Rumors that my mother had killed the woman's child purposefully with her herbs. Calls for her to attend sickbeds and childbeds tapered off and stopped. The cheese- and fishmonger stopped coming to our door. Mother ignored the sidelong glances, the empty pews around our family on Sundays. She said people had short memories and would soon forget.

"But a few months later, my mother's own labor pains began. As I said, I was just twelve, but I had helped her deliver dozens of babies. Around midnight I knew something was wrong. I could see my brother's head, could nearly grasp it. But with each contraction he stayed put, never descending, no matter how hard she pushed or in what position. He was too big.

"I didn't know what to do. Mother was too exhausted to direct me. I sent my sister and our housekeeper for help. They knocked on the doors of every midwife, every physician, every apothecary we knew. They begged for help at the gates of the convents and poorhouses where Mother treated patients and refused payment. But no one would come to the home of a 'witch.'"

I press my hands together in my lap. Almost done.

"She asked me to cut her."

My mother screamed as the blade sliced her. Then she summoned the last dregs of her strength and pushed. My brother came. He came through the slit I made in my mother's flesh, made it wider as he passed, and along the jagged tear my mother's blood flowed like a river.

"I pulled the baby free. He was already blue from want of air, long dead." But I had eyes only for her. For what I had done to her. "I tried to stop the bleeding, tried to stitch her back together, but I couldn't tell flesh from blood. My father went to Saint-Agricol for a priest. Father Loup came. He had heard the rumors about my mother. He believed them."

And you, girl. Your time will come.

A long moment passes. I fight and win a battle to keep my eyes dry. Guigo does not speak, does not reach out for my hand, and I cannot bear to look at him for fear I'll see the same contempt on his familiar features.

"She died without her last rites. My father donated a huge sum of money—a bribe, really—so my mother could be laid to rest in our family crypt at Saint-Agricol. Father Loup left for another diocese. But now he is back."

This is it, now. The most important piece.

"She was *not* a witch," I say. "But she had a gift that wasn't studied. It was *in* her."

I slide my thumbs over my fingertips, feeling Clement's boggy tissue again, the pull toward a swollen organ whose name and function I did not know, only that it was the source of his pain. "And it is in me, too, Guigo. I cannot describe it. I cannot ignore it. I know, in my bones, that I will be content with no other life than pursuing it."

I raise my eyes to find Guigo's searching my face. I cannot tell if I have convinced him, or if the priest's words have corrupted him against me. After a long moment, he clears his throat.

"I came from nothing."

My spine straightens. Guigo has never spoken to me about his past.

"My parents were pig farmers in Languedoc. They didn't have two *deniers* to rub together. I hated that farm. I hated the blisters on my hands. The shit on my boots. But like you, I, too, had a gift. From the time I can remember I could bandage a bird's broken wing or splint a calf's broken leg, suture a wound as pretty as any surgeon.

"One day the master's daughter rode out from the house. Her horse was a young thing, restless. He jumped a fence and threw her. Her thigh bone went like *that*—" Guigo makes a movement like breaking a wishbone.

I shudder.

"She was lying there in the dirt screaming, with the white bone sticking out. I was in the field and ran to her when she fell. I must have been twelve, thirteen. I'd never even *seen* a woman's leg before. I remember staring at the yellow marrow and the muscles of her legs and thinking it looked just like a ham hock." He snorts. "It was as though time slowed, and I knew exactly what to do."

I nod, remembering Mathilde. How easily the steps jumped into my mind and everything else melted away. The intoxication of finally occupying my place in the world.

"It was as simple as splinting the broken leg of a sheep or goat," Guigo continues. "Something I had done a dozen times. By the time her father had called a proper surgeon I had applied a tourniquet, relocated the fracture, and stitched her up. I remember sitting on the ground after they took her away, staring at the blood and footprints, and feeling happy. Truly happy, maybe for the first time in my life."

Guigo smiles, remembering, and I can see him as a young man, too big for the low thatch of his family's cottage, already a glimmer of what he would become beneath the sack cloth and dirt.

"A few weeks later the girl's father found me," Guigo continues. "I had seen him only at the rent collecting, and then only from afar. His clothes were so clean. There was a garnet on his finger, and I thought him as rich as the king."

Guigo looks down at his meaty fingers, turns his hand so a ring with a ruby the size of a quail egg sparkles in the firelight.

"He told me his daughter had made a miraculous recovery and had started walking again. He offered to pay for me to attend the medical school at Montpellier, told me that my skills were a gift from God and he had a responsibility to help me become a physician. The next day I rode with him to Montpellier. I had never been on a horse. I couldn't even read.

"If it weren't for these"—he holds up his huge hands—"I would be pushing a plow. You, your mother, and I are the same, though your sex bars you from licensure and stokes all the old fears in those stupid enough to believe that women are inferior to men. God put us on this broken world to heal people, to learn what we can and practice and teach, to put it back together the best we can. Our skills *are* a gift from God. And we have a divine mandate to practice them, even in the blind face of fear and mistrust."

My insides feel as light as soap bubbles.

"So do not be afraid," he says soothingly. "That priest is a nasty old bastard, to be sure. But as my apprentice, you have nothing to fear from him. And if there's any justice in the world, this plague will make pig food of him by spring."

Chapter Thirteen

March 1348

Guigo and I spend the following weeks dissecting plague corpses.

They are delivered fresh to the laboratory each day like river fish by two monks from La Pignotte. The rat-faced monk, who we first encountered at the poorhouse door, is greasy-haired and sullen and always casts hungry glances at my bodice. The other is silent and apple-cheeked and blushes whenever I catch his eye. Each morning, barely breathing, I stand at the laboratory window and wait for the corpse cart. But there is never a sign of Father Loup.

The first morning, as Guigo's scalpel hovered over our subject's gray abdomen, I felt a churning in my guts, a warning, perhaps, that we were about to commit an irrevocable sin. I could tell Guigo felt it, too; his blade tip wavered, and perspiration beaded his forehead. But then he took a deep breath and plunged metal into skin.

As best I can, I think of the bodies on the table as pigs. Nothing more than dead meat, their souls already flown.

We lay our subjects on the table with a cloth draped over their faces and genitals in Christian courtesy. Guigo does the dissecting while I take notes and make drawings. Each chest cavity contains blackened, congealed lungs, each abdominal cavity spills hemorrhaged organs onto the rushes. We know that the disease enters the body through the air and rots the lungs, then passes through the blood to contaminate the rest of the tissue. We have no idea what to do about it.

On March 14, the day before Queen Joanna's arrival in the city, Guigo sends me home.

"We are no closer to discovering the cause of this illness than we were a fortnight ago," he says, wiping the gore from his hands. "Go home. Watch the queen's cortège, but for God's sake avoid the palace. It will be full to the gills with gawkers come to watch the trial, bringing bad air from every port city in Europe. I shall expect you back in three days."

I scrape the blood from under my fingernails and walk home.

The ides of March dawns crisp and bright.

Margot and I stand in the window of Father's bedroom, eyes fixed on the street below. It feels so good to stand shoulder to shoulder with my sister in the narrow casement, inhaling her sweet smell, knowing by her warmth and breath that she is alive.

She has said nothing of Father Loup's return, of what it is like to sit in the family pew at Saint-Agricol each Sunday listening to his vitriol. In this omission, she is protecting me. She does not know I know he is back in the city, does not want to taint our rare time together with his name. So I, too, keep my words light and do not mention the priest, nor that I have spent the past weeks dissecting human corpses.

Father is at the palace. He and the other notaries have been working even longer hours than usual, struggling to balance the exorbitant debts Clement accrued in preparation for the queen's arrival. But Margot and I made him promise he would do his best to attend this afternoon's trial under the excuse of taking notes in his excellent Latin.

The cobblestones are cleaner than I have ever seen them, the corpses carted off to the new cemetery, the clogged drains flushed with water from the Rhône. Bright banners hang from the noble houses along the Magna Carreira, and the streets are lined with Avignonese, standing eerily quiet beneath us, the early-spring breeze ruffling their finest clothing.

"I did not know so many souls still lived in Avignon," I say caustically. "Mothers and fathers abandon their children to die alone, but the moment there is a spectacle they forget the threat of bad air."

"Be kind," Margot chides without turning her head. "They need to forget, if only for a short while."

The bright voice of a trumpet cleaves the morning and shakes a flock of pigeons from the eaves of Saint-Agricol. Murmurs ripple through the crowd below us. Hats are straightened, veils adjusted, necks craned to see past the curve of the street. And then, far off at the southern gate, a hundred voices rise in jubilation.

"Joanna is here," Margot breathes. "I didn't think she would come." And, inexplicably, she starts to cry.

"What?" I ask, searching the street for the source of her tears. "Margot, what is it?"

After a moment she lifts her blotchy face from her hands. "I wish Mother were here."

My own throat burns with sudden, sweet sadness. "So do I," I say, threading my arm around her shoulder. "So do I."

The cheering grows louder, closer. A trumpet sounds again, just out of sight, and the first figures of the procession come into view.

Two men, portly and smiling, wave to the crowd. The sun glints on the heavy chains around their necks. A group of red-hatted cardinals in long scarlet robes follow; I count eighteen of them, including Cardinal Romana of the rotted tooth.

Then—I hear Margot's sharp intake of breath—a man, walking alone. The handsomest man I have ever seen.

Luigi of Taranto, Joanna's new husband, is as tall and broad-shouldered as Erec. Beneath a red cap his gold hair is fashionably cropped, the sleeves of his Spanish-style jacket puffed and slashed to expose flashes of yellow silk between crimson velvet. Yellow hose hug his muscular thighs, leaving little to the imagination even from our high window. He strolls across the cobblestones with the swaggering stride of a conquering general.

And finally—"It's *her*!"—Joanna, queen of Naples, Sicily, and Jerusalem, countess of Provence, steps into our view.

Butter-yellow hair falls unbound to her waist, shining brighter than the gold crown that adorns it. She, like her new husband, wears crimson and yellow. But the queen does not saunter; she holds the folds of her gown tightly before her, revealing a bulging belly.

"Is she . . . ," Margot whispers.

"She's pregnant," I finish, stunned. "And if she fled her home, traveled a great distance, survived the plague, and is still with child—"

"Then clearly," my sister interrupts excitedly, "she is blessed by God and innocent!"

We grin at each other. Happiness—that rarest of emotions in these times—rises like a cake between us.

Margot and I spend the afternoon recounting each detail of the parade and opening the door every ten minutes to look for Father, desperate for news of the trial.

"What do you think she puts in her hair, to make it shine so?"

"And her gown! Ruby-red velvet and cloth of gold!"

"Where *is* Father?"

Finally, Anes sticks her head out of the kitchen.

"*Enough!* Both of you!" she snaps. "Your nattering isn't going to bring your father home any sooner. Margot, come peel these parsnips. Elea, fetch some water."

We get up gloomily and help.

Dinner is ready when the door opens. Margot and I rush into the hall to meet Father, speaking over each other.

"What happened?"

"Is she innocent?"

Father hangs his coat and hat, laughing. "I cannot recall the last time you were so happy to see me."

"Tell us, Father!" Margot whines. "Please!"

"All right!" he says, taking a seat at the table and holding up his hands in surrender. "I can see I won't be allowed to enjoy my supper until I've told all."

Anes comes in and pours Father a cup of wine, shaking her head at us in exasperation.

"Is she innocent?"

"She *has* to be innocent, Father!"

He raises an eyebrow and takes a slow sip. "If you keep interrupting me and speaking at the same time, it will take me longer to tell it."

As one, Margot and I cross our arms and sit back in silence.

"So," he begins, "Queen Joanna and Luigi of Taranto arrived at the palace. The court assembled in the consistory, with Clement seated on a dais head and shoulders above everyone else, dressed and crowned like an emperor."

My father shakes his head. I grin. It sounds exactly in character for Clement.

"The hall was packed from rushes to rafters with every nosy nobleman still living. It's amazing, the city is plague-ridden and dangerous and still—"

"Father!"

"Very well, very well. Where was I? Ah. The Hungarians. They looked about as backwoods as you can imagine. I'm told they smelled of onions. They presented their evidence against Joanna for murdering her husband, which I must say, girls, was very convincing."

Margot and I scowl at each other. Father's mouth twitches.

"We all know that Andreas was a plump, dull boy who couldn't hold a candle to Joanna. The night of his death, he was lured from their bed by Joanna's servant. The door of their bedroom was then locked from the inside so he couldn't return. He was attacked and dragged down the hall and thrown off the balcony with a noose around his neck. The guards heard the ruckus and discovered the boy dangling like a goose. Joanna, supposedly asleep just feet away, heard none of this."

Margot fidgets but holds her tongue. Father takes another sip of wine and continues.

"The Hungarians also brought up Queen Joanna's barely concealed affair with her cousin and the quick decision to marry him following Andreas's death. After what I heard today, I have no doubt that she was involved in the murder in some way."

"It could have been anyone, Father!" Margot bursts out. "Plenty of people are angry that Naples allied with Hungary. That's what . . ."

Her voice trails off. The joy flickers in her eyes. Silently, I finish her sentence. *That's what Erec said.*

"And then . . ." Father smiles mischievously, oblivious of Margot's reopened wound. "And then the doors opened, and Queen Joanna entered the courtroom, and we all forgot every shred of evidence against her. She walked slowly through the rows of men, but her eyes never left the pope. She knelt before his dais and bowed. Pope Clement raised her to her feet, kissed her square on the mouth, and had a chair brought so she could sit beside him."

I laugh out loud. Margot's face brightens again.

"When it came time for Joanna's defense, she insisted on speaking on her own behalf. She acknowledged that, true, her marriage to Andreas had not been a love match, and they had struggled to agree on many issues. But before his death, she insisted, they had reconciled some of their differences and were finally happy together, with their first child on the way. She reminded the court that she lost not only a husband, but also a childhood friend. And, the coup de grâce, she spoke about her beloved son, Charles Martel, who, now tragically fatherless, was snatched from her palace in Naples to be raised at the Hungarian court at just two years old. I saw some of the noblemen and even one or two cardinals dry their eyes.

"And then Queen Joanna, with tears streaming down her beautiful face, turned to the court and said, 'Proclaim to the world the innocence of your persecuted queen!'"

He pauses for dramatic effect.

"*And?*" Margot and I say desperately.

"And . . . and . . ."

"Father!"

"And . . . the court exonerated her."

Margot holds fists against her mouth, suppressing a squeal.

"Not only that," continues my father, "they declared her 'above the suspicion of guilt.' The Hungarians were so mad you could nearly see steam coming out of their ears."

Margot and I grin at each other.

"What happens now?" she asks.

"The Hungarians go back to their drafty castles," Father says, "and Joanna and Luigi return to Naples in peace. Andreas's brother Louis is still ransacking the city, but once he hears that Joanna has been declared innocent, he will have no choice but to retreat home with his tail between his legs. Little Charles Martel will stay in Hungary, I suppose, but Joanna is already expecting Luigi's child. She has proven herself fertile."

Father shakes his head and takes another sip of wine. "It was strange, girls, to be gathered again in the consistory, as though there were no pestilence in the city and court business was back to normal.

We were all shifty at first, everyone with our kerchiefs over our noses. Anyone who so much as cleared his throat found the benches around him vacated. But as the trial progressed, I forgot the plague entirely. The way she commanded that room. I'm telling you, girls, I've never seen a woman control a powerful group of men like that before. And I married your mother."

The next morning Margot and I eat breakfast together. We repeat the same questions that kept us up late into the night, snuggled tight together beneath the blankets.

"Will Joanna stay here until her child is born?"

"It seems likely; travel is dangerous in her condition."

"Do you think you will see her in the palace, Elea?"

A knock at the door makes me freeze with a piece of buttered bread halfway to my mouth. Margot is closest; she gets up and peers through the window suspiciously.

"It's a huge man," she says, "dressed all in purple."

I rise, brushing crumbs from my skirts, and open the door for Guigo.

He stands on the threshold in his long velvet coat and matching hat.

"Good day, Guigo," I say, swallowing my surprise. "Please, come in."

Guigo stoops under the doorframe and walks past me. Once inside the house his barrel-chested bulk makes the room feel small. I look around self-consciously. The house is neat as always, but dark and plain compared to the pope's palace. I remind myself that Guigo was born on a farm and probably does not even notice the low ceiling nor that the rushes could do with replacing.

Margot curtsies respectfully, and Anes, hurrying from the kitchen to see who is here, does the same, albeit reluctantly.

"Good day." Guigo pulls off his hat and bows distractedly. His eyes widen as he stares at Margot, then at me, then back to Margot.

"Please," says Margot, pulling the bench away from the table. "Have a seat."

I wonder if the bench will break.

"No, thank you," says Guigo. "I will be brief."

He says nothing more, just looks at Margot again and back to me. I clear my throat.

My sister, bless her, takes the hint. "Anes," she says, "would you assist me in the garden?"

Anes scowls, then stomps out of the room behind Margot with one final withering glance over her shoulder at Guigo, who doesn't notice.

"I am here on a matter of utmost gravity," Guigo says once the kitchen door has rattled shut. "As I'm sure you know, the lady—the *queen*—is with child."

The blood drains to my feet. Dear God, let her be well.

"She is experiencing some . . . discomfort," Guigo continues, kicking a booted foot in the rushes and looking like a boy who was caught throwing rocks down the chimney. "The pope sent me to attend her, but I regret that my experience with the treatment of pregnant women was found wanting. She sent me away and demanded I find a suitable substitute. A *female* substitute."

Guigo raises his eyes to mine. "Your mother was the midwife at many births, correct?"

I nod again, realizing with a sickening drop in my stomach that *I* am the female substitute.

"And you assisted her?"

The image of my baby brother, his face blue from want of air, comes unbidden to my mind. I smell my mother's blood.

"There must be someone else, Guigo," I say hastily. "A more experienced midwife. It is a great honor, but our work on the plague is just beginning. Does the queen not have her own physicians?"

Guigo shakes his head. "I have made inquiries. Avignon's midwives are dead or gone. The queen's own midwife and doctor succumbed on the journey from Naples. You, Mademoiselle Médecin, are our last hope."

My distress must show in my face, for Guigo says quickly, "It won't be for long. I'm sure she will be on her way soon, back to Marseille or Naples once the Hungarians abandon the city. Until then, you will examine her daily and prescribe herbs for her women's troubles. And when she excuses you, you may rejoin me."

I cannot say no. I nod numbly, feeling fifty pounds heavier on my feet.

"So?" he says, clapping his hands together. "Do you want to gather your things? Time is of the essence. You do not want to keep this queen waiting, believe me."

In the streets outside, Avignonese gossip in knots, protective kerchiefs clutched forgotten in fists. Children chase one another, the cheery banners from yesterday's parade snap in the wind. A metallic taste fills my mouth as my mind repeats an impossible truth: *I am going to meet the queen.*

Once inside the walls, Guigo leads me to the complex in Pope Benedict's old palace where noblemen and ambassadors stay while visiting, which is full of elegantly dressed Venetians and perfumed Frenchmen who attended yesterday's trial. The courtyard rings with voices speaking half a dozen languages and, far off, I hear music. After the months of silence, these sounds of life are like the first quickening days of spring.

A guard in Joanna's livery—blue velvet emblazoned with the gold fleur-de-lis of Anjou—meets us at the entrance to the tower. We follow him through a maze of staircases and hallways to a third-floor corridor where light splashes on flagstones and guards stand on either side of a painted door. I feel the touch of fate on my shoulder and obey, wading through the bright morning sun like water and trying to remember each moment, every detail, for Margot.

The guard announces our presence, and we wait, my breakfast roiling like eels in my stomach, until the doors open and a squat man in Joanna's colors says, "Surgeon, mademoiselle, Her Majesty will see you now."

Guigo nudges me across the threshold and into a magnificent chamber.

The first thing I notice is the music. Notes from a tenderly strummed lute float on the air like summer honeysuckle over the thudding blood in my ears. On the far wall, iron-latticed windows offer views of the sparkling Rhône. The floor is covered with giant Turkish carpets in patterns of flowers and geometrics. In each corner, incense burns in bronze braziers, cleansing the air and filling the room with the warm, earthy scents of frankincense and myrrh. On a low divan along the windowed wall three ladies-in-waiting, pretty as peacocks, sit in a cloud of perfume. They eye me and Guigo curiously, holding kerchiefs to their noses, and titter as we pass. I'm painfully aware of the patches on my skirt, my sloppily darned stockings.

The queen sits beside another lady-in-waiting on a low couch facing the river, shimmering like an icicle in the sun. As the usher steps beside her, she raises her head to hear him and casts her profile against the bright windows. Her nose is lifted at the tip, her chin dimpled like a peach.

The usher turns back and gestures to us to approach. Guigo and I cross the expanse toward the queen, our footsteps silenced in the deep carpets. A youth with a lute, the source of the music, looks up as we pass and, for an instant, our eyes meet.

It takes me a moment to remember where I've seen this face before, but then I place it: the bust of a Greek god in Clement's chambers. Apollo, perhaps, or Hermes. Here is the same wide, laughing mouth, the same almond eyes set close to an Attic nose. But these eyes are golden brown, not cold marble, and fringed with lashes as thick as a girl's. He smiles at me, and suddenly there is no air in the room.

"Preferirei morire mille morti piuttostoche," he sings, *"che vivere un giurno senza di te."*

I walk on dizzily, my head full of his music. I do not understand the words, but the melody speaks of love, and loss, and spring.

Joanna sits in a cushioned chair with her feet curled under her and a book open in her lap. She has kicked off her shoes—white leather slippers encrusted with seed pearls—which lie on the floor beneath her. Her famous golden hair is piled high and affixed with dozens of pearled pins, and today she wears a rose-pink gown sewn with silver thread. A dark-haired woman sits beside the queen, embroidering. Her eyes are long-lashed and golden-brown, just like the musician's, but when they lift from their work to meet mine, there is no glimpse of friendship in their depths.

"Your Majesty," announces the usher, "I present to you the Dottore de Chauliac and the Signorina Eleonora Blanchet."

Guigo sweeps off his cap and sinks into his best courtier's bow. I curtsy.

Queen Joanna tears herself reluctantly from the page of her book. Her eyes, an impossible shade of aquamarine, move dismissively over Guigo and settle on me. A dusting of freckles adorns the bridge of her nose and high, slanting cheekbones. Her face has something—symmetry, perhaps—that lifts it above simple beauty.

"You may rise," she says in perfect, bored Provençal French.

Guigo stands and begins speaking abruptly.

"Your Royal Highness, may I present—"

"Is this she?"

I look up and meet the extraordinary eyes once more. Joanna leans back in the chair and surveys me coldly, starting with my dirty boots and ending with my hastily braided hair.

"She is just a child," she says, turning back to Guigo. "This is the best that the great city of Avignon can do for their queen?"

"Your Majesty, this is the mademoiselle—"

"Can you speak, child?" Joanna asks me impatiently.

My anxiety dissolves, replaced by irritation. "Yes, Your Majesty," I say. "I can speak."

She closes the book and swings her feet out from under her. "Signor il Dottore told me you are a midwife. Is this true?"

"I am an apprentice of Surgeon de Chauliac, Your Royal Highness, but my mother was an herbalist and a midwife, and I was her assistant."

"And are you skilled? You have treated pregnant women? Delivered healthy babies?"

"Yes, Your Majesty."

Joanna lifts her arched blond eyebrows skeptically at Guigo.

"You disappoint me, Surgeon. The Holy Father spoke highly of your skills and those of this poor peasant girl who now stands before us. I see now that I must send for another physician from Aix-en-Provence, or Marseille. You may leave."

Guigo bows again, red-cheeked, and turns to go.

I feel the color rise in my face. *Peasant girl?* Does my father not work within these very walls? Did I not cure the pope himself? And this haughty queen has the gall to dismiss Guy de Chauliac, the greatest physician in Christendom, like some clumsy lady's maid.

"Your Majesty," I say, proud that my voice is strong and clear, "I may be young, but I began assisting my mother when I was seven years old. Her father was a bona fide physician trained at the Paris medical school. He taught her everything he knew. Midwifery was her forte. She treated all manner of afflictions suffered in pregnancy, and I helped her deliver dozens of babies. Under Surgeon de Chauliac I have learned proper anatomy and how to treat all manner of illness with medicines and surgeries. I know more about pregnancy and childbirth than anyone living in Avignon."

I curtsy again. The music has stopped; an uncomfortable silence settles over the room.

When I look up, Joanna is smiling.

She gets to her feet, moving a little awkwardly, and for the first time I can make out the swell of her belly under the thick robes. She addresses the room.

"Leave us," she commands.

The ladies jump off the divan and pass through a set of double doors on the far wall; the musician lifts his instrument and follows them. The dark-haired lady-in-waiting beside the queen does not move.

Neither does Guigo.

Joanna turns her white-lashed eyes on him once more. "You as well, Surgeon," she says.

Guigo opens his mouth, closes it, casts a fortifying glance at me, bows again, and exits.

I am left alone in the sunny chamber with Joanna, queen of Naples, Sicily, and Jerusalem, Countess of Provence, and her unfriendly companion.

Joanna lowers herself back into the cushions and gestures at an empty chair across from her. I sit.

"What is your name?"

"Eleanore Blanchet, Your Majesty."

"This is Donna Imilia di Rosa," says the queen. Her lady-in-waiting nods coolly. "She is my friend and confidant. You may think of her as an extension of me."

I nod cordially at Donna di Rosa. She does not return my smile.

Joanna places her hands under her belly, stretching the material of her dress tightly over the curve. I would guess she is about six months along, carrying high.

"My personal physician and midwife perished of this cursed *pestilenza* on the ship to Marseille," she says. "His Holiness has graciously invited me to stay here for the remainder of my pregnancy. From Caffa to Bordeaux, the plague rages. God in his mercy spared me, my husband, and our child on the voyage from Napoli, but I dare not tempt death again. No, I will stay here in safety and wait for the prince to come. If I deem that you are equal to the task, you, Eleonora Blanchet, will be my personal midwife during this pregnancy and birth. Do you understand?"

"Yes, Your Majesty."

"I had my first child two years ago by my husband Andreas, may God rest his soul."

She watches my expression closely, and I keep my face blank. Joanna crosses herself; Imilia and I follow suit. "The pregnancy with my sweet Charles Martel was easy. So easy! I felt no different, until the very end when I was so fat it took three men to lift me."

She lets out a pretty peal of laughter. I find myself smiling, too. This woman could charm the birds out of the sky. I must remember to keep my wits about me.

Joanna leans forward, and I copy her, as though she were a friend rather than my queen.

"This pregnancy has been quite different," she says. "I was sicker than a dog for the first three months. I could barely get out of bed, and I vomited everything up, even water. Then the itching, the terrible itching, began. Now whenever I eat, whatever I eat, my throat and stomach burn like I've swallowed poison. And the backache! The ride from Marseille, with every step of my horse there was a knife in my spine."

She shifts in the pillows and allows a little discomfort to show on her face. Imilia takes Joanna's white hand in her golden one.

"This child must be healthy, do you understand?" the queen says to me earnestly. "It must be a healthy prince for Naples. If this child is born twisted or deformed or dead, they will say, *See, Giovanna is guilty of her husband's death and God has cursed her.* And then my kingdom—the land of my forefathers, the kingdom God chose me to lead—it will fall to those hedge-born Hungarians. Do you know, when I fled my city to come here, the Napoletani screamed at me in the streets? They shouted, *Death to the whore queen!* My own people. I would gladly die for them, and they cursed me."

She wipes away a tear. I am not sure if this is artifice or sincerity, but my heart swells for her.

"Men do not understand," she continues. "They do not know what it is to be a queen and a wife and a mother. How could they? All they care for is fighting and drinking and wenching." She laughs again, but this time it rings cold and hollow.

Without thinking, I reach out and place my hand on her knee. Donna Imilia stiffens under her brocade gown, but I pay her no heed. Queen or peasant, we are women living in the world of men.

"I understand, Your Majesty," I say. "And I think I can help. But I must first tell you that you will give birth not to a prince of Naples but a princess."

I might as well be floating, my head feels so disconnected from the rest of my body as I leave the queen's chambers and walk the long hallway toward the stairs.

I, I tell myself dizzily, *am Queen Joanna's midwife. I, Eleanore Blanchet, am Queen Joanna's midwife.* I want to tell Margot. I want to shout it from the palace windows. And I want to run through the city gates and up the hill to the cottage in the meadow and never turn back.

I am Queen Joanna's—I turn abruptly on the landing and crash headlong into someone. The air explodes with flying papers.

"Christ's teeth!" I curse, landing painfully on my bottom.

"*Merda!*" shouts my assailant, also falling backward.

As the pages settle like feathers on the flagstones, I reach out and catch one.

It is a sheet of music. I look across the littered landing at my partner in clumsiness and wish I could melt into the floor.

It is the musician with the golden eyes. He sits sprawled across from me like a dropped doll, rubbing his wrist.

"*La dottoressa!*" he says, flashing me a dazzling smile. "*Cosa fai facendo qui?*"

I shake my head, feeling more foolish by the second. "*Mi dispiace,*" I say haltingly. "*No Napoletano.* I don't speak Neapolitan."

"Ah," he says, grinning. "Or you pretend not to, so that you may know our secrets?"

I flush to my hairline. His smile widens.

"I am Paolo," he says, mock-bowing from his seat on the floor.

"Eleanore," I reply. I cannot help myself—I smile back.

We gather the scattered music on our hands and knees. When the pages are all collected, I sit on my heels and hand Paolo my stack. He takes them with ink-stained fingers.

"You wrote these?" I ask.

"Yes," he says. "I am a *musicista* in the court of la Reina Giovanna."

The skin at the divot between his collarbones is brown like Anes's bread and so smooth. His cap lies a few feet away. Uncovered, his hair falls in thick, dark waves. I remember my thought from earlier and speak before I can stop myself.

"Are you related to Donna di Rosa?" I ask.

"*Si!*" he exclaims. "La Donna di Rosa is my sister."

I nod, thinking it strange that these two people could share so much and yet so little. My new friend must follow my train of thought, for he gestures for me to move closer and lowers his voice.

"You must not be afraid of Donna di Rosa, *dottoressa*. She appears very ferocious on the outside, no?"

I nod again. He smells of cinnamon.

"She would kill for our queen. But on the inside, her heart is as soft as a . . . a baby cat."

I laugh. "A kitten."

"Yes, a kitten," he says. "A wolf on the outside, a kitten on the inside. You shall tame her like *that*." He snaps his fingers together, then glances down the hallway at the closed doors before turning his eyes back on me. "La Reina Giovanna, however, is a kitten on the outside and a wolf on the inside."

He winks, then jumps up like an acrobat. He holds out a hand to me, pulls me to my feet, and gathers the stack of music. Then he performs an elaborate court bow and walks past me and down the hall with the thoughtless grace of a dancer.

Chapter Fourteen

April 1348

As blossoms settle on the cherry trees like snowdrifts and the birds return from their southern wintering grounds, Avignon continues to die.

When the new cemetery is full to bursting with corpses of the plague dead, Clement consecrates the Rhône. Instead of taking the bodies to the overflowing cemeteries to be hastily buried, stacked on top of each other like gratin, the corpse collectors drive to the center of the Pont d'Avignon and toss them one by one over the side.

And instead of trying to help fight the disease, I am beholden to Joanna's every whim.

The queen rises at terce and eats a long, leisurely breakfast. She hears mass with her priest, listens to Paolo play, argues with Prince Luigi in explosive Italian, or receives overdressed and overscented noblemen from whom she hopes to borrow enough money to raise an army against her brother-in-law. When she finally sends for me, I give her tinctures to ease her discomfort or rub her back with sweet-smelling oil until she grows bored or irritable and sends me away. Some days she does not call for me at all and I spend the day pacing the laboratory, fuming, while Guigo visits the hospitals and almshouses alone. I continue sleeping in the laboratory in case she needs me.

At the start of my tenure, a chest of clothing appeared in the laboratory, full of cast-off garments. The queen insisted I wear a different dress, even different shoes, in her presence, in case bad air lingers in the folds of my skirt, and that I be sprayed with a cologne of clove and camphor before crossing her threshold. Margot would love sorting through the brightly colored gowns with their voluminous pleats and immovable sleeves, but I picked the simplest—a midnight-blue damask—for attending Joanna.

The first few days with the queen I felt drunk, heady on her presence and my still-unbelievable circumstances. The sensation was crystallized in my letters to Margot, sent home weekly with a cart of groceries from the palace kitchens. My sister's excitement was palpable in the notes I received in return, flavoring my own interactions with the plague-hostage court of Naples as I tucked away details of clothing and conversation.

But now the novelty has worn off. As I listen to the same asinine conversations between ladies-in-waiting and reassure the queen that the mild discomfort she feels is normal, I start to dread the inevitable climax of Joanna's pregnancy. The last baby I delivered—my own stillborn brother—reappears in my nightmares, blue-lipped and swollen.

On the day the bubonic plague, the feared second form of the pestilence, first appears in Avignon, Joanna detains me late into the day. She complains of a headache that feels, she says, as though someone is boring a nail into her forehead. I give her comfrey and willow bark tea and rub her neck.

Then the baby moves as she has been doing more and more, kicking the queen's ribs and causing her to double over in pain.

"This child is torturing me," she moans. Another internal assault forces her to grab on to the arm of the chair for support. When it passes, she glares at me. "Is there nothing you can do?"

My mother always said that the movement of a baby is a good thing. I kneel beside Joanna's chair and put both my hands over her belly, close my eyes, and allow them to guide me through the layers of muscle to the fluid-filled womb. The writhing slows as the small form responds to my touch, rolling in the liquid as curiously as an otter. I can make out a pointy edge that might be an elbow, the dual pressure of tiny feet before the child turns away restlessly. Like me, she is tired of sitting indoors listening to court gossip, deprived of fresh air and movement.

"Rejoice, Your Majesty," I say with a reassuring smile, "your baby is healthy and active. When she gets a bit bigger, she won't be able to move as much, and you'll be more comfortable. But in the meantime, I think you must walk every day. This child demands exercise."

"Walk every day?" Joanna repeats incredulously. "Have you lost your mind, Eleonora? The pestilence rages outside these walls. Many members of the Holy Father's staff have fallen ill and died—even bishops and cardinals who should, of all men, be under God's protection. You would have me risk my life and the life of the future prince or princess of Naples?"

At least she has finally stopped insisting that she will give birth to a boy.

"Of course not, Your Majesty," I say, "but to soothe this child, even a few turns around the room may help."

The kicking starts again, as though the baby agrees with my recommendation. "Fine," Joanna says with a grimace, holding out a hand for me to help her up. Her ladies-in-waiting hover around us making little sounds of concern.

"Eleonora and I will go alone," Joanna announces.

My heart sinks; it must be nearly none, and I had been praying for an early dismissal so I could meet Guigo.

Joanna holds my arm for support as we take a few circles around the room with ten pairs of eyes watching us. The queen leans heavily on me twice when the baby kicks but otherwise keeps her back straight.

As we approach the door on our third turn, she says quietly, "Let's go out. I don't care to be stared at like a dancing bear."

She nods to the guard, and we step into the long hallway, where dust motes shimmer in the afternoon sun.

We walk down the hallway in silence. At the window farthest from the chamber doors I spot a bird's nest under the eaves and point it out. The starling sitting atop her eggs does not notice us behind the glass.

"I forgot it was spring," says Joanna.

The baby does not bother her again as we lap the hallway once, twice, three times. Joanna's grip on my arm relaxes, and she starts to talk.

"My Castel Nuovo in Napoli does not have windows like this. It is a fine building, a strong old fortress, but it is cold and drafty. I wonder what my brother-in-law has done to it. He's probably sitting in my bed in his dirty boots, wiping his greasy hands on the tapestries."

We have made it back to the bird's nest. Her beautiful face is, for once, unguarded as she gazes up at the little starling. I do not know if she wants me to comment, but I think of Margot's empty days and decide to press a bit.

"Surely now you have been exonerated of his brother's death, the Hungarians will be forced to abandon your city?"

She sighs. "I do not know. Louis may be an uncultured barbarian, but he is a fierce warrior. I do not believe he will stop until I am dead. Which is why it is so important to spend my time here wisely, gathering support and funds to defeat him."

The line between her brows has returned. I change the subject. "You are beloved in Provence. How do you find your kingdom here?"

"The countryside is beautiful. I had heard of the wonder of your rivers and forests, the flowers, the sunshine. On the journey from Aix-en-Provence, I finally understood why Clement loves it so. If I were the pope, I would never return to the ruins of Rome. I would stay here in the sun, drinking *my* wine, hunting *my* deer."

We have nearly reached her door again.

"My feet ache," she complains. "Let us hear Signore di Rosa sing while you massage them."

The queen's arm tugs on mine as she steps forward, but I have frozen where I stand.

"Your Majesty," I say, "as you said, the plague still rages. Surgeon de Chauliac is doing all he can to help the afflicted, but he is but one man. If there is no pressing concern for your health or the unborn princess's, perhaps you would grant me leave to join him after our morning examinations?"

Joanna stares at me, twin spots of pink kindling in her cheeks.

"I will be a call away," I say quickly, sensing catastrophe, "should you need me for anything more dire."

She draws her arm from mine and pulls herself up to her full, regal height, her features stiffening like petals under frost.

"I am your queen," she says, and her voice, too, is changed, more sonorous and commanding than I have heard it. "Do you forget this? Many would kill to be in your position."

I meet her gaze. I stand firm in my borrowed shoes.

"You are right," I say simply. "You have done me a great honor in making me your midwife. But, as you remember, I did not seek out this distinction."

Joanna's jaw hardens. I am acutely aware of the weight of her power, of the guards at the door who would do her bidding without a second thought. *A kitten on the outside,* Paolo said. *A wolf on the inside.* But I have seen glimpses of the tender kernel of her maternity. How can I appeal to her heart?

"Before I was your midwife," I press on, the words spilling over each other in my haste for them to reach her, "I was Surgeon de Chauliac's apprentice. You have been charged by God with the care of your citizens. And as a woman, as a mother, you feel this burden more keenly than any man ever could. I am no queen, no mother, but I fear for my family. My friends and neighbors. My city. As you wage war against the man who threatens your people, I wage war against this pestilence. And if anyone on earth can find a treatment and cure, it is Guigo. It is my calling to help him."

Joanna studies me with eyes as cold and blue as chips of ice. My pulse pounds in my ears but I meet them, search for a spark of companionship there. The seconds stretch between us, silent and taut.

"Who was your namesake?" she asks.

The question is so unexpected that it takes me a moment to find my footing in the conversation.

"Eleanor of Aquitaine, Your Majesty."

"I thought so." Joanna considers me as if seeing me for the first time, her dimpled chin lifted, her pale lashes wide. "My ancestor was an extraordinary woman, was she not? She did not allow the confines of her sex to imprison her. She went on crusade. She married and divorced. She held her power as surely as any man, and her people loved her for it."

"She was extraordinary," I agree, thinking of my mother, of the heroines of her bedtime stories.

"I will strike a deal with you, Eleanore of Avignon," Joanna says. "I will be mindful of your time. I will call you promptly and dismiss you quickly if I feel well. But you must agree to my terms. If I call for you, no matter where you are, what you are doing, you will drop everything and fly to my side. And when you are with me, you will be present. No rolling your eyes at my ladies. No gazing longingly at the door, counting the minutes."

My mouth falls open. "You . . . Your Majesty," I stutter. "I never—"

Joanna laughs her genuine laugh, like a tinkling bell, and the tension melts from the air.

"*Macché*," she scolds. "I have lived my life reading the behaviors of others. It is the reason I still have my throne. You have your enemy, and I have mine." She motions to the guards, who uncross their lances. "But I am still your queen. You remain in my employ. I will send for you tomorrow, or sooner if I need you. Leave a note so my pages may find you."

She disappears between the painted doors in a sibilance of silk. I stand for a moment watching them close, then run to the laboratory, exultation lightening my feet.

"You're still here," I say, opening the door to find Guigo standing over a shrouded corpse on the table. A woman, I guess, from the size. He doesn't answer.

"I thought the queen would have my head on a spike." I step behind the carved wooden screen Guigo stole from some abandoned room in the palace and summarize my exchange with Joanna while I slip out of the blue frock. I hear the elation in my voice, the words flowing as quick as my pulse. We understand each other, Queen Joanna and I.

Guigo doesn't comment, doesn't interrupt my deluge. When I emerge a moment later in my day dress, he has not moved.

"Guigo?" I ask tentatively. "Is everything all right?"

At the sound of his name he looks up from the winding cloth, his face lit with some internal fire.

"It is here," he says through the kerchief over his mouth. "The second form of the pestilence. The bubonic plague is here, in Avignon."

My happiness evaporates.

I have the sensation of watching myself, witnessing this moment, from a point outside of my body. It is here. A second enemy, when we have made no headway in defeating the first.

"And she," I begin, gesturing to the corpse, "does she . . ."

In answer, Guigo lifts the edge of the winding sheet, exposing thin legs, a tuft of gray pubic hair, and—I hear my own sharp inhale—there, below the jutting hip bones on the right side of her groin, swells a dark purple tumor the size of an egg. Black veins lead away from the growth, as stark and intricate on the white skin as leafless branches against a winter sky. I've seen veins like this before, long ago. I scour my memory. *When? Where?*

"There's another in her armpit. And look here," Guigo says, raising the sheet a little higher to expose a white arm. "As other physicians have noted, this form of the pestilence causes gangrene of the extremities."

The curled fingers are gray, tipped with black. But it is not this sight that stops my heart.

Along the woman's forearm, crosshatched like a snake's with old bloodletting scars, lies the mark of a newer wound. The line is raised and pink, studded with the punctures of sutures. I recognize the work of my hands as surely as a mason does his mark.

"First, we must dissect the buboes," Guigo is saying. "Discover what they are filled with, try to determine the cause of the corruption. Gentile da Foligno writes from Perugia that he has been excising and draining them, with some success . . . You're white as cheese, Elea. Are you all right?"

I stare at the draped face of my mother's friend, my self-proclaimed enemy. The fabric pits over her eyes and mouth, but I see her clearly as I did that November day when the madness turned its empty gaze on me. I hear her voice.

You sneaking witch.

Guigo glances from the corpse to me, realization dawning.

"Go," he says, placing himself before me and the corpse. "Go, Elea. Don't return until vespers."

When I do not move, he puts his hands on my shoulders and turns me toward the door.

"Go," he repeats, and this time the urgency makes its way to my muscles.

I am at the door, in the courtyard, through the gates of the palace and on the Pont Saint-Bénézet as though Mathilde herself pursues me, blackened fingers reaching from her shroud.

Nightfall finds me dutifully standing before the laboratory door.

Through the casement, candles glow and Guigo's hulking shadow moves from bookshelf to table. Still I linger, frightened of what I will not be able to unsee if I enter.

The decision is made for me. Without warning, the door opens. Guigo shouts in surprise as I jump out of his way.

"God's teeth!" he says, nearly dropping his candle. "I was just coming to find you." His eyes move over my face, concern threading his brows together in the candlelight. He moves out into the courtyard with me, shutting the door behind him. "Are you all right?"

I don't answer. I went to the meadow, sat with Baldoin until the sun sank so low I feared I would be locked outside the walls. I could not bear Joanna's glittering chambers, the twittering of her ladies. I could not face my sister. I had nowhere else to go.

"Oh, Mademoiselle Médecin," he says, in a tone so soft it makes my eyes burn. "Come. Let's get some supper in you."

For the first time we eat at the long table in the center of the main kitchen, ears buzzing with the mundane discussions of the scullery staff and the reassuring warmth of the cooking fires. Guigo does not ask me who the corpse was, how I knew her, just speaks broadly of dissection techniques and apostemes until the terrible afternoon feels distant. An hour later, fortified with roast chicken—Guigo made me eat two whole legs—bread with butter, and a large glass of wine, we walk back to the laboratory together.

"The pestilence did not touch her lungs," he says for the third time. "The buboes were filled with pus and blood. I saw no underlying structure, no cause of the corruption. I believe Gentile da Foligno was right: this is a slower-moving variation of the plague, which kills by pollution of blood, not air. If we can drain the apostemes—and this we can do, I believe, if we find a young, healthy patient—"

I stand apprehensively on the flagstones while Guigo opens the laboratory door. He holds it wide and stands back, giving me a view of the firelit table. It is empty.

"I had someone come by while you were gone," he says soothingly. "All clean."

I cross the threshold as cautiously as a hare leaving her warren in first light. But the table is empty, no gore lingers on the floor. I sniff the air, searching for any foul scent, but all I smell are my own sweet-burning herbs.

Guigo takes a seat and riffles through a sheaf of scattered parchment. "Here," he says, setting a few papers before me as I take my usual seat. "I am no artist, but I did my best."

The drawings are crude as a child's. A bubo—or is it an aubergine?—sits tucked between two curving lines that appear to be hills, although I know them to be thighs. Black squiggles lead away from the tumor, and I recall with a sickening rush the macabre map on Mathilde's white skin.

"What is this?" I ask, once more searching my memory for where I've seen those marks before.

"Ah," says Guigo. "Blood poisoning. It is not the bubo itself that kills, I think, but the corruption that swells it."

Suddenly it comes back to me. I could not have been more than ten when Mother and I were called back to the baker's house a week after we delivered his wife's first baby to find her unconscious and pale, with the same veins marring her deflated stomach. Some of the afterbirth was still in the womb.

I had sprinted the whole way home, repeating the herbs out loud so as not to forget what I was tasked with fetching. *Rose hip. Fenugreek. Celery. Dandelion. Clover. Crab apple.*

"Perhaps if we bleed the patient from the right arm early on—"

"Guigo," I interrupt, "my mother made a tonic for blood poisoning."

He looks up from his papers, the candle flames reflected in his eyes. "You must make it at once, and in great quantities," he says. The excitement in his voice is contagious. "Between the two of us, perhaps the poor souls who contract this form of the pestilence may have a chance of surviving."

Chapter Fifteen

Guigo and I turn our attention to the second form of the pestilence with all the fervor of the flagellants, whose numbers grow despite Avignon's dwindling population and who march daily through the streets, mortifying their own flesh to keep the plague at bay.

Each day around terce Paolo comes to fetch me, sweeping into the laboratory like a summer breeze with his jewel-toned silks and scented skin and the latest court gossip. No matter how immersed I am in a medical text or my treatise notes from the previous day's patients, he manages to pull a smile from me by pretending to faint at an anatomical illustration or by dabbing one of my medicines behind his ears like perfume.

"Did you hear?" he says, walking by my side through the silent palace. "Signore Bozzuto has challenged Signore Cosenza to a duel after he said his wife was so fat he was not sure how his lordship could possibly perform a husband's duties!"

Joanna keeps her promise, and I keep mine. I listen to her heart and lungs, take her pulse, evaluate the contents of her chamber pot. If she is feeling ill, I administer medicine for headache or nausea. If she is well, we take a few turns in the hallway and spy on the starling's fuzzy-headed chicks while the queen speaks of her beloved firstborn son, her castle in Naples, her hopes for the future. My mornings are spent in the queen's sunny rooms on the third floor, as distant from the horror outside the palace walls as the surface of the moon.

In the afternoons, the nightmare continues.

The second form of the pestilence moves more slowly than the pneumonic strain, and first strikes the very poor, the very old, and the infirm. It begins with a fever, then the telltale swellings in groin, neck, or armpit. As the poison spreads throughout the body by way of corrupted blood, diarrhea and vomiting ensue. The hands, feet, and nose grow black and gangrenous, rotting like grapes on the vine. Within a few days to a few weeks, the patient is dead.

"Too weak," Guigo mutters over patient after patient, as we search for the perfect subject on whom to attempt Guigo's first excision. "We need someone young. And strong."

In the meantime, we continue to practice on corpses.

Guigo brings me pigments and paints from the abandoned frescoes in the Palais Neuf, and I make careful drawings of each phase of the autopsy while he dissects and rehearses excising, draining, and suturing the buboes of the deceased who, as he says, cannot flinch or wail like living patients. In the lonely hours after Guigo leaves for his chambers and my nervous mind keeps me from sleep, I perfect my gruesome art. I spend hours on the texture and color of each flaccid bubo, each corrupted lung. In a few prideful moments I allow myself to imagine these illustrations copied and bound in Guigo's plague treatise, studied by medical students across Europe.

The opportunity for Guigo to practice his hypothesized technique comes two weeks after Mathilde's corpse arrived on our dissection table.

Queen Joanna calls for me late in the morning. Her child is growing and cannot thrash about as much, but still, she wants to walk. If the weather is fair, as it is today, we descend the stairs and circle the courtyard below. At first, she clutched my arm like a blind woman and pressed her kerchief so tightly against her face that it left marks, but after several weeks of walking outside without issue, her fear of contracting the plague has diminished. And she enjoys the attention of the gaping pages, the anxious obeisance of the few courtiers and clergymen who have not yet fled the city for their country estates.

We walk the cobblestones with the spring sun bright on our faces. The queen loops her warm arm through mine, and I suddenly miss Margot like a kick to the gut. How long has it been since I have seen her? Since the day after Joanna arrived. More than a month, then. She sends me notes with the kitchen boy who delivers their groceries weekly: *We are well, praise be to God, but you are missed.*

"Eleonora," Joanna's voice cuts through my thoughts, "let us visit the stable."

Caught off guard, it takes me a moment to consider. "I don't think that's a good idea, Your Majesty. You shouldn't even *really* be outside of the palace."

Joanna laughs. "Dottoressa Eleonora, my petit jailer. Relax your rules just this once. Being around the big beasts soothes my nerves. And it is a beautiful day." Her blue eyes match the sky.

Erec works in the stables.

The image of Mathilde's curling, blackened fingers makes my stomach clench. Does he know what happened to his mother's body?

Of course he knows, I silently chide myself. Father Loup would have told him, told anyone who listened, twisted the truth into something heinous. But I understand Erec's loss better than anyone. Perhaps I could explain . . .

"All right," I say impulsively. "Let's go."

The stable complex is past the kitchens. Joanna nearly skips through the packed dirt of the yard and shoots a dazzling smile at a knot of shocked scullery maids as we pass.

A groom in Clement's livery runs to meet us at the stable doors, clearly flustered that the queen is here unannounced and unescorted. "May I be of assistance, Your Majesty?" he asks with a nervous bow.

"Good day," Joanna answers. "I have heard of the pope's famous charger, and I should like to see him."

"Of course." The groom bows again. "Follow me, Your Majesty, mademoiselle."

We pass out of the sunshine into the cool shade of the stable. The pleasant smells of hay and manure and big warm bodies fill my nostrils. I peer into each cell we pass, dreading and hoping to see Erec, but the long aisle is empty but for the three of us.

Horses stick noses over stall doors to watch curiously as we pass, nickering to one another. The largest stall contains the pope's charger, the massive white stallion I've seen in parades and processionals. He raises his head from a bucket of oats as we approach.

"This is he, Your Majesty," says the groom. "Pope Clement's pride and joy, although he has not ridden in months."

Heedless of his size and power, Joanna reaches a hand over the door and strokes the stallion's long neck. He lifts his great head to sniff her, blowing foamy pieces of oat into her golden hair. She laughs.

"Do you ride, Eleonora?" asks the queen, scratching the horse's nose with manicured fingernails.

I shake my head. "No, Your Majesty. My father was injured when he was thrown from a horse as a boy and never kept them."

"A pity," says Joanna. "I have never known a purer joy than riding my Topolino. At least Louis knows the value of good horseflesh and will take care of him." She shakes the bitterness from her voice and smiles at me brightly. "Here, Eleonora, I shall teach you how to feed him oats without sacrificing your fingers."

We spend half an hour with the horses. The fine lines around Joanna's mouth soften into an easy smile as she questions the groom about horseshoes and explains to me the telltale signs of colic. I laugh in delight when the charger's velvety snout tickles my palm. The outside world, with all its horror and strain, seems miraculously distant.

As we thank the groom and walk reluctantly down the aisle of stalls, another groom crosses the entrance. For a moment his silhouette is stark against the bright light, and I am certain he sees us, recognizes us, but he turns abruptly and stalks away. I would recognize Erec anywhere, but there was something menacing in the broadness of his shoulders, the arms with their new muscles from months of hard labor. Joanna doesn't notice; she chatters happily and tugs on my arm, leading me toward the door where, a moment before, the man stood.

Erec occupies my mind as I take my leave of the queen and walk back through the palace corridors. I try to imagine if it were my mother's body taken for dissection. I see her open on the table, her chest pried apart like wardrobe doors, her lovely face intact. An image to haunt the waking hours and chase sleep from one's bed.

Guigo is waiting for me in front of the laboratory door, arms crossed over his chest and a booted foot tapping the flagstones.

"I'm sorry," I say, picking up my pace across the courtyard, "Queen Joanna wanted to visit the stables—"

He waves a giant hand, cutting me off. "Grab your things! I have had a message from Dr. Farissol. His nephew has the bubonic plague."

I jog to keep up with Guigo as he weaves through the streets, remembering David's blanched face on that terrible night in the Hôpital Saint-Antoine. He watched his entire family die of the pestilence, and now it has finally come for him. I cannot imagine a more frightening nightmare. Mother Mary, may Guigo's technique save its first soul today.

"I thought Jews could be attended only by Jewish physicians?" I ask when a passing corpse cart forces Guigo to stop and I finally catch him.

Guigo nods, turning down a narrow side street which opens onto the Place Jérusalem. "That is technically true, but as you know, Dr. Farissol is an exceptional doctor. He knows of our research and would try anything to save his nephew."

Guigo pauses before a handsome building on the square made of the same golden stone as my family home, raises the heavy brass knocker, and lets it fall. We wait in silence. I clasp and unclasp my fingers with an anxious energy that is not only for David and the task ahead: I have never been in a Jewish house.

After a moment, a plump, pretty woman opens the door.

"Good day, madame," says Guigo. "I am Surgeon de Chauliac, and this is my apprentice, Mademoiselle Blanchet."

I curtsy.

"I believe Dr. Farissol expects us."

"Please, come in," she says, opening the door wider to admit us. Her face is rosy, the skin around her lips and eyes creased into smile lines. But she is not smiling today. "I shall fetch him."

Guigo removes his hat and crosses the threshold. I follow.

My first impression is one of extreme cleanliness. The pleasant smells of fresh herbs and olive oil soap hang in the air. The bare flagstones of the floor, the walls, even the thick beams crossing the whitewashed ceiling appear to have been recently scrubbed.

The woman leaves us to find Dr. Farissol, and I glance about greedily in her absence. The furniture is simple but well-made: a long table with benches on either side, two comfortable-looking chairs upholstered in red Spanish leather on either side of the fireplace. Besides the lack of rushes on the floors and tapestries on the walls, there is no difference between this home and that of a Christian *bourgeois* family—mine included—except the shining cleanliness. I do not know what I expected.

Dr. Farissol enters from the same doorway through which the

woman vanished. "My friends." He looks like he hasn't slept since the last time I saw him. "Thank you for coming."

"How is he?" Guigo asks, clasping Dr. Farissol's proffered hand. "When did he fall ill?"

Dr. Farissol runs a hand over his beard. "He was feverish for a week. The apostemes surfaced this morning: one in each groin, another in his armpit." He sighs, shakes his head. "He is brave, but in such pain."

"Lead us to him," says Guigo. "I pray we can help."

We follow Dr. Farissol down a hallway, up a cool stone staircase to an airy second-floor landing. He stops before a door and pulls a kerchief from his pocket, ties it over his nose and mouth. Guigo and I follow suit.

"You should know," he whispers to Guigo through the fabric. "He thinks the world of you. He's read every treatise you've written."

He opens the door. Bright sunlight pours from tall windows; through them, the sycamore trees of the Place Jérusalem sparkle. The stench of the illness is made tolerable by overtones of soap and clean linen.

David lies sleeping in the bed. It is the fine-featured face I remember from the Hôpital Saint-Antoine, the straight brows and serious mouth. But now his hair is wet with sweat, his lips colorless. Dr. Farissol sits at the edge of the bed and takes his nephew's hand.

"David, are you awake? You have visitors."

David's eyelids flicker and I am struck, suddenly, by the memory of his dark eyes the night Arye died, how the room around us blurred. But the gaze that meets mine now is glassy and unfocused. He blinks, struggling to orient himself through the fog of fever. When he recognizes me and Guigo, he tries to push himself to seated.

Guigo sits on the stool beside the bed. "Save your energy, son. I'm afraid you'll need it."

David collapses back on the pillows, the pulse jumping in his throat. Judging by his wide-eyed stare, he does not know whether this is a hallucination or reality.

"Your uncle tells me you have already become an excellent physician. What better way to learn than on oneself, eh?" Guigo smiles ruefully, leans closer. "I believe there is a chance you may survive this plague if the swellings are lanced, drained, and sutured. A strong young man like you would be the perfect patient. But I must warn you that I have never performed this surgery before. It will be dangerous and extremely painful. There is a very good chance that you will die."

David swallows. His cracked lips part. "I understand," he whispers.

"Very well," says Guigo. He glances at Dr. Farissol, then at me. "Shall we begin?"

Guigo sends me to Dr. Farissol's wife, Sarah, for clean linen and hot water. I wait in the hall, listening to the pleasant kitchen sounds: the bubbling of a carafe being filled, the click of metal against ceramic. But my mind is upstairs, with David. I try to imagine myself in his place. My family dead and buried, the same disease making its home in me. I think, with a pang of shame, that I would give up. I would let death have me. But David is still fighting.

Sarah returns bearing a steaming pitcher and a stack of muslin. "I'll be up to remove the soiled cloth and bring more water. Should you need anything else, come find me."

"Thank you," I reply, taking the items from her. Then, before I can stop myself, "Madame Farissol?" She turns on the threshold.

I cast a glance over the spotless room, wondering how to phrase my question politely.

"Your home is so . . . *clean*."

She smiles. The expression illuminates her features like sunlight on water at the bottom of a well. "Thank you, mademoiselle. Last week was *Pesach*. My servants and I worked very hard."

I blink.

She explains, "In the days before Passover we clean our homes from top to bottom and remove all *chametz*, every piece of grain. It makes the rats furious."

I want to ask more questions, but Guigo is waiting for me, and my arms ache under the weight of the full carafe. "I've never been in a better-kept home," I say, and Madame Farissol rewards me with another smile.

Upstairs, Guigo and Jacob speak quietly in the corner. David has drifted into unconsciousness again, the fever blazing in his cheeks.

Guigo gestures for me to join them. "I don't pretend to know the course and outcome of this surgery," he says quietly. "It is very likely the young man will die. Are you sure you wish to proceed, Jacob?"

Dr. Farissol nods. "The alternative is certain death. David knows what he faces. It is worth any chance, Guigo." And he adds, with a raw edge in his voice, "He is like a son to me."

Guigo places a hand on his old friend's shoulder. "Just as we have planned, then," he says. "May God be with us."

Dr. Farissol rouses his nephew. "David," he says gently. "David, it is time."

I help him pull David upright. Dr. Farissol unstoppers the aqua vitae and administers it in gulps. Perspiration beads David's forehead, and his eyes are cloudy, but he opens his mouth again and again, seeking as much numbness as possible from the pain ahead.

When the bottle is half-empty, Guigo holds up his hand. "Enough," he says. "We can't have the poor boy vomiting in the middle of surgery." Then, to me: "Are you ready?"

I blink away the image of David's long-limbed body on a corpse cart. I nod.

We lower David to his back. Guigo removes the sheets and raises the hem of the nightgown to David's waist. I force the shadow of discomfort from my mind as we examine him; he is a man, just like any other man, any other patient, even if he is young and handsome. And he is dying.

A large bubo swells in the left groin and two smaller ones in the crease of the right, but—thank the Virgin—the veins crisscrossing the abdomen and thigh are blue, not black. The poison has not yet entered his blood.

Guigo turns to ready his scalpel out of David's sight. I clean the two small buboes with more aqua vitae, then drape his abdomen and genitals with a clean cloth.

"Hold him," Guigo whispers, moving into position beside me. I put all my weight onto David's thigh. On the opposite side of the bed, Dr. Farissol does the same.

Guigo grasps the smallest bubo between thumb and second finger, and David bucks beneath me. I flatten my entire torso over his leg as Guigo whispers, *"One . . . two . . . three."*

David screams—a horrible choking sound—and Dr. Farissol and I hold him still with all our strength. Guigo has done it. The smallest bubo is lanced: pus and blood dribble from the incision. I clean it with shaking hands as Guigo readies his thread and awl.

Dr. Farissol and I once more hold David down while Guigo stitches up the wound. He does not struggle, does not cry out again, just takes great shuddering breaths each time the needle punctures his skin.

"I don't know many men who could have handled this better," Guigo says, tying off the last stitch. "You have more courage than I did at your age. You'll make a great physician one day."

David's face is very white, but he tries to smile.

He faints when Guigo lances the second bubo. We take advantage of this, working quickly to spare him the agony of a conscious surgery. All three buboes in his groin are lanced, drained, sutured, and bandaged by the time David comes to. Only the aposteme in his armpit remains.

"Almost finished, son," Guigo says, tossing sweat-soaked hair from his face. "Just one more."

I extend David's arm over his head and pin it against the pillow to give Guigo the clearest view of the bubo, which swells poisonously between the muscles of his axilla. Dr. Farissol holds his hips down. Guigo takes a deep breath and lowers the scalpel.

David screams, thrashing hard as the metal bites, and Guigo's hand stutters. A jagged line dissects the bubo and runs, bleeding, into the skin of his chest. But it is done.

"A few extra stitches," Guigo says bracingly, threading his needle again. "And ladies love scars, isn't that right, Elea?"

David's breath comes quick and shallow as Guigo sutures the cut. When he has finished, I clean the wound, apply a poultice, and pack it with clean muslin.

"You're a tough man to kill," says Guigo, taking David's pulse at the opposite wrist. "I daresay you'll outlive us all."

Once David is asleep, his chest rising and falling in slow, even intervals, I pack our supplies and Guigo and Dr. Farissol fall into a tense, quiet conversation.

"It's the Pastoureaux all over again," Dr. Farissol whispers. "In Barcelona and Strasbourg, it is said that Jews spread the illness by poisoning the wells. In Carcassonne there are pogroms already, buildings burned, homes raided. Those who have escaped are lining up at Avignon's gates, seeking sanctuary in the pope's city."

"That is wise," Guigo says bracingly. "Pope Clement will not allow any violence against your people here. You have nothing to fear." He claps Dr. Farissol on the shoulder. "Get some rest, Jacob. We shall return tomorrow. Now it is up to David and God."

Guigo and I walk to the palace silently, wrapped in twilight. He says good night and leaves me in front of the laboratory. I stand still for a moment and take a deep breath of cool spring air. Overhead, the bats swoop over the courtyard and the first stars shimmer. I close my eyes and think of David, fighting his silent battle all alone, and pray with every fiber of my heart that he wins it.

Chapter Sixteen

Joanna did not sleep well; she is cross and short-tempered and does not want to walk the next morning. I give her a dose of valerian root tonic that would put Guigo to bed and, as soon as she is resting, fly to the laboratory. Guigo and I do not speak as we make our way through the city, so nervous are we both for what awaits us in the Place Jérusalem. But Madame Farissol admits us with a curtsy and a smile.

"Jacob was called away, but he should return soon," she says, leading us upstairs.

My heart climbs higher into my throat with every step.

The door of David's bedroom is open, and light pools at the threshold. Guigo reaches it before me; I hear his sigh of relief.

"There is the man!" he booms, and anxiety flutters from my body like a flock of roosting doves.

David is seated in bed, propped by pillows. He is still pale, the bones of his cheeks and jaw too pronounced, but under the dark, wavy hair his eyes are clear and bright. His mouth curls into a smile as we enter, and I try to ignore the sensation that a colony of termites has suddenly made its home in my belly.

"How do you feel?" Guigo asks, settling on the stool beside the bed and taking David's pulse at the wrist.

"A bit sore," David admits.

Guigo throws back his head and laughs. "A bit sore!" he repeats. "God's teeth, you are a tough one."

We inspect the incisions, which are red and swollen but show no signs of corruption. The long, jagged cut on David's chest where Guigo's scalpel slipped weeps a little, but the fluid is clear and odorless. Downstairs the front door opens and closes, accompanied by Dr. Farissol's rumbling voice.

Guigo beams at David. "Excellent! We could not have prayed for a better patient." He turns to me. "I'm going to speak with Jacob. Will you change the bandages and administer another dose of the blood-cleansing tonic?"

"Of course." My stomach flips at the thought of being alone with him, but I try to keep the nervousness from my face as I roll up my sleeves and unpack my basket. Guigo pauses at the door and looks back at David as if to say something more, then shakes his head and walks away. I hear him whistling the whole way down the stairs.

I channel my mother's brusque professionalism and pray David does not see me blush when I raise the bedsheets. *He's a man,* I tell myself. *Just a man.*

"How did you sleep?"

"Fine," he replies, but as I remove the bandage on his left inner thigh, he winces. What little color there was drains from his face, and my own girlish jitters follow. My patient is not out of danger. I have a task to perform.

"Guigo is gone," I say quietly. "You may tell me the truth. Was it an awful night?"

I pack the new herbal poultice as gently as possible along the crease of his groin and wrap it lightly in muslin. David takes a long, steadying breath.

"To be honest," he says, rearranging his face so no pain is evident, "the swellings were so painful that even the pressure of clothing against them was excruciating. When Surgeon de Chauliac lanced them, it was something like relief. I did sleep. A little."

His voice is deep and warm and moves over my skin like velvet. I avoid his eyes, remembering how they trapped mine beneath them that night in the Hôpital Saint-Antoine, but I keep him talking to distract him from the discomfort of the dressing changes.

"Why did you wish to become a physician?" I ask, moving to the opposite side of the bed. David gazes out the window at the shivering leaves, considering the question. The thoughtfulness of his expression is jarring in so young a face.

"There is so much suffering in the world," he says after a moment. "To help our fellows is surely the highest calling, other than religion." His face splits into a self-deprecating smile. "And I fear I lack the constitution to be a rabbi."

I smile, too, unable to picture this young man trapped indoors, poring over holy texts by candlelight, and for a moment his eyes catch on mine. I drop them hastily, wishing Guigo would return and hoping he does not in the same breath.

Focus, I scold myself, moving on to the final incision, but as I untangle his arm from the bedclothes, I am acutely aware of the smell of him, of olive oil soap and sweat and something deeper, musky but pleasant. The skin of his chest is smooth and pale as marble. I have a wild urge to trace the line of muscle from sternum to shoulder, but I feel David's eyes on me and chase the thought from my mind.

He inhales sharply as I raise his arm overhead and expose the bloodstained bandage. I search for another train of conversation to occupy his mind, but he asks me first. "And you? Why did you wish to become a physician?"

A physician. The word reverberates in my head like the metal tongue of a church bell. Not a midwife, apothecary, herbalist. A physician.

I open my mouth to repeat his words about being of service, but they do not come.

"Because of my mother," I say.

"Oh?"

I feel the heat of David's gaze as I peel the muslin away.

"What is she like?"

"She's dead."

The words are harsher than I intended; they linger in the air like the smell of something burnt.

After a moment, David says, "I'm sorry. What *was* she like?"

"She was . . ." I mean to tell him she was a midwife, a good one, and leave it at that. But my tongue no longer seems governed by my mind. The story pours out of me from the very beginning as I clean and dress his wound: watching her heal illnesses and injuries when I was a child, accompanying her on house calls. Delivering babies and setting bones. Making it all look so easy.

"The blood-poisoning tonic, for instance," I say, gesturing to the bottle. "I was with her at the bedside. The woman was dying. Her stomach was crisscrossed with black veins, like some horrible spiderweb. Her husband was there, with the screaming baby in his arms. My mother knew exactly what to do. She made the tonic in about five minutes, like other women make biscuits. And then she put her whole arm inside the woman and pulled out a putrid, decomposing afterbirth . . ." I glance quickly at David, but there is no disgust in his face.

"Any other midwife," I continue, "any university-trained physician, and that woman would have died in a day. But that was how my mother was. It was second nature to her."

"She sounds extraordinary," says David quietly.

"She was. She was extraordinary," I repeat. "If she had been born a man, she would have been as famous a physician as Guigo. He was born the son of a pig farmer, and now he is the pope's personal physician. And she, practicing the same skills, could have been burned at the stake as a witch." My voice is suddenly bitter, remembering the scrape of Father Loup's cold eyes over my face. *And you, girl. Your time will come.*

I don't remember the last time I talked this long. The thrilling discomfort of being alone with him evaporated with the ease of speaking with him, like frost under sunlight.

David clears his throat. "I understand," he says.

My belly twists at the honesty in his voice. No one else in my life understands how it feels to reach for something forbidden. Not Guigo, not Margot.

"Every day I face the same risks as you, the same mistrust. But I cannot turn from my faith, nor my calling."

An expression that I can't quite fathom flits across his face, something between longing and hope.

"And there is power in possessing something that no one can take from you."

He meets my gaze and holds it.

Footsteps fall on the landing. The door swings open.

"Well, mademoiselle?" Guigo asks, entering with Jacob. "How is our patient?"

I turn away to pack my supplies and hide my blazing cheeks. "The incisions are cleaned and dressed."

Guigo claps his hands together. Jacob beams at his nephew. It is too early to celebrate, of course, but if David recovers, there is hope for Avignon, for Provence, for the world.

The other men crowd around him, speaking to each other as they take his pulse and listen to his lungs. I fold and refold the squares of gauze, rearrange the bottles in my basket. When I can busy myself no more, I glance at the bed. Guigo asks a question; David mutters a response. But his eyes, like embers, black and burning, are fixed on me.

The following day is Easter Sunday. Joanna excuses me from her service, so Guigo and I attend Clement's mass, then spend a few hours excising a young nun's buboes at the Hôpital Saint-Antoine. As we exit the hospital into the bright afternoon, the streets are full of Avignonese scurrying home for their Easter supper. Like at Joanna's processional, it is unnerving to see so many moving bodies in the typically sparse streets, and I stand for a moment, watching them.

"Guigo," I ask, "may I have the rest of the day? I'd like to see my family."

Guigo looks up from his boots, clearly not having heard my question. "Hmm?" His mind is often elsewhere these days.

"I said, may I go home? I'll be back tomorrow at dawn. And you know where to send, should the queen need me."

"Go," he says distractedly, waving a blood-spattered hand in the air. "Be with your family. I have correspondences to write."

I join the uneasy crowd and follow the street home.

"There you are!" Anes exclaims, opening the door and immediately pulling me into a tight hug.

"Anes," I say, trying to break out of her embrace, "I've been in the hospital. You shouldn't be so close to me."

But she doesn't let go. "The plague hasn't come for you yet, despite all the time you've spent with the sick. God is listening to my prayers."

"That," I say, "or it might be the burning herbs and fires, purifying the air."

Under the gray homespun she is thinner, her vertebrae rising from soft flesh like rocks in the river, but the familiar smell of her—baking bread and cooked onions—makes my throat tighten.

After a moment she releases me and holds me at arms' distance, her blue eyes moving shrewdly over my face and gown. "Too skinny," she declares. "Do they feed you?"

"Not nearly as well as you," I say, laughing.

"Don't linger on the threshold like a stranger," she says, steering me through the door. "Come in, come in!"

I step inside, into the warm embrace of my family.

After supper, Anes insists I bathe while she beats my filthy day dress into submission in the kitchen sink. I sit in the tub until the water is cold and the surface rimed with gray soap rings. My belly is full of Anes's cooking. My father naps before the fire. And upstairs, Margot is waiting for me. For these precious moments, all seems right in the world.

Clean, dry, and dressed in an old dress of Mother's, I pick my way up the stairs, careful not to wake Father. Margot sits cross-legged on our bed with her dark hair drifting about her shoulders. Amber sunlight fills the room.

"Come," she says, patting the coverlet beside her. "Tell me everything."

I sit with my knees touching hers and tell her about Queen Joanna, the progression of her pregnancy, her love of the horses. I tell her of Guigo's treatise on the plague, of my dream that Mother's tonic might be used across Europe to combat blood poisoning.

"There is some hope," I say, squeezing her hand. "We may be on the path to the cure. At least for those who contract the bubonic form of the disease."

Margot looks down at her lap, blinking hard.

"What? What's wrong?"

She shakes her head. A teardrop, glittering like a jewel, falls on the bodice of her linen gown. "Perhaps you did not hear. Mathilde Dupont is dead."

My stomach feels like a struck drum. I see the white arm again, the fingers blackened as if by fire, the skin marked with so many scars that it was more like fabric than flesh. And the sign of my own needle, as clear as a pilgrim's tattoo.

"I only wish she had fallen sick later," Margot says quietly. "You and Dr. de Chauliac might have saved her."

I imagine her body open on the table like all the others. What would Margot say if she knew of Mathilde's dissection, of the part I've played in mutilating the dead? Without the autopsies, Guigo wouldn't have developed the excision techniques that might save countless souls. But I do not think my sister would understand.

I squeeze her hand again and try to keep the guilt from my face.

"But never mind that." Margot wipes her eyes and forces a thin smile. "There is an overabundance of sadness in the world, and I only have you for a few more hours. Tell me a tale of hope."

I have no stories of hope yet, save one. So I tell her about David: the details of his surgery, how well he is recovering. But I cannot help myself; I hear my voice, more animated than it has been in months. I feel the color rising in my cheeks. It feels so good to talk about him.

"Elea." A true smile spreads across my sister's face and chases the shadows from her eyes. "If I didn't know better, I'd think you were in love with this man."

I press my lips together to stop from grinning.

"You are!" Margot exclaims, taking both my hands in hers. "You must tell me everything. Every little detail."

The words tumble from me. How handsome, how serious he is. The milky paleness of his skin, his dark hair. His eyes. The way he speaks to me, as an equal.

"And his family?" Margot asks excitedly. "Would Father approve?"

The giddiness drains from me like blood to a letting bowl. I drop my sister's gaze.

"Elea," Margot says gently. "What is it?"

I know it could never be, of course. No world exists in which we could be together. But still, to say it aloud is to smother a dream.

"He is Jewish."

Margot's fingers go limp in mine.

"You must quash this foolish attachment immediately."

I look up in wounded surprise. I knew my sister wouldn't approve. But the harshness in her voice, when she speaks, kicks the breath from me. The lovely lines of her face are hardened into an expression I haven't seen before. But when she recognizes the pain in my eyes, her mouth softens.

"Who knows what it is to love what you cannot have better than I?" she asks quietly. "But you are too important—to me, yes, but to Guigo and the queen and . . . to the world, Elea!—to risk a hair on your head for a love that cannot be. You already have a target on your back as a woman practicing medicine, and the penalty for miscegenation is *death*." Her bright eyes search mine. "You have heard that Father Loup is back?"

Reluctantly, I nod.

"I sit in Saint-Agricol each Sunday and listen to him preach hate and suspicion against the Jews, against gypsies and witches, against anyone who thinks differently than he. I hear the talk in the streets. Everyone has lost someone. Everyone is frightened. They want a scapegoat."

We will be blamed for this, David said on the night Arye died. And Dr. Farissol's uneasy whisper. *It is said the Jews spread the illness by poisoning the wells.*

Rage bubbles up inside me.

"This plague is a force of God," I say, fighting to keep my voice even. "No different from an earthquake or a storm. It is no one's fault. And these stupid men are making a war of it, like they make a war of everything."

"And just like any war, those without power are the first to suffer."

"So we should just let this hatred run roughshod through our city? Close our windows, bar our doors, and hope—this time, at least—that they take others and leave us be?"

"You can do nothing to stop it," Margot says. "You have no power. No husband to protect you."

"Here we are again," I say with a hollow laugh. "Back to the old argument. Just because I have no husband does not mean I cannot speak out against what is wrong."

"That is *exactly* what it means," my sister replies. "You are a single woman in a strange profession drawing attention to yourself. Do you not know what our neighbors say about you? I hear their whispers, Elea. It is like Mother all over again. How do you not see how vulnerable you are?"

"I work for Guigo and the queen. I am not so powerless as you think. And I would rather stand for what is right than stay inside with my embroidery while innocent people are killed."

Hurt flashes across Margot's face. "Is that what you think?" she snaps. "You think I sit here and *embroider* all day? I have *nothing*, Elea. I have no mother, no husband, and my sister might as well spend her days on a battlefield without armor. The fear has eaten a hole in my heart."

"I am afraid, too," I retort. "I fear for you and Father and Anes. But I also fear that this hatred will boil over and innocent people will die."

Margot nods. "It will. They will. It is terrible, I agree. But they are not *our* people, Elea. Do not put yourself in danger for a race to which you do not belong."

I stare at her for a long moment. Then I stand and slip on my shoes.

"Where are you going?"

"I must get back to the palace."

It's a lie, of course, but I cannot bear to sit in this room another moment. Margot's mouth falls open in hurt and surprise.

"Wear your kerchief," I say, not meeting her eye as I tie my laces. "Burn herbs in the fire. Don't speak to anyone. I'll come home when I can." Although I know it will be a long time before I set foot here again.

As I turn to the door, my sister calls, "Elea. Please be careful. I couldn't bear to lose you, too."

I don't reply.

Downstairs I make some flimsy excuse to Anes that the queen needs me. I ignore the question in her face, the way her eyes follow me as I reclaim my basket.

I pause at the front door and glance over Anes's head to where my father is still asleep before the fire.

"Tell him goodbye," I whisper.

"Be safe," she replies.

I walk to the palace, bunching my fingers into fists. *How could Margot be so small-minded?*

But as I pass a gaggle of old women on a street corner, I imagine their eyes on my back, their tooth-poor mouths forming the word. *Witch.*

My sister is wrong. Wrong about standing by when innocent people are blamed for crimes they did not commit, wrong about choosing a side in this nationless war. But when my mind repeats her last sentence, I hear, for the first time, the helpless panic in her voice. I have spent the last months fighting an invisible foe. Her fear has faces and weapons. Her enemy enters through the front door.

Chapter Seventeen

Guigo and I return to the Farissols' house every day for the next week. David's wounds heal well. As he becomes stronger, Guigo stops hovering over my shoulder like a great, hairy gargoyle. He spends hours with Dr. Farissol, performing his lancing technique on the plague-afflicted in the Jewish quarter, and leaves me with David. I think Guigo senses the affinity between us and makes me a gift of this time. And a gift it is.

I awaken with a crawling sensation in my belly that lingers through my morning examination of Queen Joanna and grows stronger with every step from the palace to the Place Jérusalem. If this feeling is hunger, then being alone with David is the most satisfying of meals. For a few blissful hours I forget the bodies stacked at street corners, the inescapable smell of decomposition. There is nothing but his face, illuminated by the window overlooking the sycamore trees.

I avoid home, even when our work brings me and Guigo down the eerily empty rue des Lices and past the big house on the corner. I imagine Margot in our family pew in Saint-Agricol, listening to Father Loup sow fear and suspicion. I imagine her lying awake in our bed, her eyes open on the black ceiling, fear wedged in her throat. And as I walk through the sunlit Place Jérusalem, I imagine her closing her heart to these people with whom she shares so much more than she will ever know.

Under Madame Farissol's careful ministrations, flesh creeps back into David's hollow cheeks, the fever clears from his eyes. And—thank the Virgin—there are no signs of blood poisoning.

I ask all the appropriate questions as I unwind his bandages: "How did you sleep? And your appetite? Was your urine clear or cloudy?"

Then we talk. I sit in the chair beside the bed and watch David's pale hands move like birds as he describes growing up in Marseille, his beloved dead sister and parents. I tell him more about my mother, and then about Father, Margot, even Baldoin. David's spirit is familiar to me, as though we have known each other since childhood.

"What is it like to be a twin?" he asks me on the fifth day.

I hesitate. *They are not* our *people,* my sister said. But this is not the Margot I want him to know. This is not the Margot *I* want to know.

I cast about for a memory that will encompass what Margot and I are to each other. The truth of it. Before the plague, before Erec, even before Mother died. Like a leviathan from the deep, the memory of that terrible night surfaces before I can drown it.

"Elea," David whispers. He is watching me carefully, concern dragging at the corners of his mouth.

I shake my head, look out the window. *Breathe. Here is sunlight.*

"Elea," David says again.

I pull myself back to him, focus on his face, on his eyes as soft and dark as open doors.

"You can tell me anything."

I want to. I want to tell him everything.

"When my mother died, Margot and I took turns with the grief." I shift a little, reaching for words that will explain. "We took turns breaking apart and coming back together. I could set my own despair aside to hold her while she wept. And when she stopped crying, she held me while the grief swallowed me. I could not have survived that night alone."

Something bottomless wells in David's face, but before I can name it, he drops his gaze to the sheets. For a moment I feel hurt and foolish, as though he has left me alone in the dark. But then I see the white knot of fingers in his lap. I hear my words as he must have heard them, and it takes every ounce of control I possess not to climb into his bed and curl myself around him, as though by doing so I could staunch the wound I have reopened. I still have Margot, Father, Anes. He has lost everyone.

Without thinking, I take David's hand. He glances up, surprised, and I think of Baldoin's wild eyes, uncertain and afraid. My heart hurls itself against my ribs, but I hold his gaze, try to ignore the thrill of warmth coursing through my body from the point where we are pressed together. After the week of professional contact between my fingers and his skin, this is something different.

"I'm sorry," I say. "I'm so sorry, David. You shouldn't have had to bear that alone."

The muscles of his throat ripple as he swallows.

"Every day after they died," he says, "just opening my eyes felt like trying to start a fire with wet wood." That is exactly what it felt like, those first weeks Mother was gone. "My uncle wrote, invited me here. I packed my things and came to Avignon. Then that night in the Hôpital Saint-Antoine . . ." He trails off.

I think of how David withdrew into himself as Arye's cough worsened. He knew the enemy we faced long before the rest of us.

"It was like the plague was mocking me. *You couldn't save your family, and you can't save him.*" He shakes his head. "I haven't saved anyone. I haven't done anything these past three months but stand by my uncle's side and watch our patients die. So when the disease finally came for me, all I could think through the fever was *Don't let it win. Don't let it win.*"

"You didn't," I say, blinking back a film of tears. "You are here, David. You are strong. You are alive. You didn't let it win."

He nods slowly, his eyes still holding mine.

"Even though I have lost more than I thought possible," he says, "I see that there is still beauty and grace in the world. It is worth fighting for."

He slides his fingers from mine and cups my hand, slowly turns the palm to face the ceiling. With his index finger, he traces the long line that cuts across the center of my palm. Something blooms behind my navel, spreading quick and hot as blood.

"You are an extraordinary woman, Elea," he says, and releases me.

I am awake half the night remembering his words, the feeling of his touch. I make a fist, trying to grasp the sensation. I have no future with him—the penalty for miscegenation, as Margot reminded me, is death. We will never have more than this stolen time. But there is something between us, something rare and alive that grows stronger with each visit. And I know he feels it, too.

On the seventh day after the lancing, the last day I will change David's bandages, our conversation turns to the future.

"What will you do, Elea?" he asks me. "If the plague ends, if you survive, what will you do?"

I have not imagined a time after the pestilence. I feel like a person stumbling around a dark room, unable to think of anything except lighting a candle.

What life had I dreamed of, before the plague?

"I suppose I'll keep apprenticing with Guigo," I say slowly. "Learn as much as I can. Perhaps set up my own practice as an apothecary and midwife one day." My vision is two-dimensional, flimsy. But something vivid and tangible shines in David's eyes.

"And you?" I ask.

"There is a kingdom," he says slowly, looking through the open windows, "south of Navarre, south even of Castile, called Granada. Christians, Muslims, and Jews live in harmony there, free to worship their gods and free to marry who they will. It is ruled by a sultan who is fair and just, who encourages the sharing of learning and ideas. He has built a university where Jews may study medicine."

I imagine David dressed in the white robes of a Moorish doctor, his dark hair wrapped in a turban. I watch him walk through light-speckled corridors, through courtyards perfumed by flowers and echoing with the music of fountains. I see him attending lectures, his eager face radiant in the crowd.

There is a hollow ache in my stomach. Jealousy, for the opportunity to pursue his dream where I am unable to follow? Perhaps a little. But mostly sadness. Mostly loneliness. He shall leave, as he should, for a life of learning far away from here. And I shall miss him.

I force myself to smile. "And you will go there, when you are recovered?"

David nods, looks as though he is about to say more, but the downstairs door opens. I hear Guigo's deep voice.

We fall silent, knowing this is the final moment we will be alone. My eyes move over his face like a blind person's fingers, trying to memorize every curve of cheek and brow.

Guigo's heavy steps fall on the stairs, in the hallway. "We will return in a fortnight," he says to Dr. Farissol, "to remove the stitches."

The door opens, and it is time to go.

Guigo and I spend the next two weeks training nuns and monks throughout Avignon on our technique to lance, drain, and suture the apostemes. The pneumonic form of the plague still rages in the city, but as we have nothing to offer these patients except prayers, we focus our attention on those poor souls who have contracted the bubonic strain. I brew dozens of bottles of blood-poison tonic and copy out the recipe to be sent in Guigo's correspondences to medical schools across Europe. Our days are so busy that I hardly have time to eat, but each night I lie in my cot in the laboratory, tracing my palm where David touched me and wondering if he lies awake with the same pulsing ache.

On the morning we are to return to the Place Jérusalem I am up at matins, unable to sleep for excitement. When I catch a glimpse of myself in the mirror over the basin in his room, my eyes are preternaturally bright, my cheeks flushed. I remember Margot, waiting for Erec, and recognize the same fierce glow in my reflection. Her words from our argument echo back to me: *Do not put yourself in danger for a race to which you do not belong.* But still the thought chases itself through my mind like the chorus of a song. *Does he think of me, too?*

In Joanna's quarters I am forgetful and distracted. After asking me three times to pass her a book of poetry, the queen grows irritated and sends me away. Paolo looks up from his lute with a question in his eyes as I pass, but I give him no clues. I fight my feet from running.

I do not hear a word of Guigo's lecture as we walk to the Place Jérusalem. The sensation of moths fluttering against my ribs intensifies as we approach the golden house in the square with its neat row of Hebrew numerals.

Sarah meets us at the door. Dr. Farissol, standing behind her, is elated.

"Surgeon, mademoiselle! I am so very pleased to see you. David asks every day when you will return." He bows politely to me and clasps Guigo's hand. "You have won an admirer for life in that boy, Guigo."

As Dr. Farissol leads us up the stairs, Guigo mutters under his breath, "I believe it is *you* who has won an admirer."

I press half-moons into my palms with my fingernails to keep from grinning.

The blood hums in my ears as I follow Guigo down the hall and into the room where just a few weeks ago David lay dying. The bed is empty. David is seated on a stool by the window with a book in his lap.

"Surgeon, Mademoiselle Blanchet," he says, getting to his feet with a little difficulty.

The change in him is remarkable. I'd forgotten how tall he is—a full head taller than me, and only a few inches shorter than Guigo. The bones of his face are still exaggerated following the illness, the cheekbones a little too sharp, but his eyes are bright and clear. As they lock on mine, a hot flush rises up my neck like fire consuming parchment.

Guigo surveys David like a proud father. "Look at the state of you! Healthy as a horse, are you?"

I stand inside the door, unsure of what to do with my arms.

David smiles, looking at Guigo and then at me. "Yes, sir. Thanks to you and Mademoiselle Blanchet."

"And have you been eating?" Guigo asks, walking around David to view him from all angles, like a prospective buyer surveying a cow.

"Yes, sir," David replies.

Guigo turns to Jacob. "He's still too skinny for my liking."

Jacob laughs. "Sarah has been trying her best to fatten him up, believe me!"

"Well, David?" says Guigo, clapping his hands together. "Shall we take out your stitches?"

A shadow of discomfort crosses David's face. "Yes, please," he says vehemently. "It has taken all my will to not cut them myself. The itch is terrible."

Once the sutures have been removed, we wait in the hallway while David dresses. Guigo and Jacob speak quietly together.

"And your people, Jacob? How many more have you lost?"

"No family is unscathed," Dr. Farissol replies, running a hand through his beard. "The coughing plague killed one in four of us and continues to kill. We are not free of it. But as for the bubonic strain, I have performed your procedure on several patients. About half survived."

Guigo nods at me. "That is about our percentage as well. I have high hopes for the treatment, but many more will die."

The door opens. David stands on the threshold, striking in a tunic and loose linen trousers.

Guigo's face brightens again. "Look at this handsome young man!" he says with a grin. "How do you feel?"

"I feel nearly normal," says David, smiling at us all. "Thank you again, Surgeon, Mademoiselle Blanchet. I will never be able to repay the debt I owe you."

"*You* owe *us*?" Guigo repeats. "My dear boy, you gave us hope again. It is we who should be thanking you. You will make a damned good physician."

David's face reddens as he shakes Guigo's hand.

A moment passes. Guigo looks at me expectantly: it's my turn to say something, to take my leave of David. But then I remember.

"Oh! I brought you a salve for the scars," I say, rummaging for the jar. With all eyes on me, the basket feels very full of other objects. My clumsy fingers close on every item except the ointment.

"Elea can explain her salve on her own," Guigo says, the corners of his mouth twitching. "I want to pay my respects to Madame Farissol. Jacob, will you join me?"

Guigo and Jacob are halfway down the stairs when I finally extricate the small pot and hold it out to David.

"Here," I say, trying not to think about the brush of his fingers on mine as he takes it. "This will help the scars heal."

"You made it for me?" he says, holding the vessel like a jewel, turning the dull clay this way and that way as though catching the light.

"Yes," I say. "No. I mean. I made it for you. But I needed to make it anyway because we always need ointment for scars, and I was out . . ." I trail off.

David smiles. "Thank you," he says. "I shall treasure it, knowing your hands made it."

I have no reply.

"What does it contain?" he asks gracefully, turning his attention to the jar and uncorking it, giving me time to compose myself. "It smells lovely."

"Olive oil, lavender oil, rose hip oil, calendula." I wave my hand airily. "My mother's recipe, with a few additions of my own."

He holds the jar with both hands like a hot cup on a cold morning. We stand in silence.

"I'm so pleased you're better," I say, meaning it.

"It is foolish to wish I had suffered more, taken longer to recover," he says quietly. "But I do. Because then I would have seen more of you."

He makes no move to step closer, to touch me, but the distance between us is suddenly charged.

"I know that no reality exists in which we can be together," he says, "but this time with you has changed me."

My awkwardness evaporates with the honesty of his words, echoed these long weeks with each throb of my heart. He is no lovesick boy, and I am no lovesick girl. We are kindred spirits brought together by fate or God. I reach out and take his hand. He turns the palm up to the ceiling slowly, lifts my hand to his lips and kisses the place where wrist meets palm, where my veins stand out as clear and blue as a road and the blood beats just below the skin.

The sensation spreads up my arm, across my chest and belly, raising the hair along my forearms and at the nape of my neck. I look at David and try once more to memorize his face, secure all the details of this moment in my mind forever. Then I let go and walk down the stairs.

The feeling of David's lips on my skin lingers the entire walk back to the palace; I long to jump in the air and cry into my pillow at the same time. It is an overwhelming emotion that bubbles up and overflows, demanding to be shared. But there is only one person with whom I wish to share it, and Margot has made her disapproval clear.

As Guigo and I cross the courtyard to the laboratory, something flutters on the laboratory door. A piece of parchment stuck there with a pin. Guigo pulls it free and reads it. The happiness slides from his face.

"Elea."

The tone of his voice sends a ripple of fear down my spine. Whatever news the note contains, I do not want to hear it.

"It's your father, Elea. He's fallen ill."

Chapter Eighteen

I run through the streets with Guigo following behind me. With every pounding footstep I pray. *Not Father. Not Father. Not Father.*

The house is dark but for a taper burning in the bedroom overlooking the street. The door is unlocked. I enter as Guigo, huffing, rounds the turn of the street behind me.

"*Father?*" I shout, sprinting up the stairs. "*Anes? Margot?*"

Anes meets me on the landing, handkerchief tied over her nose and mouth. Her apron is spattered scarlet. I push past her into my father's room. Margot rises from a chair beside the bed. She says something through her own face covering, but I do not hear.

He is lying on the bed, his white nightshirt stained with black tissue and blood.

"Get out!" I shriek at Margot and Anes. They do not move. In the hall below, Guigo calls my name.

"*Get out!*" I repeat, grabbing them each by the arm and dragging them from the room.

Deaf to their protests I close the door, slide the heavy wooden bar across it and fumble in my pocket for my kerchief. I pull it over my mouth, tie it behind my head.

Then I turn my attention to my father. I pull back the sheets and tug up his nightdress, praying to find a bubo in his groin, in his armpits. At least then he might have a chance. But his fever-damp skin is smooth.

The disease has progressed quickly. My father—my handsome father—looks like an old man. His face is gray, his eyes sunken. How many patients have I seen like this, and only ever one outcome? But not Father. Please, not Father.

"Elea," calls Guigo from the landing. "Let me in, for God's sake."

I stand numbly, unbar the door.

Guigo pushes past me, his face already half-covered, and bends over the bed. He rests an ear to my father's struggling chest, listens to his lungs, his heartbeat.

After a moment, he stands. With a movement almost imperceptible, he shakes his head.

My blood turns to smoke.

"Elea. You must listen to me," Guigo says quietly, placing a hand on my shoulder. "Your father is dying. He has the pleural pestilence—already it is in his lungs."

The words make their way through to my mind. With effort, I attach meaning to each one. *My father. Dying. Already in his lungs.*

"We both know that there is nothing we can do." He looks at me intently. "Do you understand me, Elea? *Nothing.*"

My father is dying. There is nothing we can do.

"But they"—Guigo points over my head to where Anes and Margot stand, no doubt listening at the closed door—"do not know that. And the next few hours will be terrible. Only you and I know how terrible they will be." He searches my face grimly. "As I see it, you and I have two responsibilities tonight. The first is to offer your father whatever comfort we can."

He drops his voice. "The second is to keep them"—he inclines his head to the door—"calm. People are most calm when they have a sense of purpose. They must keep out of the room. I will give them things to do. You will think them useless busywork, and they are. But it will help them through tonight, to think they are being useful."

I nod.

"Your family will look to you now. This is the responsibility to which you agreed when you asked me to take you as my apprentice. This is the covenant that every doctor makes: to stand between the living and death. You and I know what this death is, but they should not."

He squeezes my shoulder. Then he releases me and opens the door.

Guigo's words shake me into reality. Grief and panic rise in my throat like bile and I force them down. Later, there will be time. I take a deep breath and follow Guigo onto the landing.

While he assigns Anes a list of tasks, I bring Margot downstairs to make more of the tonic I gave to Arye. I have nearly a full bottle, but the process of steeping and straining the herbs will take hours. I tell her it's very important.

"He didn't go to the palace this morning," Margot murmurs. She sits at the kitchen table, staring at the scrubbed surface with unfocused eyes. "I saw his cloak on its hook and his boots when I came downstairs. We found him in his bed. He was delirious. He thought I was Mother."

I should have been here. I left her alone to face this.

"We sent for you at the palace." Margot continues in the same flat tone. "You told us, I remember, that the breath of the afflicted is poisonous, so we burned your herbs, tied kerchiefs over our faces. We didn't know what else to do, but every hour he grew sicker." Her voice thickens with tears. "He didn't know me, nor Anes. I didn't know what to do. But I couldn't leave him, Elea. I couldn't."

She buries her face in her hands. I wrap my arms around her, hold her tight to my chest like Mother would have done.

"Guigo and I are here now," I say. "We will take care of him. But you did exactly right. I'm so proud of you."

My sister takes slow, shuddering sobs into my shoulder. I think of the night Mother died, when we took turns with the grief. I rest my head on hers.

"You are myself," I whisper. The anger I harbored against her is small against what we now face.

"You are myself," she repeats.

I stroke her hair and try not to think of the last time I was here, the last time I saw my father alive, sleeping before the fire. I would give anything to live that moment again. To turn from the door, sit beside him at supper, listen to his snores from the next room. But instead, I left without a backward glance.

I leave Margot with hastily scribbled instructions and climb the stairs. Guigo and I sit in silence, watching my father. He has sunken into the stupor that accompanies this phase of the disease, when the fever still rages but the patient is exhausted, working too hard at the task of breathing to move or speak. Guigo checks his pulse and listens to his chest when Anes comes into the room with a stack of firewood or clean linen, so it appears as though we are doing something.

The seconds drag to hours. I have watched so many die of this illness, I have the course of it memorized. But tonight, as death creeps through the casement to steal my father away, each change is a terrible surprise.

The waiting is torture. Each extra moment between inhale and exhale makes my pulse quicken. I want to jump out of my skin, to run down the hall and out the door and not stop until I am alone in the woods, calling out for Baldoin. But instead, I sit in stillness, with my hands clasped uselessly in my lap, and watch my father die.

Guigo does not rest even as the moon rises and the cold river air pools under the open window. He builds the fire higher, drips water between my father's slack lips, lets Margot watch from the doorway as he administers her medicine in the black hours before dawn.

"Well done," he says soothingly. "See how his breathing is quieter? You have eased your father's suffering."

Margot says nothing, just stares at the form in the bed with her soul in her eyes. I catch Guigo's gaze as he turns away from my sister. I know what he's thinking.

Not long now.

When a smudge of gray appears on the black horizon heralding the edge of the endless night, Guigo forces me from the room.

"You know how it ends," he whispers. "And no one should watch their father die like this."

"What about his last rites?"

"I will read them. Go."

I force myself to my feet. I look, for the final time, into my father's face.

In the plague-pale cheeks, the bruised lids, I superimpose the man I knew. Smiling at Margot. At Mother. Carrying me upstairs when I fell asleep after supper. Pressing a kiss to my temple as he pulled up the covers. I reach down and cover his cold hand in mine, feel the familiar dimensions of palm and fingers.

I glance around the room, at the trappings of my father's life. The books stacked beside the bed, the manuscripts and scrolls on the table. The embroidered handkerchief—Margot's Christmas present—folded carefully beside the bottle of scent I made him. A cache of worthless treasures kept as carefully as jewels. I swallow a sob. Suddenly the endless night feels too short. We should have done more; surely there was more to be done. . . .

"Elea," Guigo says. "*Go.*"

I descend the stairs alone.

The dawn light glows pink through the window when Guigo's step falls on the kitchen threshold. We stand from the table together in silence. Margot reaches for my hand; I take Anes's.

Guigo enters, looking exhausted. His eyes linger for a moment on our clasped fingers.

"His suffering is over," he says quietly. "His soul is with God."

Margot drops to the bench with a stifled sob. Anes wails. I feel a dreadful relief. It is over. He is free.

"We must burn everything," Guigo says, "all his clothing, all the linens. But first I will make arrangements for"—he glances at Margot and Anes on the bench behind me—"for the remains."

The remains. My father's body growing cold in the bedroom overlooking the street. I close my eyes against this, think instead of falling asleep in his lap as a little girl, the sounds of conversation and laughter drowned out by the steady thump of his heart. How unassailable he seemed, as eternal and enduring as stone.

Guigo takes care of everything. He disappears for a while and returns with two men who leave muddy footprints on the stairs. While they stomp about overhead, I close the kitchen door and insist we bathe: first Anes, then Margot, then me, in the big copper tub. I try not to listen to the sounds of the door opening, the men's footfalls heavier under their burden. Margot makes a movement toward the door, but I shake my head.

I have seen too many plague corpses with their gray and twisted faces. They will remember my father as he was: healthy and strong and handsome. This is a horror from which I can protect them. This is a gift I can give.

By the time it's my turn, the water is lukewarm and dirty, but I stay in the tub for a long time. I scrub every inch of my body until the skin is pink, push too hard with the horsehair brush. It is good to feel pain instead of raging grief.

At terce, Guigo has still not emerged. I rise from the table.

"It's time to go to bed," I say. "There is nothing more to be done now. Tomorrow we will clean the floors and change the rushes. But now we must sleep."

Too tired to argue, Margot and Anes shuffle before me, through the hall and up the stairs. I pause on the landing.

"Go on," I say to Margot, who stands with her hand on our door, waiting for me. "I'll be there in a moment."

I knock lightly on the door at the end of the hall. Guigo opens it.

The bed is stripped bare and the smell of burned fabric singes the air. The wardrobe stands empty. Guigo has taken no chances; anything that could harbor the plague miasma was taken away to be burned. All my father's clothing, the simple black doublets, the velvet he wore on his wedding day, are gone. Gone, too, are the few things of my mother's that he hid, tucked away in the back of the wardrobe. Her cloak, the green dress she wore when she married him. Gone.

Guigo opens his arms.

He embraces me, holds me the way my father hadn't held me in years. Wrapped in his big arms, held tightly against his chest, all sound is muffled except the beating of his heart.

The grief that I locked away is released. Like water from a dam, like blood from a wound, it pours from me in great wracking sobs. My legs shake, I think I will collapse. But Guigo has me.

I cry until I have no tears left, until the storm inside me runs out of rain.

Chapter Nineteen

We move slowly in the days following my father's death. Time seems to stand still with no agenda, no list of tasks to complete before supper. Margot, Anes, and I drift in and out of the rooms like ghosts, meeting in the kitchen for a cold meal or a cup of ale at midday or midnight. A strange quiet settles over the house. The walls themselves seem to lean closer to listen. Our brief conversations are whispered; a knife clattering on a plate or a log falling in the fire is deafening. The closed door of my father's bedroom looms across the hall. Sometimes I catch Margot pausing as she passes it, as though hopeful she will hear him stirring on the other side. I do it, too.

Margot has nightmares. She moans, tossing and turning, or cries out. I shake her gently, hold her until she cries herself to sleep again. Memories of that night wait for me, too, like thieves in the shadowy corners of my mind, replaying over and over. I never got to say goodbye.

We watch ourselves, each other, for any sign of the plague. I lie awake at night listening to my sister's breath, feeling my forehead for the first flush of fever. I think of David, of the terrible days after his family died, all alone in that empty house. I hold Margot tighter.

On the third morning after my father's death, there is a knock at the door.

Guigo stands on the threshold with a plucked chicken in one hand and a loaf of bread in the other.

"Good day," he says pleasantly. Then, when I make no move to admit him: "May I come in?"

I step out of the way with a muttered apology. Guigo heads straight to the kitchen where Margot and Anes sit in silence at the table, sipping mugs of hippocras. They stand in surprise as he enters unannounced and places his gifts on the table.

"Surgeon de Chauliac," says Anes, her hands flying to the frizzy curls escaping from her bonnet. The way he cared for my father has quelled her suspicions of him. "Please, have a seat. May I bring you something to drink?"

Guigo lowers his bulky backside onto the bench across from Margot and smiles at her.

She does not return it, and instead looks up at me with an accusation in her face. *What is he doing here, interrupting our grief?*

"A cup of whatever you are drinking, please," he says. Then, to me, "I have spoken to Queen Joanna. She has excused you for another week."

I nod numbly. Guigo looks around curiously in the silence that follows, taking in the bunches of herbs hanging from the ceiling, my jars of medicines on the shelves. Anes sets a steaming mug before him.

"Thank you."

Anes nods mutely and sits beside Margot.

"I'm glad that the whole family is here," he says, blowing on the hot wine. "I need to speak with you about your finances, Elea."

My thick mind moves slowly. "What?"

"Your father surely left you some savings. Have you opened the strongbox in his room?"

I shake my head, feeling foolish. I have not even thought of how we would manage without my father's income and no male relatives to take us in.

"I made inquiries at the palace. Your father earned eighteen *livres* per year and lived quite modestly. I expect he left you and your sister respectable dowries. But if you are to keep this house, and Anes on as housekeeper, you need to make more than the measly *sou* per week you are earning with me. So, I have spoken to the pope and your Queen Joanna. We have all agreed to increase your income to total sixteen *livres* per year."

Anes gasps. It takes me a moment to work out the math. An eight-fold increase.

Guigo sips his wine. "That, combined with your dowries, should set you all up for lives of moderate comfort."

I search for the words to convey my gratitude for all he has done. "Thank you" is all I can manage.

He pats my arm. "You deserve it." Another silent minute passes. Guigo clears his throat awkwardly. "I thought, perhaps, that the chicken would be best served roasted?"

In the week that follows, we begin to emerge from the stupor of our grief. It lingers—an ache in the bones, a heaviness in the air—but there are glimpses of normalcy as daily tasks force their routine upon us. Guigo makes a point of stopping by almost daily to bring us gifts: links of sausages, candied fruits, a bundle of jonquils. And whenever Margot and Anes are out of earshot, he tells me news of the plague.

"The pestilence in both forms now rages in Paris and London," Guigo whispers one afternoon as I walk him to the door. "And everywhere the same conspiracy Jacob told us, that Jews spread the plague by poisoning the wells. In Barcelona, Carcassonne, even in Narbonne, those who did not flee were rounded up and burned."

The floor feels unsteady beneath my feet. Dr. Farissol, doing everything in his power to keep his patients alive. Madame Farissol in her gleaming kitchen. David.

Although grief still hangs like a stone about my neck, a spark catches inside me. Suddenly I am eager to return to Guigo's side and fight not just the plague but this dangerous and swelling hate.

The morning before I return to the palace, Margot sits at the kitchen table watching me pack supplies while Anes scrubs the flagstones in the hall. I spent the last day brewing blood-cleansing tonic; the little glass vials clink against each other pleasantly as I tuck them in my basket.

"I'm leaving three bottles here," I say, placing them on the bare shelf that once held all my medicines. "Just in case."

My sister doesn't answer. She stares at the scrubbed wood with far-seeing eyes.

"Did you hear what I—"

Margot looks up suddenly. "Would you do something for me?"

Her gaze does not focus on my face. She looks through me, past me, like someone watching a fire. The intensity of it unsettles me. We have been so careful with each other since Father died, neither mentioning the argument over David, not speaking of anything more straining than what we should have for supper.

"Anything," I say.

"Would you deliver a letter? To the palace stables?"

Mathilde's corpse beneath the winding sheet, her curling black fingers. I swallow.

"To Erec?"

Margot's eyes sharpen on mine. "Yes. To Erec."

I know what this letter will contain. I force down the creeping dread and reach across the table, cover her clasped hands with mine. "Of course."

My sister smiles. In the curve of her thin cheek, the sudden brightness in her eyes, hope flickers. "Thank you, Elea. I'll write it tonight."

Anes tromps in, lugging a bucket of soapy water. "I didn't know all the work was done," she says, crossing the kitchen toward the back door. "Here I am, breaking my back to get the floors clean when I should have been sitting at the table—"

Margot and I exchange a glance and get to our feet. But before we can follow Anes through the back door, she freezes on the threshold.

"Girls," she whispers. "There is an animal in the yard."

We crane our heads to see over her shoulders. Sitting beside the well, basking in the morning sun, is Baldoin.

He leaps to his feet when he sees me, wagging his tail. He looks larger than ever in our yard, easily twice the size of an average dog.

"How . . . how did he know where I live?" I stammer.

Anes shoots me a reproachful look.

"You *know* him?" asks Margot delightedly.

I step slowly into the courtyard. Baldoin trots over to greet me and butts his nose against my hand.

With a squeal, Margot abandons the safety of the kitchen and runs to my side. Baldoin sniffs her, black ears erect and interested. She places a hand on his great head, runs it down his spine to his wagging tail. The joy on my sister's face is as welcome as sunshine after months of rain. She looks up at me with a laugh on her lips. I arch a brow. Just as when we were children, no words are necessary.

We turn, as one, to Anes.

Her blue eyes flit from me to Margot as realization dawns. "Absolutely not," she says.

"Please, Anes," begs Margot. "We never had a pet before. Father forbade it. But look at him—poor thing. He would die on the streets."

Baldoin sits still between us, wagging his tail pleasantly. I know he would most assuredly *not* die, but I hold my tongue.

"Elea returns to the palace tomorrow," my sister continues. "And now that Father is gone, he can protect us."

She kneels and scratches his ears. "Please, Anes," she repeats.

Baldoin licks her face so hard she falls backward into the muddy yard, giggling. The scene swims before my eyes.

Thank you, Baldoin. Thank you for bringing my sister joy.

Anes crosses her arms over her chest in a posture of inflexibility, but when she runs her eyes over Baldoin, lingering on the twigs and mud stuck in his coat, I know Margot has won.

"Very well," Anes says at last. "But you have the charge of him, Margot. I will not clean up his messes. And if he causes any trouble, he is *out,* and I will not hear another word about it!"

I throw my arms around Anes, who tries valiantly not to smile. Margot springs to her feet and runs a circle around the yard with Baldoin chasing her, barking and bounding. As they pass close, Anes pinches her nose in distaste.

"He stinks, Margot," she calls as the pair circle the well again. "You must bathe him. And he may live here in the yard. I'll fetch some straw for his bed."

Margot stops abruptly, and Baldoin bumps into her legs. We speak over each other indignantly.

"He will freeze!"

"What if it rains?"

Anes holds up her hand, her face reddening.

"That is enough!" she shouts. "I said you can keep him. Your poor father is watching from heaven, shaking his head at my weakness." Anes casts her milky eyes skyward as if she could see my father wagging his finger at her. "He will sleep under the eaves, he will eat scraps from our table, but over my dead body will he set one filthy paw inside your father's house." She narrows her eyes. "Do I make myself clear?"

"Yes, Anes," Margot and I chorus.

By evening, Baldoin is curled up before the fire in the hall, and Anes has fed him the better part of one of Guigo's roasted chickens.

Early the next morning I return to the palace, content in the knowledge that Baldoin watches over my family like a strange, shaggy guardian.

I finger the letter in my cloak. Margot slipped it to me last night; I glimpsed *Erec* written in her curling script and Father's seal in the red wax before tucking it into my pocket. In the dirty light of dawn, in the awakening city, I allow myself to think her thoughts. Mathilde and Father dead, the world remade. She and Erec might finally be together. I imagine them sleeping in our parents' bed, Margot dozing in the sun with a child in her arms, Anes buzzing around the house like a contented bee. If there is any hope for happiness left in the world, I would give it to my sister. But is he the same man he once was?

When I present myself at Joanna's quarters, the queen rushes to greet me, walking a bit wide-legged but still gracefully.

"*Tesoro,*" she exclaims, taking both my hands in hers and kissing me on both cheeks. She smells of violets. "We are so sorry to hear of your loss."

"Thank you, Your Majesty," I reply woodenly. *I will not cry,* I tell myself. *I will not cry.*

"Let us go for a walk," she says, linking her arm through mine like an old friend. "The horses tell me they miss you."

In the cool, dark stables, Joanna stops at a bay mare's stall. We stroke her neck, feed her oats from the bag hanging on the door.

"My father died when I was an infant," she says in a breezy voice, as though speaking of the weather. "My grandfather raised me. But God called him to heaven when I was seventeen, just like you. He was the last of my kin. Have you any family left?"

"I have a twin sister, Margot," I reply. "And Anes, our housekeeper, who is really a member of the family. That is all."

"Soon you must marry and start your own family. A child is the best antidote for sadness. Are there any young men who hold your affection?"

"Elea?" someone calls from behind me.

The queen and I turn. Erec stands outlined in the light from the doorway as though summoned by the folded parchment in my pocket—or by the queen's inquiry about men in my life. He walks toward us uncertainly, eyes widening as he recognizes my companion.

"Your Majesty," he murmurs, sweeping the hat from his head and dropping into a deep bow. His cheeks are narrower; his eyes, sunk deeper in their orbits, give him the expression of something hunted. We are both orphans now, I realize, and the empty chambers of my heart ache for what we have lost.

Joanna lifts her eyebrows at me over Erec's bent head. "You may rise." And then, "Do you know this young man, Mademoiselle Blanchet?"

"Yes, Your Majesty."

Erec stands. I search his expression for anger, for the burning knowledge of what transpired to his mother's corpse. There is a hardness to his mouth that I have not seen before, the last vestiges of boyhood scrubbed clean.

"We are old friends."

"Excuse me." Joanna sneaks me a wink, then glances down the aisle of stalls to where the head groom stands with a curry brush in hand. "I must ask Monsieur Thion his opinion on horseshoe calkins."

Erec and I stand in silence while the queen's footsteps fade and her silvery voice rises, punctuated by Monsieur Thion's gruff reply.

Erec toes the stable dirt, turning his cap over in his hands.

"How are you?" I ask.

He doesn't respond. His eyes are fixed on the ground between us.

Then Joanna laughs, and Erec starts. I am reaching for Margot's letter when he speaks again.

"Is it true?" he asks huskily.

My fingers freeze. I think, for a moment, that he speaks about my father. Sorrow and gratitude well up inside me.

"Is it true that you opened her, Elea? Turned her inside out so that not even the saints will recognize her at the gates of heaven?"

His words kick the breath from my lungs.

Erec raises his eyes. They are tortured, blue as a wind-wild sea, the whites shot through with red. "I can't sleep," he says miserably. "Every time I close my eyes, I see her walking the streets, holding her organs."

"It wasn't me, Erec," I say, taking a step toward him. "I swear on the memory of my mother that I did not touch her."

His furrowed brow clears as he searches my face, reads the honesty written there. But that is not the whole truth. And he deserves it.

"But Dr. de Chauliac did," I say, wishing this heavy task did not fall to me. "He dissected her, as he has done many of the plague-dead. With each piece of knowledge we understand more." I'm speaking fast, trying to make him understand. "It is science, Erec: no different from plotting stars to chart a course. Your mother gave us all a gift. If she had fallen ill now, we may have saved her."

"I didn't believe it." His voice is empty, hollow. "When the priest told me it was you, helping the surgeon. I didn't believe it. But now I see how misled I have been."

"Erec," I plead, taking another step toward him, so close I can see the grime caught in the lines about his mouth, "you know me. I would never—*could* never—have touched Mathilde. But the pope raised the ban on human dissection. Guigo says—"

"Ah yes," he interrupts. "The pope. He who allows those who spread this vile pestilence to grow fat and rich while faithful Christians rot of it."

"That is not true." I fight to keep my voice steady. "The Jews are dying of it just like the rest of us."

But Erec has stopped listening. "I have been a fool," he says. "A blind fool. I'll hear no more of your lies."

He turns on his heel and walks toward the stable doors. Too late, I remember my promise to my sister.

"Erec, wait!" I reach for Margot's letter. My fingers close around the edges, the smooth circle of wax.

He pauses, glances back over his shoulder, his profile so clear against the daylight that it could be carved. The long nose, the strong jaw. But his mouth twists with a cruelness I have not seen there before, and my spine prickles when I recognize the coldness in his eyes.

"My mother was right about Bietriz," he says. "And she was right about you."

As the sunlight swallows his black shadow, another voice echoes in my head.

If she were not already dying, I would burn her myself.

I try to put Erec out of my mind and focus on the queen as I concoct a tonic for her headache, but a bitter taste lingers through Paolo's love songs and the ladies' gossip. At sext the queen becomes snappish and sends us all away, retiring to her bedchamber.

Back in the laboratory I pace from door to cot with Margot's letter clutched in my hands. Through the windows, the courtyard bustles with the energy of a beehive. I glance again and again to the archway which leads to the stables, half of me hoping to see Erec's long silhouette, hoping for the chance to explain; half of me sick with worry, replaying his words.

I can guess what the letter will say. But I must know for sure. I whisper a prayer for Margot's forgiveness. I crack the wax and open the parchment.

My love,

I do not recognize the world anymore.

I do not recognize myself, except the parts of me that love you. It is your heart I carry in my chest, not my own.

Every night I close my eyes and pray that the hurt of losing you will subside. Every morning the sting is stronger.

I do not need a fine house, nor rings on my fingers nor feathers in my mattress. I would share a stable with you and make it a home.

Our parents' souls are with God. Nothing now stands between us. I beg you: make me your wife for whatever time we have left on earth.

—Margot

My tears blur her signature. Margot, Margot. I expected some of this: the hope, the plea. It is the pain in my sister's voice that sinks me like a ship.

Guigo's heavy steps fall on the cobblestones. I just have time to tuck the letter beneath my mattress before the door opens.

"You're back!" Guigo closes the door and turns to face me with a grin. "You have already seen the ice queen?"

My cheeks burn as if Margot had interrupted me, not he. "I have."

Guigo takes a seat at the table. "How is she?"

"Irritable."

"I knew she would be," he says, pouring himself a cup of wine from the carafe. "When did she hear?"

For a moment I forget the letter. "Hear what?"

Guigo looks puzzled. "That His Holiness is leaving the city."

"He's *what?*"

"He will wait out the plague at Étoile-sur-Rhône, where the air is better, and the pestilence has not yet struck. I thought the queen—"

"He is abandoning Avignon? Now, when the plague rages more virulently than ever?"

Guigo nods.

"People will despair." I drop heavily into the chair across from him. "And what of Queen Joanna? It is too late for her to travel any distance. Is she to remain here, pregnant and alone? Shepherd of the world," I say traitorously, "abandoning his flock in our time of direst need."

Guigo holds up a finger. "Do not *ever* say such a thing again." He glances through the window, then back to me. "Women have burned for less."

I drop my head, admonished.

"I told His Holiness to go," Guigo says. "His health is my greatest concern. And the soundest advice I could offer was for him to leave the city. I've been begging him for months, but he wouldn't, as you say, abandon his flock."

I stare at my lap, feeling miserable. When I look up again, Guigo's face has softened. I take in the bags under his eyes, the permanent frown lines, the new streaks of gray at his temples and in his beard. A hollow pit gapes in my belly, too dark and deep to contemplate. *I cannot lose Guigo, too.*

"And you?" I ask quietly. "You have already done so much. No one could blame you for leaving with the pope. You are the greatest physician in Europe: the world requires you to survive."

"And you, Mademoiselle Médecin?" His lips twitch with the ghost of a smile. "Would you fly with me to Étoile-sur-Rhône? Eat sweet meats and hear music with the pope and his retinue while Avignon's bakers, butchers, priests, and prostitutes fall in the streets? Would you have me face infamy for all time as the surgeon who abandoned his city in its time of greatest need?"

"I would have you live," I say. "More than anything, I would have you live."

Guigo reaches across the table and rests his hand on mine.

"My life is in God's hands," he says simply. "As is yours. I must stay. I know that is his plan for me."

To awake in dread and fall asleep in dread, day after day for months on end—it is an exhaustion for which the human mind is not designed. Such is life in the time of the plague: a grueling march from catastrophe to catastrophe, an endless parade of suffering. I grow paranoid that the illness has attached itself to me. My sleep is riddled with nightmares. I awaken wringing-wet with cold sweat.

When Guigo and I pass the rue des Lices, I feel Margot's longing for me burning like a candle in a window. But I do not stop, do not rap my knuckles on the front door. My sister's letter lies under my mattress, undelivered. She will see the betrayal in my face, written clear as daylight. I cannot bear to shatter her hope.

When sleep evades me, when the guilt over Margot chews at my edges, when the faces of the dead march across the dark laboratory ceiling, I go to the stables.

The horses reach their heads over the doors of their stalls as I pass. I filch withered apples and carrots from the kitchen cellars and listen to the sound their enormous teeth make as they grind my offerings into frothy saliva.

The first few times I came here, I searched for Erec's broad-shouldered figure in the dark. In my head I strung words together into speeches. Words to explain what happened to Mathilde. Words to remind him who I am, who my sister is. Words to pull him from the ice-slick slope of hatred. But night after night, I am alone.

I hold the despair at bay by going through a cache of happy memories that I hold in my mind like rosary beads. My mother picking wild roses in the meadow, braiding them into my hair. Father kissing her one late night, long and tenderly, when he thought me asleep. Margot laughing as Baldoin licked her face. I replay them, try to remember every detail of light and color and scent. *There is still beauty and grace in the world,* as David said. *It is worth fighting for.*

I think of him often, as April gives way to May. Reading in his sunny room, attending patients beside his uncle. But Margot, for all her ignorance, was right. My feelings for him only place us both in greater danger.

The days are easier. There is so much to do that there is no time to remember. But at night the sadness creeps in like a storm, and I can no sooner hold it off than return rain to the clouds.

Two weeks after my father's death I stand in the darkness before the bay mare's stall, stroking her neck. And suddenly, superimposed on the true image before me, I see my father as he lay dying. His face gray and eyes sunken, his life rattling in his lungs.

I take a deep breath. *Feel your feet on the ground,* I tell myself. *Smell the hay and horses. The spring air on your skin. The firm muscles under your hand.*

It is no use. My memories cannot be dammed—they flash before me, too fast, too numerous, too much to bear. Stacks of wax-skinned corpses, the smoke of bonfires and rattle of carts, the splash of bodies hitting the surface of the river. Mother. Father. The hundreds we could not save. Mathilde. Father Loup's jeering face. Mother. Father.

The stables spin. I clutch the stall door, squeeze my eyes shut against the deluge, but still the memories come. Mathilde lying in blood, shrieking. *Witch.* My baby brother, growing cold in my arms.

Mother's black hair wrapped about her neck like strangling hands. Brother Christophe, small as a child in death. Father, shrouded in his sheets and dropped in the river, another anonymous corpse. Mathilde's scarred arm glaring up at me from the dissection table like an accusing eye. I could not save them. I could not save them. They are dead and cold in the ground, and any day it could be Anes, or Guigo, or Margot. I cannot save them. I cannot save any of them.

The sobs come in great shudders, and I cannot breathe, cannot breathe, and the earth is tilting off its axis, I cannot hold on. I cannot breathe.

I collapse onto my back and try vainly to inhale, but my lungs don't cooperate. I gasp like a fish, but the air will not come.

"Elea?"

Footsteps fall in the straw.

"Elea!"

Through my breath-starved brain, I smell cinnamon.

Paolo kneels beside me. He takes me by the shoulders, lifts me, leans my back against the stall door.

"Breathe," he says, gripping my arms. "Breathe with me."

He inhales deeply. I try to copy him in stuttering gulps.

"Good, now slowly out through the mouth." He exhales through pursed lips. I follow.

"Good," he says. "Again, in through the nose . . . And out through the mouth. Good. Again. In through the nose . . ."

Slowly the earth stops spinning. The ground is once more solid beneath me.

"Good," Paolo says gently. "*Bellissima.* Do you feel better?"

I nod, still following his inhale and exhale. I am aware of the warmth of him, of cool night air caressing my skin. He says nothing, just matches his breath to mine, keeps his hands on my shoulders like anchors.

After a few moments I trust myself to speak. "I thought I was going to die." The words sound foolish. To cover up my embarrassment I add, "How did you know what to do?"

He releases my arms and leans against the stall door beside me. "After my mother died, I had the same sort of attacks. My sister held me like that, taught me to breathe like that. It was the only thing that helped."

We sit in silence for a moment, listening to the big animals shift and sigh around us. Suddenly it strikes me that I am alone, in the dark, with a man. There was a time when this would have mattered. There was a world in which this was forbidden.

"Why did you come here?" I ask. It must be midnight.

"I was looking for you," he says. "Since your father died, you are not yourself. I, too, could not sleep tonight. I thought to walk by your room to see if you were in the mood to talk. The candles were lit but there was no sign of you. Her Majesty speaks of your mutual love for the horses."

He came searching for me. He was worried.

"Thank you," I say, grateful that my voice is even and clear.

Paolo places his hand over mine, his eyes glimmering like a cat's in the darkness. "Would you like to speak of him? Would it help?"

I shake my head. If I speak of Father, the floodgates will open and I will not be able to close them. There are too many dead, too many lost. Too many I could not save. I take another breath like Paolo taught me. *Feel the ground beneath you.*

"No," I say, "it is kind of you. But I cannot. Not yet."

"I understand," he says, leaning back. "After my mother's death, my sister used to tell me stories. She would talk for hours about anything I asked, and when she didn't know, she made it up. Would that help?"

I smile, imagining the indomitable Donna di Rosa performing this act of tenderness for her little brother. "Yes, I think it might."

Paolo stretches his legs long and reaches an arm around me.

"Here," he says, patting his chest. "Rest your head. Close your eyes. What would you like me to speak of?"

I think for a moment. "Yourself," I say simply. "I know nothing about you. Sing me the ballad of Paolo di Rosa."

He laughs. "Very well. I was born in Firenze, the greatest city on earth, in the year of our Lord 1329. . . ."

I listen to his warm voice and the sound of his heart beating, steady as a drum. He tells me about growing up in Florence with three sisters and an older brother. He tells me of his father, a banker of great wealth. Mostly, though, he speaks of his mother.

"She was an angel," he says. "I am certain most boys would say this about their mother. But I speak the truth, Eleonora: she was the most beautiful woman in the city. And she was famous for her singing—she had a voice like a nightingale.

"My father could not believe his luck when she agreed to marry him. She could do no wrong. But he is a proud man, with a vein of cruelty in him like a fault in a piece of marble. He was hard on his sons. My brother rose to the challenge, succeeded in everything he did. But I, the younger son, the musician, the artist, I did not impress him. I was too sensitive, too *femminile*. Not interested in swordplay or horsemanship. Not what he thought a son should be. My mother shielded me from the worst of his disappointment. I was her favorite, you see. I was twelve when she died of the sweating sickness, and my father could not bear to be reminded of her. He performed his role, did his duty for the city and his businesses, but every night he drank until he couldn't walk. He beat me. Small scuffles at first—a shove or a clumsy punch. But the blows fell harder and harder. He came into my room one night when I was playing the lute, took it from me, and threw me against the wall. I woke up hours later with a bump on my head the size of a goose's egg."

His story cuts to my bones. I cannot imagine Paolo—gifted, playful, exquisite Paolo—the victim of such ugly violence. "How did you escape?"

"My oldest sister, Imilia, married a Neapolitan nobleman and became a lady-in-waiting to Giovanna. I wrote to her, begged her to send for me. She found me the position and made my introduction at court. I owe her so much. I doubt I would have survived another year in Florence."

Paolo speaks for a long time, his musical voice light and flexible. He tells me about the death of Andreas and the terror when Louis's Hungarian army descended on Naples.

"We never thought we would survive," he says. "The court raced to the boats, but citizens gathered in the streets, throwing stones and rotten food. They were furious that Giovanna was abandoning her city, but she had no choice. Luigi barely made it onto his ship. Louis killed his entire family."

He shifts beneath me. "Are you still awake, Eleonora?" he whispers.

"I'm awake," I whisper back.

"It's very late," he says. "So late that it's almost tomorrow. You should get some sleep."

I do not move. I am suddenly aware of the muscles of his chest beneath me, the fast thud of my own heart beside his. I sit up, feeling the same hollow ache in my belly as when I said goodbye to David. The same loneliness.

"Paolo," I ask, "why did you tell me all that?"

He laughs. "Because you asked me to."

"But why did you tell me the truth?"

I sense him smiling through the darkness. "Because, little lioness," he says gently, "I know this: when you are in the grief of your life, when it is so dark you cannot see the next step, it is good to remember that you do not suffer alone."

His arm around me is so warm. All those long nights, remembering David's lips on my wrist. I ache for that all-encompassing hunger to engulf me, drown out the pain. But Margot was right. David was right. No world exists in which we can be together.

I lean forward slowly, inch by inch, until I feel Paolo's warm breath on my face. I kiss him.

He does not turn his head away. But neither does he reach up and hold me to him. His lips beneath mine are soft but unmoving.

I pull back.

How stupid I am. I do not feel the same deep thirst for Paolo that I felt for David. I kissed him because my body is starving for comfort. And now I have ruined our friendship, which I cannot afford to lose.

"I'm sorry," I say, covering my face with my hands. "I'm so sorry. I wasn't thinking—"

Paolo reaches out for me, gently pries my hands from my face and holds them tightly.

"Eleonora," he says quietly, "I shall tell you one more truth tonight."

I open my eyes on the dark shape of him, shame still burning my throat.

"If it were in my power to give you what you want, as God is my witness I would do it," he says. "But I cannot. I shall never send you love letters. I shall never kiss you. It is not from lack of love that I tell you this, but quite the opposite. I shall never lie with any woman. I shall never marry, unless my family forces marriage upon me."

He raises my hands to his lips, presses a kiss into my fingers.

"I love you," he whispers, "as a friend and a sister, but I shall never *love* you."

I sit, frozen, as his words sink in, the honor and weight of what he has shared with me. This is a man who came to find me tonight, who shared a secret that could end his life. I reach my arms around his neck, as a friend, a sister would do. I breathe in the peppery smell of his skin.

"I am your friend," I say, "now and forever."

His arms encircle me. We hold each other tightly in the darkness; another memory for my cache of hope.

Chapter Twenty

June 1348

One morning in early June, a month before her child is expected, Joanna complains of labor pains.

They are not true contractions: the pain is irregular, and there is no other sign the baby is coming. But they distress her. She paces the room like a cat, her mind tuned anxiously to the subtle language of her body.

I search my mother's book for a tea that will calm the womb. I find the recipe, run my fingers along the slanting letters, scan the row of ingredients. *Nettles. Red clover. Peppermint.*

Thank God it is summer. Peppermint I have, but red clover and nettles will require a trip to the banks of the Rhône. I could send Briant or another boy from the kitchens, but it is a hot, clear day, and I relish the thought of walking through the north gate with the sun on my face, alone.

Guigo is out, so I leave him a note and walk through the guarded gates of the palace. Clement left for Étoile-sur-Rhône three days ago and the city is oddly quiet in his absence. Although I hear the far-off call of the corpse cart driver, and the smoke from Guigo's bonfires smudges the blue sky, my spirit rises. Today there will be dirt under my fingers instead of blood, the smell of living, growing things in my nostrils.

But as soon as I turn north on the Magna Carreira, I know something is wrong.

The wide road is full of people, more people than I have seen since Queen Joanna's procession, all walking south. They march alone or in knots, and the air buzzes with their voices, as angry and indiscernible as a swarm of wasps. Most of them are peasants, but there are noblemen, too; here and there a chain glints, the sun catches on jewel tones amid the sea of brown homespun flax. There are no kerchiefs held to faces, no amulets gripped like crucifixes. My skin prickles as I realize every face, noble or rustic, wears the same expression: fury.

Without thinking, I join the crowd.

I am borne through the street like a leaf in a stream. With every street crossed our numbers swell until, jostling and elbowing, we pour into the Place Saint-Agricol.

The sun glows on the church's golden stone walls, where a hasty scaffold has been built. Pacing across it, his black cassock streaming behind him, is Father Loup.

Fear floods my veins. I must get out of here before he sees me.

"Not two months past, my children," he rasps, his tattered voice already hoarse from shouting, "we marked the rebirth of our Lord Jesus Christ. But so joyous were we to celebrate his miraculous return from death, to break our Lenten fast, that we forget who killed him! Who crucified Christ and left him to rot on the cross? Who killed God's son?" He gazes out over the packed square, his gnarled hands outstretched and quivering. "*Who?*"

"*The Jews!*" shrieks the mob.

"And who alone, in our great city and our sister cities, is unmarked by this pestilence? Whose children still live? Whose parents still care for them?"

"*The Jews!*" the mob repeats.

Lies, hateful lies. But these people do not know, would not care, that the Jewish cemeteries are as full of plague dead as their Christian ones.

A woman with long, greasy hair standing before the makeshift pulpit raises her arms to the sky and screams, "They killed my children! They killed my children!" until the man standing beside her pulls her back and she collapses, sobbing, against his chest.

"Here," Father Loup cries, "under the nose of God's vassal on earth, Jews have been caught poisoning our wells. And what has the Holy Father done?"

"*NOTHING!*" answers the crowd furiously. Cold sweat beads my forehead. I must get back to the palace, I must tell Guigo—but then I see him, standing five paces from the hateful old priest, his traitorous hair gleaming like a coin. Erec. As I watch, he turns to say something to a pockmarked youth beside him and shows me his unmistakable profile.

I look about wildly for my escape. Fifteen paces backward and to my right I spot the mouth of an alley that, I know, twists sharply away from the square and back to the palace. I will have to elbow my way through.

"In Carcassonne and Narbonne our brothers and sisters have wisely burned these vipers in their nests," shrieks Loup. "And the pestilence has already released its hold in their city. But here, in Avignon, the seat of the Mother Church, what have we done?"

"*NOTHING!*" repeats the mob.

With my heart in my throat, I sneak another glance at the scaffold.

Erec is staring right at me.

Every muscle screams to run, but I force myself to be still. I stand up straighter. I meet his gaze.

He holds my eyes for an endless moment. Then he smiles, a cold and wolfish smile, and turns back to the priest.

A shiver runs through me. Erec is no longer my friend, my sister's lover. In this war against an invisible foe, he has chosen an enemy he can see. The Jews are his enemy. I am his enemy.

"I ask you, brothers and sisters in Christ," cries Loup, his voice carrying to every corner of the square, "to take it upon yourselves and do what the pope in his foolish weakness will not. I ask you to protect your families from this threat. . . ."

Pushing through the wall of people behind me, keeping my head down, I force my way to the alley.

As I reach the twisted cobblestones, the crowd behind me roars.

I run straight to the Place Jérusalem.

Madame Farissol opens the door to my frantic hammering, her surprise quickly replaced by a bright smile.

"Mademoiselle Blanchet!" she exclaims, ushering me inside. "We did not expect you. Is Dr. de Chauliac—"

"Guigo isn't here," I interrupt breathlessly. "Just me. I need to speak to David."

She arches an eyebrow as she takes in the red splotches in my cheeks, the strands of hair escaping their pins. "Are you all right?"

"I'm fine," I lie. "Forgive my rudeness. It's urgent."

"David's just down the street," she says, reaching for her cap. "I'll fetch him."

I pace the flagstones and chew my fingernails, rehearsing the words that will explain the force of the threat he faces. But when the door opens and David stands on the threshold behind Madame Farissol, looking tall and concerned and so, so beautiful, the script flies from my head.

"Elea?" His dark eyes hook into mine. I want to run to him. I want to throw my arms around him and bury my face in his neck. "Is everything all right?"

I nod, hide my shaking hands behind my back. "I need to speak with you."

He takes a half step toward me, concern creasing his forehead. "What has happened?"

I glance at Madame Farissol. It doesn't seem right for her to hear the hateful words from my mouth.

"You may speak in the kitchen," she says, inclining her head in its direction.

David walks behind me across the hall, past the dining table and the fireplace with its red leather chairs. Feeling Madame Farissol's eyes, I resist the urge to look over my shoulder at him. She might see something in my face that I haven't yet named.

The kitchen is as I remembered it, gleaming copper pots and whitewashed walls. David pulls a chair away from the table for me, but I make no move to sit in it.

"Elea, what has happened? You look as though you've seen a ghost."

I wrap my arms across my chest, afraid I'll reach for him. "There was a mob in the Place Saint-Agricol."

His eyes narrow. "What kind of mob?"

"The lynching kind," I say. "The priest repeated the old lie about poisoned wells, urged the crowd to take matters into their own hands. There were so many of them, David. And Pope Clement has left the city."

David's eyes drift from mine. He catches his bottom lip between his teeth, thinking.

"This is just the beginning."

His words have the hollow objectivity of prophecy. I ball my fists, remembering the palpable excitement in the Place Saint-Agricol. This fear, this hatred is a weapon searching for a target. I know this is the truth: that many, many more Jews will die.

I take a step toward him, the fear of losing him greater than the unspoken understanding keeping us apart. "You are not safe here. Not you, not your aunt and uncle. No one with a yellow circle on their sleeve."

His knuckles whiten on the chair back.

"What will you do?" I ask.

"I don't know yet." He shakes his head. "I need to think."

"I should go." I force the words out. There is nothing I want less than to leave this quiet kitchen and face the world outside. Nothing I want less than to leave him. "I'll talk to Guigo, convince him to send a message to the pope."

"I'd offer to walk you back," David says with a self-deprecating smile, "but I fear I'd offer you more danger than protection."

I swallow. I must walk past him to reach the door.

"Be careful, Elea," David says earnestly. "Go straight to the palace. Go nowhere without Guigo. No one who thinks differently than they do is safe."

I nod. I force my feet to move toward him, past him. I have nearly slipped the warm inches of air when his fingers close around my wrist.

"Just tell me this," he says softly. Turning toward his deep voice is like shutting a door on a storm. "You are well?"

"I am."

"And your people?"

The dam inside me cannot break, not here, not when there is so much at stake.

"Elea." It is not a question. The gentleness of his voice brings pricking tears to my eyes.

I shake my head, choke down the rising lump in my throat. *Not here. Not now.*

David cups my chin with his hand. The motion is so natural, so intimate that for a moment, I forget it is forbidden. He raises my face to his.

We have never been this close. In all our time together, through the hours of talking and daily wound changes, I have never felt his presence the way I feel it now.

"What happened?" His fingertips are gentle around my jaw, the expanse of him so warm and human and alive. I breathe the way Paolo taught me. *Feel the ground beneath you.*

"My father is dead." The words come out before I have the chance to swallow them.

Something deeper and sharper than sorrow flickers over his face. It is the twin of the ache inside me, the throb of a fresh wound on a scarred heart.

"Elea," he whispers. "I'm so sorry." He wraps his arms around me and pulls me to his chest.

I let myself be held. I let myself press against him the way I have wanted to for so long. In the circle of his arms the rest of the world fades, the horrors of my mind return to their tethers.

The linen of his tunic is soft under my cheek. I have seen every inch of him, but now, clothed, his body is a mystery. His heart thuds beside mine, too hard and fast for standing still. His throat contracts against my temple as he swallows.

Something opens inside me like petals unfurling, revealing a center too tender to be exposed. In this moment I want nothing more than to come apart, to dissolve into him. I want nothing more than to give myself to him, all my grief and love and desire.

"David?" Madame Farissol's voice calls from the hall.

We spring apart.

"Is everything all right?"

My heart clatters in my chest and suddenly I am sheepish, the ease of being close to him replaced by the awkwardness of separation.

"Everything is fine," David calls back. The color blazes in his cheeks. I see my own want mirrored in his face and fight the urge to rush back to him, feel him against me again. But Madame Farissol's shoes click over the flagstones in the hall. My fears and responsibilities rush in, drowning desire like the tide.

"You will tell them?" I ask.

David nods. "I'll tell them. And I'll send word to the palace when I decide what to do."

We stand for another moment, looking at each other.

"Be careful," he whispers, and presses a kiss into my hand.

Guigo looks up from the letter in his hands as I throw open the laboratory door.

"What is it?" he asks, taking in my disheveled hair and red cheeks. "Are you all right?"

"There was a huge crowd in the Place Saint-Agricol," I say, setting my empty basket on the table with a thud. Joanna will have to bear the premature contractions until I can send one of the kitchen boys to the riverbank for clover and nettles. "Father Loup incited them to take matters into their own hands, to burn the Jews like they've done in Carcassonne and Narbonne."

Guigo pours me a cup of ale, frowning. "It will never happen in Avignon," he says confidently. "The ignorant might rant and rave, but they will not act. The pope's power is too great."

"But the pope is gone!" I place the cup, untouched, on the table. "You didn't hear it. You didn't see it. We must get a message to Clement; surely he will return when he hears what has already transpired in his absence."

Guigo shakes his head. "He already knows, I assure you. His Holiness has better informants than any king. And do not forget that he left a large contingent of his guards here; they will uphold his decree, keep the city order in his name. No harm will befall the Jews in Avignon." He stands, stretches. "Do you want anything from the kitchens?"

I shake my head and resist the urge to scream.

When the door closes behind him, I walk the length of the laboratory with my fingernails between my teeth. Clement is gone, and with him, any hope for protection. The palace guard will do nothing to stop the mob's violence unless they storm the palace walls. Of this I am certain.

I feel infected by the wild energy of the crowd. Father Loup's voice scrapes through my head. And Erec. The man my sister loves. Standing front and center, smiling.

I slide Margot's letter from under my mattress.

I do not read my sister's words again. I have them memorized. But he does not deserve the gift of them. I would save her the grief of losing her love, not to death, but to hatred.

I light a taper. I kneel before the empty fireplace and touch flame to parchment.

Chapter Twenty-One

I sleep fitfully and rise early.

The sun climbs up the blue sky, but there is no sign of Guigo. This is not unusual; sometimes, these days, the exhaustion catches up with him and he oversleeps. I try to occupy myself with our plague treatise, but I am too full of anxious energy to sit still. I pace across the laboratory, the memory of David's body against mine hijacking my mind like a highwayman. I wrap my arms around myself, trying to feel him again.

At terce, Paolo arrives with Queen Joanna's summons.

"*Buongiorno, dottoressa!* It is a beautiful day and our beautiful queen is in an ugly mood."

I pull a face and follow him through the door.

Paolo is right—Joanna is in a foul mood.

"Everyone is gone," the queen mutters, staring down at the empty courtyard from the hallway windows. The little starling and her chicks are long flown, the nest in the eaves empty but for a few feathers caught in the twigs. "Safe in the country. And I, their queen, abandoned here, in this dying city."

I say nothing. Before demanding to walk, Joanna threw a shoe at her redheaded lady-in-waiting like an angry fishwife. I don't want to be the next to have my head bitten off.

"If I die," she says quietly, "my death and my child's death will be on his hands."

Her black temperament continues through the rest of the morning. I manage to avoid being a target of her ire, but she makes another of her ladies cry and sends Paolo away for playing too cheerfully. At noon she retires to her bedroom and dismisses me.

Back in the laboratory, there is still no sign of Guigo. Normally by this time he would have finished his midday meal and be halfway to a hospital or almshouse. But he has always left me word of where to meet him. Something is wrong.

My stomach rumbles, and I realize I have not had breakfast. Maybe the cooks have seen him.

The kitchens are a shadow of their former bustling glory; three-quarters of the staff, at least, have followed Clement, and those left behind have a surly look about them and do not offer me help. I spot the boy who brings my family their weekly groceries and my news to Margot. I call to him as he passes carrying a basket of eggs.

"Briant!"

He turns and smiles in recognition. "Bonjour, Mademoiselle Blanchet!" he says, setting the basket down. "Is Surgeon de Chauliac hungry?"

My heart sinks. "You have not seen him, then?"

Briant shakes his head. "Not today, mademoiselle. He usually comes by for breakfast, then again at noon. Perhaps he is still in his rooms?"

I realize that I don't even know *where* in the massive palace complex Guigo's rooms lie.

"Briant," I ask, "do you know the way to Guigo's chambers?"

He nods.

"Would you take me there?"

"Of course, mademoiselle!" he says cheerfully. Abandoning his eggs, he leads me back toward the central courtyard.

I follow Briant down the empty servants' hallways and staircases. I am thoroughly lost by the time we emerge into a hallway much like the one before Queen Joanna's chambers, although the view from the windows informs me that we are on the opposite wall of the courtyard and on the second, not the third, floor. Halfway down the corridor, Briant pauses before an unmarked door and knocks.

"This is Surgeon de Chauliac's room, mademoiselle."

There is no answer. Briant knocks again, more loudly. After a moment, he shrugs.

"He is not in, mademoi—"

I hold up a finger to silence him.

A low moan, barely audible. I try the handle—the door is unlocked. I open it onto a fine room with high ceilings and hangings on the walls, bookshelves and two chairs and a table arranged comfortably before the hearth. On the opposite side of the room stands another door that must lead to the bedchamber.

"Guigo?" I call. After a moment, I am rewarded by another low moan. I cross the room and throw the door open.

Guigo lies motionless in the bed, his face gray and beaded with perspiration.

"Guigo!" I rush to him, place a hand to his forehead. He is hot as—my heart stops—as Arye was. As my father was. His eyes flutter under my touch, but he does not try to speak.

Not again, shrieks the voice in my head. *Will this nightmare never end?*

"Briant," I say quietly, pulling the kerchief from my pocket and tying it over my nose and mouth, "fetch some water."

The boy looks to the water jug on the table, then back to me. He has not crossed the bedroom threshold. "Water, Briant," I repeat.

He avoids my eyes. "I should not be here, mistress," he says nervously. "Neither should you. The plague is here, the air is bad—" He starts to back away.

"Briant!" I shout, but he turns and runs from the room.

I take a deep breath against the rising panic. Guigo cared for my father when I could not. Now it is my turn.

I open the windows, although the day outside is hot and still, and light a fire in the hearth. Then I untangle Guigo's legs from the twisted sheets, unbutton his night shift to expose his damp skin to the air.

With a sliver of embarrassment, I raise his nightgown. My blood curdles in a mixture of hope and dread. If it is the pleuritic plague, he will be dead in a day, just like Father. If bubonic, I might be able to save him.

On Guigo's upper left thigh swells a small, purple aposteme.

The next two days pass like a waking nightmare.

I split the hours between Guigo and Joanna in a flowery haze of cleansing perfume, massaging the queen's back and pouring my medicines down Guigo's throat, my shoelaces and buttons half-undone from constant changing.

I check Guigo's bubo obsessively, waiting for it to ripen so it may be lanced and drained, but it hardly seems to grow at all. I debate calling for assistance from monks we've trained or sending for David and his uncle, but without Guigo to guide me, my confidence falters.

From the depths of his fever, he raves. But the first morning he is lucid for half an hour after his dose of feverfew tonic and walks me through the surgery.

"You must wait until it ripens," he says weakly. "Until it looks as

David's looked, remember? Large and purple and ugly, like a great shiny grape. But before the poison enters the bloodstream, you must lance it as you have observed me do countless times, clean it, and suture it. Do you understand?"

"Let me fetch someone else," I plead. "Dr. Farissol—"

Guigo shakes his head. "A Jewish physician cannot attend a Christian one. I would never ask Jacob to risk so much. And those monks have less skill with a scalpel than does a butcher. You know the steps better than anyone but me."

"But the queen," I press on. "Her child could come any day—"

"Have you told her I have the plague?" Guigo asks, his dulled gaze suddenly sharp.

"No." I have kept it from her, from Paolo and the rest of them, as if by speaking the words Guigo's illness would suddenly become real.

"Good. Don't. If she knows, she may forbid you from treating me."

"I can find someone else to attend to the queen," I say frantically. "There must be someone, some midwife—"

"No one else in Avignon can deliver that child safely but you," Guigo interrupts. "It is not fair, what God demands of you. It is not just. But this is what you asked me for, Elea. This is what a physician is."

Twenty minutes later he does not know I am in the room.

That night I collapse into bed, my mind and body exhausted, and drop immediately into sleep. But terrible dreams wait for me on the other side of consciousness. Joanna calls me to her quarters, but she is not pregnant, she has the plague; an enormous bubo the size of her swollen belly balloons on her neck. I ask Guigo what to do but he just laughs. Joanna screams, the room swims with jeering faces. I lance the aposteme: pus and blood drench the walls, the floor. And inside the loose skin, at the heart of the bubo, lies a stillborn baby.

On the third day of Guigo's illness the bubo has swollen to a tumor the size of a strawberry and he does not surface from the fever, not even after my medicine.

Tomorrow, I think, readying my supplies on the table beside his bed. *Tomorrow I will excise the bubo, and suture it, and Guigo will live.*

I calm my nerves by naming the items as I place them in a neat line. *Awl. Sheep's gut thread. Scalpel.* As I lift the bottle of blood-cleansing tonic, it feels too light in my hand. I hold it up to the window; there is only enough for two or three more doses. It would take a full day to brew more, so I tromp to the kitchens for someone to send for the bottles I left at home.

A week ago, the long hall bustled with people and smells; now half a dozen men and women remain to perform the work of twoscore.

"I need someone to run an errand," I call. A few of them raise peaked faces. "I need medicine fetched from the rue des Lices."

No one steps forward.

"I will pay a *denier,*" I say. "A *denier* for twenty minutes of your time."

A man tending the roasting fire wipes his forehead with his sleeve. "You won't get no one to leave the palace for a *sou,* mademoiselle," he says. "No one will risk the bad air."

He turns his attention back to the flames. There is nothing for it, then. I must go home.

The streets are empty and silent, but as I walk the familiar route, the back of my neck tingles with the unshakable feeling of being watched. I swivel my head from one dark-windowed house to the next, but no faces peer back from the gloom, no eyes glimmer between the boards. I pick up my pace.

At the turn of the rue des Lices, one of Guigo's bonfires smolders gamely on the blackened cobblestones, its ashes thickening the air like snow. I brush them from my sleeves as I pass and try not to think of Margot's desperate plea to Erec curling in the fire, swept up by the scullery maid like common cinders.

Perhaps she will not ask, I think as my feet follow the curving street. Perhaps I will not have to lie to her.

I hear Baldoin's happy bark a block away.

Anes opens the door before I even have the chance to knock. "My lamb!" she exclaims, trying in vain to keep Baldoin inside. He muscles past her, tail wagging, and sniffs my skirts.

Anes moves to embrace me, but I hold her off.

"Is everything all right?" she asks. In the darkness behind her, I hear Margot's footsteps.

"Guigo has the plague," I reply dully.

Anes's hands fly to her mouth.

"The bubonic form. I came for the bottles of tonic."

"I'll fetch them," she says. "Straightaway."

And I am left alone on the threshold with Margot and Baldoin.

My sister's cheeks have lost their bloom; the crescents beneath her eyes lie deeper. She frowns, and I wonder if she marks identical changes in me.

"I am sorry about Guigo," she says. "But he is strong. And he has taught you well."

"I am sorry that I am his only hope."

Margot makes an impatient sound. "He is lucky to have you. No one else would have stayed."

The silence stretches between us like arms. "Elea," she says, more gently. "I hope you have not stayed away from home these last weeks because of me."

My eyes jerk up to her face. But there is no blame there, no anger.

"You don't have to avoid me, Elea. I have my answer."

"You do?"

Margot nods. "Erec hasn't responded to my letter. He doesn't want to marry me."

My heart drops like something swallowed. "Margot," I begin, "there's something you should—"

"He was always proud." I hear the tightness in her throat, the effort it costs to keep her voice steady. "But I thought . . . I thought—"

"He's different." It takes all my willpower not to reach for her hand. "He is changed, Margot. You must believe me when I tell you he is not the man you loved. He is harder."

She drops her eyes to the rushes. "And I am softer," she says quietly. "All those rules. All that misery, all that suffering. For what?"

Erec chose hatred when he could have had happiness. Fear and blame have pulled us apart when we should all be mourning together. Will nothing come of all this suffering but more suffering?

"I am so sorry," Margot says.

An unpleasant jolt, hearing the words I should be saying to her. "What for?"

"For telling you to kill your feelings for that man." She looks up, looks past me. "What was his name?"

"David." The two syllables seem to conjure him, and I close my eyes against the sensation of his lips on my wrist, the memory of his long, tapered fingers.

Anes's footsteps fall in the hall. Our time is short.

"David," my sister repeats. His name sounds so sweet in her mouth. "Make me another promise," she says. The fogginess has evaporated from her eyes; a brightness glows in each like a little flame. "If you have another chance for happiness, take it. I wish I had."

Chapter Twenty-Two

The next morning after a cursory hour with Joanna, I send to the kitchens for aqua vitae, hot water, and linen to be brought to Guigo's quarters. As I climb the stairs, I repeat the steps of the surgery for the hundredth time and wish, wildly, that David were here. That *anyone* were here. That the surgery that may result in the death of the most famous doctor in Christendom did not fall to me and me alone.

I approach the bed, speaking through my kerchief as though he can hear me.

"Queen Joanna was in a rare state this morning," I say, lifting the sheets. "She is as temperamental as a nest of hornets. The baby had better be born soon or Donna di Rosa—"

The bubo is dark purple and so swollen that the skin around it is tight and shiny, like a ripe plum. And through the ashy skin, the veins leading away from it stand out starkly black.

The blood poisoning has started. I waited too long. Am I too late? Have I killed him?

When Briant raps on the door with the supplies, I have threaded the awl and re-cauterized the scalpel. There is no sign of the boy in the corridor, so I carry the steaming pitcher, alcohol, and stack of linen into the room myself. I swab the aposteme with aqua vitae, then reach for my mother's blade. I say a prayer that my hands might be as steady as hers, my mind as clear.

"I will cut on three," I say to my unconscious mentor, taking the edges of the bubo in my left hand and hovering the scalpel tip above the engorged skin. "One . . . two . . . *three.*"

I cut through the tight skin like paper, and the thick contents burst, dribbling in a viscous river down Guigo's thigh. He jumps at the incision but then lies motionless.

I squeeze the edges of the bubo to ensure it is fully drained, then pour alcohol over it once, twice, three times. I sop up the mess and drop the rags on the floor. Then I reach for the awl and thread.

It takes me three times as long as Guigo to close the wound, and my stitches are uneven and sloppy, but I finish it.

I pack the wound with the poultice and wrap it, pour blood-cleansing tonic between Guigo's lips and watch him swallow. Then place a hand on his shoulder and pray that far below the surface of his consciousness, in the depths of his fever, he hears me.

"I have done what I can, my friend," I say, watching the even rise and fall of his chest. "It is up to you now. If anyone can fight this plague, it is you."

I force myself from the room, out of the fetid air and into the breezeless afternoon. I don't remember walking through the halls, down the stairs, but the next thing I know I'm standing in the laboratory, blissfully alone.

I take a double sleeping draught and collapse into bed, swallowed, at last, by sleep.

BAM BAM BAM.

I sit straight up in the cot with my heart hammering against my ribs.

BAM BAM.

Through the fog in my head the events of yesterday come, interwoven still with strange dreams. *Guigo.*

With shaking hands, I feel for the flint on the bedside table.

"Eleonora! Are you there?" Paolo's voice calls through the door.

"Paolo?" I murmur, lighting the candle and reaching for my robe.

"Of course it's Paolo, you ass! Who else would it be, in the middle of the night? *Porco cane!*"

I raise the bar and open the door.

My flickering candle falls on Paolo's tousled hair, his face puffy with sleep. "What is it?" I ask, still thick and slow from the valerian tonic.

"*What is it?*" he echoes in a hiss. "Oh, nothing, I just thought I would come serenade you in the middle of the night. Regina Giovanna is in labor, you dolt!"

It takes a moment for his words to permeate, like syrup poured on a cake, but then my mind starts to move and my body follows. I dress hastily behind the screen, then race to the shelf of herbs and sweep them all into my basket. I take my mother's book from its safe hiding place inside a mildewed medical atlas on the bookcase. All the while Paolo mutters under his breath in Neapolitan.

Together we jog down the dark hallways, up two sets of staircases and past the guards, to the queen's bedroom door.

Paolo squeezes my shoulder. "*Buona fortuna, dottoressa.*"

I face the painted wood, raise my hand, and knock.

A very harried-looking Donna di Rosa opens the door.

"What kept you so long?"

I ignore her—she doesn't know this is my second medical emergency of the day—and step into the room. It is like walking into a furnace. Despite the warm summer night, the heavy curtains are drawn and a fire blazes in the hearth. Joanna's ladies-in-waiting stand at the foot of the bed, their lovely faces bright with perspiration. One of them raises a bottle and spritzes me with the cloying scent of tuberose.

Joanna sits up in bed, her golden hair plastered to her forehead. Her cheeks are flushed with the heat, but the rest of her face is very pale. An image of my mother flashes through my mind, and I shake my head to clear it. *No. This child, this mother will live.*

Joanna glares at me as I enter. "Where have you—" she starts, but another contraction overtakes her; she cries out through gritted teeth. I set down my basket and hurry to the bedside.

The queen's pulse is fast and shallow. The wave passes, and she collapses against the pillows.

"How long between contractions?" I ask Donna di Rosa as I feel Joanna's forehead. Hot and damp, not cold and clammy. Good.

"About three minutes," she says.

"Has her water broken?"

Donna di Rosa nods. "Half an hour ago."

"Good." I turn to the ladies-in-waiting. "Kill the fire. Open the windows. Her Majesty needs air."

As they flutter about the room like a flock of unhelpful birds, Donna di Rosa and I position ourselves on either side of the bed and hold Joanna's hands as the contractions come quicker and harder.

"Dio è con te," Donna di Rosa whispers through each. *"Dio è con te, Mia Regina."*

The queen does not answer. She pants like a dog, face still scarlet despite the breeze from the open windows, her chemise plastered to her breasts and belly and translucent with sweat.

When I assisted my mother there was always a moment when the laboring woman—no matter how noble, how beautiful, how rich—

transformed before my eyes. When the body took over, discarding the trappings of society at its feet and reminding us of what we truly are.

Not a minute later another contraction grips her. When it is over, I touch a wet cloth to her forehead. "Your Majesty"—her exhausted eyes flutter open and focus on me—"are you ready to push?"

She takes a deep breath, gathers her strength. She nods.

"By dawn," I say bracingly, "Naples will have a new princess."

Joanna smiles. Then the next wave of pain begins and her grip on my hand tightens.

"*Push!*" I yell. Joanna screams, bearing down with all her might.

"That's it," I shout, "*PUSH!*"

I raise the hem of her chemise and position myself before the birth canal. The opening is wide and red. With an effort that bulges the veins in Joanna's temples, a bit of pink liquid dribbles onto the coverlet. But no child is yet visible.

Donna di Rosa wipes the queen's brow and clucks over her like a Neapolitan mother hen.

Another contraction comes quickly, and Joanna pushes again, hard.

I can see the baby's head now, covered in sticky blood and damp hair. With another powerful push, the forehead comes into view.

My heart stops. The baby's face points up, toward Joanna's pubic bone, instead of backward toward her tailbone.

Time seems to slow as I flip back through my memories, through dozens of births, to a wintery night, a first-time mother and a baby boy, stillborn with the umbilical cord tight around his neck.

But before that, before the dead child was delivered and the mother's sobs filled the air, my mother had tried to turn him.

"Your Majesty," I say, "I need you to move. Your baby is facing the wrong way."

Panic flashes across her face.

"It's all right," I say in a voice that sounds much more confident than I feel. "I can turn her. But you must get on your hands and knees."

Joanna looks from me to Donna di Rosa, who nods encouragingly.

"Trust Eleonora, Your Majesty. She is skilled beyond her years."

I could kiss her.

Joanna obeys. Donna di Rosa and I help her clumsily to her hands and knees on the high mattress. I must act quickly, before the next contraction comes.

"Excuse me, Your Majesty," I say, "I must reach inside you to move the child."

Without pausing to think, I reach my fingers through the delicate pink tissue of the birth canal and feel for the edges of the baby's soft head. Joanna's breathing quickens. How painful it must be. My fingertips inch over the skull like pincers, grasping below the tiny ear . . . and my stomach plummets. Just as I feared, the umbilical cord is wrapped around the child's neck like a noose.

A vision of Andreas of Hungary materializes unbidden in my mind, his body hanging limp and lifeless from the balcony. I chase the specter from my thoughts.

This child deserves to live. I pray with all my might, feeling the life creep out of her with every strangled heartbeat. *She is innocent. She deserves to live.*

Joanna's cry splinters my focus. Another contraction is starting, she must push. Her body will do it even if she tries to fight the urge. If she pushes the child out in this position, the cord will tighten, and the princess will die.

I grasp the child's head with my fingers and press it up, back into the womb.

Joanna screams, but she does not flinch. Very slowly I turn the child's head to the right—my fingers meet tension, the cord tightens—and then, with sweat dripping into my eyes and Joanna bellowing like a cow, I turn her to the left. The cord loosens a little.

I fight for every hairsbreadth, feeling the baby start to shift and the noose loosen, willing my fingers not to cramp.

Joanna screams again as another contraction takes her but this time, I am ready. When she pushes, I turn the child, riding the force of the contraction. I catch the slippery baby in my hands.

Joanna gives a final shuddering sob and collapses. I stare at the child in my hands, blue and bruised, silent. Still.

My mother's voice cuts through my mind. I flip the curled baby face down and hit her between her shoulder blades.

"Breathe, damn it!" I cry, just as my mother yelled on that cold winter night.

There is an earsplitting silence. No one moves. No one breathes.

And then, from the shape in my hands, a rattling gasp. A sticky gulp of air. And a wail.

Joanna names her daughter Catherine. The baby is undeniably homely with her bruised face, weirdly elongated head, and flattened nose—all marks of her position in the pelvis—but Joanna coos over her adoringly. Her ladies shoot one another apprehensive looks from the corners of their eyes, but I know the bruises will fade, her head will become round, her nose will grow normally.

Childbirth is hard on the baby as well as the mother. One would think God would have designed the process by which we all come into the world better, but of course the Church tells us the pain of childbirth is punishment for original sin. That reasoning always made my mother snort.

"And horses?" she would mutter. "Cats? Dogs? What sin have they committed?"

Once the cord is cut and tied, the afterbirth delivered, and little Catherine latched contentedly on Joanna's breast, I collapse into a chair in the antechamber. One of the ladies brings me a plate of food and a cup of wine, but I am too tired to eat. I gaze silently out the window, my mind blank and my body exhausted in a satisfied sort of way.

If I had not been the one to deliver her, if my mother had not been the midwife she was, Joanna might have lost her child this morning. Beneath the new-baby mews emanating from the queen's bedchamber, I whisper a prayer for those I could not save. My little brother, who was never given the chance to breathe. My mother, who rescued so many women from childbed only to perish there herself. But as dawn breaks over the city and sets the Rhône sparkling, I cannot help but smile with gratitude and—God forgive me—pride. I did it. Catherine lives. Whatever is to come, whatever horrors still await, I pulled a new soul into the world today.

Paolo pads into the room on his cat's feet and spots me with a grin. "*La dottoressa!* How is our queen? Does Naples have a new prince?"

"Prin*cess*," I answer. "The queen is well. She is resting."

Paolo drops into the chair across from me and filches a custard tart from the plate in my hands.

"Women always make such a fuss over these things," he says, putting the whole pastry in his mouth, "but they seem to always work out in the end."

I open my mouth furiously.

"I was only joking, *leonessa*!" Paolo says thickly. "One look at your face would tell me that you had a most trying night. What do I know about the miracle of birth, eh? Only you will be wanting to be not *so good* at delivering babies, otherwise our queen will never set you free. Joanna and Luigi are certain to have enough babies to man the army of Naples."

As if summoned by Paolo's words, the door bursts open and Luigi enters the antechamber. His face is bloated with interrupted sleep, but his expansive happiness fills the room.

"Where is she?" he booms. "Where is my daughter?"

I rise from my chair with some effort and manage an ungraceful curtsy. "Her Majesty and your daughter are resting, Your Highness."

Luigi bounds over to me, takes me in his arms, spins me around, sets me back down on my chair, and kisses me on both cheeks. He smells very strongly of wine.

"*Grazie mille, dottoressa!*" he says happily, striding to the door of Joanna's chamber. "You have done God's work tonight!"

Heat flushes up my neck and across my face. "I'm going to bed," I announce, avoiding the hilarious expression on Paolo's face. "Her Majesty may call if she needs me."

"And Prince Luigi, too?" Paolo adds.

I ignore him. He puts another tart in his mouth and watches me leave.

Chapter Twenty-Three

Guigo hovers between safety and disaster like a ship caught in a storm.

The fever waxes and wanes. He speaks through his dreams; mostly it's gibberish, but occasionally I pick out a sentence. "*Yes, Your Holiness*," or "*Write this down now*," which always makes me smile—even from the edge of oblivion, Guigo bosses me.

The wound heals well. I dress it by feel: sometimes a bit more comfrey, a little less yarrow. When the tissue is dry, I use an ointment of duck grease and rose oil to moisten it. When it is weepy, I leave the bandages off for a few hours and let it breathe.

Joanna is as love drunk as any mother I've seen. All day she sits up in bed with baby Catherine on her breast, cooing down at her and stroking her tiny fingers with tender adulation. She refuses to hire a wet nurse, and although Donna di Rosa asks me privately to change the queen's mind—*She must conceive again, as quickly as possible, a boy this time*—I do not try to convince her. It warms my heart to see Joanna enjoying so deeply one of the few unadulterated joys of womanhood.

By the end of the second day, Guigo recognizes me between the bouts of fever. With my assistance he can sit up to take my tonic before collapsing back into fitful sleep. On the third day, he swallows a few spoonfuls of broth and, in a first glimpse of his old self, he asks for meat and cheese.

"If I brought you that now you would lose your bowels, and I would have to clean it up," I say, checking his wound. Guigo laughs a little feeble laugh that turns into a cough. When I come back that night, the fever has returned, and he does not know who I am.

Five days after Princess Catherine's birth, I pass the morning applying hot compresses to the queen's clogged milk duct, then return to the laboratory to wash my face and eat something before spending the afternoon in Guigo's quarters.

I freeze halfway across the courtyard. There is a man standing before the door.

My pulse races as I think, suddenly, of Erec, of his broad-shouldered silhouette in the Place Saint-Agricol. But the man who now steps from shadows into honey-thick sunlight is well-dressed and slender.

The blood spins to the tips of my fingers. It is David.

We stare at each other for a long moment. The buzz of cicadas and the damp press of summer fade until there is just him, just his dark eyes and fine-boned face, the corners of his mouth tugging up into a smile.

We speak at the same time.

"I thought you'd—"

"I came—"

We stop mid-sentence, waiting for the other to finish. David laughs, and relief washes over me: he is not here with bad news. But he is still here, in Avignon, after all my prayers for him to be far away and safe.

"Can I speak with you?" he asks, stepping closer. The yellow felt on his arm blinks like an eye.

I glance around the courtyard. It is empty, the archway to the stables filled with nothing but slanting shade.

"Of course." I walk past David and pull the laboratory key from the pouch on my waist. "Come in."

My fingers fumble on the metal under David's eyes. The smell of him envelops me, olive oil soap and sun-dried linen. The key clicks, the bolts turn. The door sighs open.

I step aside and hold my breath as he brushes past me, acutely aware of his dimensions, his long-limbed body taking up so much more than its fair share of space.

"You are well?" he asks.

I close and bar the door, turn to face him with my back against the oak. "I am. But Guigo has the plague."

David's face falls.

"He's all right," I say quickly. "At least, I believe he *will* be. It was the bubonic form, thank God. I lanced the bubo a week ago, but since then—"

David takes a step toward me. "You lanced it?"

I nod.

"And sutured it?"

"Yes."

"By yourself?"

"I begged him to let me send for you and Dr. Farissol, but he wouldn't let me. He didn't want you to risk—"

"Elea," he interrupts, his face cracking into a smile. "You are extraordinary."

I fight a grin for his pride in me. "Guigo is not out of danger. He is still feverish and weak."

"I am sure he will survive. If anyone can save him, it is you."

"What are you doing here?" The words come out before I can soften them. "I mean. I'm glad to see you, of course." I flounder. "I just thought you'd be far from Avignon by now. Somewhere safe."

"We leave tomorrow for Marseille," he says, his face serious once again. "My aunt, uncle, and a few other families. It will be much safer there for us. I wanted to leave sooner, but it took time to convince them that the threat they face here is greater than the risk of plague on the journey."

"And now?"

His mouth twists into an expression I have not seen on it before. Anger. "Last week a mob came through the Jewish Quarter," he says. "They threw stones through business windows and took anything of value. A moneylender's shop was set on fire, the strongboxes taken. But he and his family escaped. They are coming to Marseille with us."

"And the papal guard?" I ask, already knowing what the answer will be.

He shakes his head. "They did not come. We put out the fire and boarded up the shop windows. But the mob will return."

We stand in silence, drinking each other in like the first warm day of spring. Then I remember my manners. "Please, sit down." I press past him, feeling my skirt catch on his shoes as I walk to the table. "Would you like something to drink?"

He shakes his head, his eyes following me. "I can't stay—"

But then he sees the bookshelf. His mouth falls open in awe, as I was, of the volume and quality of Guigo's library. "My goodness," he breathes.

With his gaze elsewhere, I run eyes over the room and realize how messy it is. There are plates and cups in the basin, the table is covered with papers. And I did not make my bed.

"Have you read all these?" he asks, stepping closer and inspecting the titles on the spines.

I take advantage of his distraction to hastily pull the coverlet over my crumpled sheets and stack the leaves of parchment on the table.

"All the ones written in French and Latin."

David turns away from the bookshelf.

"Some of them are in Greek, which Guigo can read," I ramble.

He steps closer. The look in his eyes takes my breath, like he is a man lost in the desert and I, a river.

And he kisses me.

His lips are warm, and against their insistent strength my defenses melt. His hands snake through my hair, around my waist, pull me closer and tighter, and although I sense he is trying to be gentle, I feel the power and hunger behind the pressure of his body against mine. The heat spreads across my chest and belly to throb deep within me and in this moment, I want nothing more than to be consumed by it.

But David's fingers slacken. He pulls his lips from mine, releases my waist. Cold air floods the space between us.

"I'm sorry," he says. His color is high, his eyes brilliant.

His chest rises and falls with the effort of breaking away from me. The parts of me that were pressed against him ache. I yearn to cross the desolate inches and feel him again.

"There is nothing to apologize for."

"I did not only come here today to say goodbye." I watch him gather courage, swallow. "I told you, once, about the Kingdom of Granada. It is warm there, I am told, and very beautiful. People like us are left alone, to live our lives as we see fit."

Suddenly I know what he came to ask me. It takes every ounce of strength I have not to close the space between us again, silence his voice with a kiss, because I know what my answer must be.

"I want you to come with me."

Something in my face makes him open his empty palms to the ceiling. "Do not mistake me," he says quickly. "I am not trying to trap you in sin. We could travel under the guise of brother and sister, sleep in separate rooms. You would owe me nothing, Elea. But I could help set you up as an herbalist in Granada with your own home, your own business. Your own life. And when we are gone, this hatred will need another target. I fear for you, for anyone who thinks differently than they do."

"David." His name comes out of me the way I might, in another life, sigh it into the smooth skin of his neck.

He lowers his hands. "You need not give me your answer now. Think on it. I'll stay in Marseille a week or so, ensure my aunt and uncle are comfortable in my family home. Then I'll take a ship for Valencia, and travel on horseback to Granada."

Make me another promise, my sister said. *If you have another chance for happiness, take it.* But I would never forgive myself for leaving her.

"I cannot go with you," I say, my voice breaking. "I cannot leave Margot. And Guigo is not yet recovered. They need me."

David drops his head.

"I am sorry," I whisper.

He lifts his eyes to mine, the fire in them extinguished.

"I understand." His voice is so gentle it makes my throat burn. He reaches out and takes my hand in his, raises it to his mouth. My eyes close as his breath brushes my skin, followed by the soft pressure of his lips. Desire for him rises inside me, desire to knot my wrists about his neck and taste him again, to make good my promise to Margot. But he lowers my hand, relinquishes my fingers, steps away. When I open my eyes, he is standing at the threshold.

"Be well, Elea," he says. "I will never forget you."

I watch him from the windows until he disappears from my view. I press my fingernails into my palms to hold myself here, to quiet the voice inside me screaming to run after him. I imagine him walking through the sunshine to the Place Jérusalem, packing his belongings in the bedroom overlooking the silvery sycamore trees. The shadows stretch, the day dies, but still I do not abandon my vigil, wishing he would reappear and run across the courtyard and take me in his arms again.

But he is gone.

The next morning, there is a knock at the door.

I open it, expecting Paolo. But a manservant, dressed in Joanna's livery, stands on the threshold.

"A message for Mademoiselle Blanchet." He holds out a letter sealed with the crest of Anjou. "From Her Majesty the Queen."

"Thank you." As soon as he has bowed and turned away, I break the seal.

We require your presence in our chambers at noon.

GR

As I change Guigo's bandages and administer his medicines, I consider the possible reasons for Joanna's summons. She cannot be ill, nor Catherine, or she would send for me at once. Perhaps she is happy with my service and wants to award me with a gift—I have seen her do so for other members of her household. How pleased Margot would be.

At a quarter to noon, I don my blue dress, tidy my hair, and make my way to Joanna's quarters. Instead of admitting me at once, the guards wait with their lances crossed until I have been announced. The door opens.

"Dottoressa Eleonora, Your Majesty," proclaims an usher. The guards uncross their lances, and I enter the room.

Queen Joanna sits in a chair in the center of the antechamber, dressed in her azure-blue gown sprinkled with silver fleur-de-lis. She is the monarch I remember from the parade, the haughty and beautiful ice queen from our first meeting all those months ago, surrounded by elegant courtiers. She gives me no smile, no warm greeting. There is no trace of the hard-won trust and respect I have cultivated these last four months.

Expectancy thickens the air. I look to Paolo for a hint, but he merely raises his eyebrows.

"Dottoressa Eleonora," Queen Joanna says imperiously, "we have received excellent news today. Praise be to God; the usurper Louis of Hungary has abandoned Naples. My city is once again free."

Her voice is measured, but I sense the exultation behind every word. I smile, so happy for her. She may finally go home.

"We will, of course, return to Naples as soon as we are packed and supplied. My advisers assure me that the plague has loosened its grip in Napoli, and we will be much safer there than we are here in Avignon. In acknowledgment of your service during our time here, and especially during the birth of the Princess Caterina, we offer you the position of midwife to the queen. You will accompany us to Naples, where you will live in our palace with your own staff. And, of course, you shall be awarded a very generous income."

My mouth is dry as kindling.

I've spent my entire life in Avignon and never thought to leave, yet here is the second offer in as many days to begin a life elsewhere. For a heady moment I allow myself to imagine it: me, Margot, and Anes sharing fine quarters in the queen's palace, a new city glinting through the windows.

Reality pulls me back into my shoes. Margot and Anes would never leave Provence, never abandon my father's house. And even if I convinced them, what then? A dangerous journey to an unknown land where they have no friends, do not speak the language nor know the customs.

And I would be a midwife. Not a physician, not Guigo's assistant, free to learn and study as I wish. Paolo's words from the morning of Catherine's birth echo in my head. *Joanna and Luigi are certain to have enough babies to man the army of Naples.* I saved Princess Catherine; I might not be so lucky a second time.

A fist closes around my heart, but I know what I must do.

"Your Majesty," I say, "your generosity astounds me. I am humbled by you and forever in your debt." I take a breath. "As much as it pains me, I cannot accept your offer."

Joanna's smile flickers.

"I have a twin sister here whom I cannot leave," I continue. "Surgeon de Chauliac and I have our work, our research on the plague. Avignon still suffers, Your Majesty. I must stay and help my city in whatever way I can. But it was the honor of my life to serve you in your pregnancy and childbirth."

The room is silent. None of the ladies meet my eye. Joanna's beautiful face is stony.

"Your refusal is disappointing," she says icily. "You have served us well and have our gratitude. You are dismissed."

I curtsy. As I rise, Joanna turns away to say something to Luigi. I walk to the door, feeling the eyes of all in the room boring into me.

"And Mademoiselle Blanchet," Joanna calls.

I freeze, my heart leaping with hope for a word of kindness, a token of our friendship—

"We shall not call for you again."

I walk back to the laboratory numbly, playing and replaying the exchange with Joanna. I know the queen's moods well enough to understand this is a response I could expect from refusing her offer, but I can't shake the nauseating feeling that I've been kicked in the gut.

Pages in Neapolitan livery rush hither and thither, their faces brighter than they have been in months with the news that they are finally, *finally* headed home. First Clement abandons Avignon, now Queen Joanna. Soon the palace will be empty but for me, wandering the echoing corridors with only the rats for company.

I try to occupy my mind by going through my notes on Guigo's illness, organizing them so, God willing, he can review the course of his symptoms and treatment when he is fully recovered. But I cannot focus. By midafternoon I give up, pour myself a cup of Guigo's wine, and open one of his romance novellas.

When the sky outside darkens and bats flit and dart above the courtyard, someone knocks on the laboratory door.

"Eleonora?" calls Paolo's voice.

I jump to my feet and open it.

Paolo stands on the threshold with a velvet bag in his hands and a scroll of parchment tucked under one arm.

"*Buonasera,*" he says, gleaming in saffron-yellow velvet. "I come bearing gifts. From *la Reina Giovanna.*"

"Gifts?" I repeat, stepping aside to let him enter. "I did not think I warranted further discussion in the Neapolitan court after the way I was dismissed, let alone gifts."

Paolo sets the bag on the table with a metallic clink and waits patiently until I meet his eyes. One cheek dimples.

"My little lioness," he says with a tease in his voice, "you are new to the ways of court. The queen was upset at your refusal, it is true. She had grown to trust you—to love you, even—and for our tragic queen, trust is worth more than gold. Of course, she was frustrated that she had lost you, your skills as well as your companionship. And your refusal, in front of all, with such lavish gifts at stake—it was humiliating for her."

I open my mouth to defend myself, but Paolo lifts a hand.

"I once told you that our queen is a kitten on the outside, a wolf on the inside. This she was forced to become to survive. She has been betrayed by her family, her friends, by those she trusted most. And so, she is fierce. She is proud. But she knows the debt she owes you. And I have the happy task of being her messenger." He hands me the sealed scroll.

Heart thudding, I break the wax and pull a candle closer to read the elegant script.

By Order of Giovanna, Queen of Naples, Sicily, and Jerusalem, Countess of Provence, we hereby award our most loyal and commendable servant Dottoressa Eleonora Blanchet the title of Midwife to her Majesty the Queen, three hundred sous for her service to the Crown, and a guarantee of safe passage throughout our kingdom.

And below, in elaborate lettering, Joanna's signature.

I stand still with the letter in my hands, reading and rereading it, but not fully comprehending.

"But this means—this means—"

"It means," Paolo interrupts me gently, "that you are a rich woman, little lioness. And you have the affection and protection of the queen. You will always have a place in her court, should you wish it." He gestures to the bag of gold on the table. "I would put that in a very safe place, Eleonora. Men would slit your throat without batting an eye for three hundred *sous*."

I cast a dubious glance at my new fortune. "I will."

Paolo peers through the window to the patch of gloaming sky. The hour is late, and the queen will want him.

"When do you leave?" I ask, desperate for him to stay a little longer.

"Tomorrow at dawn," Paolo says. "Or as close to dawn as the household can be ready, so closer to midday, I would guess. We will spend a week or so in Marseille, then take a ship to Naples."

Marseille. Where David will be, too. I dispel the thought and focus instead on Paolo, casting around my mind for something to say that will convey my feelings for him, my appreciation for his friendship.

"I . . . I will miss you, Paolo," I say lamely.

"And I, you, Eleonora." He steps forward and catches me in a tight hug. I wrap my arms around him. We stand for a long moment, Paolo's chin resting on my head, and I breathe in his smell, feel the warm velvet of his doublet against my cheek.

He releases me and strides to the laboratory door.

"Addio, leonessa," he says, tossing me a grin over his shoulder. *"Addio."*

Despite the ruckus of the Neapolitans' departure, I sleep late the next morning.

When I open my eyes, the cot is drenched in summer sunshine and the sky above the courtyard is the intense, cloudless blue that heralds another hot day.

I stretch my arms overhead and listen to the sounds of the palace: shouts in French and Italian, closing doors and wooden wheels on stone.

I stand and pour myself a cup of water from the pitcher beside the basin, eyeing the innocuous velvet bag on the table while I sip. Three hundred *sous*. More than enough to take care of Margot and Anes for life.

As I dress and braid my hair, the feeling that fills me—a gentle, seeping warmth, like the creep of sunlight over the coverlet—is so unfamiliar that it takes me a moment to name it. *Contentment*. Guigo is recovering. Princess Catherine lives. David, please God, is safely out of Avignon. After all the months of plague, of dread and suffering, I see for the first time the promise of a life after all this death.

I hum a song my mother used to sing as I slip on my shoes and pack my basket with gauze and salve. I'll check on Guigo, change his bandages. Then I'll visit my family.

A knock sounds on the laboratory door.

Imagining Paolo, come to give me a final hug, I open it with a smile. But it is not Paolo. Another man stands on the threshold. He is young, with pockmarked skin and dark hair, dressed simply in worn but clean clothing. His face is vaguely familiar, although I can't place him.

"Mademoiselle Eleanore?" He sweeps a shapeless hat off his head as he bows.

"Yes," I reply. "Who are you?"

"I was sent to fetch you," he says, straightening. "Your sister is not well. She told me where to find you."

The words make their way through my brain like honey. "Margot is ill?"

"I'm afraid so," he replies, turning his hat round and round in his hands. "Anes is with her. She thinks"—he gestures for me to step closer, drops his voice—"she thinks it is the plague."

No. No, it cannot be true. Not now, not when the tide is finally turning.

I race through the room, stuffing my basket with rolls of bandages, bottles of herbs, Guigo's surgical instruments.

My mind has already flown to the task ahead. Please, God, let it be the bubonic plague, if it is the plague. I saved Guigo. Let me save Margot.

Without another word I push past the man through the door, pick up my pace down the courtyard corridor until I am running. It is not until I have stepped into the thick summer morning beyond the palace walls that I remember the bag of gold on the table, my letter of safe passage from the queen. But those things hardly matter now.

"Mademoiselle," the young man calls, following me down the staircase to the empty plaza. "Mademoiselle!"

I take the steps two at a time, only one thought in my mind. *Margot.*

"Mademoiselle!" he shouts.

"What?" I wheel on the bottom stair and he almost crashes into me.

"Forgive me," he says anxiously, "but I was ordered to accompany you. Since His Holiness left, the city has become very dangerous."

I gaze out at the empty cobblestones. I have never heard my city this silent. No voices ring through the air, no bells, not even the rattle of corpse carts. I remember David's words, the broken shop windows and stolen strongboxes.

The man steps level with me. "Please, mademoiselle. Anes said I must stay with you and not let you out of my sight. I am to take you the back way and avoid the main streets."

"Avoid the main streets?" I repeat skeptically, turning my eyes on his scarred face. "If it is as dangerous as you say, would it not make more sense to avoid the back alleys, monsieur . . . ?"

"Henri, mademoiselle, just Henri," he says. "Anes wanted me to take you through the back streets because"—he swallows—"because a mob roams the main streets. They captured a Jewish family just three days ago. And they're on the lookout, forgive me, mademoiselle, for"—he looks around the empty plaza—"*witches,*" he whispers.

Fear drenches my spine. "Lead the way."

Henri casts a nervous glance in all directions and guides me down a smelly little alley off the plaza.

It is eerily silent between the tottering walls. Our footsteps echo against the faces of empty homes, empty businesses. A city of ghosts. And Margot, sick, scared, alone. I resist the urge to bypass Henri and sprint home, back the way I know down the Magna Carreira.

I am coming, Margot.

Henri looks over my head at the street behind us as though determining if he went too far. His profile jars me.

"How do I know you?" I ask as he pauses at a fork in the alley.

"Eh?" he mutters, looking both ways and gesturing to the left.

"I said, how do I know you?" I repeat, following him.

He looks straight ahead as he speaks. I strain to hear him.

"I lived down the street from your family," he says. "My father is the blacksmith."

"Oh. Yes, of course," I respond automatically, though I have no recollection of this. I flip through the memories of what feels like someone else's life, searching for this man's face. With difficulty I pull up an image of the forge at the end of the rue des Lices, where the street connects with the rue des Teinturiers.

Monsieur Rondet. No, Roulet. I can see him, stocky shoulders and scarred forearms, smiling at my father. Bowing as he introduces me, a child of no more than ten. And then my fingers clench into fists. Monsieur Roulet only had daughters.

I remember where I have seen that waxy, pockmarked face before. This man stood beside Erec in the mob at Place Saint-Agricol, cheering at Father Loup's speech.

My brain starts to spit up facts that don't make sense, facts that I ignored in my worry for Margot. Neither Margot nor Anes have ever been to the palace: how could they tell him where to find me? How did he get past the guards in the first place? My family did not send him. Which means—I realize, with a combination of relief and dread—that perhaps Margot's illness was fabricated to get me out of the palace. I slow my pace imperceptibly, putting a little more space between us. My eyes shoot down each street we pass, looking for anything I recognize, a sign or door or turn in the road, but I am completely lost. We have taken so many turns I don't even know in which direction we are walking. As Henri pauses at another intersection, looking right and left and then continuing straight, I turn and run.

At the next fork I turn right, then right again. I hear Henri call from behind me, "Mademoiselle? Mademoiselle Eleanore?" Then he yells at the top of his voice, "She's getting away! She's getting away!"

There must be more of them. I turn right again and nearly slam into a wall—a dead end. The brackish odor of canal water hangs in the air. If I can find the Sorgue, I can find the rue des Teinturiers, which I could navigate with my eyes closed. I backtrack and go left instead, following the smell down the narrow street as it slopes steeply, twisting like a serpent.

Another dead end. Footsteps fall behind me. I freeze, plaster myself against the wall. They pass me and turn down another way. I listen for more.

A figure appears at the turn of the street. He sees me—he shouts. I race down the steep cobblestones, slide in the muck, turn again—I feel my heart will burst before my pursuers reach me—I can hear them now, hear them calling to each other like fox hunters—I turn left away from their voices and the ground drops steeply away again, another twist and—*another dead end.*

I stare at the wall. My chest heaves. *This is the end,* I think. This is where I die. *How could I be so stupid?*

And then I remember: my mother's scalpel. I plunge my hand into the basket and search furiously—the footsteps are getting louder now, they are nearly here—and my fingers close around cold metal.

Henri rounds the corner, flanked by two men in black robes. I recognize them as the monks who brought the plague bodies to the laboratory: one with eyes set too close against a long, twitching nose, the other with cheeks like apples.

I scream. I scream as loud as I can, but there is no one to hear me in this city of the dead. Henri runs toward me, lifts his hands to cover my mouth, and I pull out the scalpel and stab him hard between the ribs. I feel his lung puncture under my blade, and he collapses with a horrible gurgling sound. The rosy-faced monk holds back with fear in his eyes, but the rat-faced monk shouts something and comes at me with his arms up. I slash wildly, and he falls back with a shriek, blood streaming from a long cut across his eye. I hold the scalpel before me like a sword as Rat Face makes another grab for me, his good eye on the blade. I hit him hard with the basket in my left hand and cut his forearm, but he catches my wrist. Metal clatters on stone as the scalpel hits the ground. I scream again, writhing, trying to throw off his grip, but his fist connects with my temple. My head explodes with color and pain. Darkness closes in, and I know no more.

Chapter Twenty-Four

The next thing I am aware of is a terrible throbbing in my head. For a while it eclipses all other senses, all thoughts.

My mind works very slowly.

Where am I?

I am lying face down on a stone floor. I try to open my eyes, but the muscles do not cooperate. I attempt to wiggle my fingers and toes, but they seem very far away. My hands, pinned underneath me, have fallen asleep and my wrists are bound. I try to bend a knee; my ankles are tied as well.

The chase comes back to me in fragments. Henri's pockmarked face. The two monks, who I've seen with Father Loup before. Pain sears above my left eye as I remember the blow.

I tune my ears to the sounds around me. My own uneven breathing against the dusty stones. Far above me, muffled male voices, footsteps. A distant rushing sound that I cannot place.

I think I am alone.

With great difficulty I roll onto my left side. The pain in my head crescendos with the effort. I try again to pry my eyelids apart. My left eye seems to be swollen shut, but my right opens a sliver.

It is very dark; the only light comes from the wooden slats of a trapdoor in the ceiling on the opposite end of the room. Barrels line the walls. An acrid smell hangs heavy in the air. It is familiar but I cannot place it.

Think, I command my waterlogged brain, *where are you?* Clearly in a cellar. Possibly a home, but more likely a business. Or a warehouse. And what is that rushing sound? Water.

Suddenly, I realize where I am. The Dupont warehouse. The water I hear is the canal in the rue des Teinturiers. The smell comes from the barrels along the wall, full of chemicals used to fix dye in wool. I have smelled it on Erec so many times.

The voices grow louder. Dust falls from the cracks in the floorboards like snow as someone walks above me toward the trapdoor.

"I'm going to wake her," says a deep male voice I do not recognize. "It is time."

The speaker grunts as he lifts the door. Light pours into the cellar; hot, bright afternoon light.

My spirits rise. If it is afternoon, then hours have passed since the chase through the street, my capture. Surely someone will be looking for me . . . but then, I remember: I left no word with Guigo that I was leaving the palace. And Clement, Joanna, my protectors, are gone.

With my pulse throbbing in my temples, I close my eyes and feign unconsciousness as a man walks down the stairs and across the stone floor toward me.

Through my eyelids I sense the light of a candle. The intruder kneels beside me and sets something on the ground, then reaches out to lift a fallen strand of my hair. He inhales sharply when he sees my face.

Supporting my head with a hand, he rolls me carefully onto my back. His gentleness surprises me. I hear the sound of cloth dipped in liquid, wrung out. Wet cotton touches my brow. The light pressure is such a shock on my bruised skin that I cannot help it—I wince.

"Apologies," he whispers, decreasing the pressure even more.

The cloth moves across my forehead and cheeks, then pauses over my left eye. "This will hurt."

The soft fibers of the cloth might as well be boar bristles. I press my tied wrists together in an effort not to cry out. After what feels like an eternity, he finishes and turns back to the tray. I open my swollen eye a crack to see his cameo in the candlelight. It is the apple-cheeked monk.

He looks at me before I have the chance to shut my eye again. "Mademoiselle," he whispers, "you must rouse yourself, eat and drink something."

I glare at him, unable to speak through the gagging cloth between my teeth. "This evening," he says, "at sunset, you will be tried for the crime of witchcraft. You will stand before Father Loup and give evidence of your innocence. I am afraid it is your only chance. Otherwise, at first light, you will burn."

Witchcraft. The world crashes around my aching head like a cymbal.

I look up into the monk's solemn face. He did not have to tend my wounds, did not have to warn me of what is to come. He is my enemy's servant, but perhaps he is not so indoctrinated as to be blind to Father Loup's hateful hypocrisy. With great effort, I nod.

He helps me sit up, removes the cloth from my mouth and the cord from my ankles but leaves my wrists bound. My ribs ache, my head pounds. My vision blurs in and out of focus. I take slow breaths like Paolo taught me, suck down stale air, wait for the world around me to stop swaying. Fear rises with stomach acid, and I force them both down. *Feel the ground beneath you.*

"Here," says the monk, holding out a cup. "Drink this." I take it awkwardly in my bound hands and drink it all in one go, not caring if it is poison.

It's water. He pours more and I empty it, feeling I will never quench this thirst. After three cupfuls he does not fill it again.

He hands me a hunk of bread that I devour, although the cut inside my cheek reopens as I chew. When I have finished, the monk packs the tray and helps me heavily to my feet.

I lean against the wall until the stone floor beneath me stops pitching. When I open my eyes, the monk is holding out a noose with an apologetic look on his face. "It is time," he says.

Cold comprehension dawns. I am to be dragged through the city like a pack mule. The trial he spoke of is nothing but an excuse for a spectacle; they have already decided I am guilty, that I will burn.

I lunge past him and run toward the staircase, each breath a dagger in my bruised ribs. I hear him following but my battered body obeys—I am up the staircase, through the trapdoor into the dazzling light of the storehouse—

And right into the rat-faced monk's arms.

He wrestles me to the ground and pins a knee painfully against my ribs.

"You're a feisty bitch," he says with a sneer. I note with grim satisfaction the jagged, disfiguring cut over one eye. "Maybe I'll let myself into your cell tonight, have a bit of fun before you burn. I might even bring some friends. What say you, Brother Remy?"

The other monk surfaces. "Gentle, Brother Thomas," he says quietly to Rat Face. "Father Loup insisted that she be delivered unharmed."

I look up into Brother Thomas's ugly face. I muster the last dregs of my strength and spit.

He digs his knee into my diaphragm. I vomit up the bread and water.

I am still retching when they pull a black hood over my head, followed by the hard bite of the rope around my neck. They drag me, coughing, to my feet, out of the empty storefront where, in another life, my sister chose the fabric for her wedding gown, and into the stifling summer afternoon.

I stagger between them, stumbling over the uneven cobblestones, but Brother Remy walks behind me, steadying me with a touch at my shoulder and hip. I do not know where we are going, only that we are moving away from the river, uphill, toward the center of the city.

I hear the crowd long before we reach it.

Hundreds of voices rise like a wave, then die abruptly as though conducted. A hoarse, reedy cry carries down the twisting street and crawls over my skin.

Father Loup.

We turn a corner into a wall of humanity. I feel their heat, smell the odor of hundreds of unwashed bodies as they shift and breathe amid the buzzing of flies.

"And now," rasps the priest, "in the wake of those hated Jews, who have fled our fair city in response to your righteous violence, God shows us the presence of another viper in our nest."

The mob holds its collective breath.

When Father Loup speaks his voice is low, but it carries all the way to the edge of the crowd where I stand, hooded and trussed like one of Clement's hunting falcons.

"I speak, good Christians, of *witches*."

Despite the sweat rolling between my shoulder blades, I shiver.

"The word of God is absolute," Father Loup continues. "'Thou shall not suffer a sorceress to live.' And yet here in the heart of Christendom, beneath the watchful eye of the Holy Father, here in this very plaza, stands a woman so skilled in the art of sorcery that she seduced God's vassal on earth himself!"

Whispers ripple through the crowd. I sense heads craning, fingers pointing in my direction. Cold fury pulses in my veins. My abused body feels taut as a bowstring, ready to fly. In a moment he will call me to him. In a moment I will walk through this crowd to stand beside him. Somewhere in this crowd stand my neighbors, my friends, my patients.

I must be strong. I must be calm. For Margot, for Anes, for Mother, I must defend myself.

"And here is the wicked mistress of Satan, to be tried for her sins!"

The mob howls as the hood lifts from my eyes.

I stand at the edge of the Place Saint-Agricol before a massive crowd, larger even than the last I saw here. Once again, Father Loup stands upon the makeshift dais erected before the golden walls of my family's church, holding an arm overhead to block out the setting sun. He waits until the entire congregation has turned, elbowing and jostling, standing on tiptoe to catch a glimpse of the dirty, bloody girl with the noose around her neck. And then he smiles at me.

Those closest to me scream and throw elbows in their desperation to put more space between my unholy body and theirs.

Idiots, I think furiously. *What have I done to you, other than offer my help and knowledge? What did my mother do to warrant your hatred?*

Brother Thomas makes a show of pulling hard on the rope as if I am a bear for baiting, and I have no choice but to stumble behind him toward the dais. An old woman spits in my face as I pass her. I blink the burning saliva from my eyes and struggle to keep my balance.

A group of children emerge in the path before me with handfuls of spoiled food. To catcalls and cheers, they raise their treasures overhead and throw. Something wet and stinking lands in my hair, a rotten egg cracks against my chest and fills the air with sulfur.

The sky and the crowd start to spin. Faces pass in a blur.

A few jar my memory. I work hard to place them as I fight to stay on my feet, fight for every step. A squat woman with lanky hair hisses *witch* as I pass—she is the butcher's wife. And this old man with the walking stick—do I imagine pity in his eyes? He was the cobbler; he fixed my mother's favorite pair of shoes. Do I have any friends, any allies, here?

Someone sticks out a foot. I do not see it and fall, hard, on my knees, my bound hands cannot catch me. The screams and jeers grow louder—I cannot get up, there is no space—someone steps on my ankle, I scream and hear an answering laugh—something hits me. Something harder than vegetables.

Another lands on the ground before me, and my mind works to make sense of it.

Stones. The first few bounce painfully off my bodice, but the next hits my head and I see stars. I hold my bound arms overhead in protection and someone kicks me, hard, in my bruised ribs.

A shout. The pelting stones stop. Someone kneels beside me, hooks an arm under my shoulder. Dazed, aching, I open my eyes. It is Brother Remy.

He helps me to my feet, half pulls, half carries me through the parting crowd to the platform where a group of black-habited monks waits. I cast a final glance at him as he hands me up to the others but he does not meet my eyes, not even when I cry out as their fingers dig into my flesh.

At the center of the dais Father Loup waits, tall and twisted as a wind-tortured tree.

The monks release me but stand close, ready to grip my arms again with a word from their master. A grim satisfaction curls the corners of the priest's mouth as he takes in my bruises, my blood-matted hair, my swollen eye.

"Well, witch," he says quietly, so none but I can hear, "we meet again. Your heretic master and your whore queen cannot protect you now."

I meet his pale gaze, willing myself not to blink. My knees shake with the effort of standing. *Mary Mother of God,* I pray, *do not let me fall.*

"Behold!" Father Loup shouts, raising his voice and brandishing a long-nailed finger at me. "Behold, good people of Avignon, the mistress of Satan, a serpent in our midst!"

Hisses and boos. I take a deep breath. Soon it will be my turn to speak, to defend myself. I must be calm. I must meet these heinous lies with truth. It is the only chance I have. I stare at the white skin of the sycamore tree at the far end of the square, watch the leaves shimmer in the last of the sun's rays.

"This sorceress used her unnatural powers to weasel her way into the pope's household," Father Loup shouts. "Once ensconced there like a snake in a hole, she seduced the pope's own physician, Surgeon de Chauliac. You know of Surgeon de Chauliac, a model of Christian virtue?"

There is a muttered accord, a few men shout "Aye!"

"And do you know what this foul enchantress did? She led him from the path of righteousness with *these*."

A monk hands him a stack of parchment. My heart sinks as I recognize them: my illustrations and notes on our human dissections. And, at the top of the pile, my mother's book. Someone must have gone to the laboratory, opened the door I did not lock in my haste to reach Margot.

"Look here!" Father Loup shrieks, raising the unmarked leather binding high. "This is her book of spells, recipes for concoctions and potions that produce most sinister and unnatural effects."

He flips it open, displays the carefully lettered pages. Very few of these people can sign their own name, let alone read the lists of herbs. I watch them draw back in horror as though confronted by satanic symbols instead of the ingredients for comfrey tonic and repress an insane urge to laugh.

"And do you know where the celebrated Surgeon de Chauliac is now?" the priest cries, dropping my mother's book like a spider. "He is dead! Poisoned by this foul sorceress!"

A gasp ripples through the crowd. Guigo is beloved, larger than life, the peasant boy whose skill and hard work won him wealth and renown. And suddenly I can hold my tongue no longer.

"It's not true!" I shout raggedly. Silence falls over the crowd.

Father Loup crosses the dais toward me.

"It's not true!" I repeat. "Guigo had the plague, but he survived, he is recovering! I saw him yester—"

Father Loup hits me full in the face with a gnarled hand. I lose my balance and fall to the platform, screaming as exquisite pain sears across my swollen knees. I hear hushed whispers, uneasy murmurs.

Hot welts rise on my face. I glare up at Father Loup. If only I possessed the unnatural power of which he accuses me. If only I could curse him, transform him into a worm to be ground under my heel. An eternity in the inferno would be worth it if I could end this man's life.

The rage inside me claws at my throat and forces its way out.

"I am no witch," I cry. "And you are no priest! You preach only hate and fear! God knows the truth. He knows what you are. It is *you* who will burn in hell!"

The blood rushes in my ears. The roar of the crowd dies away. I focus all my being on this hateful man before me, willing him to catch fire, to be struck by lightning. The priest's eyes narrow, and I swear a flicker of fear crosses his face.

"Elea! Elea!"

The voice breaks through the pounding in my head.

"Elea!"

I turn away from the priest. At the far edge of the crowd gold hair glimmers, the face beneath bright as a torch. It is Erec, fighting his way toward the dais.

"Witness this!" Father Loup howls happily, pointing. "This poor foolish boy! He, who came to me sick and lost, after this witch stole his mother's corpse. Only under my instruction, with daily flagellation, fasting, and prayers, did he finally come to his senses and step back into the light of God." He picks up my mother's book again, waves it overhead. "See how easily she enchants him again! See how even now he cannot fight her power!"

"You promised you would not hurt her!" Erec shouts.

Four black-clad monks slip off the platform behind me and move through the crowd like shadows toward him.

"She has been misled," Erec cries, "but she is no witch! She is no—"

He swallows the next word as the monks overtake him. Erec lands a few hard blows, but they outnumber him. After a brief tussle they strap his arms to his side, mouth bleeding.

"Erec!" I cry, my voice thin over the cries of the crowd. "Erec, get help!"

He shouts something back to me, but I cannot make it out. The monks turn him harshly, drag him away through the rippling mass.

"This poor fool!" crows Loup. "He must appeal to God for forgiveness. But it is *she*"—he points at me, his eyes burning like brands—"who is to blame! She worked alongside the Jews, assisted them as they poisoned our wells! It is she who murdered your children! It is *she* who, when we needed him most, bewitched the Holy Father to abandon our city!"

Father Loup strides to Brother Remy and rips the final papers, the coup de grâce, from his hands.

"And it is *she*," he shrieks, holding the papers aloft, "who practices necromancy! See, good people of Avignon, see the proof of her sorcery! See this foul evidence of the most heinous of crimes, the disembowelment and mangling of Christian corpses for Satan!"

The crowd recoils. My careful drawings—the hours I spent documenting every turn of vein and bone, every subtlety of flesh and organ—twisted into immutable proof of witchcraft.

"How, I ask you, will these poor souls be recognized by their maker?" Father Loup cries. "Shall they wander purgatory forever, holding their cut skin together to keep the entrails in?"

"Burn her!" a few townspeople begin to chant. *"Burn her!"*

"And what does the Bible say about necromancers?" shrieks Father Loup. "'Therefore, in one day, her plagues will overtake her. Death, mourning, and famine. She will be consumed by fire, for mighty is the Lord who judges her!'"

"I am no witch!" I cast the words with every ounce of strength I still possess. "I am no witch!"

But no one hears. The chanting swells until the walls of the square ring like church bells.

"BURN HER! BURN HER!"

The priest holds an arm overhead, calling for silence.

"Good people of Avignon," he shouts, his cracking voice triumphant, "you have spoken! Tomorrow at sunrise we shall send this witch to her master, where she will burn forever in the eternal fire of hell!"

The crowd explodes.

Rough hands jerk me to my feet. I am half led, half carried by the monks. Down the stairs of the platform and toward the church doors I stumble, out of the chaos of the square into the cool, dark interior. The doors close behind me with echoing finality.

It is over. I am dead.

The mob roars through the four-foot-thick walls of the church. The stones that heard my parents' marriage mass, my and Margot's cries in the baptismal font. Mother is buried here, somewhere beneath my feet. As the monks drag me between the wooden pews, I cannot help but turn my head and catch a glimpse of the seats where my family sat together. Strange that I should die before this place, which witnessed so many thresholds of my life.

They lead me past the altar, lift a trembling torch from its wall socket to light the way down the steps into the crypt.

As we descend into the darkness beneath the church, the scent of cool earth mingles with the sweet odor of decay. Torchlight jumps on damp walls and stone coffins, casting strange shadows. The monks around me are silent and press together closer than is necessary, frightened of the dark, the odor of old death. Fools.

We reach a heavy door with an iron lock. Brother Remy takes a jangling ring of keys from his robes and selects one. With a metallic moan, the door creaks open.

The torch illuminates a low-ceilinged room. The stone walls are beaded with condensation, moss covers the mortar between the bricks. Brother Thomas shoves me into the cell.

"Sleep well, witch," he sneers.

The door closes. The key turns in the lock. I hear nervous laughter, the echoes of retreating footsteps against the crypt walls. The band of light beneath the door grows dim, and I am left alone in the dark.

Rats patter, water drips on ancient stones. My breath sounds irreverent in this kingdom of the dead. My eyes strain against the blackness but it is useless, there is no light here.

I am too tired to cry, too tired to get to my feet or try the door. I do not dare to hope that Erec heard me, that he went to the palace for help. Even if, by some miracle, he found Guigo, enlisted others to accompany him, how would they find their way to this crypt in the dark? And even if they did, even if they broke the lock and freed me, Father Loup surely has guards stationed in the church above.

Tomorrow at sunrise I will burn. It is said to be the most painful death. I imagine my skin crackling, my hair ablaze. And what follows that torturous end? Heaven? No. I have not lived in perfect piety. Perhaps the flat plain of purgatory, as Dante describes it, until I have paid in time for my small sins: wrath for the people who turned on my mother, who imprison me here. Pride for my own skills and knowledge. Lust in David's embrace.

I will never walk through my beloved woods again, nor embrace Anes. Nor sit with Guigo in the laboratory. Nor feel the summer sun on my face, nor watch living things grow. How precious each mundane moment now seems with death looming before me. Never again will I sleep beside Margot.

Margot.

I close my eyes and search for her, scour the sensations of my body for the piece of her that I carry with me. I find it, deep and throbbing, like a soldier who knows his wound is mortal.

I hold this ache tight, lift it to the surface of my consciousness, wrap my arms around myself and feel my sister's glow like an ember inside me. It is incomprehensible for me to imagine the world without her in it. What will it be like for her, when I am gone? We came into this life together. As long as there has been me, there has been Margot. I would die a second death for the chance to say goodbye.

I crawl to the wall beside the door and lie with my back against it.

After trying desperately to untie Death's knots, to pull Mother, David, Father, and Guigo back from life's precipice, it was always waiting for me. My battle has always been with Death. Now I see how foolish I have been.

I see Death now as Baldoin, a wild and untamable thing, not a specter to be feared, not a mysterious enemy, but a piece of nature older than stones. Death was never the foe.

Fear is the foe. Hatred is the foe. Ignorance is the foe.

My mother is here, somewhere. As exhaustion overtakes me, I stretch out my bound wrists, reach my fingers for her.

Are you there, Mother? I need you.

But she does not respond.

Chapter Twenty-Five

I dream I'm flying over Avignon, gazing down at the rooftops and cathedral spires, the night air cool on my face. There are no bonfires, no piles of corpses, only neat, empty streets. The Rhône glimmers in the moonlight, and I think how pleasant it would be to glide across its surface and trail my fingers through the water, but instead I float higher until I can see the whole city beneath me, miniature and perfect.

I turn east toward the black mass of Mount Andaon. A few pin-pricks of light mark the walls of the fortress, the abbey windows. I fly above the deserted bridge, too high to hear the rush of water between its arches, over the Île de la Barthelasse, and feel the damp breath of the trees on my skin.

I am across the river. Through the dark carpet of trees, I make out the path, like a ribbon, that leads to the fort. I drop lower. I know where I am going now. The tallest branches are mere feet below me: if I stretched my legs, I could brush my toes against their topmost leaves.

The trees suddenly give way to a clearing—my clearing—but the cottage in the center is whole, the roof thatched. Candlelight glows through waxed linen windows.

My feet land softly in the dewy grass. The smell of honeysuckle hangs in the air like stars. After the wind in my ears, it is so quiet here: no sound but the music of crickets, the cozy hoot of an owl. And voices.

I pad soundlessly to an open window. I know what I will see before the room comes into view, and my skin prickles with anticipation.

My father sits in a low chair with an elbow resting on his thigh, his chin in his hand. He is younger than I ever remember him, his face unlined, his hair dark and thick. Never have I seen him look so careless, so deeply content as he is now, gazing at the figures before him. I long to run to him, leap into his lap and throw my arms around his neck like I did when I was a girl. I long to feel his scratchy cheek against mine again. But I do not feel my loss of him. I feel only joy, only hunger to be with him.

My mother sits on a woven rug in front of the hearth. She looks just as I remember her, all creamy skin and dark eyes and shining hair. I drink in the sight of her greedily. On her knee she bounces a baby boy. He laughs, pink gums gleaming, and dribbles spittle down his front. My mother laughs, too, wipes him clean, says something to my father that makes him smile. She speaks to my brother in the singsong that babies like. I watch my father watching her.

A sudden movement makes me start. On the far side of the fireplace, cast in shadow, a huge dog raises his head. Baldoin's eyes glow like rubies in the firelight. He stares right at me.

My mother glances at the dog, follows his gaze to the open window. Her eyes look straight into mine.

She makes no sign to my father. She gets to her feet, the baby on her hip. "The breeze is cold tonight," she says.

My father looks at the open window without seeing me, starts to stand.

"I will go," my mother says. She places the writhing baby on my father's knee, kisses the top of his head. She walks toward me and suddenly I am paralyzed with the realization that I am intruding, that this scene is not for my eyes. But my desire to be with them is too great. I stay where I am.

My mother comes to the window. In her face, younger and more beautiful than I remember, is written the same thirst, the same deep longing that shudders in my chest. Her hands ball into fists with the desire to hold me. I feel like an empty cup about to be filled. Behind her, oblivious, my father bounces the baby on his knee and coos.

"It is late," she says to me quietly.

I hear my father mutter an assent behind her, thinking she speaks to him.

"So late that it is nearly tomorrow. There will be time enough tomorrow, and the day after tomorrow. But now, we should sleep."

She places her hand on the windowsill before me, close enough to touch her, close enough to smell the lavender oil on her throat and behind her ears.

I open my mouth to say something, anything, to call to my father, to push through the door. But my mother shakes her head imperceptibly, and I remember that I am not supposed to be here.

Someone else steps into the room behind her—I glimpse a familiar willowy shadow, a mass of long dark hair.

And then my mother closes the window.

I awaken on the cold stone floor, still caught in the floating web of the dream, still under its spell. Could it be a glimpse of what's to come? My mother, close enough to reach out and touch. My baby brother, healthy and whole, all smiling eyes and chubby cheeks. Father.

I sit upright, remembering the dark-haired woman. I know who she was, why she was there.

It was me.

A sense of peace comes with this realization, as though my death in the morning is the predictable climax of a passion play. All that remains is acting it out, seeing it through to its conclusion. And perhaps, if God takes mercy on my imperfect soul, my family awaits me in the cottage in the woods.

"Thank you," I whisper. "Thank you for the dream. I will try to be brave."

My body aches. How strange to fall asleep in darkness and wake in darkness. Somewhere, on the other side of these walls, it will be morning soon. Somewhere birds are tucked safely in their nests and grass reaches tender fingers through damp earth, and today, or tomorrow, or the day after that, the sun will shine.

There is a sound in the hallway. Vermin, perhaps. Or—with a chill, I remember Brother Thomas's cruel words—*Maybe I'll let myself into your cell tonight, have a bit of fun before you burn. I might even bring some friends.* I hear voices, quick footsteps, growing closer. My traitorous heart pounds, longing to fight, to flee. I try to hold on to the sense of calm, remember my mother's sad smile as she closed the window.

Someone whispers furtively outside my cell. My joints protest as I pull myself to my feet, stand with my shoulders set toward the door.

I will not try to run. I will not beg nor plead. I will meet my fate with eyes open, back straight, as my mother would have done.

A rasp of metal on metal, a few hissed words. The door scrapes against the stones as it swings open.

My visitors are lit only by a torch that flickers over their faces, twisting their features into unrecognizable masks. The taller of the two raises the torch higher, pooling the light like gold on the floor of my cell.

"Eleonora?" he whispers.

It cannot be. This must be another dream.

"*Paolo?*" I step forward into the circle of light, my heart leaping. "What are you doing here?"

"There is no time to explain. We must hurry. Come now, come!"

He ushers me through the open door and drapes me in a heavy riding cloak. It is warm and smells like him. "This way," he whispers, starting down the passageway with the torch held high. The other man follows behind me. The light reflects off the walls and illuminates his face.

"Brother Remy?" I whisper. The monk holds a finger to his lips.

I do not dare to trust the hope swelling in my chest. Even if we are caught, I think, even if I burn just the same, it is enough that they tried.

We turn and walk down another long passage, then another, zigzagging out of the crypt. Once Paolo pauses, unsure of which way to go, but Brother Remy points to the left. A locked gate bars us. The monk opens it, his shaking fingers jingling the other keys on the ring. Paolo holds his breath. We pass through, reach the stone staircase, and start to climb. The temperature rises with each step.

I wonder if they can hear my heart pounding. I wonder who else can.

We surface into the breathless church, dark except for a few candles guttering under the crucifix. At any moment I expect Father Loup to appear like a ghoul from behind a column or pew. But nothing stops us.

Brother Remy unlocks the double doors with another key. They creak open—an alarm will sound, someone must hear—but we are out, down the steps, into the silent plaza and the thick summer night. Paolo grabs my hand and drags me down a side street, twisting away from the Place Saint-Agricol, turning again, and again. I look over my shoulder, but Brother Remy did not follow. I wish I could have thanked him.

Paolo slows as we approach another corner, and I hear low voices, the sound of horseshoes on cobblestones. *They have caught us,* I think. *It is over.* I remember my promise to be brave, but disappointment burns bitter on my tongue.

Paolo pauses at the turn in the street, holds out an arm for me to stop. He whistles a long, low note.

And the whistle is returned.

Paolo jerks his head at me and strides around the corner. I follow.

Four hooded figures stand together in a square beside two horses. The smallest figure barrels toward me and collides with my chest, throws her arms around me. It's Anes.

"Oh, my lamb," she whispers in my ear. "May God keep you safe."

"Where's Margot?" I whisper back. "Is she all right?"

"She is well." Anes kisses me; her face is damp with tears. "She wanted me to tell you she loves you and she will pray for you."

"Tell her I love her," I whisper. "I'll write as soon as I can."

Anes nods, releases me to wipe her eyes with her sleeve.

The third hooded figure grabs my hand.

"Elea," says Erec's strangled voice, "Elea, please forgive me—"

A shadow cloaks his face, but I imagine it as I saw it in Father Loup's mob, lit by a fanatical light. God help me, I cannot forgive him. I say only, "Take care of my sister."

The largest figure turns to Paolo.

"It's time to leave," says Guigo's rumbling voice. "We have only a few more hours before dawn." He hands the reins of the horses to Paolo and catches me in a hug, his wasted body unrecognizable under my arms after the weeks of fever. He makes a choking noise as he releases me and whispers, "Go now. *Go.*"

Erec lifts me lightly into the saddle. The little mare shifts beneath me, tossing her head.

The fourth hooded figure says nothing, just leans against the wall—another monk, perhaps? I don't have time to wonder because Paolo clicks his tongue; his horse starts off down a narrow alley and mine follows obediently.

I turn back in the saddle for a final glance of them, wishing I could say more, thank them, say goodbye, but the street twists, the square disappears, and we are swallowed by the night.

Paolo and I ride east through the gray light before dawn. We meet no one. A few stone cottages pepper the landscape, their inhabitants dead or gone. No smell of woodsmoke laces the air, no bellow of oxen nor the thud of an ax interrupts the calls of birds and the droning insects. The unharvested hay stands taller than my head and the wide road is overgrown from lack of traffic. Birds call sleepily, cicadas make their first scratchy preludes in the trees. The morning is warm, heralding another sultry summer day. I think of the frescoes in Clement's chamber, the deer and hounds and beautiful maidens, their arms laden with flowers.

It feels as though Paolo and I are the last people on earth. I watch the line of his perfect shoulders as he rides in front of me, the dark hair peeking out from under his cap cut close to his neck in curling whorls. We have not spoken for hours, since he told me how I was sprung from my prison in Saint-Agricol.

Erec escaped the monks and sprinted straight to the palace, where he found Guigo still in bed, weak from his illness. It was Guigo who recommended that I travel with Paolo who, thank the Virgin, had not yet left for the coast and had the good sense to rescue a few of my things from the laboratory. Miraculously, he found Joanna's letter of safe passage and the bag of gold untouched.

We will ride for two days to Marseille to meet the Neapolitan court, and then onward by ship to Naples. I pray that the plague will burn itself out in my city, that Pope Clement will return and douse the dangerous flame of fanaticism. Then, when it is safe, I will come home to Margot and Anes. I will write as soon as we reach Marseille.

We stop by a clear brook and eat a little bread and cheese while the horses drink. The sun breaks over the edge of the earth.

Paolo is tightening up the saddle girths when I smell the fire. It's close; I look up sharply, half expecting to see the tree line behind us smoldering.

"What is it?" Paolo asks, following my gaze.

"Do you smell that?" I ask. "Smoke?"

It's getting stronger, closer, as is the crackling smell of a hungry fire. Soot fills my lungs although my vision is unclouded, the morning clear and cool. I start to cough and cannot stop, every breath thick and black and greasy, and it is suddenly so hot, I am suffocating, I cannot breathe, I cannot breathe. Paolo watches me with wild eyes, looking around for his water skin which he holds out to me but I cannot take. The cool, extinguishing water of the stream might as well be miles away.

I am frozen in place, cannot move, strangled by the heat and the smoke as my mind tries to process what is happening, so stupid for lack of air. My feet are on fire. I look down with a smothered shriek and see only my shoes in the grass, but I can feel the flames crawling up my body.

Paolo throws the water on me, but it does nothing to quench the fire which creeps up to my chest now, liquefying the wool of my dress and igniting my eyelashes. My heart slows, my lungs collapse. *Jesus, God, just let me die this pain is too much to bear—*

Suddenly, miraculously, the agony abandons me. For a moment I feel my body illuminated from the inside and I know what it is to be a coal, or a sword, or a star, before I explode into a million tiny pieces.

Someone is screaming.

"Elea! *Elea!*"

I open my eyes.

I am lying on my back on the ground under a pale morning sky. For a moment I do not know where I am, who I am.

Paolo kneels beside me with his hands on my shoulders. He helps me sit up, holds a cup of water to my lips with shaking hands.

When I can speak again, I ask, "Who was screaming?"

His face blanches. "You were screaming, Eleonora."

The memory of the fire floods back to me. I can still feel the greedy flames licking my body. Paolo watches me carefully, his face etched with fear and worry. And another emotion—guilt.

I push away the cup.

"Tell me," I say, my eyes locked on his. "Tell me what happened."

I see him make the decision to tell me the truth, his face incapable of a convincing lie. He prepares himself, glances down at the cup he holds, back to my face. He takes a breath.

Suddenly I want to run as fast and far as I can.

"She insisted," he says quietly. "She said if they found you gone, they'd burn another innocent woman, and they would not stop with just one. She had the plague. That part of the monk's ruse was true. She coughed blood, she vomited blood. She was so weak. She willed herself to stay alive so she could take your place. She should have died yesterday, or the day before. But Guigo came to care for her, even though he was not fully recovered. He gave her water and changed her bedclothes as tenderly as a father would. He helped her put on your dress and carried her under the cover of night to Saint-Agricol. Brother Remy led them back to your cell. She knew she just had to breathe long enough to take your place. She died on the pyre this morning."

Paolo moves closer, puts an arm around me. I sit rigid in his embrace, fighting down bile.

"No." I break free, get to my feet. "You are lying. It is not true."

I back away from him, hot tears welling in my eyes. I raise my arms up as though he will hit me. I wish he would.

He stands, holds his open palms out to me helplessly. "I am so sorry, Eleonora. She lived longer than she should have for your sake, but there was no saving her. I am so sorry."

Something nags at the back of my mind.

"Who was the fourth monk?" I ask. Paolo looks up in surprise. "There was Guigo and Anes and Erec. Who was the fourth?"

Paolo looks miserable.

"Tell me."

"It was her—it was Margot," he says.

I knew it. She was right there. I could have reached out and thrown off her hood. I could have stopped her.

Tears fall from his eyes. I turn and run from him, sobbing. I run through the untended field into the trees, running like an animal with no thought of where I am going, only that I must keep moving, away, *away.* My knees protest with each footfall but I do not stop.

I catch an ankle on a root and fall hard on my hands and knees. I cannot breathe for sobbing, and I am glad for it, glad for screaming pain in my ankle and the frantic need for air, the physical struggle distracting me for a few seconds from the horror that waits for me in every corner of my mind.

I squeeze my eyes shut and force myself to breathe slowly. I search for her presence, call out for her, make my soul a beacon. *Margot.*

If I ever had any powers, if I am a witch, to Mary and Jesus and God and the devil and all the dead pagan gods, I would trade my soul for hers. Please, let me find her now.

I concentrate every ounce of my being. I reach out fingers of consciousness across the miles, searching for her. I walk the empty streets of Avignon, climb the stairs of our home, search the plazas and hospitals and jails. *Margot.* Her name resounds in my ears. *Margot.* She does not answer.

Her light has gone out.

She is gone.

I know it is true now.

This world is an empty house without her.

I hear Paolo cracking sticks, looking for me. I watch the scene from outside myself like a bird on a branch, witness rather than feel him kneel beside me, say something soothing, so careful with me. I think of Baldoin in the trap. I think of the night Mother died, weeping all night together, taking turns, the loss too big to face alone. Our empty home, which was once full of laughter and sunlight and the smell of baking bread.

The rooms of my mind are filled with my dead, voices and shadows moving in the slivered light under closed doors. What I would give to join them. I remember the fire in David's plague-fevered eyes when he faced the same foe who took all his family. I know now, as I knew then, that I do not possess that kind of strength. I cannot face this sorrow alone.

Paolo has his arms around me. His shirt is wet with tears. Mine or his? It does not matter. He rocks me, repeats something over and over. Forward and back. Forward and back. He is shaking. No, it is I who am shaking. I shiver uncontrollably, my teeth chattering so hard that my head aches. Suddenly I am so, so tired.

Paolo says something. I think he is asking me to stand. I look down detachedly at my ankle. I don't recognize it as mine at first—it is purple and swollen, the outlines of the bones no longer distinguishable. With Paolo's help I stand on my good foot, try a little pressure on the twisted ankle, cry out. He loops one arm under my shoulder and together we make our way out of the cool darkness of the woods.

The pain is distant, like a sound heard through a dream, but I am grateful for it. It is a sorry companion to the shrieking pain in my head and my heart, but every step brings me back a little, keeps me rooted in the present. I notice little things, one by one, easing across my consciousness like clouds. The sound of the cicadas. The warm breeze. My own harsh breathing. The walk back to the brook takes a lifetime.

Now it is dark, and Paolo must make a fire because orange light plays over his face. I am sorry to cause him so much trouble. He gives me some bread, which I take and forget I am holding. He takes a cloak from his pack and drapes it over me. A sigh of lavender fills the air. The tiny stitches catch the firelight—flowers and leaves. The cloak Margot embroidered. As I wrap it tighter around me, something rustles in the inner pocket against my breast.

Paolo says a few more things, brushes the hair from my face, kisses me softly in the center of my forehead, the way my mother used to. Then he wraps himself in his cloak and rests his head on his pack on the opposite side of the fire. The flames reflect in his open eyes. He watches me until he can no longer keep his eyes open, and then he sleeps.

When Paolo's breathing has been steady for an hour, I pull the piece of paper from its hiding place in the inner pocket of my cloak. It is a small scrap, torn from the edge of a book. In Margot's hand, wobbly with fever but unmistakably hers, is written,

You are myself.

Epilogue

Baldoin loathes the ship.

He weaves back and forth across the deck like a drunk, crouched so low his belly touches the gangplanks. But he howls if I lock him in my cabin.

The Marseillais point at him and laugh; the Spaniards spit over the rails to demonstrate their displeasure. None of the sailors speak to me. I have spent our four days at sea standing at the stern while they shout and sing their lewd songs around me, but they will not meet my eyes. Women are bad luck on a ship, and although there are other wives and daughters onboard—other refugees of plague and violence—they hide in their airless quarters, vomiting into chamber pots.

I want to take the sailors by their shoulders and shake them. I want to tell them this superstition is just another excuse for mistrust and hate, and look, *look* at the sky, if our presence has brought them anything it is fair weather, look at the sail bellies full of wind, pushing us south. But I say nothing. Instead, I put my hand in the pocket of my borrowed gown and finger the folded parchment there. I do not pull it free, do not trust the wind to not take it from me, but I have the words memorized.

Mademoiselle Médicin, the letter begins, in the familiar, sloppy handwriting that makes my chest ache,

I am improving every day. Your sutures have healed well, though they itch like the devil, and thanks to your medicine there is no sign of blood poisoning. You have saved my life, and I will never forget the debt I owe you. Your mother would be proud.

Anes is settling into palace life. With most of the staff still in Étoile-sur-Rhône, she has taken over the operation of the kitchens. I have never seen the floors so clean. The quality of the food, too, has improved substantially. It would warm your heart to see her bossing the young men and women over their chopping and scouring.

I have tried to revisit our treatise, but so far the inspiration to continue has not come. Perhaps I am still too close to my own illness to be objective, or perhaps I have become accustomed to collaboration. You are missed.

We hope you will return to Avignon once this cursed plague passes, and His Holiness reestablishes order in the city. But until then we are confident of your security in the employment of the queen. Know that we think of you often and remember you in our prayers.

Safe travel and
God's speed.
Guigo

I read the letter morning and evening in the light from my little window, trace the signature with my fingertips, comfort my tattered heart with the knowledge that Guigo is recovered, Anes is with him.

But the final paragraph twists my stomach. I am not in Joanna's employ. Not safe onboard the ship to Naples.

I spent the week in stinking, cheerful Marseilles in a sort of numb nightmare, sleeping through the days, emerging from the tangled sheets only when Baldoin's bark alerted me that Paolo was at my door. He stood on the threshold with a meal in his hands and pity in his eyes, begging me to bathe, take a walk with him, eat something. But it was Baldoin who dragged me from my self-imposed prison. The day after our escape from Avignon he met us like some strange, shaggy envoy, standing in the middle of the road with his tongue out and ears high. All through the sultry Provençal afternoon he trotted beside my horse. Once we were safely through the city gates and ensconced in the palace, Paolo brought him food and water and tried to force him from the room so he could relieve himself, but the stubborn dog would not leave my side.

On the second evening, I limped over the battlements of the seaside castle on my twisted ankle for the first time. I didn't speak, just leaned on Paolo's arm and breathed the briny air. The next afternoon I did it again. The third morning, I was surprised to recognize the ache in my belly as hunger. On the fourth day I forgot Margot for a moment and laughed as Baldoin chased a seagull that wheeled and cried, taunting him, twenty feet above his head. But then I remembered, and grief buried the sunlight.

Paolo stroked my hair while the wave passed through me.

It was Paolo who packed my bag, laced me into his sister's gown, smuggled me past the guards. Paolo who saved my life a second time.

"Addio, leonessa," he whispered, kissing me like the brother who never reached this life. *"Addio."*

I inhale the hard press of sea air. I will write when we reach port. I will write to all of them, Guigo and Anes and Joanna and Paolo, and try to explain.

"One more day." The voice comes over my shoulder. "They say we'll be in Valencia before sunset tomorrow."

Over the pine tar and salt, I smell olive oil soap. "Careful," I reply without turning. "If we're thrown off course by a storm, I'm the first they'll toss overboard."

David scratches Baldoin between the ears, then takes his place beside me, leaning his elbows on the railing. I know without looking at him the expression he wears, mouth carefully neutral, brow furrowed against the reflection of sun on water. His closeness lights me like a lamp, the realization that I could reach out and touch him and no one would care. Four days together and it has not left me, has only grown stronger, this flickering feeling of possibility.

"I won't let them."

"You'll be the second."

He laughs. Something inside me rolls over with the pleasure of it.

"Are you hungry?" Then, when I say nothing, "The bell for supper rang ten minutes ago."

I tear my gaze from the distant shore and turn to David. His eyes hold mine the way, I know, his arms long to hold me. With tenderness, understanding. With love.

Make me a promise, my sister said. *If you have another chance for happiness, take it.*

She gave me a gift, and I will not squander it. I reach out and take his hand.

To get back up to the shining world from there
My guide and I went into that hidden tunnel,
And following its path, we took no care
To rest, but climbed: he first, then I—so far,
Through a round aperture I saw appear
Some of the beautiful things that Heaven bears,
Where we came forth, and once more saw the stars

Historical Note

In the summer of 2018, I took a trip to the South of France with my mother and aunt who, like Elea and Margot, are identical twins. I was captivated by Avignon's twisting medieval streets; take one too many turns, it seemed, and one might be transported back to the fourteenth century. A year later I was on my honeymoon, in the bathtub, when the entire plot of this novel leaped into my head. I jumped out, dripping, and started scribbling on a hotel notepad.

Then COVID-19 hit. I was working as a physical therapist, not a frontline worker, not an ICU nurse nor environmental services worker nor pulmonologist, but like so many others, I left my home each morning, donned my PPE, had my temperature checked, and spent the day seeing patients. *Eleanore of Avignon* was my companion through the long hours and empty weekends.

At the height of the pandemic, my husband tested positive. I cared for him at a distance and dreaded the possibility that I would have to leave him at the hospital, unable to accompany him past the front doors. Thankfully, his symptoms remained mild. But I was struck by the parallels in my novel and in my life: the fragility of modernity, the limitations of medicine, and the power of fear.

Eleanore and her family are inventions of my imagination, but the events through which she lived and the figures she encountered were very real.

The Black Plague made landfall in Europe in 1347. By 1351, it had killed roughly 40 percent of the continent's population. We know now that the disease was caused by *Yersinia pestis*, a bacterium that thrives in the intestines of rat fleas, but medieval medicine was centuries away from germ theory. Physicians, apothecaries, and other early health care providers did what they could with the limited skills and knowledge they possessed, but the suffering and loss of life was, to a modern mind, unfathomable. The treatments for and hypothesized causes of the disease as described here are taken from the firsthand accounts of physicians who lived during the plague.

As the pestilence raged, so did anti-Jewish violence. The lie that Jews had spread the disease by poisoning wells traveled like wildfire across Europe and was fueled by confessions coerced under torture. Historians estimate that between 1348 and 1351, 510 European Jewish communities were exterminated. The lengthy list of horrifying pogroms includes the 1349 Strasbourg "Valentine's Day" massacre, in which more than two thousand Jews were burned alive, even though the plague had not yet reached the city.

Clement VI, lover of finery, feasts, and spectacles, was pope from 1342 to 1352. Eschewing his monastic vows of chastity, he lived like a secular king, patronizing artists, poets, musicians, and scholars, and elevating his court to one of the most cosmopolitan and sophisticated of the time. He suffered from kidney stones throughout his life. During the plague, he published two strongly worded papal bulls decrying violence against the Jewish people and urging the clergy to take action to protect them.

Queen Joanna of Naples, countess of Provence, lived a turbulent, scandalous, and ultimately tragic life. Famously beautiful and intelligent, she fought fiercely to maintain control of her kingdom against scheming relatives, duplicitous nobles, and four husbands. After being accused of her first husband's murder, she fled a besieged Naples for Avignon to stand trial for the crime. Pope Clement VI and his tribunal found her innocent, but shortly after the trial, Joanna quietly sold the city of Avignon to Clement. Many historians debate whether any money exchanged hands, or if the cost of the city was the price she paid for her innocence.

Joanna was, by all contemporary accounts, an affectionate and natural mother, but none of her children survived past infancy. Her first child, Charles Martel, died in Hungary while Joanna was in Avignon. Her daughter Catherine, whose birth I describe in this novel, did not live a year. Her second daughter by Luigi of Taranto, Françoise, died at eight months old. Joanna miscarried a fourth child, and there is no evidence that she ever conceived again.

Joanna was murdered by Charles of Durazzo, her cousin and the chosen heir of Louis of Hungary, after he took Naples by force in 1382. Some contemporary accounts state that she was strangled with a cord while at prayer in restitution for her first husband's murder by hanging. She was fifty-six years old.

Guy de Chauliac, the peasant boy who became chief physician to the pope, is another larger-than-life character who really lived. When the plague decimated Avignon, other physicians, and Pope Clement himself, fled the city. But Guigo stayed on, contracting and surviving the disease using the same techniques he had developed to save his patients. There is no record of who performed the surgery.

After he recovered, Dr. de Chauliac published a widely read treatise on the plague in which he described the two strains of the disease and, using scientific language, discredited the rumors that it had been spread by Jews poisoning the wells. His masterwork, *Chirurgia Magna,* was widely translated and remained one of the most important reference manuals on practical medicine for at least three centuries. He is known today as the father of Western surgery.

I read dozens of books and scientific and academic articles in my research for this novel, but I would like to especially note John Kelly's *The Great Mortality* and Barbara Tuchman's *A Distant Mirror: The Calamitous 14th Century*, both of which brought medieval Europe to life so effectively that I could nearly smell the bonfire smoke.

Acknowledgments

Writing a novel is a lonely task. I'm grateful to many excellent people who helped bring this book into the world.

Thank you to my mother and aunt for loving books so much. For all the vacation hours spent sprawled by a pool or on a couch or in a big bed together reading Poldark, Lymond, and Mary Renault novels aloud. Thank you for listening to so many rough, early pages of this novel. Thank you for your enthusiasm at every step of this process.

Thank you to Andie Jokerst for taking time out of your incredibly busy life to read, edit, and listen to me complain, for believing with your whole heart in the far-fetched fantasy of getting this novel published.

Thank you to Amy Wallen for providing such helpful feedback on a very early draft, for talking me through every step of the querying and publishing processes, for being coach and cheerleader and friend. Here's to many more walks and glasses of wine.

Thank you to my rock star agent, Stacy Testa, for taking a chance on a debut author and believing in this book. For all your thoughtful edits, your weekend and holiday reading, your tireless championship of *Eleanore*. I am so grateful to be on your team.

Thank you, thank you, thank you to the team at Dutton. To Lexy Cassola, whose brilliant editorial work made this book the sharpest, best version of itself—collaborating with you was a dream. Thank you to Cassidy Sachs for stepping in at the eleventh hour, for your passionate advocacy and for shepherding this novel through publication. Thank you to LeeAnn Pemberton, Melissa Solis, Hannah Dragone, Erica Ferguson, Nicole Jarvis, Diamond Bridges, and Juli Meinz for all the behind-the-scenes production work. Thank you to Laura Corless for the beautiful book design, which is so much better than I could have ever imagined.

And thank you, finally, to my husband, Garrett, who has supported this dream from its nascency. Thank you for folding laundry and cleaning the kitchen and giving me time and space to write, for listening to the constant litany of plotlines and self-doubt over dinners and dog walks. Thank you for all the ways you quietly take care of me and act like it's no big deal. I am so lucky to build this life with you.

About the Author

ELIZABETH DELOZIER holds a BA in Spanish literature, a BS in biological anthropology, and a doctorate in physical therapy. An avid traveler, animal lover, and history nerd, she lives in Southern California with her husband, twin sons, and rescue dogs.